SUNFLOWER DOG

Share Your Thoughts

Want to help make *Sunflower Dog* a bestselling novel? Consider leaving an honest review of this book on Goodreads, on your personal author website or blog, and anywhere else readers go for recommendations. It's our priority at SFK Press to publish books for readers to enjoy, and our authors appreciate and value your feedback.

Our Southern Fried Guarantee

If you wouldn't enthusiastically recommend one of our books with a 4- or 5-star rating to a friend, then the next story is on us. We believe that much in the stories we're telling. Simply email us at pr@sfkmultimedia.com.

SFK
PRESS

SUNFLOWER DOG

Dancing the Flathead Shuffle

KEVIN WINCHESTER

For Ava—may the laughter in your life
be exceeded only by love.

Contents

"We're all damaged. It's a universal component of the human condition, like the stages of grief, déjà vu, and expired coupons."

–TIM DORSEY, *Nuclear Jellyfish*

1

Take the Next Left to Salvation

When Salvador Hinson rounded the corner, he saw two men in matching suits, obviously employees of the funeral home, trying to restrain Bill's wife. It was a struggle—Jolene was an ample woman.

She bobbed between them, flailing her arms like a kid in a schoolyard fight. One swing connected with the usher on the right and when he stumbled, she lunged for the opening, throwing a roundhouse right at the equally ample female the men were separating her from. An unidentified arm shot from the knot of relatives behind Jolene, grabbing the back of her dress and slowing her, allowing the usher to re-grip. Sally's first thought was to keep walking, sneak up the steps and avoid the whole mess, but the sight of the other woman dodging Jolene's fists made him pause. Two more ushers stood between the second woman and Bill's wife, not physically holding her but feebly stretching their arms wide as if to corral her.

She looked to be about the same height as Jolene, a little heavier, maybe. She wore a matching outfit with the word "JUICY" stenciled across her ass in blocked blue letters. As he moved closer, Sally could see her jabbing a finger toward Bill's wife. A few more steps and Sally heard her yelling, "Sinner" and "Heathen" with each thrust of her finger, which only caused Jolene to swing harder and wilder, the blows from her thick forearms pummeling the two ushers as she screamed, "You killed my Billy. It was you."

A fat baby in a wispy bleach-blonde's arms started squalling. Finally, the usher who took one to the ear took another across the mouth and stepped up his efforts. He managed to push Bill's wife backward and yelled, "Everybody shut up. This is a solemn occasion, damn it. The man's dead, for God's sake."

Everything stopped. The pause hung in Sally's gut, like that moment of weightlessness when you're on a rope swing. Instead of bolting up the steps, he froze, and that was it. Caught. Bill's wife yelled, "Salvador Hinson, get your greedy ass over here," and the sensation of falling rushed over him. The crowd turned as one to look at him, and his moment of escape vanished.

"Hello, Jolene. Sorry about Bill," Sally greeted her as he ambled closer, both hands stuffed in his pants pockets.

"Don't start with me, Salvador Hinson. I am not in the mood."

"Paying my respects, Jolene. That's all."

Sally felt everyone staring at him, including the woman in the matching outfit. He rubbed the buckeye in his pocket between his thumb and forefinger.

"You know this, this—*her*?" Jolene thrust her chins at the other woman.

Sally looked at the woman, who grinned back at him. Beyond them, a steady line of people filed up the steps to the chapel, more cars pulled into the lot. Better turnout than he expected. What if it'd been him? Who would bother?

"No, Jolene, can't say as I do."

The woman stepped toward him with her meaty hand outstretched, a ring on each of her fingers. "Hi. I'm Mary, like in the Bible," she said. "Pleased to make your acquaintance—Salvador, is it?"

He let go of the buckeye and shook her hand. The lightness of her touch surprised him, not what he expected from a woman her size.

Still, strong enough that he was caught between the two women. "Likewise. Call me Sally. Everybody does."

"Nice to meet you, Sally."

"Oh, stop that," Jolene grumbled. "You two aren't fooling a soul. Salvador Hinson, you know well as I do, that—that trollop is Billy's mistress. Or was. Look at her, all painted up, wearing them rings. *Pfft.* A common whore, that's what she is, and you knew about the two of them."

"Now Jolene, I haven't seen nor talked to Bill in over two years."

"Do I look stupid, Salvador? Do I? The two of you been covering each other's tracks for years. Now Billy's laying in there deader than four o'clock on Tuesday, so just stop your lying, for once."

"Damn it. It's been almost two years since I last talked to him, I swear."

"That's right," Mary chimed in. "Bill mentioned it during our sessions. He missed you, Sally. Really, he did."

Sessions? Missed him? Funny way of showing it. All those years speculating on real estate, flipping properties, hustling land deals. They'd been through a lot. Partners, best friends, Sally thought. Each knew plenty about the other, things nobody else knew. Shady business deals, hand-shake arrangements, back room promises. Then, after the real-estate bubble blew in 2007, Sally noticed a change in Bill. He didn't talk as much, started leaving the room to take a call, acting secretive. He was up to something. There were still some deals to be had, mostly snapping up foreclosed properties (everybody and everything was shaky), but if Bill was working on something, Sally couldn't imagine why he didn't bring him in on it. Finally, one day when Bill had asked Sally to meet him at the Red Apple Bar & Grill, Sally decided to call him on it, demand an explanation. Instead, Bill began talking all that nonsense about finding Jesus and joining the church.

Sally hadn't bought it, but Bill had insisted it was genuine. "Sally," he'd said. "Think what you want, but—"

"I intend to."

"Yeah," said Bill. "I know, but listen. I'm a couple years older than you. My diet's for shit, I'm just saying, if I check out before you, there's a safety deposit box Jolene doesn't know about. Mason City Bank, Number 313. It's yours." He walked out the door without looking back and Sally'd not spoken with him since.

Sally took a hit when everything went south, they both did, but he had a little put by. He was far from well-off, but Sally knew he could make it without the income. For a while. He'd take some time off, a month, two at the most, and consider options for what might be next. Two months became three, then four, and Sally drifted. Nothing held his interest, everything bored him. He rumbled around his house, room to room, felt the walls moving in closer around him. He joined a gym, but after three weeks, stopped going. Started, and stopped, a long list of hobbies, habits, and causes. He wouldn't admit he missed Bill, missed chasing deals with him, wouldn't admit that he was more jealous than angry. Bill was always the face of the business, Sally was better working behind the scenes—he preferred it—and without Bill out front, there wasn't much left. He'd always thought Bill would come around, that things would go back the way they were, but now the finality of it hit Sally harder than he'd expected.

Jolene didn't give him long to contemplate it.

"See?" she said. "See, right there. He *talked* to her. During *sessions*. He, oh he . . ." her face grayed, her mouth gaped open for a few seconds before folding closed, her chins began quivering and tears rolled down her cheeks. After a few moments, she whispered, "He died in her arms, Sally. In her *arms*."

The usher cleared his throat and looked at his watch. "Uh, folks," he started, "it's almost time for the service. The minister would like a few moments with the family. Could we go inside?" He placed his hand on Jolene's back to herd her toward the chapel. Jolene and the rest of the relatives filed by, each casting their own unique and condemning glare toward Mary and Sally as they did.

Once the last of them passed, Mary turned to Sally. "Sally, I don't want you to get the wrong impression. I'm forty-two years old, and never in my years have I even considered doing what she's suggesting, especially not since I joined the church, but I forgive her for thinking as much. Would you like to sit with me during the service?"

Sally took a long look at Mary, took it all in. He suspected there was a lie in something she said, he just needed to find out what part. He didn't know any of the details about Bill's death, what if Jolene was right? She seemed certain about Bill dying in Mary's arms, and when it came to wedding vows, Bill gave *love, honor, and cherish* an honest shot, and to a lesser degree, *in sickness and in health*. History'd shown he leaned toward the plus-sized. *Big women need loving, too,* he always says. Said. Mary knew more than she let on, maybe she knew about the deal Bill was working.

Sally didn't want to admit the existential reasons that brought him to the funeral, so he convinced himself that going to the service might provide a clue about Bill's previous silence, the lack of contact. Maybe he'd spot something, anything that might give him a clue why Bill had suddenly cut him off. Yeah, the crash had been bad, but not bad enough for Bill to start asking the baby Jesus for help, not bad enough to just drop their friendship with no explanation. And there was the question of the safety deposit box. Of course, he couldn't lean over the casket, poke Bill a time or two and ask, "Hey asshole, do I still need to check the safety deposit box?" but he had no better starting place. He couldn't expect any help from Jolene, either, especially not if she were right about Bill dying in Mary's arms. Jolene didn't know about the extra safety deposit box anyway. Mary would have to do.

"Sure, Mary. I'll sit with you," he answered.

The preacher kept the eulogy portion as short and impersonal as possible, moving quickly into a sermon that began with a vague mention of Bill's giving up his ways of the past, how he was lost until he found the Lord. Sally drifted. Found Him? How'd that happen? MapQuest? GPS commanding, "Take the next left to salvation"? The Trinity on a milk carton? Sure, Bill had told him about his conversion, his moment of clarity, but Sally didn't buy it.

Finding religion. Sally thought it as much vanity-fueled superstition as anything else out there. And he'd tried his share of what was out there, especially over the past two years. Shrinks, expensive entitlement cars, slow-witted and younger women, Xanax, coke, vegetarianism, and a long list of various other "isms." The combined weekend of aromatherapy and colonics was a total waste of time and money. Oddly soothing and slightly disgusting, but Sally's boredom returned while eating a four-cheese quesadilla a week later. Making a deal . . . that worked. Ferreting out an opportunity, working the angles, estimating margins. Buy low, sell high, count your money. It worked for P.T. Barnum, the Rockefellers, the Carnegies, a slew of tele-evangelists and snake oil proprietors. Sally loved it, same as Bill. For most of his life, the next deal had sustained Sally, pulled him along toward . . . There it was again. Pulled him along toward *what*? It had left him here, his best friend—his only friend—dead, and not much else. Nothing around him seemed any more real than googled images on the computer screen and that created in him a hollow longing for the past and an anxious, confused view of the future. Those feelings followed Sally around like a stray dog he'd tossed a scrap.

The preacher droned on, laying down a thick blanket of Baptist guilt, working into a pitch. He'd moved down from the pulpit, waving his good book in the air every so often. Bill lay behind him, ignored.

When the preacher gave the altar call, Sally leaned to Mary and whispered, "Let's go."

Mary's hands rose to her jowls and tightened, causing her lips to pucker slightly as she spoke. "Oh, Sally," she said. Sally grabbed the hock of her wrist, and quickly led her out the door toward his Lexus. She struggled to catch her breath as he helped her into the passenger seat. "But the altar call," she huffed.

"Next time, Mary. You look like you could use a bite to eat."

"But," Mary stammered. "Well," she glanced back toward the funeral home doors. "I do get light-headed when I don't eat. And all the excitement with Jolene. Oh, this is nice." She smoothed a hand across the leather dash, down the fake, burl mahogany console.

"Thanks," he said as they rolled out of the parking lot. Mary didn't strike him as much different than the folks he and Bill convinced to sell their land. They kind of people who wanted to believe, who needed to believe, what someone told them. She'd tell him what he needed to know, eventually, because she'd believe she was helping. He'd make sure of that. He was never comfortable being the front person, that was all Bill, but this, this he could do.

A FEW MINUTES past nine, James Flowers strolled out of the Mason County Detention Center, sat on the curb and thumbed Colton a text. Colton hadn't responded to all the messages James had sent before they took his phone, but it was a new day and the sun shined bright.

Be there in 15, Colton finally texted back.

It had not been the best of weeks for James. Sunday evening, he dropped Brittany in front of her house and pulled away, knowing her parents waited inside. She was past curfew and at least one Smirnoff Ice past her limit. An hour later, James sat in his parents' house with the lights off, hoping they'd stop for ice cream after church and not come home until Britt's father, who was screaming about statutory and strangulation, had stopped banging on their front door.

By Monday night, he'd read Britt's text saying her parents didn't want her to see him anymore, endured *his* parents' wrath for over an hour, during which they recounted everything Brittany's father told them over the phone. all before James stormed out with a handful of clothes and landed at Colton's house, where he settled into their converted garage. *But only for a night or two,* Colton's mom said.

This time would be different. He'd show all of them. James had a buyer lined up for his truck on Wednesday morning and was taking the Marine Corps test again that afternoon. Third time's a charm. Couple of months and he'd be in Afghanistan, killing towel heads, like *Tour of Duty* on the Xbox, instead of worrying about the curfew of a sixteen-year-old who couldn't hold her booze, or his parents insisting he grow up. He was nineteen, for Christ's sake, a man. How much more grown up could he be?

After selling his truck, James took the bus to the recruitment center, took the test, and then waited for the officer to return. The Marines needed him. He was one of the few, had always been one of the few. Not every orphaned kid got adopted. Most of them slinked from foster home to foster home, but not James. Adopted young. And proud? Well, yeah. He'd not really done anything yet to be proud of, school wasn't really his thing, not sports, not friends — but, well, that's what the Marines were for — he'd find something there, and be damn proud to do it.

The recruiting officer came back, shaking his head. "Hell-fire, son," he said, "two wars on and a hundred places in the world going to shit, needing us to bail their sorry asses out. We don't cull much, but . . . damn. Ain't got to be that bright to run toward the bullets," he looked at the test again, "but this? You thought about trade school?"

The air blew out of James in a low, steady gush and the rest of that day and then Thursday kind of ran together. Thursday night, well, early Friday morning, he got popped at the bus stop in front of Dale Junior's Whiskey River. Couple of cops saw him stumble into a middle-aged couple while trying to get on the bus. Several overnight hours at the County spa now left him on the curb, the morning heat already baking a crispy edge on his hangover.

At 11:30, James saw Colton's red Ford Ranger round the corner. He slumped into the passenger seat and stared out the window.

"Dude. You know Mom's not gonna let you crash at the house after this."

James shrugged but didn't look at Colton. "Figured." He tapped the dash twice. "Let's ride."

Colton eased onto the highway and asked, "DUI, underage drinking, or something new?"

"Public intoxication."

"Huh. Boring. You should try something new."

"Thinking I'll start smoking weed regular, this drinking thing's not working so well."

"You and weed? I don't know. If it wasn't a DUI, where's your truck?"

"Sold it Wednesday. I'm set, though. Got three grand for it."

"Thought you paid fifty-five hundred for it, not more than a month ago."

"That was a month ago. Market's changed. Gas is going up again."

The light caught them, and Colton turned toward James while they idled, his dark face split with a sardonic smile. "That was your sixth vehicle since sixteen, J. Four just since we graduated," he said. "I gotta admire that."

"Shut up."

"Three G's the last of the money?"

A few days after turning eighteen, James cashed in a stock trust account his grandfather had left him, seventeen thousand dollars' worth. The Wall Street geniuses had flushed the market by that time, but it was coming back around. Had James not blown through the money like a former debutante goes through merlot, there'd be nearly thirty thousand on paper now.

"For the most part," James answered. "Well, less what I spent at the Whiskey. And my fine. Where we headed?"

"Your house. Mom says it's best."

"That won't be pretty. Let's ride a while instead, I need to work on plan B."

The light changed. James scrolled on his phone: Instagram, CarMax, Craig's List—Apartments, Facebook, ESPN, NRA, Porn Hub, bored. Still no wheels, and no place to crash.

"Last I saw you, you were off to take the Marine test again. All you got to do is hang on until Parris Island, right?"

"Those assholes. Screw their dumbass test. What's a test got to do with killing camel jockeys? I got their *Marine material* right here."

"Racist much? And if Brittany hadn't of done all your homework the past two years, you could've passed, you know."

"It wasn't like what they wanted us to learn had anything to do with anything that mattered. Screw 'em all. Everything you need to know is on the Internet anyway."

"There's this song you should listen to." Colton made a right turn. "John Mellencamp. Something like, *I like to fight authority, but it always wins. That's you, man. That's you.*"

"Sounds about right." James stared out the window, where the buildings had changed to houses and now the houses to scrub oaks and pine trees interrupted every so often by a fresh gash in the earth where the red dirt waited for the next housing development. None of it seemed real. Cardboard cutouts of how life was supposed to be. The buildings were empty, the housing developments sprung from the dirt but lacked even the shallow roots of the scrub oaks and pines they'd replaced. Somewhere past the boredom and the facades, James' real life waited, concrete and three-dimensional. All he had to do was find it.

He knew it existed, knew he had a place in it, had even seen a glimpse of it once, years earlier. It was during a non-descript baseball game most of his teammates thought important. Championship of Shitville or something. School had ended for the year and a couple of kids were out of town on vacation, so James swatted gnats in right field and took his obligatory three strikes batting ninth in the order, instead of his usual position as chief disrupter of dugout karma. The game was tied, last inning, one out. James wanted it to end. The pitcher walked a batter, then another. James kicked at the bare spot in right field, pounded his glove, kicked the dirt again. Then, he heard a low rumble coming down the street, growing louder. The motorcycle, a chopper, eased into view from behind the bleachers on the right field side. Painted orange flames curled down a purple gas tank and lapped across the front and rear fenders. Lots of chrome shining in the late day sun. The rider, an old guy, wore a leather vest and a black t-shirt, a faded USMC tattoo on his forearm, black cowboy boots resting on highway pegs, his gray goatee waving in the wind. It was a Harley, James saw that immediately, and he watched the machine glide past. The guy saw him and flashed a peace sign and a wide grin. A younger woman, the most beautiful James had ever seen, rode on the back. After the driver shot him the peace sign, he tapped the girl's leg, pointed again at James as he said something to her over his shoulder. She turned toward James, pulled down her tank top and swung her tits from side to side. As she did, the batter connected and the line drive bounced past James and rolled untouched to the fence. It didn't matter. At that moment, even if he couldn't name exactly what it was, James knew he wanted it, and one day, he'd have it.

James stretched his arm back to the jump seat of Colton's truck, fished around beneath the clothes and backpack. "Your .22 back here?" he asked.

"Yeah. Somewhere."

"I need to clear my head, do some thinking. Let's go to the dump."

"A'ight. Wanna pick up a twelve pack first?"

"Colton the psychic."

DR. KATHERINE SARDOFSKY sat at the bar in Red's Pure Country Saloon, tearing her cocktail napkin into tiny bits. It was three in the afternoon, and the place held only a handful of scattered people: a few construction-worker types, some bikers, and three random women casting occasional glances in her direction. Kat evaluated her dictum that arriving on time was to be late, and arriving early meant being on time, thinking college professors meeting a local in a country bar might warrant an exception to the rule. Three-thirty came and went with no sign of a guy wearing a Carhartt jacket and a Braves hat. More peopled filed in, the first shift at the last mill in town had ended. Still no sign of Arlen Johnson, only an assortment of locals, ordering shots. She glanced at the mirror behind the bar and wondered how, exactly, she had slipped to this particular station in life.

The noise in the bar grew louder; Kat felt overdressed. She ordered a second glass of chardonnay, which the bartender—a skinny, tattooed man with a thin ponytail and no eyeteeth, delivered with a grin and a new napkin. "That wine alright?" he asked. "Bottle's kinda dusty." He nodded toward the door. "You waiting on somebody?" According to her mother, she should be.

"A gentleman named Arlen Johnson. Do you know him?" She ripped the first corner of the new napkin and glanced over her shoulder.

"Darling, you can do better than Johnson. He ain't worth shooting and he sure as hell ain't a gentleman." He winked and flipped his ponytail off his shoulder. "I get off at six."

"I'll wait on Mr. Johnson, but thank you."

"Suit yourself. He usually rolls in around four. That'll be three-fifty for the wine."

Kat waited. At 4:05, a short, fat man waddled through the door carrying a manila envelope and wearing a Carhartt jacket and a Braves cap. He stopped and looked around the bar. Kat's breath caught, and she subconsciously touched her right index finger to the tip of her nose. For her summer, non-academic reading, she loved detective novels, a fact she hid from her colleagues, but the novels were no help now. She remained unsure of how *this* should unfold, which made her uneasy. The man approached and she touched her nose once more.

"Are you Arlen Johnson?" she asked.

"Depends. Who's asking?"

The cliché surprised her. "Why . . . well . . . I'm Dr. Katherine Sardofsky. Assistant Professor of Botany at Mason University," her voice wavered. Yes, maybe she should have been Associate by now, but she still wanted her job title to explain who she was in the same fashion that other titles for other people portrayed exactly who they were, but she remained unconvinced that it accomplished this. She continued, nonetheless. "My arrangements were to meet a Mr. Arlen Johnson here, at three-thirty." She looked at her watch. "Again, are you the Mr. Johnson in question?"

"You don't look like a doctor or a professor, not even the TV ones."

"I don't watch television. I find it obtuse, mundane, consistently derivative, and lacking in verisimilitude."

"Hmm. Me, either. Except for TruTV, they've got some good shows. Course, I'll watch a NASCAR race now and again. All the *CSI* shows, *Law and Order.* Oh, and *Celebrity Rehab,* that's funny. And *Wipeout,* I love the big balls. I think they should combine *Wipeout* and *Celebrity Rehab.* Now that's a show everybody'd watch." He paused, then leaned closer. Kat leaned away. "Don't tell anybody, but I watch *Oprah,* too. I'd be watching her right now, if it weren't for meeting you here. I figure it'll help me *evolve.*"

"So you are Mr. Johnson?"

"That's me, two hundred pounds of twisted steel and sex appeal. I reckon you want to see these." He pushed the envelope toward her.

Kat looked over both shoulders before opening it and sliding out the pictures. When she saw the first one, an "oh" slipped from her lips in a half-word, half moan, pre-orgasmic sort of way. Kat composed herself and whispered, "*Helianthus schweinitzii.*" For the first time she could recall, Kat felt herself balanced on the precipice of professional validation, not in the sense of her job, well, maybe that too, but to the world beyond academia. To her sister. To her mother.

Johnson nodded and adjusted his work pants. "Yeah, that's what I'm talking about. Wait . . . what?"

"It's Schweinitz's sunflower," she told him. "Where did you take these pictures? You've got to take me there."

"Now hold on. That weren't part of the deal."

"Is it on your land? Where did you take these pictures?"

"It ain't my land. I don't know who it belongs to."

"How'd you get the pictures, then?"

"What's all the fuss? Sunflowers? Look like weeds to me."

"They're endangered, practically extinct, and extremely rare. I've been trying to establish them in the lab, both hydroponically and in soil mediums, but I've failed. This could make my career. You didn't Photoshop these, did you?"

"Photo-what? Lady, I don't know what you're talking about. I'll fess up, I didn't even take the pictures."

"Internet? You downloaded them from the Web, didn't you? I knew it."

"I don't ride that superhighway. No sir, it's a conspiracy, that's how they track you. No, I got them from a friend of mine. His brother's wife's second cousin's daughter took them."

"I've got to meet her."

"Well, I don't know how you're gonna do that, I don't even know her. I told you, it was a friend's brother's . . ."

"Yes, yes, I know. We'll start there."

"Nope. That weren't part of the deal. But you buy me dinner and we'll talk about the future possibilities. Ain't no such thing as a free lunch, I know that."

The idea repulsed Kat, but not for long. "Fine then, tomorrow night."

"Naw, tomorrow night won't work. *World's Dumbest* comes on TruTV, and *CSI*. I don't miss those for nothing or nobody. Make it Friday night, Captain Steve's Fish Camp. Where can I pick you up at?"

Kat shuddered. "I'll meet you there. Seven-thirty."

"Naw, seven-thirty won't work. People bring lawn chairs to wait in line at Captain Steve's. Take forever if we wait until then. Better make it five o'clock."

"Fine, then. Five o'clock Friday it is."

A BOWL OF hushpuppies and honey-mustard butter sat on the table in the corner booth of the Brown Fedora Restaurant. Mary dipped hushpuppies in butter and popped them in her mouth, one after the other.

"So, how did you know Bill?" Sally asked.

"I'm sort of a counselor at church. For Preacher Mike." Mary ate the last hushpuppy and took a long drink of her tea, then waved the empty bowl at their waitress. "Before you join our church, you meet with a member for several weeks. Bible study, life lessons, church history, stuff like that. I helped him see he had to give up his old ways, why they were wrong."

"That's what you meant when you told Jolene about the sessions?"

"I would've never done the sort of thing Jolene suggested. Never. *Never.* I've been praying for her though."

Sally wanted to believe her, but the way she insisted caused some doubt.

The waitress brought a new bowl of hushpuppies. "Ready to order, hon?" She looked at Sally. Mary grabbed two puppies on her first swipe.

"Oh, I'll just have the salad. Extra ranch dressing," Mary said.

"Burger and fries," Sally ordered. "Giving up his old ways—I can't wrap my mind around that. Not Bill."

"It bothered him you couldn't accept his being saved. He wanted you to see the Light, too. I thought you had when you said, 'Let's go.' Bill would've been smiling down from Heaven if you'd walked down that aisle."

"I have enough imaginary friends, Mary. Tell me more about the old ways Bill needed to give up." She knew something, Sally was sure of it.

"I can't. That's between a parishioner and their counselor. Well, them and Preacher Mike. And the deacons, I could tell them about anything from a session, too."

"Jesus, Mary. You can tell all them, but you can't tell me? Me and Bill were best friends, you said that yourself."

"Don't blaspheme."

The meals came as Mary finished the hushpuppies. No help on what Bill was chasing nor the safety deposit box. Bill had been up to something, though, Sally was sure of it. They'd talked for years about churches having the biggest source of untapped cash, just hadn't found the right way of getting to it. But why didn't Bill share it with him? Something to do with Mary, or what she knew, no doubt. They finished the meal in silence.

Bill pushed his plate to the edge of the table and leaned back in the booth. "So tell me about how Bill died. I only read it in the paper."

"Oh, Sally. It was beautiful, in a way. Like the Rapture."

What was it with Jesus groupies? All that longing for heaven stuff made no sense. Getting there meant you were dead, and dead's dead any way you look at it. Sally shook his head. "Beautiful, huh? Go on."

"Bill talked about you a lot, what the two of you did over the years. Especially taking advantage of all those old folks. That was Satan's work, Sally. The Devil had his talons in both of you, Bill realized that. You should too, before it's too late."

"Yeah, I'm gonna work on that. How'd he die, Mary?"

"Last Sunday, we were on the campground side at the lake, holding a baptism service. Bill was last in line. He waded out to Preacher Mike. You should've seen it. When the water got deeper, his white baptism robe spread out like the wings of an angel. Since I was his counselor, I stood next to Preacher Mike. Preacher Mike said the words, placed his hand on Bill's forehead and pinched his nose while I wrapped my arms around his shoulders to support him as he went under.

"Preacher Mike said 'in the name of the Father,' and we leaned him back the first time. When Bill came up, he coughed and sputtered a bit, then sucked in a big breath as Preacher Mike said 'in the name of the Son,' and lowered him again.

"When we brought him up that time, he didn't make a sound, didn't even take a breath, but we didn't think nothing of it. Preacher Mike said 'in the name of the Holy Ghost,' and dunked him good, one last time. Bill twitched just a little while he was under the water, but he relaxed soon enough. I figured maybe it was the excitement of it all, the Spirit filling him, like when a sudden shiver runs all through your body. Then he just went limp. I almost dropped him he grew so heavy, but Preacher Mike helped me raise him back above the water. He fell back into my arms with the most peaceful smile a body's ever seen. Never took another breath in this world, got baptized and went straight to his mansion on high."

"Drowned?"

"No, they said it was a heart attack. Massive."

"Damn." It was like hearing about a car crash or a tornado destroying houses or something. You didn't really want the details, but it created an odd sense of satisfaction knowing it happened to someone else, not you. But this was Bill. They were practically the same age. Sally rubbed his left arm.

"Sally, watch your mouth."

"Sorry, Mary. Now much as I've enjoyed this, I need to stop by the bank before five."

"Me, too. Enjoyed it, I mean. I don't need to go to the bank. We should do this again."

The conversation with Mary didn't answer any questions or provide anything about the safety deposit box, but Sally realized, for the first time in months, all those other questions of his didn't seem as loud. He even felt pangs of his old self returning, a shoot of excitement about tracking down Bill's motives had appeared, frail as the first spring bud. Still, there was more he needed to know. "I'll call you," he said.

"That won't work, not right now. I forgot and left my cell phone in my dress pocket during the baptism. I'm on Facebook, though. Friend me."

2

Never Saw It Coming

Donnie Flowers liked Budweiser beer, every song George Jones ever recorded, and his job dispatching the trucks at the county dump. James liked Uncle Donnie, thought they were cut from the same cloth. Donnie always looked out for him, or at least tried to when his wife would let him.

The summer James turned ten, his parents sent him to Math & Science Bible Camp for a week, hoping James would gain an outside perspective on guilt while learning the fuzzy math needed to properly calculate the age of the earth to explain dinosaurs and disprove evolution once and for all. Donnie rescued him on the fourth day, claiming a family emergency. He spent the next two days teaching James to chew tobacco and shoot empty Bud bottles with a .22. Donnie dropped James at the camp's front gate on the last scheduled day and drove away, making James swear not to tell his parents when they arrived an hour later to take him home. It was a bonding experience for both, and James appreciated it still.

Donnie waved when they neared the fence. "Hidee-ho James. Colton, what's happening, homey? You boys shooting rats today?"

"Hey, Uncle Donnie. Which yard's open?"

"East lot. Nobody's working over there until end of the week. Won't nobody bother you. Fresh stuff, too. Stinking like a dead pole-cat in August. Be plenty of rats out."

James and Colton kept walking. Donnie eased the four-wheeler along on the opposite side of the fence. "Must be something heavy on your mind," he said. "You ain't been out in months."

"Thinking about a career change, is all."

"Well, shooting rats'll sure clear your mind. You remember where I cut the fence for you, right?"

"It ain't been that long, Uncle Donnie. We got it. Want us to leave you a couple beers in the usual place?" Colton held up the twelve pack, which now held eight beers.

"Naw. Much as I'd like one, better not chance it. Old Barack Hussein Obama's got the economy so screwed up, they're even laying off county workers. Best not give them a reason. No offense about the Obama stuff, Colton."

"None taken, sir."

"Good, good. I best get back to the dispatch shack. You boys have fun."

James and Colton settled in on a small pile of garbage partially covered in dirt. The ground was uneven, but James found an old cooler and Colton a five-gallon plastic bucket for seats. They wedged them into the dirt and trash, trying to get a stable foundation for aiming. In a few minutes, the first rat crawled to the top side of a freezer that lay on its side forty yards away. James took a pull from his beer and pointed at the varmint with the can. "Fat one. You take him."

"You can have the first shot if you want it."

"Go ahead. I'll take the next one."

Colton raised the rifle, sighted and squeezed. His shot drifted off target by a couple inches and hit the rat in the hindquarters. It fell spread-eagled, its front claws trying to gain traction on the slick sides of the freezer as it slid toward the edge. It caught itself on the rubber gasket where the door once connected and hung by its front paws, swinging slightly left to right as it tried to haul itself to safety.

Colton sighted again. The force of his second shot knocked the rat inside the freezer.

"Good one," James told him and took the rifle. "Extra points for style."

"So what's next?" Colton asked.

"It'll come to me. You just got to stay open to the possibilities the universe offers, C-note. Chill-ax. You worry too much."

Two more rats appeared and crawled inside the freezer to inspect the damage inflicted upon their cousin. After a minute or two, one waddled out and started edging its way along the backrest of a broken sofa, its body silhouetted in the slanted rays of sunlight.

"Not worried about me. I start classes this fall, remember?"

"Oh yeah. College man." James pulled the trigger and the rat fell out of sight behind the couch. "Classes, tests, reading, for God's sake. Bor—ing." He handed the gun back to Colton.

The second rat followed the same path toward the sofa and Colton tracked him through the scope. "Why do sorority girls wear fur lined panties?" he asked. James grunted. Colton squeezed off the shot. The rat squealed as it died. "To keep their ankles warm," Colton answered his own question.

"Not for me. Got bigger things in mind."

"What about Brittany?" Colton reloaded the magazine, slid it back in place and chambered a shell.

"Britt?" Yeah, that was a question. Plenty of hints and innuendo lately. They'd been hooking up for well over a year, but, with graduation looming, Brittany now mentioned things like plans, responsibility—a job, often enough that it made James uneasy. Sure, she was a hook-up, at first, but somewhere along the line he realized that, even when she wasn't around, he thought about her, remembered something silly she'd said, the way her forehead furrowed just so when she concentrated on getting the right angle or focus for a photo. But that wasn't the kind of thing he could tell Colton, or anyone else. "Brittany's just a hook-up. There any time I want it. Damn, look at that one." James stood and pointed to the corner of the garbage pile where a larger rodent had just come into view.

"Yeah, you keep thinking that, it'll be you and Rosie." Colton looked through the scope. "Ain't a rat. That's a possum." He stood up for a better look. "Yep. Possum."

"My shot, gimme the rifle."

Colton took a step toward James with the gun outstretched. The rubbish beneath him shifted and he lost his balance. When the gun hit the ground, it went off and the shell Colton had chambered rifled out of the barrel and through the top of James' right foot before thumping into a discarded bassinette.

James grabbed his right ankle with both hands and started hopping around, yelling, "ow, ow, ow," until he finally fell over backward. He let go of his ankle but kept his foot in the air. Colton got up, walked over and leaned in for a closer look. He inspected the top side of James' shoe which was now staining red. He grabbed James' heel and turned his foot to inspect the damage from the bullet's exit. James "ow-ed" a couple more times.

"Ha. Went right through," Colton said.

"What's it look like on the bottom?" James winced.

"You remember that commercial where they shot an apple in slow motion? How it kind of exploded out, all jagged and stuff? Looks like that." He took his finger and pushed on the sole of James' tennis shoe an inch below the wound. "That hurt?"

"You bastard," James said and jerked his foot away. "Help me up."

Colton looked toward the trash pile, then picked up the rifle. "Hang on a second," he said. The possum never saw it coming.

Colton went for Donnie and the four-wheeler. After making sure James could move all his toes, Donnie wrapped gauze from the first aid kit around James' foot. The tape had long since disappeared from the kit, but Donnie improvised with the roll of Duct tape he kept for occasions such as this.

"Should I take him to the emergency room?" Colton asked.

"Naw." Donnie hitched up the right sleeve of his work shirt and pointed to a puckered scar just above his elbow. He turned his arm and showed them another, slightly larger spot on his triceps. "Old girlfriend give me that one. Went clean through, like James' here. Ain't seen a doctor yet. Poured some mint gin on my arm and rinsed it out with the garden hose. Little tape and a couple of weeks — good as new. James'll be fine. No need to alarm no doctors."

"Thanks, Uncle Donnie. Help me up, C-note." They helped James over to Colton's truck, let him swing his legs inside, and Donnie eased the door closed as Colton went to the driver's side. Donnie leaned on the passenger door and looked at James for a long minute.

"You okay?" he asked.

"Right as rain. Thanks for taping me up." James finished another beer and dropped the empty in the bag between his feet.

"No, I mean are you, you know, okay? Talked to your daddy. He's my brother and all, but he can be an asshole."

"Oh. That."

"I'd let you stay with me, James, but Ruth Ann, you know how she is. You got some place else in mind?"

"Been crashing at Colton's. I'll figure something out long term." He pounded his fist on the dashboard and then shook his finger at Colton. "Drive me to the store, Miss Daisy. Thanks again, Uncle Donnie, for everything. We're gonna split."

"A'ight then. You boys keep the shiny side up."

After three selections, Colton finally settled on a live, bootleg Modeski, Martin, and Wood CD and the jams were the only sound in the truck for the first several miles toward town. The throbbing in James' foot distracted him. Colton had not asked where, and James didn't know what he'd tell him if he did. He needed to think. He couldn't go back to Colton's. Don't like the message this sends, Colton's mom said, and James knew exactly what she meant. He'd overstayed his welcome for one thing, but she was a parent first and letting him crash there violated some kind of parent code.

James closed his eyes and leaned his head on the headrest. After another few miles, the word homeless scrolled across his brain. He had cash left, just pick a place. No more homeless. The plan had been to live wherever the U.S. Marine Corps told him to live. Picking a place of his own stunk of resignation, an admission that . . . that . . . screw it, they found him as a baby on the steps of Sister Hosanna's Fortune Telling, Tarot Readings, & Consignment Shop, that meant something. And the biker dude and his old lady, they wouldn't mope around feeling sorry for themselves, would they? Hell no. This was America, damn it, and if the Marines wouldn't have him, he'd find another way. He had options. He'd find something that'd work, and make Brittany proud, too.

"C-note, you know that no-tell motel? The one on Roosevelt?"

"Sketchy place. The Budget-Tel Motel, right?"

"One and the same. We'll go by your place, pick up my shit, and I'll get me a room there, they rent by the week. Good place to start the rest of my life."

"Hells yeah. Wait, start your life doing what?"

"You worry too much. There's possibility all around, you just got to see it. Take a chance, Columbus did. That's my new saying, my new rule."

Colton slowed to a stop. They were in town now, a half mile from the Budget-Tel. Colton craned his neck out the window, looking at the line of cars in front of him. "Why the traffic jam?" he asked.

James looked out his window. "Funeral home up here on the right. Some stiff bought the farm."

They crawled forward a few car lengths.

"Is it the processional?" Colton asked.

A few more car lengths.

"Nope." James pointed toward the funeral home parking lot. "Pull up some and stop."

"What is it?"

James held his phone out the window. "Stop, stop. I gotta get the pic. Two fat chicks fighting." Click. "Look, now they're turning on the older guy. They're gonna kick his ass. Dude needs to bounce, he shoulda known better."

Colton shook his head and pulled forward, accelerating up to speed. "That's not right, man."

"Dude. This is my new profile pic. Check it." James held the phone in front of Colton's face.

Colton swatted it away. "Let me drive. We're coming up on the Budget-Tel. Last chance, you sure about this?"

"Base camp, brother. I'm going to the top of the mountain from here. Wait on me, I'll check in, then we can go get my stuff."

For most of his life, everything came relatively easy for Sally. He made decent grades in school with little effort. He played JV baseball and basketball. Never a star, but he managed to earn playing time and could have made the varsity squads had he bothered going to tryouts. He didn't date cheerleaders, but he never had a problem finding company on the weekends, either. Never the big man on campus, but everybody knew him and, in general, liked him. Sally had a way of making people feel at ease—when asked if they considered Sally a friend, most kids in his class would have shrugged, considered it for a moment, and answered, "Yeah, I guess." Pose the same question to Sally and he'd have shrugged, considered it, and said "No, not really."

After high school, he managed to sit through his first two semesters at the local college, earn C's, but made no real friends there either. After the spring semester, he took a summer job at the local manufacturing plant. The only dark cloud in his life passed over him a few weeks later. His father, who'd been a moonshiner long after the profession's appeal waned, drove Sally's mother and his younger brother, Artie, to Lake Fontana for a vacation. One night, they crossed the Tennessee border headed for a barbecue place in Alcoa, where his father had too much to drink. Coming back, their Plymouth missed a curve on Highway 129, ran off the mountain, and all three died. Sally dealt with the news like everything else—navigating the grief and the legal issues of settling an estate with relative ease and detachment. That fall, a full-time spot driving a forklift opened and Sally quit college to begin his real life.

It didn't take long before boredom won out, and as the male species will do, Sally and his co-workers conceived the First International Fork Lift Time Trials to keep them entertained. They designed a course that snaked in and out of aisles C and D in the warehouse, then down the long straightaway in the center of the plant before making a ninety-degree right at the bar stock racks. After the racks came a series of S turns through Tool and Die, then another, shorter, straight section past Assembly before a final ninety-degree left-hand turn into aisle G of the stockroom, and then a short dash to the finish line. Everyone took turns, Bennett kept records of the best times, and the Trials kept boredom at a manageable level for a while.

As male genetics require, healthy competition soon developed, then a points system, which naturally led to elaborate wagering. When the initial interest waned, the boys on the dock instituted a playoff system. For the first time in his life, Sally found himself genuinely excited about something, challenged even, and the feeling overtook him. He made his way up the chart, came through the regular season unscathed, and landed in the playoffs. They raced against the clock, always using the same forklift, and best times came down to driving skill, how the driver handled the corners. Sally understood this and knew he could finish as champion based on his technique alone, which, as always, came naturally.

That wasn't enough. Sally became obsessed with winning, spent hours thinking of ways to go faster, turn sharper. He bet heavy, took action on the side, and parlayed it into a payday that would equal his weekly check. If he won.

It came down to him and Hurley Knaus, and once again, serendipity smiled on Sally. A few days before the finals, Shot Baucom's appendix ruptured and they asked Sally to cover his spot on the graveyard shift for the week he was out, which provided opportunity for Sally to open the governors on the fork lift a bit. Hurley wouldn't know the difference and with the extra speed from the horsepower, he'd never be able to keep it on the track.

Hurley started his run and held it steady for a while, but then cut the last turn too short and his left fork caught the outside support of the shelving on aisle G. The support leg ripped from its concrete mooring, unleashing racks from the top down, and skids crashed to the floor. Thousands, tens of thousands, of rogue ball bearings, gear blanks, and housing assemblies rolled to every corner of the plant. Management wrote Hurley up—three days without pay and loss of his fork lift license for a year, which meant demoted to working with the stock girls, pulling parts for sub-assembly. Sally won by default, but Management ended the Time Trials.

Sally collected his money, but the guys were suspicious. They'd known Hurley a long time, Sally was still the new guy. It didn't surprise or bother him to eat lunch alone. That lasted two weeks. One day at lunch, without warning Bill Tucker plopped down across the picnic table from Sally. Bill was only a couple years older than him, but Sally couldn't recall ever speaking to him before. Bill didn't say a word, eating in slow and deliberate bites. Sally concentrated on his bologna sandwich, wondering for a moment if Bill had been sent by the others, maybe to ask him to return the money. He had no intentions of that, he needed cash more than he needed friends.

When Sally finished eating, Bill cleared his throat and leaned forward.

"So okay," he started. "I know you tinkered with the governors." Sally stared at Bill. He had no intention of admitting anything one way or the other. Just as the silence grew heavy, Bill continued.

"Well, I gotta respect that. You saw an opportunity and you took advantage of it."

Sally grinned.

"Here's the deal," Bill leaned closer, "I started a little real-estate investment business on the side a few months ago, and I could use a partner. We'll never have a thing working here the next thirty years. It's a way out."

Sally considered himself a pretty good judge of people, had a knack for sizing them up quickly and then shaping his reaction to them accordingly. Most people he initially viewed with disdain or condescension, but there was something about Bill he instantly liked. "I don't know a thing about selling houses," he told him. "Sounds boring."

"You don't have to know about selling houses. It's like you winning this race, you gotta know how to take advantage of an opportunity. Now, I got a little cash put back. Heard you had some estate money. We pool our resources, we can make some deals, make some real money." Bill looked at the distant tables where the other fellows sat. "This county's full of *them*," he jutted his chin toward the men.

Sally knew what he meant by *them*. He nodded.

Bill continued, leaning closer still. "I'm telling you, next twenty, thirty years, what with Charlotte and everything, real estate's gonna be the thing around here. Whatta ya say? I'll handle all the public stuff, you work the locals."

That was that. More than friends, Bill became the closest thing to family Sally knew. Almost thirty years together, and they'd been through plenty. Made a ton of money, a pile of deals. Sally never grew tired of it, not the chase, at least. The money? After cleaning up in the early nineties land rush, the money didn't matter anymore. Chasing the deal, that mattered, kept him going.

But that feeling began to fade soon after he and Bill stopped talking. In a few months, it disappeared altogether. Sally went from one mid-life crisis to the next, bored with each as quickly as he'd found it until his days began to ooze together in a pointless, mind-numbing and spirit-crushing drift that led to him daydreaming about his eventual demise. Other than the occasional lunch at the Brown Fedora, Sally spent most of his time sitting at home.

But now . . . now, well, Sally felt something stirring again. He had to know what happened, had to know what Bill was working on and why Bill had felt he'd had to keep it secret.

Mary knew, and all he had to do was get it out of her.

When Dr. Ransom Leaderlick threw the photos on the desk, they slid toward the edge, teetered, wavered—Kat reached too late—and they spilled across the floor at her feet. She bent to gather them, fully aware of Dr. Leaderlick leering down her blouse. He was that guy, most of them were. May as well use it to her advantage. Other than that, he was harmless. She lingered, what could it hurt? It might help. Kat knew the pictures provided nothing without documentation, the photographer, the location, anything to prove their authenticity, but she needed his departmental approval to continue.

"It's a ruse, Dr. Sardofsky. Any six-year-old with a computer could produce these photographs," he said.

"Yes, but . . ."

"This hardly qualifies as research under the new Strategic Revision Plan. You will never receive tenure if you insist on following this path. And continued funding? I don't think so. Selecting this—this weed as the focus of your research project based solely on these photographs borders on malfeasance."

"Malfeasance? How . . ." Kat touched the tip of her nose.

"Malfeasance, yes. Misconduct, the commission of an unlawful act."

She thought of a few unlawful acts she'd enjoy at the moment. Strangulation by kudzu. Feeding tiny but copious bits of Leaderlick's flesh to a Venus flytrap. She'd use tweezers, of course, the thought of touching his skin was unbearable.

He was her boss, the department chair by default, nobody else wanted the position. Leaderlick the Administrator. Hadn't published a paper in over a decade, but he could recite the University's new Twelve Point Strategic Revision Plan verbatim, all eighteen pages. Everyone knew each of the twelve points originated not in the cloistered halls of academia but in the trustee boardroom. Give them credit, the suits understood subtext. The points sounded as if the best interests of first the students, then the faculty, were considered, but the astute reader saw each point for what it really was—unabashed homage to the bottom line. Leaderlick understood the bottom line like a mountain climber understood gravity, and Kat knew he'd untie her belay without hesitation, letting her career plummet toward the rocks below.

"Yes, I know what malfeasance means, Dr. Leaderlick, and I know using the photos without the source constitutes plagiarism. But I can find the source, the photographer. She's local. I have a contact who knows her. I'm meeting him tonight for dinner."

Leaderlick removed his glasses and blinked. Kat looked away. Leaderlick had a tick, either a flaw in his DNA or a misfiring synapse that would not allow his eyes to blink simultaneously. The right eyelid always snapped closed a millisecond after the left. Or perhaps the left eyelid was early, no one was sure. It had been discussed for years, though, and not just among colleagues in the Science building. Even the freshmen entering Leaderlick's Intro to Botany class somehow all knew in advance. More than one had invested far too much time and effort into staring at Leaderlick's blinking eyes and wondering what else about him might be off kilter. Some days, Kat admired that his dedication to the University bordered on the obsessive. Most days, Kat found herself mentally constructing detailed plans for his murder.

"Oh, I didn't realize you were dating. Perhaps your time might be better spent developing a more relevant research project rather than pursuing social gratification."

What? Had her boss and her mother started meeting to discuss the state of her social calendar? Actually, for once, she agreed with Leaderlick. Get her career in order, move a few steps closer to tenure, maybe then she'd consider a date. She shook her head, trying to clear the picture of Arlen Johnson from her mind. "It's not a date, it's research," she answered.

"Dr. Sardofsky, the Twelve Point Strategic Revision Plan is very clear on matters such as this. Research projects must be viable, useful, in the world outside of academia. Student assistants must learn applicable skills, employable skills. I fail to see how study of this," he looked at his notes, "this *sunflower* satisfies any of the criteria."

Kat had waited for this moment, prepared for it, stood naked in front of her bathroom mirror and rehearsed her answer for hours.

"Schweinitz's sunflower was indigenous to the Eastern Piedmont Prairies for centuries. Its tuberous roots served as a food source for local Native American tribes. By identifying prairie remnants, finding and protecting native populations, and re-establishing the species, the possibility exists of creating, or reintroducing, a new food source that may eventually be viable as a cash crop for farmers." Just as she rehearsed—had she stopped there. She couldn't resist adding, "And they're pretty."

Leaderlick eased back in his leather chair. "Hmm. A cash crop, that's something to consider." He leaned forward and blinked twice. Or four times, if Kat counted each individual eyelid. "I suppose I could grant some leeway under the auspices of the Twelve Point Plan."

"Thank you, Ransom. Dr. Leaderlick. Thank you."

"I'll expect detailed reports as you progress. And no additional funding. Not yet. I expect results, Dr. Sardofsky. Your future at Mason, in academia itself, rests on this project, be it fortuitous or calamitous."

"Absolutely, yes."

Kat briefly considered wearing her black dress and heels to Captain Steve's Fish Camp that night, but decided against it. Too soon to celebrate.

In Statler Town Park—a one-and-a-half-acre patch of crabgrass, a seesaw, picnic table, three swings and a half dozen park benches—the crepe myrtles bloomed. A few of the transplants convinced everyone else that annexation by Charlotte was imminent and they incorporated a patch of land surrounding the local crossroads. But incorporation, becoming a town, brought its own share of detritus. A town council was needed, and a mayor. Jobs were created. And taxes. The group who'd fanned the rumors of Charlotte's possible expansion appointed themselves as council and elected a mayor from their ranks. A town needs officials; officials need corruption to self-validate. The newly appointed mayor had a brother-in-law who owned a landscaping company suffering from poor management and a lack of profitable contracts. A park was proposed, land was condemned, contracts were awarded, the brother-in-law kicked back the appropriate amount to the mayor, and now the crepe myrtle blooms draped like heavy clusters of fat grapes around the edges of the park.

A young girl sat alone, eating an ice cream cone and listening to Kellie Pickler on her iPod. On the bench beside her rested a bag of Skittles, her camera, and a laptop. She wore Daisy Duke cutoffs and a lime green halter top, and her tanned legs stretched out in front of her like a river of clover honey. A small plane passed overhead. She kept crossing and uncrossing her legs at the ankle as she licked the cone. Closing her eyes, she felt the sun hot on her bare skin. In the distance, the moan of an approaching train. Another taste of the ice cream and she closed her eyes again, arched her neck and tilted her face toward the sun as she swallowed, enjoying the feel of the cool dessert melting down the back of her throat.

Directly across the park, a man in an Atlanta Braves hat sat on another bench, eating a livermush sandwich while watching the girl enjoy her ice cream. When she tilted her head upward and swallowed, he bit his tongue. Every job has its hazards.

3

Opportunity

Sally liked to know who he was dealing with, it made negotiating easier. Now, standing in front of the Mason City Bank, he wished he'd been a bit more visible in the operation with Bill. If he had, he'd have a better feel for how to handle the whole safety deposit box situation. It was a small bank, owned and operated by Hanley "Boot" Jackson. Sally had history in Mason County, knew a lot of people, but the circles he ran in didn't include bank presidents, or people like them. Bill always handled folks like that. So, Sally didn't know Jackson, but he knew of him. Not being exactly sure how to navigate this first meeting with Jackson, caused a touch of the resentment he'd secretly held for Bill to surface. As close as they'd been, Sally had always felt second, somehow.

Sally looked up at the building, followed the sweeping line of the marbled steps to the heavily-carved oak doors. He appreciated the building's sturdiness, its longevity. He knew it was built in 1875 and at the time, was considered a garish monument to the owner's sense of self-importance, which was out of character for its purpose—a general store. But here it stood, and it'd be here longer still. A man could be remembered for worse things after he was gone. Or not remembered at all.

He sighed and started up the steps. After the Big Crash in '29, Boot's great grandfather, Hanley "Root" Jackson bought the property and started Mason City Bank. Boot took over just before the Reagan years anointed capitalism the national religion. His loans were good, albeit old-fashioned, and his policies sound. He had a reputation for keeping his mouth shut when a situation—a second account, a sudden safety deposit box—required it. Sally knew this, and it explained why Bill Tucker preferred Jackson's—and Mason City Bank's—services.

Sally also knew Bill kept several accounts, some Jolene knew about and some she didn't. Sally wasn't concerned about any of those. Bill had told him years ago that every account Jolene didn't know about had already been designated to a daughter from a "brief indiscretion" in the next County. Sally's only concern was the remaining safety deposit box, the one Bill told him was his if he died, and Sally wondered what, if anything, Bill's banker friend knew about its contents. Sally swallowed any thoughts of being second and opened the door with confidence.

THE MAID VACUUMED in room 115 of the Budget-Tel Motel, which caused James to turn up the volume on the TV. Gajendranath and Eenakshi Dasgupta advertised the Budget-Tel as locally and independently owned and offered rooms monthly, weekly, and nightly. Adding the hourly rental option proved to be the carrot that kept them solvent, though. That, and a willingness to accept cash without a credit card or photo ID behind it. The credit card and expense account crowd always stopped at the Hampton Inn or the Holiday Inn Express eight miles west. It took a certain amount of conviction to drive past those establishments and settle into the Budget-Tel.

The clientele oozed conviction: long-haul truckers over their hour limit and low on speed, low-level Republicans and their same-sex partners, lower-level Democrats and cheap hookers. Fundamentalist preachers with their church secretaries, both of whom always thumbed through the Gideon's in the nightstand drawer. And there were the regulars: the Hispanics who booked rooms 118, 119, and 120 by the month. On Friday, James watched them lead a goat into room 120, and on Saturday they invited all the current guests, James included, to join them in the motel's small dirt and gravel recreation area for a barbeque.

The maid stopped the vacuum and settled into the room's plastic deck chair as she aimlessly dusted the table. She stared at the TV. James looked at her, the TV, back at her, the TV. The noon day anchor for WAOC out of Charlotte droned about an overturned eighteen wheeler carrying chickens and the cops' efforts to arrest the residents of the nearby low-income housing project for stealing the freed birds. The screen switched to a video of uniformed policemen, tasers ready, chasing the people, who were chasing the chickens. When the anchor reappeared, the maid pointed at the screen and smiled at James. "Ese hombre tiene pelo agradable," she said.

"It's W—A—O—C," James pronounced each letter, each word, slowly. "We—Air—Only—Crime."

"Pelo agradable," she repeated, touching her hair with one hand and pointing at the screen with the other.

"See," James told her. "You want cerveza?"

She shook her head no and resumed dusting and watching the TV.

The next story was brief and James only gave it passing notice as he lifted his Budweiser for the maid to finish with the tabletop. The anchor mentioned an information session scheduled for that evening from six to eight at the local college. A politician would discuss the bill he planned to introduce calling for the legalization of medical marijuana in North Carolina. The piece immediately following that one caught more of James' attention. The screen filled with DEA agents and local deputies throwing armloads of pot plants on a blazing fire. They all grinned at James from the TV. James grinned back.

The maid shook her head. "Norteamericanos han perdido su sentido de ironía," she mumbled.

When she said it, James jumped to his feet, bounced one-legged on the center of the bed, and shook his finger at her. "I'm trying to get an idea here, Juanita," he yelled. "If you gotta talk, speak American."

The maid looked frightened, then indignant, and gathered her dust cloth and vacuum before marching out the door. She quickly returned with a small stack of clean towels and washcloths, which she dropped just inside the doorway. "You Americanos have lost your sense of irony. You are being no fun anymore," she snapped, then slammed the door.

James turned the TV louder, found a pen and tore a page with plenty of white space at the top and bottom from the Gideon's.

The agents led the guilty grower, Timothy Phillips, past the camera. James wrote down the guy's name. Phillips looked innocent—early forties, khakis, light blue button-down oxford shirt, handcuffs, short black hair and a paid-for porcelain smile. James wrote *dress like a nerd* on the Gideon's page. The voiceover told James the authorities seized one hundred and twenty-three plants with a street value of 250 K. James wrote *think big*. The report took a personal turn. Phillips had a wife and three kids, the youngest of which had a disease James couldn't pronounce, but it sounded expensive. Phillips worked for one of the mega-banks until the bogus loans took them down a couple notches, leaving Phillips jobless, overqualified and without a bailout bonus. His benefits ran out several months back, the bank he used to work for started foreclosure proceedings, the sick kid's medical bills rolled on, and Mrs. Phillips, who was kinda hot for an old chick, cried on cue, telling the camera "he only wanted to provide for us."

The anchor reappeared, bantering with the female co-anchor. "Michele, I wonder if Phillips had planned to attend the session on legalizing medical marijuana tonight at the college?" he asked.

"Well Howard, if he did, those plans have changed now," Michele answered. "Next up—new leash laws have one local neighborhood hot under the collar."

James jumped from the bed. "Thank you," he told the TV. "Legal weed, that's it. But what session? When? Where?"

The station went to a commercial advertising a new prescription drug for fibromyalgia. James grabbed his phone and scrolled for the WAOC web site. He found the link to the report about that night's session and jotted down the details. James reached for the remote, but paused when the anchor returned. That guy's got nice hair for an old dude, he thought, then turned off the set and called Colton. Voice mail: "C-note, pick me up at the No-Tell Motel. Four'ish. Wear shoes, we're going to college. Hit me back." He hung up and texted just to make sure.

SOMEBODY ONCE SAID if you picked America up by the east coast and tilted it on edge, everything not nailed down would slide right into Hollywood. That tilt began in the 1920's with talking movies, but the angle steepened when Elvis hit the stage. It went full vertical in the summer of 2000. The Y2K meltdown didn't happen, Brittany Combs turned eight, and also that summer, after modest failures in both Britain and Australia, *Survivor* aired in the United States of America and a spectacular convergence of ever-diminishing American intellect, crippling narcissism, and lazy voyeurism occurred. The tilt completed, a downward slide on the scale of the Roman Empire's rushed westward toward Cahuenga Pass and the corner of Fairfax and Melrose.

Sally had never seen *Survivor,* but he knew all about America's rise and its subsequent slide. The real-estate market went crazy soon after the turn of the century—ridiculously high prices for land and property and banks loaning ten, twenty, even thirty percent over value with nothing down—until 2007. Then, the real-estate bubble burst and the banks, deemed too big to fail, failed. Sally took a hit, but Boot Jackson kept Mason City Bank solvent and healthy.

The guard directed Sally toward Boot's office, where Sally handed the assistant a copy of his and Bill's partnership agreement and the note from Bill about the safety deposit box.

"Mr. Jackson has someone in his office, but he should be finished soon, if you'd like to have a seat," the assistant told him.

"Thanks," Sally answered, then took a seat.

A few minutes later, a young blonde came in, spoke to the assistant, then took the seat next to Sally. Sally guessed she was about eighteen or nineteen, but he'd reached the age where he couldn't really tell the age of anyone younger than mid-thirties. He had nothing against young people, didn't hold them in any disregard like so many his age did, he was just never around them enough to have much opinion at all.

The girl fished a book from her backpack and flipped to a page she had marked. Sally noticed the paperback was dog-eared and worn; she'd obviously spent a lot of time with it, but it didn't look like a schoolbook. Sally glanced at the title—*Survivor Auditions for Dummies*. He didn't recognize it. The girl glanced up and smiled at him.

"You like *Survivor?*" she asked.

"No, no. I've not read it," Sally grinned. "I'm more of a *Sports Illustrated* guy."

The girl looked confused for a moment, then realized he was talking about her book. "Oh," she said, "you mean the book." She held the paperback up for him, as if that would help him understand. "I'm gonna be, like, a reality TV star. This book is to help with the audition for *Survivor,* the TV show," she explained.

Sally was vaguely aware of the concept of reality TV, but even the concept seemed absurd to him.

"What the hell's a reality TV star?" he asked.

"There's *Survivor.* That's the best. Then *Big Brother, Amazing Race,* there's lots of them, *Dancing With the Stars* is big, but you need to win one of the others first, you know, so you'll be a star and all, before you can be on that one. Don't you watch TV?"

"But what *is* it? I get the reality TV thing, but *Survivor,* I mean. What do you do on the show?" Sally asked.

"You have like, challenges and stuff. Make alliances, vote people off. Then you win a million dollars and you're a star."

"So that book tells you how to win the million, does it?"

"Not how to win," she said. "How to audition. What they're looking for. You need a video. That's why I'm opening a savings account, to pay for my audition video. Then there's implants, get my nose fixed, stuff like that. They vote the ugly people off first. And a tattoo, I'll need a cool tat. I need twenty thousand, total."

"Sounds like you have a plan and a budget."

"Oh, totes."

The office door opened. "Mr. Hinson. Come in. How might I help you today?"

"Well, that's me. Good luck with your contest."

"Thanks. I'll be on in a year or two, watch for me. My name's Brittany, but my reality TV name will be Luna. Luna Marze."

"Luna, huh? That'll be your reality TV name?" He chuckled. "Well, you got my vote, Luna."

4

Do It for Love

In the summer of 1973, Livingston Carr's father walked along the South Carolina shore, sounds from a prototype personal metal detector beeping in his ears. A few miles north, at the Myrtle Beach Municipal Airport, another man, a pilot, launched his aircraft. The plane was a Cessna kit model, assembled solely by the pilot. When he felt liftoff, he swelled with patriotic pride. He lovingly tapped the plane's console. This kind of ingenuity is what made this country great.

He flew south, toward Charleston, then circled, and buzzed Edisto Island before heading back north. Ten miles south of Murrell's Inlet, the pilot noticed a thin spray of oil hitting his windshield. Two miles south, the plane's single prop worked loose and spun harmlessly into the Atlantic. The pilot wrangled the plane into a downward glide, aiming for the hard-packed sand at the water's edge, too distracted and terrified to notice the man walking alone on the sand.

As the plane drew nearer, only feet from the sand, Livingston's father listened as the beeping in his headphones increased. His anticipation increased proportionately. The buzzing and the anticipation both ended when the plane hit him. Livingston, eight at the time, clutched at fuzzy memories of his father to this day.

His father was an influence, though. Genetics installed the father's neuroses into the boy and Livingston's mother told him everything about his father, imprinted his work ethic, his morality. Repeatedly. She buried those lessons deeper than the shrink's brand of detectors could fathom. By the time Livingston graduated college he'd wrapped his dead father's dogma around him like a prophylactic.

When something challenged Livingston, he silently repeated his life's mantra: honest, stable, dependable, loyal. He even developed a series of tics, twitches, habits, and rituals to remind him of the mantra when he faltered.

His boss at the Orangutan Condom Company appreciated that about Livingston, especially the loyal part. He focused on it as he waited for Livingston to appear in his office.

"Liv, come in, have a seat."

"Thank you, Mr. Arnold." Livingston took a seat.

"Listen, you're a valued employee, a straight-shooter, so I'm just gonna get straight to it."

"Yes?"

"We gotta let you go. Nothing personal. We're cutting nine others. This damn economy, nobody wants to fuck when their house is being foreclosed. You know what I'm saying? Nobody but kids anyways, and hell, most of them don't wear rubbers. Then you get more bastard young 'uns, more sucking the government tit, more drain on the economy, more lay-offs. It's a vicious cycle, I tell you. I hate to start your new year off this way. Corporate wanted it done before Christmas, but hell, we been fighting this shit nearly two years, I told them we'd wait until after the holidays. Appreciate you working the overtime last week to finish up the year-end inventory, by the way."

"But, effective when?"

"Oh security's cleaning your desk out right now. It's today buddy. Sorry about that."

"Well...I guess...Is there a severance? What about my retirement? I've been contributing for all of my twenty-two years here."

"Here's your last check. And you need to sign this."

Livingston signed it and slid the paper back toward Mr. Arnold. "What is it?" he asked.

"About that retirement." He waved the signed paper in the air. "This here is a confidentiality agreement you've signed, so what I'm about to tell you, you can't tell anyone, capisce? I know a man like you would never think of such a thing, right?"

"Okay. I guess."

"Our retirement fund, all of it, every freaking cent, was invested with Bernie Madoff. That shit's gone. It's like Elvis, Livingston. It ain't ever coming back."

"But what am I . . ."

The door opened and two security guards entered. One of them carried a small box of personal items from Livingston's desk and the other gave Arnold a thumbs up. "Good to go," he said. Arnold nodded and stood.

"Well, Livingston, it's been a pleasure working with you. Joe and Bobby here will walk you to your car. Let's see," he shuffled the papers on his desk. "Yeah, here it is, all your paperwork."

Livingston stared at the manila envelope in his hands.

"Oh, I almost forgot." He reached in the credenza behind his desk and tossed a box of Orangutan Brand Condoms on the desk. "Corporate said to give everyone a box when they left."

Livingston picked up the box and read the slogan: *Orangutan Brand—For Those Times When Only Wild Monkey Sex Will Do.* How could he tell Trudy?

He couldn't, and that presented Livingston with a problem. In sixteen years of marriage, he'd never lied to Trudy. Not once. Sure, he told her the poodle perm looked great, he adored her mother, and he agreed that Barry Manilow was a musical genius, but those weren't really lies. Sometimes Trudy needed reassuring, that's all. She'd endured enough in her life, she deserved that much. Even something as simple as grocery shopping challenged her. Everyone knew they always put the best selection of fruits and produce at the top of the pile.

Trudy depended on him, counted on him to provide. The news would upset her too much, he was certain. But lying to her violated everything for Livingston and that violation, combined with having no job, would upset the order of their lives. Liv held that order above all else. He rose each morning, weekends included, at precisely six o'clock, enjoyed a breakfast of bran flakes, one slice of wheat toast—no butter, a glass of orange juice and a cup of coffee as he read the Local section, obituaries first. Always.

In winter, he warmed the Volvo's engine for seven minutes before leaving for work at twelve past seven. Tuesday nights were lasagna; Wednesdays, meatloaf; salmon patties with garlic-mashed potatoes, on Thursdays. Every light switch in the house pointed down before Livingston retired to bed. He and Trudy reserved Sunday mornings from nine to nine-thirty for sex, missionary position, followed by cuddling, unless a Sunday fell on February twenty-ninth. Then it was leap year sex—still basically missionary, but Liv would move his right leg *outside* of Trudy's left leg, for variety.

Rock met hard place. Livingston saw no option, so he did what any sane husband, any man would do, and he did it for love. He got up each morning, followed his routine, spent the day at the library reading Walker Percy novels, and came home at the usual time. He'd simply avoid the subject until an idea presented itself. Liv considered his bank account, the likelihood of finding another job at his age, with his qualifications, in the current economy, and convinced himself he could continue the charade for six, maybe seven months. By then, he'd have an idea. Until then, he'd follow the routine and keep his mouth shut.

Like Christ in the tomb, Livingston lasted three days.

The first thread in Livingston's plan freed itself on the Thursday after Arnold fired him. Liv was reading a particularly riveting section in Percy's *Love in the Ruins* when he heard a commotion at the front desk. The discussion grew loud, even by coffee shop standards, let alone a library, and Liv couldn't concentrate. Apparently, word had just come down that, due to budget shortfalls, several branches of the library would close. He ignored the discussion until he realized *this* library, his sanctuary, was on the list. A second thread worked loose. Liv abandoned his Percy novel and chose a volume of Yeats poems lying inconspicuously across the table. He opened the book and stared at the same page until his shift ended three hours later.

The unraveling continued when he arrived home. It being Thursday, the scent of salmon patties frying and garlic-mashed potatoes ... well ... mashing, he supposed, should have greeted him. Instead, he smelled pork chops and asparagus. No, no, no. That was Saturdays in months with thirty-one days. She knew. She *knew*, she had to. He closed the door, placed his briefcase in the appropriate location, kissed Trudy on the top of the head as she stood on her stool by the stove, turning the chops, excused himself to the bedroom under the auspices of changing clothes before dinner (which he *never* did), went into his bathroom instead, closed that door, turned on the fan, lifted the toilet seat, and threw up. How did she find out?

It didn't matter. How he handled it, what he said, *that* mattered. He rinsed his mouth and looked at himself in the mirror. Wait. If she knew, shouldn't she be angry? If she were angry, she'd serve Spam and sauerkraut for dinner. Sunday's evening meal, his least favorite. Pork chops over wild rice and asparagus was his favorite, favorite meal. No, no, no, no. Everything was fraying. The center cannot hold, he thought, and now I'm the slouching beast. Livingston turned toward the kitchen. Act natural. Be unaffected. Deny. Let her talk first.

"What's for dinner?" he asked.

"I thought I'd change things up a bit." Trudy turned to smile at him. "It's your favorite, honey glazed pork chops, wild rice, and braised asparagus."

"Is something wrong? What's happened?"

"Nothing's *wrong*, Liv," she answered. "I'm just feeling . . . I don't know, *not* like salmon patties. Does that make sense?"

"But, but . . . it's Thursday, Trudy. Thursday."

"I know." She flipped the last pork chop and shuffled around on the footstool until she faced Livingston and then held the spatula above her head and shimmied the short length of her body, starting at her shoulders and ending at her hips. "Exciting, don't you think?"

Livingston swallowed hard, then swallowed again, his mouth suddenly so dry he'd need the spatula to prize his tongue from his palate. "Well, sure. I guess. That's great."

It wasn't great. Deep in his gut, Livingston felt his universe beginning to shift, yet again. He choked back the urge to blurt out the whole story, confess even if she already knew every detail. Beating her to the punch might restore some sense of order. He wished she'd just say it, he hoped equally she wouldn't, and he wanted his salmon patties and garlic-mashed potatoes.

Trudy served dinner and Liv concentrated on devouring every morsel. Each bite tasted of guilt, deception, condemnation and fear. Trudy made small talk and Liv answered, as always, but was suspicious. *The news said there'd be nice weather for the weekend.* A trap. *I'm thinking of painting the guest bathroom.* Full of subtext. *We need milk, but there's enough for your morning cereal.* An accusation? *I'll pick some up when I get groceries tomorrow.* Does she buy groceries near the library? Wait, they're closing, but when? *How are things at work?* Oh, dear God.

"Work's fine, everything's good. You know, business as usual, the daily grind. Yes, everything at work is perfectly normal." Livingston's last bite left his stomach and lunged up his esophagus, gripped the back of his tongue and threatened to reappear on his plate. He cleared his throat, swallowed. "Another delicious dinner, Trudy."

"Thank you, Liv. See, a little variety can be a good thing."

"I suppose. Yes, occasionally."

The rest of the evening proceeded as usual. Trudy worked on her latest cross-stitch project while Liv tried to watch a Discovery Channel show about the mating habits of spiral-shelled snails. At the commercial break, Trudy announced she was going to bed and a new wave of fear drenched him. Ten o'clock was *his* bedtime; Trudy always watched the news then Letterman before turning in, well after he'd fallen asleep. Her plan revealed. She'd confront him as he drifted toward sleep and his defenses waned. Trudy kissed first his forehead, then shocked him with a lingering kiss on the lips before going to the bedroom.

Livingston walked to the kitchen, drank a glass of water, walked back to the den, to the dining room, to the kitchen, drank more water. Sat down, stood up, ate Tums, then sat down again before giving up and quietly brushing his teeth and sliding stiffly into his side of the bed without checking to make sure all the light switches pointed toward the floor.

Trudy faced the opposite wall, and for a few calming minutes, it appeared to Liv that he'd survived.

Then, Trudy turned and snuggled against him, her hand slipping beneath the elastic band of his pajama bottoms as she did. He wanted to scream: *It's Thursday, for God's sake, this is not right. It'll upset our schedule. What's gotten into you?* But he feigned a yawn and turned his face away from her instead. In his head, he began repeating *do not get an erection* but he soon felt that method failing. He thought about Mr. Arnold, he thought about the trade deficit, he thought of a tribe of indigenous Inuit living within the Arctic Circle. He thought about spiral-shelled snails, and still his blood rushed south. Too much variety for one night. What did this mean for Sunday morning? Did this advance change the terms for Sunday? Replace their usual session? Or was this in addition to?

Trudy's plan lacked all fairness, which began to make him even more nervous than usual. Unfortunately, that didn't work either as now, were he to stand up, he could hang a pair of wet dungarees on his erection. He yawned again, but this tactic had no effect on Trudy. As she slipped his pajamas down past his knees, he vowed he'd admit nothing.

Trudy worked the pajamas free. His breath caught in his throat. *Oh my god.* He'd overheard some of the guys at work talk of this. He'd always ignored them, but—*oh my god.* No, no, no, no. Not fair. Concentrate. Use the anger. Not playing fair. Oh . . . The light switches. What about the light switches?

Trudy sat up, then straddled him. Okay, he thought, I have no idea what this means for our usual Sunday session, but there's no turning back now. Focus. Try not to enjoy it too much or she'll want to change the schedule. Focus. Snails. Nancy Pelosi. Nancy Pelosi. There, that's some better. Let her do all the work. Trudy positioned herself, cowgirl style, and grinned at Livingston. Liv closed his eyes. Eskimos. Multiplication tables. Mmmm. No, no, no. Golf. Nancy Pelosi. Golf. Spiral-shelled snails. Nine holes at Augusta. Azaleas. Amen Corner. Trudy's motion increased in speed and efficiency. What *was* she doing? She couldn't possibly know about work. "Yes, yes, yes . . ." Wait, that came from Trudy. But usually, she never made a sound. She *must* know.

She didn't know.

It had never been like this. Maybe she did know. Maybe she thought of him as dangerous now, maybe she found the lie made him more mysterious. Livingston eased one eye open, and once he saw

Trudy's eyes closed, he opened the other. Her head tilted back and her breath came in bursts, faster, quicker, making an abbreviated "hee-hee" sound with each exhale. The expression on her face was foreign to him. She seemed content to continue doing all the work, but Liv couldn't help himself; once he saw the look on her face, he pitched in. The other images had not helped so he switched to his usual Sunday morning method, counting each thrust. One. Two. Three. Four—why delay the inevitable for her sake, she'd started this. Besides, the quicker this ended, the quicker they'd both fall asleep, which meant another day passed without Trudy's discovering the current job situation. As soon as he made that decision, he was lost. Maybe she . . . Oh, oh, oh—the pressure rising. No, no, no, not yet. Snails, spiral-shelled. The lie. The light switches. Snails. The lights. Snails-the lie. Snails-lights-snails-lights-snails-lights-lie-Lie-LIE-LIE—"I LOST MY JOB!"

"You *WHAT?*" Trudy stood straight up, and even at three-foot-ten, towered over him.

Too late. The last thread had released and one of Liv's swimmers made it all the way home.

ONE DAY, COLTON tried to explain to James that he thought of himself as an enigma. James didn't understand all of it, no matter how much Colton talked.

"Is that a bad thing?" James asked.

"No, not really," Colton answered. "It's better than being a cliché. Or a geek. Or an asshole. It keeps people off balance, which is good because I don't really fit anywhere."

That much James understood. He liked that about Colton.

High school was all about cliques and it didn't take him long to see that he and Colton were their own clique. The blacks, your peeps, as James called them, had little to do with Colton. He had no street cred, wasn't from the hood, didn't speak Ebonics. Dwight Yoakem, Robert Earl Keen, Wagner, and Vivaldi filled his iPod. He drove a stock Ford Ranger. No twenty-six-inch 2Crave chrome rims, no nitrous kit, no bass booster. His pants fit around his waist, he hated wearing a ball cap, and he made A's and B's all through high school. He thought Obama's election might help, but it didn't. The black kids started calling Colton "Prez." Their tone was less than endearing.

The white kids were also unsure what to make of Colton. After all, he had no street cred, wasn't from the hood, didn't speak Ebonics. And, he was kinda tall and skinny, like Obama, who the white kids thought was either a socialist anti-Christ, the savior, a Muslim, mostly Caucasian, or the secret love child of Pat Robertson and Oprah.

Colton said that was exactly what made him an enigma, but James still didn't understand.

"That's okay," Colton offered. "Nobody else does either. I'm like a super hero, that way. Captain Enigma."

"Yeah, you should get a big-assed 'E' printed on all your t-shirts," James offered.

"Captain E, coming to all those marginalized by society," Colton mocked.

"Marginalized? W-T-F, dude?"

"Let's just say Captain E comes to the rescue of folks who might not really know they need to be rescued."

So, when James called Colton for a ride to the college, Colton didn't hesitate. Captain E to the rescue.

James stopped as soon as they entered the foyer to Sanders Hall. "Lotta po-po in here," he whispered to Colton. "Don't sign your real name to nothing. You'll be on their list."

"Didn't plan on it. I'm just driving Mr. Lazy to the store," Colton answered.

"Reckon they'll have free samples after the meeting? Maybe some special brownies."

"You haven't had the best of luck with weed in the past."

"Aw come on, C-note. Where's your sense of adventure?"

James only smoked pot on special occasions and he invented those special occasions five or six times a year when he felt the need to impress someone, usually a female. The last special occasion was Janie Anson's eighteenth birthday party. Her parents were out of town again so everyone was at Janie's party. Janie came from money, and lived in forty-five hundred square feet of opulent materialism with the latest of every gadget imaginable. Way out of James' normal field of play. James and Janie's cosmic biorhythms had somehow synchronized so that every time she felt the need to punish her father for some slight, it coincided with another of James and Brittany's infamous breakups. They never actually went out, Janie would never stoop to that, but they both played up the possibility enough to bring her father and Brittany back in line.

Some premium grade Hindu Kush floated around the party and then someone brought out a vaporizer. James, having never used a vaporizer before, kept hitting the tube and complaining he wasn't getting any smoke. Colton found him an hour later in Janie's parents' bedroom, leaning against the fluffy pillows and carved headboard of their bed, naked. He'd smeared crunchy peanut butter over most of his body and was finishing off the second jar, using an eighteenth century, carved ivory letter opener as a spoon and drinking draft Coors Light from an L.C. Tiffany vase.

"I don't know," Colton said as they moved to the front door of the auditorium. "Remember Janie's party? Keith Moon would have been awed, man."

"Well played, my dark brother from another mother. Well played. But this is a business venture. I'm thinking to get on the growing side, not the toking side. Plus, Britt's needing twenty-K for *Survivor*. I get some cash flow going, I'll cover that nut. That'll show her." As James spoke, a female approached, then paused, obviously angling to get past James and out the door.

"Excuse me," she mumbled.

"Well, yes ma'am." James hopped aside and the woman shouldered around him and walked toward the exit.

"That's her." He punched Colton in the shoulder. "That's my cougar."

"Too flat-chested. Too smart. She's probably a professor here."

"Naw, she's perfect. That brown hair up in that little bun with the ringlets falling down. Those sexy librarian glasses. Did you get a load of those legs? All the way up to her ass. Professor, huh? Even better. If you don't do it right the first time, they make you do it over again. Un-huh. Woman like that'll make you do freaky shit for love."

"She'd eat you alive."

"Exactly. That's what I'm talking about." James turned to a nearby student who was handing out information for the meeting. "You know that lady going out the door?"

"Dr. Sardofsky. Science department, I think."

James turned back to Colton. "Hear that, C-note? *Doctor* Sardofsky. Bet she knows stuff, kinky doctor stuff."

"All college professors are called doctor, Einstein. Thought you and Brittany were getting back together?"

"Coconuts and toilet paper. One's got nothing to do with the other."

"Come on, let's go inside. Think of it this way. I'll guarantee you there's somebody somewhere who's had enough of Dr. Sardofsky's shit. Now find us a seat."

James looked out the glass doors once more before entering the lecture hall, watching Kat Sardofsky walking away. "Mmm. Like two speckled pups wrestling under warm a blanket," he said

5

Friday Night in America

Sally sat in the plush leather chair in Boot Jackson's office, smoothing his hands along the arms and appreciating the craftsmanship. He gazed at the photos on the back wall as Boot shuffled papers. A younger Boot with Ronald Reagan. Boot with Karl Rove. Boot with Rush Limbaugh. On the other wall, more pictures. Boot standing on the metal tracks of a bulldozer, wearing a hardhat and a tie, a thick stand of trees directly in the dozer's path. Boot squatted in camouflage coveralls, a rifle barrel leaning against his shoulder as he held up the antlered head of a mule deer.

Boot stacked and re-stacked the papers, dropped them in a file, and reached for another form. "That your daughter?" He nodded toward the waiting area outside the office window.

"Her? No, no. Don't know who she is. Friendly, though." He glanced over his shoulder, looked at the girl still waiting. "You got kids?"

"Two boys. Grown. And neither one worth a shit, lazy as the day is long."

"Hell, they'll come around. Give 'em time."

"Time's getting short. Ask Bill."

"Tell me. Still, you reach a certain age, you start thinking, you know?" Sally's voice trailed.

"Least he went quick." Boot pulled another file from the drawer. "You got other family? Wife, kin?"

"Nope. Just me. Had a sister, twin actually, but she died years back."

Sally shook his head, unsure of why he couldn't keep his mouth shut. "You find the paperwork?" he asked.

"Yeah, here we go." Boot pulled out a form. "Bill set everything up, looks like. You two close, huh?"

Sally paused. "Business associates, mostly. You knew Bill a long time?"

"Oh, for years. Practically grew up together. Good man. It's a bitch what happened. I don't recall ever seeing you and Bill together. He did all his banking with me, seems we'd've crossed paths."

Sally wanted to admit he'd been thinking the same thing. Boot seemed like any other guy. Did Bill not think it necessary—or did he really view Sally as somehow less than, good but not quite equal? Didn't matter, especially not now. "I was more a behind-the-scenes kind of business associate," he said.

"Everybody needs one. Come on, I'll show you to the safety deposit vault."

As they walked down the hall, Sally felt another twinge of the old excitement returning, and it reminded him of how much he used to enjoy the first time he eyed a prospective property. Everything potential, nothing tainted, no encumbrances. If the lay of the land was right, had some frontage, good access . . . yeah, it had been a while, but he remembered this feeling. Maybe what waited inside the box could bring it back for good. Boot left him alone and Sally slowly raised the lid.

"What the hell is this?" Sally took a pen from his pocket and used it to lift the first item from the box—a large, red, silk, thong. Sally gripped the strings on either side, raised the underwear to eye level, and stretched his arms in opposite directions. And stretched. "Jesus," he whispered. "You were one sick puppy, Bill." And old Virgin Mary's a liar, he thought. Had to be hers. He dropped the thong on the table.

Next, he found a gray poker chip from the Tropicana in Atlantic City. "Five grand. Nice of you to leave me a tip for disposing of Big Mary's drawers, Billy Boy."

An eight by ten, black and white aerial photo lay folded in the bottom of the box, and nothing more. Sally opened it, moved the partial panties out of the way, placed the picture face up on the table, and smoothed the creases. Bare trees surrounded an open, weedy area. No markings, no outlines, no buildings, no roads. Nothing he recognized and Sally couldn't tell how many acres it might be with no point of reference. He turned the snapshot over. On the back was a note that read: *LC on the deed as a life tenant. No plans to live there or develop. Might sell, but wants covenants. Or, change to tenants in common. Working on it.* Below that were more words: *Done Deal. RFR. Will changed—tell Sally???*

Bill's last deal. He'd swindled somebody else out of their property and left it to Sally before joining the God squad. Bless his heart. But why? And where was it? Who was LC? There was nothing else inside, no indication of what he should do next.

Sally closed the box and slid it back into the wall. He picked up the photo, dropped the chip in his pocket, and considered the expanse of thong still lying on the tabletop. What the hell, he thought, it's leverage, and he stuffed it in his other pocket before leaving. Not much to go on, but he knew where to start. He needed a pilot and a plane, a road trip to Atlantic City, and a date with Mary.

Dr. Kat Sardofsky usually enjoyed her late afternoon *Plant Life* class. It was a survey class, primarily lecture, and her TA graded any work not suited to a Scantron form. The students, non-science majors, never asked questions, content to text or catch an afternoon nap. Once she dismissed the students and they cleared out, she'd often sit in one of the front row desks for a few moments, relishing the echoing silence of Sanders Hall and reflecting on her days as an undergrad. She wasn't nostalgic; there was nothing about undergrad life that she missed. The workload of a bio major had left no time for a social life, and the underlying competitiveness, the jockeying and posturing for grad school recommendations from favored professors, coated everything in stress. Still, distance made undergrad life feel simpler and if anything, she missed that.

Too, her mother started dropping the husband hints when Kat was a sophomore. *A girl can find a good husband at college, Katherine, don't spend all your time studying,* she'd repeat. Sure, there were times now when she wished there was a significant other in her life. She had more free time and it would be nice just to have someone there in the evenings, but she didn't regret any of the choices or sacrifices she'd made. She hoped one day she'd meet a man who wasn't afraid of her intellect, but she was not about to tell her mother as much. She didn't miss her mother's needling, then or now.

There was no time for reflecting today; a presentation or forum of some sorts immediately followed her class. Kat didn't know the topic, but she knew she didn't like it when the attendees began filing in even as her students were leaving. This was a different crowd. There were several obvious college students, but none she recognized. None of the motivated, over-eager geeks. None of the arrogant pre-pharmacy students, either. She especially disliked those students, even though she knew their tuition dollars carried a large portion of the undergraduate programs, hers included. That didn't give them the right to be such . . . such . . . asses. Glorified pill counters, not *scientists.* The students gathering in the lecture hall were oddly worse, she decided, and they made her somewhat uneasy. Artist types, probably Philosophy or English majors. They smelled of patchouli.

The event had apparently been opened to the public as well. Not much better clientele. They also stunk of patchouli, and worse. She saw dreadlocks and tie-dye, bare feet and Earth shoes. One man walked past wearing a tall *Cat-in-the-Hat* style hat on his head. Another stood in the aisle kicking a hackey-sack. Disgusted, she elbowed her way toward the exit.

A young man, boy really, blocked the rear door. She paused, hoping he'd move without her insistence. He was talking to a bright-looking young black man. The boy didn't fit, not with either group, student or the general public. His friend could easily pass for a freshman, but there was something about the boy. He wore Wrangler jeans, faded by wear, not the factory-faded designer brands the students favored, and a John Deere t-shirt. His shoes, white Chuck Taylors, the old canvas style, had holes in the sides of the fabric and the remnants of frayed duct tape around the right shoe. His right shoe also had a larger hole in the tongue and was stained a dirty rust color.

He didn't move, didn't seem to notice her at all. Typical with the generation, she thought. She waited. No luck. Kat took a deep breath. "Excuse me," she finally said.

The boy looked up and the azure intensity of his eyes caught her off guard. She instantly felt an urge to reach out and straighten the boy's hair, make some attempt at organizing it into a style.

He grinned and said something but Kat lowered her head and edged past him without responding. He hopped out of her way, favoring his right foot.

She felt a release once outside and quickly tried to separate herself from the growing crowd streaming into Sanders Hall. As she walked away from the building, she had the sensation that someone, the boy, was watching her. Normally, such a feeling would have been annoying. The boy was harmless, not so different than many of her male students, but something about the him—either his complete lack of self-awareness or his total commitment to his simplicity—caused a smile to crease her face.

6

An Itch That Needs Scratching

The year his son was born and seven years before the small kit plane obliterated him on the sandy shores of the Atlantic, Herschel Carr invested in a hundred-acre tangle of land. Herschel had never grown so much as a tomato plant, so he'd never considered farming the property. The acreage consisted of pines, oaks, and undergrowth circling an almost eight-acre open patch of weeds, broom sedge, and briar brambles. Herschel had had no plans to develop the property, either. It was miles from Mason and nothing resembling a community existed nearby. The closest main road ran south out of Mason to the state line, but finding the parcel meant following a series of unmarked side roads to a barely distinguishable dirt lane leading to the property. He had no real reason for buying or keeping the land but something about it touched him and in a strange way, made him think of his child.

Livingston had been to the property once since his father's death. He hadn't known the place existed, or that he owned it, until he graduated from Mason University. His mother presented the deed as a graduation present, which disappointed Livingston a great deal—he'd hoped for a leather briefcase and a monocle. All that summer his mother insisted, and finally, in September, he'd agreed to visit his holdings.

Livingston initially missed the dirt road, turned around, then made a cautious left onto the property. Weeds had taken over and as Livingston bounced along the path, he worried that snakes might somehow slither into his old Volvo. When he reached the clearing, he stopped, rolled down the window, and looked around before gingerly stepping out of the car. A couple of grasshoppers took flight near his feet and he stumbled back against the car. I have to do this, he thought, my father left this to me. *To me.* Perhaps there's some remnant of him here. Something he found important, necessary.

There seemed to be a natural path where the woods met the field, and Livingston crossed in front of his vehicle, angled right, and began slowly making his way around the circumference of the open area. He never looked up, never looked in any direction, but kept his eyes trained for any danger lurking in the grass. After an hour, he'd made it halfway around the clearing. He even managed to glance at his surroundings from time to time. He realized the plot would have been a perfect wonderland for a normal young boy. The woods guarded secrets, the honeysuckle jumbles created imaginary forts and hideouts. Birds flitted and called, and Liv was certain interesting and potentially dangerous wildlife lurked deeper among the trees. But Livingston had never been a normal young boy, had never felt the call of the outdoors.

A hundred feet before Livingston returned to his car, a thick tangle of flowers blocked his path and he saw no way around. To his left, an impassable briar thicket. To his right the undergrowth threatened to choke the outside edge of the tree line. The plants looked harmless enough. Some stood waist high, still others reached his shoulders and beyond. The flowers themselves were small and bright yellow with a cluster of tiny pods in their center. Livingston found the hue striking—a butter color at first glance, but no, maybe egg yolks. That was wrong still. It was a yellow more stark and brilliant than he'd seen before and he had no comparison. The stems fascinated him almost as much as the flower petals. They appeared sturdy, even as the stalks bent slightly in the early autumn breeze, but what caught his attention was their unusual purplish color. He'd not seen anything like it before, either. For some reason, the plants reminded him of something older, of another time long passed, and he thought of his father.

Still, they were imposing, clumped tightly together with grass and weeds rising at their base. No telling what that might hold. He could see the Volvo, right there. Livingston felt his heart quicken. He swatted at the gnats swirling around his head. Scratched his ankle, then his arm. Who knows what lurked in that thicket. Snakes? Mice? Even the plants themselves looked threatening. He took a deep breath. Scratched his other ankle. The flowers loomed. He had no choice. Livingston closed his eyes and began running toward his car, waving his arms at the flora, trampling them beneath his shoes, breaking others mid-stalk. He collapsed across the hood of his car, his chest heaving.

Days later, following his oatmeal bath, his mother dabbed Calamine lotion over the sections of his body he couldn't reach. "Your father believed that land would be useful one day," she said. "Your future, he called it."

"Has anyone ever been hospitalized from poison ivy? Died from it?" Livingston asked.

"No Liv, it'll dry up. You'll be fine. Just don't scratch."

"Well, maybe he thought it was my future, but I'm never going out there, ever again."

"It's yours to do with what you like. Maybe one day you'll change your mind." She capped the bottle. "There, all done."

"How long before this clears up?" He asked.

"Week, maybe."

"But I have . . . I'm meeting . . . There's this—a girl. Trudy Yathers. We're having coffee Saturday."

"Ah, a date. You should've told me."

"It's no big thing, not a date. We just met. It's coffee, that's all."

"I see. So, this girl, what's she like?"

"I don't know," Livingston shrugged. He knew his mother intended well, that she would want to know details about the girl, her background, her parents, all of it, and once he started, she'd keep at it. And what could he tell her at this point? That she was a little person? That her laugh instantly relaxed him? That something about her reminded him of her—his mother? No. He needed to give her some detail, though, something specific enough to staunch the avalanche of questions for the time being.

"I met her at the library. She seemed nice. She's younger than me, I think. Maybe ten years, and she likes reading biographies."

He could feel his mother's stare in a physical way and she paused much too long—please, please no more questions.

"A younger woman. Hmm. You know your father was thirteen years older than me." She dabbed an extra layer of Calamine on a large row of blisters.

Livingston nodded and his mother closed the bottle of lotion.

"Well, I'd wear long sleeves, if I were you," She said.

Livingston met Trudy Yathers for coffee that Saturday, and if she noticed the welts from the poison ivy, she didn't mention it. He eventually went back to the property, but a long time passed before he did.

"Think it's infected?"

Colton leaned down for a closer look at the top of James' foot. "Lemme see the bottom."

"It itches like a bitch." James leaned down, grabbed his pant leg, then raised his leg, which caused him to tip over and fall back on the bed. A hot pain stabbed from his instep and past his ankle until it faded near his calf.

"Could be itching 'cause it's healing. Could be 'cause it's infected." Colton cupped James' right heel and lifted, inspected, then lowered it and gripped James leg just above the ankle. Once he had him, he poured a stream of Bud Light across the wound. James screamed and jerked his foot away.

"Damn it, C-note," he moaned. "What the hell'd you do that for?"

"Alcohol's good for infection."

"So it is infected. Shit, I knew it."

"I don't know. It looks nasty, but you got ugly feet to start with. Makes it hard to tell."

"What if I get gangrene?"

"You'll have to see a doctor, then. Unless you want *me* to cut it off. I'd do it for you, but that's the sort of thing you ought leave to a professional."

"Let's start with some Neosporin."

"You should at least let my dad take a look."

"No thanks." James picked up Colton's laptop and googled gangrene. Colton might be his best friend, but his dad was a different story. He was thirteen percent Cherokee, forty-seven percent white, twenty-one percent Asian, thirty-four percent Latino, and a hundred percent leftover hippie vegan. Those numbers didn't add up for James, and he knew whatever holistic, naturalistic, and imperialistic salve Colton's dad whipped up for his gunshot wound would make a voodoo priestess run trembling for the nearest Free Will Baptist cinder-block sanctuary. "Here," James said and slid the laptop next to his foot, turning it so the screen faced Colton. "Does the bottom of my foot look like that, or not?"

"You get Wi-Fi here?" Colton asked.

"Boosting it from the guy in the next room, I think."

"What kind of guy? Who is he?"

"I don't know. Button down, Johnny Corporate type. Keeps to

himself. I don't think he'll last long, plays bootleg Grateful Dead constantly. What difference does it make, do I have gangrene or not?" On cue, the music started in the next room and the volume pushed the tune through the motel room wall.

"Hey," Colton said, "that's 'Dire Wolf.' I like that one." He picked up the verse and sang along as he twirled around in a circle with both hands in the air above his head.

"If you don't look at my damn foot it's gonna be worse than murder." James hopped over and banged on the wall. "Turn it down," he yelled. "That shit's wearing thin."

The music stopped. James sat in the plastic chair and propped his leg on the cooler with his foot hanging over the edge. The music started again, louder this time. Colton strolled over, carrying the laptop, his head bobbing to the beat. He looked at the screen, at James' foot, at the screen again. After a moment, he shook his head no.

"Walk it off, man. It's not gangrene. The bullet probably nicked a bone going through, that's all. It's about healed."

James put on his Chuck Taylors. The Dead extended the 'Dire Wolf' jam into a cover of 'It's All Over Now.' James stood up. "Come on," he said.

"Where to?"

"Gotta come to an agreement with my neighbor. That stuff's better than the wetback gibberish, but not by much. I need a little peace and quiet to work out plans for our grow operation."

"James, James. Easy, man. That's racist."

"What? They were Mexican, not black. Now come on."

When James knocked on the door of Room 114, the music stopped but no one answered. He knocked again and waited. A third knock. "Dude," he yelled into the peep hole, "I know you're in there, I heard the music cut off. We need a pow-wow." He banged on the door again. It cracked open a few inches.

"Yeah?"

"Hey man, I'm James from 115. Next door."

"Yeah?"

"Need to talk to you a minute, neighbor to neighbor. Open up, it's just me and my buddy, Colton."

When Colton heard James announce his name, he yelled "Ssshh" and punched James hard in the center of the back. The blow caused James to shift his weight onto his right foot. The flash of pain made him lose his balance, he fell against the door, throwing it open and causing the man to stumble back against the wall as James sprawled inside. A bright yellow-amber light flooded from the room out into the natural sunshine. As Colton stepped over James, all three men yelled "Shit!" at the same time.

James rubbed his eyes and grinned. The room had been transformed. Thermal blankets covered the walls and ceiling, shiny side facing inward. Fans and a charcoal filter system to blow the smell out of the room and into the common area behind the motel. Two computers controlling the water, nutrient, and lighting systems. Beneath the lights, a series of six-inch PVC tubing in five rows formed a square that filled most of the room. Holes had been cut into each of the five center tubes. In the holes grew thirty healthy babies cloned from a high-grade Cali Mist mother plant. The plants were beautiful and the whole thing looked simple, which impressed James.

"Dude," he said from the floor, "you can't trust those cheap-ass safety chains. I've been telling Gajie he should upgrade. People like to feel safe."

"Jesus. Get in here and close the door, assholes," said Finn Strickland. "Let me figure out what I'm gonna do with you."

MOST OF HER clothes had been folded, pressed, or hung; only one pair of jeans and the cotton top remained. She touched the tip of her nose and approached the dryer holding her breath. Please, please, please, she thought. It was her favorite pair of jeans, one of her favorite blouses and she'd washed them both twice now since that night. She eased the dryer door open and raised the garments slowly toward her face. So far, so good. She stopped a few inches from her nose, gathered herself, and drew a timid breath. "Nooooo," she moaned. The stench of fried seafood rose and hung around her like a fog in August, thick and humid. Kat put the jeans and top in a garbage bag and carried it directly to the outside bin, bypassing the trashcan, then opened a new carton of Ben and Jerry's Vanilla Heath Bar Crunch, slumped into her couch and cried.

A disaster didn't accurately describe that night a couple of weeks ago at Captain Steve's Fish Camp. Shocking, disgusting, repulsive—maybe. The smell of her clothes reminded her of details Kat couldn't fully choke back and the ice cream couldn't dilute. The same smell had greeted her when she walked through the doors of the restaurant. The place appeared clean enough, and rather quaint given the size of the dining room. She liked the koi tank in the lobby, and the 97.5 Sanitation Grade framed above the aquarium eased some of her initial trepidation. The interior décor was less appealing. Pictures of lighthouses and seashores hung between stretches of fishing nets. Above them, several large stuffed fish mounts leered down at her. She touched her nose and asked if Arlen Johnson had arrived.

The hostess led Kat to the table and when Arlen rose to meet her, his belly jostled the table, causing some of his tea to lap over the edge of the glass. He apologized, shook her hand, then yanked a red bandana from his hip pocket, and wiped the spill before the hostess had a chance to respond. His belly performed the same stunt when he sat down and he labored to draw the bandana back out of his pocket and apologized again as he dabbed at the tea.

It didn't get any better.

When she ordered a salad and broiled scallops, Arlen rolled his eyes. "Take forever," he said. "It's a fish camp, nobody orders broiled." He turned to the waitress. "Bring mine when it's ready. No call to wait, I'll still be working on it when hers comes out."

And he was. Kat had never witnessed a human eat so much in such a manner. Arlen devoured a bowl and a half of hushpuppies before his food arrived. For dinner, he ordered the fried, three-way combo: popcorn shrimp, whole flounder, and deviled crab, with a baked potato (sour cream, extra butter) plus a side order of salt and pepper catfish. His left hand alternated between breaking off bits of the flounder and stuffing them in his jowls and reaching for another hush puppy, while the fork in his right hand followed a counter-clockwise pattern of shrimp-baked potato-deviled crab. Once he conquered that plate, he started on the catfish, grabbing the crispy tail in one hand and the head in the other, biting down in the center and pulling the meat away with his teeth. He'd then flip it over and repeat the procedure, leaving only a cartoonish fish skeleton and the crispy tails when he was done. The complimentary coleslaw that came with his meal went untouched.

Between—well, during bites, he told Kat about the developments with the girl who'd taken the pictures of the Schweinitz sunflowers. "It's going good," he mumbled. "Found her, been following her. She'll lead me to them flowers soon enough." He grinned. The more he explained, the more Kat began to think he might be a stalker, possibly even a pervert. When he took a mid-meal bathroom break, Kat scrolled her iPhone, checking the sex offender registry on-line. It listed no Arlen Johnson, but that could just mean he'd not been caught, yet.

The end of the evening found Kat disheartened but not defeated. Johnson had not made direct contact with the girl. He invited Kat to another dinner at the local barbeque rib joint, which she declined for the time being, and he promised to call as soon as he had more definite news.

A couple weeks passed and her worries grew. Leaderlick wanted updates on her research progress and every other day or so he made it a point to stick his head in her office to remind her of the Twelve Point Strategic Revision Plan requirements and the necessity of her being a team player. He never failed to follow those comments with a quick mention of the economic situation and the bearing it had on the college and her employment. She tried her best to ignore the implications, but once she realized the school rented Sanders Hall for the information session on legalizing medical marijuana as a means of raising additional revenue, the weight of it all settled drearily around her.

She finished the last of the Ben and Jerry's, dried her eyes, and looked at the phone. She could sit and feel sorry for herself, but that wouldn't help the sunflowers. Time to take action, give Arlen Johnson a nudge. She touched her nose and found his number. The flowers needed her.

ARLEN JOHNSON KNEW a lot about Brittany Combs. Knew where she lived, knew she liked to eat ice cream in the park, knew she'd turn seventeen later that summer. Of course, he had the basics nailed: average height, dirty blond hair that she sometimes twirled around her left index finger while daydreaming. Right handed, spent more time texting than talking on her phone. Carried a camera with her almost all the time. A small diamond nose ring in her left nostril. Arlen found it sexy, but wondered how she blew her nose when she caught a cold. She'd recently opened her own bank account. He also knew she spent a lot of time at her grandmother's place, a little brick ranch-style house out in the country on a couple acres. He'd followed her there. The first time, a scruffy looking kid a few years older than her had picked her up, stayed at the grandmother's with her for an hour, then left.

Development had begun creeping toward the house in the past few years, but hadn't taken over yet, which made following her there difficult, and Arlen worried about being spotted. Traffic helped conceal him as they rode out of Mason, but once they turned, the traffic thinned. The final few miles were the most dicey, especially after he passed the last housing development. Arlen relied on every trick he'd gleaned from *Law and Order* and *CSI*. On stakeouts, he filled his passenger seat with fried pork skins, barbecue potato chips, Little Debbie crème-filled oatmeal cookies, and spicy beef jerky for sustenance. A large cooler sat on the passenger side floorboard where he kept a couple of two-liter Pepsis to wash down the snacks, and an empty two-liter Mountain Dew bottle to relieve himself. In a plastic Wal-Mart shopping bag, he carried a legal pad and four, sharpened Ticonderoga number two pencils for making notes, and a pair of binoculars he'd scored at a yard sale. The glass for the left lens was missing, both ends, but they worked well enough and had only cost a quarter.

In spite of the details he'd gathered about Brittany Combs, plenty remained that he didn't know. Arlen didn't know that the scruffy looking boy was her on again, off again boyfriend that she considered a convenient, low maintenance hook-up but didn't see any long-term future for the two of them. No ambition. Plus, too little sexual creativity for her tastes, unless he'd been smoking weed, and then things just got, well, weird. Brittany thought the boy's issues stemmed mainly from a lack of focus, and that held for everything in his life.

His plusses were he had somehow figured out a way to get her alcohol, he liked every photo she'd ever snapped, and he was easily manipulated.

Arlen also didn't know she was actually intelligent and highly inquisitive, even though she found school more boring than a *60 Minutes* documentary on retirement planning. Or that her main reason for wanting to be on *Survivor* and then parlay that into appearances on other reality shows was to create some buzz for her photography. Or that she'd never considered anything other than photography as a career.

These were hard things for even a seasoned detective to garner, and Arlen, in the beginning, readily admitted he was a rookie.

There was more he didn't know. He didn't know where she'd taken the flower pictures. But the college teacher, Kat, kept leaving messages, and while her tone was a little harsh, Arlen knew she was warming up to him. If he could find out about the sunflowers, he had a chance with her. He needed a break, some sign, maybe a snitch, and soon. Being around that professor lady gave him an itch that needed scratched.

7

Landings

The small plane taxied, then paused for clearance. As they waited, the pilot took a sterling flask from his boot, enjoyed a quick gulp, winced, and offered it to Sally. "Flying makes me nervous," he said.

Sally looked at the flask. "No thanks, I'm okay for now."

The plane rolled forward once they received word from the small tower and as it gained speed and rose, the man at the controls asked, "So where we headed?"

"I'm looking for this piece of land." Sally showed him the picture. "I think it's around a hundred acres, give or take, and it's bound to be in this county. Everything in Mecklenburg is built out, and everything else is too far from Charlotte. Bill wouldn't go after anything he'd have to wait that long to flip. Gotta be here."

"I'll head east, then. Doubt you'll find a piece that size anywhere west of Hwy 200 in the south or 601 in the north."

"Circle the county first, outside in."

"It's your nickel."

They flew south, then banked west and north. From the air, patchwork housing developments and shopping centers circled dwindling dots of open land. Those were the likely targets, or would have been. At one time, there were opportunities to buy in low, convince the old-time natives or their heirs the land was best suited as pastureland, that most of it wouldn't perc and it would be decades before the county ran sewer lines. Then, line up developers by giving enough sketchy details regarding the locations so they'd be willing to fork over cash that Sally and Bill used to leverage the purchase, only to flip the property for hefty profits six months later.

They had a good run, but even before Bill's conversion, Sally could see it all coming to an end. In the beginning, several things converged to create a real-estate tsunami. The outer loop around Charlotte, I-485, had been rumored for decades and once construction actually began, officials slated the southeastern corridor as the first leg for completion. Most of the clannish landowners in the bordering county were too senile or stubborn to realize what that really meant. Sally and Bill weren't.

It helped that the generation who owned most of the land was fading and their kids no longer felt an obligation to the home place. No, they'd scattered, leaving Mason and the surrounding county during the seventies and eighties, searching for better paying careers, culture, adventure, anything other than a job in the dying textile industry or working the production line at a low-level manufacturing plant. Forget farming as a viable option. And they were quick to stick Mom and Pop in one of the retirement center-slash-nursing homes springing up like dandelions and then cash in their land inheritance.

For ten years, everything was great. Bill was ruthless, could turn a reluctant son or daughter in one or two visits, and Sally was happy to play his part. Bill laid out the facts, pointed out every downside to holding a piece of property. Then, Sally moved in, playing the "local" card. "My family's been in this county for generations, too," he'd tell them. "But you can't stop progress. Used to be, we looked to the land to take care of us, provide." Sally'd pause, let it sink in while they nodded agreement. "It'll still do that," he'd reassure them, "just in a different way. The money from the sale provides now. Those retirement communities are nice. Set your folks up, have someone on call 24-7. They'll be happier knowing they won't be a burden on you."

Sometimes, Sally almost believed it himself. He wondered what he might do if he still had family, if it was their land. Other times he pondered what would become of all he did own when he was gone. Who'd care? In the past, every check he put in his bank account helped push those thoughts away. It'd been a while since he'd made a deposit. Now he felt possibility stirring again.

A hundred-acre swath on the west side of the county? Well, the Tea Partiers worshipped Reagan but the rich knew nothing trickled down. Those that had money before the real-estate crash had more now, and offering such a piece of land would flush it out into the open. Putting a deal like that together would help more than Sally's bank balance.

They circled the county once, but Sally didn't see anything promising. He told the pilot to begin working a grid from the west. He figured the land would be on the fringe of the western development. On the east side of the county, other than Mason University, there wasn't much more than chicken farms and trailer parks.

An hour passed with no results and Sally began worrying about his pilot. He'd re-visited the flask a couple times already, and as he banked the plane in another slow arc, he started singing David Crosby's "Tree Top Flyer."

"That Highway 75?" Sally asked.

"Think so. Why's this land so important but you don't know where it is?"

"Somebody left it to me."

"Wasn't the info in the will?"

"No will. Off-the-record kind of thing."

"Had a few of them deals myself, so I won't ask any more questions. 'Cause I'm a . . ." he picked up the chorus of "Tree Top Flyer" again.

"Over there," Sally pointed. "Take me over there."

A side road weaved vein-like eastward for a mile or two before branching. Sally followed the right fork with his eyes and then pointed. "There, see that patch? Circle it up high, then take us lower."

"Aye, Captain."

Sally studied the picture, compared it to the county map spread across his lap. Maybe, but he couldn't be certain. The piece was large enough and there was the clearing in the center, but a small brick ranch on a couple of acres bordered one side of the tract that didn't appear in the photo. "Turn around and fly the same path, just a bit lower."

From that direction, Sally was sure. He peered out the window, back at the photo. The land beneath him was the same land in the picture. He had it. Sally circled the spot on the map and wrote the word "house" in the location he'd seen the brick ranch. He could get the address now, maybe pay those folks a visit, see what they knew.

"You sober enough to land this thing?" Sally asked.

"Landing scares the shit outta me. You don't want me trying that sober." The pilot took another swig from the flask and grinned.

COLTON LOOKED AT his notes. "Nope, Finn didn't mention anything about spots." He scanned another page.

"Well, something's wrong." James counted again. "We've only got four left, and two of those look shaky. No hope for the rest."

"Finn won't be happy to hear that."

"He said we'd probably lose a few first time around."

"A few, yeah. Not all of them. And this is the second batch."

"Yeah, this is getting a little frustrating."

"Finn'll be more than frustrated."

James wasn't worried about Finn. The man had an established grow operation, distribution, too, but he wasn't gangster about it.

Nope, Finn was smooth, laid back. A real boutique feel to everything. When James and Colton first barged into his hotel room, it only took James a few minutes to calm things down. He bargained, offered ways Finn could punish them. "Tub of water and a toaster," James suggested, grinning. "Jumper cables on my nipples? Ice-water enema?" Finally, Finn laughed and James played the only card he had, casually mentioning an anonymous call to the cops before proposing a partnership of sorts.

"What the hell," Finn answered. "I'm starting to like you a little bit. You got gumption. Here's the deal. I'll set you up with a few babies, teach you everything I know. You give me ten percent."

"Deal." James didn't hesitate.

No, handling Finn wasn't the most frustrating part. Instead, James saw in the ailing plants another chance to impress Britt wilting away. Another chance for his real life to begin now drooping to a halt. Again. It wasn't his fault, though. A hydroponic grow was complicated. All the chemicals, the right amount of light, when to feed, what to feed, playing Grateful Dead tunes for the plants constantly so they'd produce kind bud. And then the PH balances, sexing the plants, vegetative state versus flowering state, indica or sativa strain—too much thinking not enough growing. There had to be an easier way and it had to be easier than admitting to Britt he'd failed again.

James looked at the four remaining plants and felt an idea forming.

"Help me out, C-note."

"Okay."

"Why do you think they call it weed?"

"Well . . . hadn't ever thought much about it."

James pounded the fingertips on both hands into his forehead. "Think, damn it, think. They call it weed because it *is* a weed."

"Well sure, there's that. I thought you meant that commercial—*why do you think they call it dope.*"

"And a weed'll grow anywhere, all on its own. People buy that Roundup shit trying to kill weeds, and they still grow."

"Yeah, but . . ."

"We're going old school. If it's good enough for Mexico, Colombia, and Jamaica, it's good enough for us. We're gonna plant this shit outdoors in the dirt like God intended, and lots of it. Screw this scientific crap, let Mother Nature do all the work. All we gotta do is harvest and collect the profit."

Colton shook his head. "But what about quality? And the Dead tunes? It won't be kind bud."

"We'll make up for it in quantity. It'll still be kind bud—the kind that makes us some serious cash."

"I don't know, sounds risky. It needs to be out somewhere, away from people. Where you gonna find the land?"

"I know just the place." James grabbed his phone and started a text.

Colton shrugged. "Whatever. Mind if I hang onto the Dead tapes?"

AFTER THE INITIAL shock, Trudy calmed down. They talked for hours—well, Trudy talked, Livingston cowered. First came the questions. Liv labored though the details in short answer form, sprinkled with repeated apologies. He tried to listen, but he couldn't focus, and when Trudy's comments slowed and her breathing became measured, Livingston was relieved. He'd survived, so far, and Trudy even seemed okay with everything by the time she drifted to sleep.

Trudy turned away from him and within a minute or two, Livingston's thoughts screamed louder. Was she really okay with it? Why'd he scream out the truth? Why had he lied about not going to work every day? Would they be fine? Liv remembered the evening news comment that the recession would lag on for another fifteen to eighteen months. Their savings wouldn't carry them that far.

Technically, it was her fault. She'd upset the schedule, starting with the evening meal and lovemaking on Thursday night. She knew initiating such a foray would unsettle him. And the . . . he couldn't even think it. She'd *never* done *that*. Where did she learn about something like . . . *that*? What made her think of such a thing? Was it something he'd said? Done? Maybe one of her girlfriends? *Oprah,* she probably heard about it on her show. Should he bring it up later? How did he begin that conversation? He'd be willing to give it another chance, if it was something Trudy wanted. True, the act deviated far from what had served them well all these years, but in light of his lying about his job situation, Liv supposed he could make the effort.

Livingston pulled up his pajama bottoms, trying not to wake Trudy, and settled back on his pillow. He turned to his right, then his left, on his back once more. He tried his body relaxing technique—concentrate first on the toes, deep breath, relax the toes with the exhale. Then his feet, his calves, thighs, buttocks. He abandoned the process before completing his torso and padded through the house checking all the light switches. All pointed down, but still he couldn't fall asleep.

He replayed Trudy's conversation, looking for anything that might provide an answer, some insight into her strange behavior, but found nothing. He approached the situation as if it were an accounting discrepancy from work. He analyzed the words and phrasing, the sentence structures. Useless. Syntax, connotation, and denotation provided no clues. If any subtext or metaphor existed, he missed it. He hit rewind and started over, this time delving into the tone. As he neared the end of the inquisition replay, he noticed something. It was slight at first, but as he considered it more closely, he brightened. There was a shift, a perceptible change in her tone. Was it more wistful? Not quite, no, there was more to it. Maybe remorseful. Yes, a twinge of guilt underscored both her words and her voice. Wistful guilt, that was it, that was it exactly.

Satisfied, he felt sleep approaching and he gave in to it without once thinking of the possible origins of his wife's wistful guilt.

He woke with that very thought, though, and it gnawed at him for three days. Worse, the wistful, guilty tone continued to permeate everything Trudy said, no matter how trivial, but nothing provided any indication of the tone's foundation.

Until Sunday morning. Their Sunday morning lovemaking proceeded as usual, returning to the normal missionary position with no extra-curricular activity. They had progressed into the post-coital cuddling section when Trudy spoke.

"Liv, honey, I need to tell you something."

"Sure, Trudy. What's on your mind?"

"Well, I've been keeping something from you. Nothing bad."

"That's perfectly fine, Trudy. I understand." He didn't know what else to say. Whatever it might be, he didn't think he wanted to know. But he did want to know. No, he didn't. He had to know. "Go on."

"I've been going to my doctor . . ."

Oh God, something's wrong. Not now, not without insurance.

". . . I stopped taking the pill several weeks ago. I know we should have discussed it, and I'm sorry, but I wanted to surprise you."

Thank goodness. A major illness would have wiped out the savings in no time, not to mention the stress it would cause. And Trudy—he loved her more than anything. What would he do if something happened to—"You stopped taking the pill? But . . . you could get pregnant." He thought about the box of Orangutan condoms he'd left in the Volvo.

"Silly. That's the point, that's why I've been going to the doctor. For tests. She says we can have a healthy normal baby, and that I'll be fine. I want a baby, Livingston. I want us to have a child, and I'm running out of time. There's not that many ticks left on my clock."

For the second time in less than two weeks, Livingston felt his universe shift. Before, finding a new job would have easily righted his world on its proper axis. This latest tilting settled upon him with a permanence Livingston immediately sensed. North became south, east became west. When combined with his being jobless and the recession, this shift might require a complete rewiring of his insulated world. He instantly became obsessed that every light switch in their home must now point upward each night. No, every light in the house would be on, that would only make things worse. He felt himself circling above what was once his ordered and predictable life. He could see it as before, each detail sharp but no longer in reach. Now, he circled as if in some strange and unending holding pattern, waiting for clearance and a safe landing.

"Well," he paused, unsure of how to respond now that he'd slipped his mooring, "If your doctor said you'd be fine, okay then." No answer was the best answer. Yes.

Later that day, Livingston took a small firebox from the back of his closet. It contained their life insurance policies, marriage and birth certificates, and the deed to the land his father had left him. Paper clipped behind the deed was an unmarked envelope. Inside the envelope rested a newspaper obituary for William (Bill) Fitzgerald Tucker and a handwritten note, also from Bill Tucker. Livingston looked at the deed and the obituary, but didn't unfold the note. He didn't need to; he knew what it said. *Right of First Refusal,* the promise he'd signed to Bill Tucker. "It gives you piece of mind," Tucker had said, "like money in the bank. Besides, it's just a right of first refusal. All that means is if you decide to sell the property at some point in the future, I get the first chance to buy it. That's all." Liv refused, told him no several times, but Tucker kept coming back. And he always had the lady from the church with him. She talked too much, Liv couldn't get his thoughts straight. Finally, Tucker told him, "I know you'll do the right thing and I trust that so much I'll even let you keep both copies of the *Refusal* note." He even had the church lady notarize them, so Liv felt sure he could make the claim against Tucker's estate. In fact, it would be even easier with Tucker not around.

Liv thought of his father, the job he no longer had, Trudy's desire for a son or daughter of their own. Once more, he looked at the deed, the note, and obituary. He remembered the day long ago when he first went to the property, the conversation he'd had with his mother afterwards. "It's yours to do with what you like," she'd said. "One day you'll thank your father for this."

JAMES KNEW THAT to impress Britt, he needed to step up his game. It had to be a big step, though, he had more on his plate than just Brittany. Standing outside Finn's door, James had—not so much a plan, but more of a notion how to make that happen. He needed a little nudge, a little help to set things in motion, and much as he hated to admit it, Finn was his only option.

"Finn, open up, we need some 4-1-1," James pounded on the door to Finn's room.

"Who is it?" Finn grunted.

"Me and C-note. Got some weed questions. Open up."

The door opened and Finn jerked James and Colton inside quickly before closing and locking the door.

"Look, I said I'd take you under my wing, but damn son, you can't be announcing weed shit for the whole world to hear." Finn took a pull from his beer and pointed toward two plastic chairs in the corner of the room. "Whatta you want?"

"We're thinking to move our grow operation outdoors, you know, go old school. You got another one of them beers?" James asked.

Finn snickered, but didn't produce a beer. "What happened?"

"The cuttings you got us started with, they're—" Colton began to explain.

"Nothing happened. What C-note is trying to explain is that we figure we should go bigger, move our operation to the great outdoors where we'll have more room," James said, "more room means more profit."

"You think so?" Finn looked at Colton.

Colton glared at James, then shrugged and nodded. James nodded too.

"Well, in a way, it is easier. Mother Nature'll do most of the work. You got a spot in mind?"

"Oh we got the place. It's out in the county, off 75. You go toward Waxhaw and turn—"

Colton kicked James in the shin.

"God, what?!" James asked. "That's my bad foot, Bro."

"You gotta tell everything you know?" Colton warned him. "To everybody?" He tilted his head toward Finn.

Finn laughed. "Relax. You can trust me."

"Yeah," James agreed, "Finn here's like family, C-note. Chillax, dude."

Colton looked at Finn then shrugged again. "Sure." He didn't sound convinced and continued to eye Finn. "So, then, we're gonna need some seeds, or more cuttings, because—"

"Yeah," James, cut Colton off once again. "That." He glared at Colton. "And you know, if you'd tell us about growing outdoors, like you did with the others."

"Not much to tell. Take the babies I gave you, keep 'em in the buckets until you get to the site, dig a hole and stick 'em in the dirt. Plant them kinda deep, though, bury 'em up to where the first stem of leaves branches off."

"Well, the babies, we need more than that, what with the extra room. That's the point. You got some seeds or maybe some more of those babies?" James started.

"He killed all but a couple of the babies," Colton admitted.

Finn shook his head, then turned his beer up and drained it. "Well," he tossed the bottle into the plastic trashcan, which turned over, spilling the contents across the floor, "you caught me in a charitable mood." He walked to the kitchenette area of the room, bent behind the cabinet, then stood to place a paper grocery bag on the counter. "I trimmed most of my mothers today and don't have room to start the cuttings. I was planning on tossing them so I didn't put any FastRoot on them, but they're fresh. Odds are they'll take root if you get 'em in the ground and water 'em in real good. Hell, it's already late May, so you boys better get them planted quick."

"Thanks, bro," James said as he retrieved the bag and looked inside. "Now tell me one more time what we got to do?"

Colton pulled a notebook from his backpack and started a new section of notes on growing outside, copying as much as he could of what Finn said while James asked questions. An hour later, they had an education, a plan, and were ready to leave.

"So that's all there is to it?" James asked. "When can we harvest the weed?"

"If you get them planted next day or so, you should be able to sex them first week or two of July, probably harvest by middle of September," Finn answered. "Assuming."

"Assuming what?" James and Colton asked in unison.

"Well, assuming we get rain, or you water regular. And you gotta worry about cutworms, deer, root rot, blight, amount of sun. Somebody finds your grow. And don't forget about curing and drying. Hang it upside down. If it gets moldy, it ain't no count. It's a lot of shit, man. And you're not gonna be able to play Dead tunes for 'em, so, you know." Finn smiled.

James thought about it for a minute. It was a big risk, but hell, the bigger the risk, the bigger the payoff. And he needed a big payoff, he needed it in the worse sort of way. If this failed, he didn't know what he'd do. He had to be sure, and he needed some insurance. Finn had been at this a long time and James suspected there was something more, some secret that could guarantee a solid crop with plenty of kind bud.

"I need this to work," he told Finn. "It's got to work. I know you got some insider tips that you're holding back. You know, pro-level secrets. I'll cut you five percent more on the profit we agreed on for the first batch of babies. That'll put you making fifteen percent and we're doing all the work. Hook us up, man." He was desperate.

"James," Colton whispered, his tone urgent.

Finn didn't say a thing, his face blank as he stared at James eye to eye. After a long pause, he answered.

"I got something. Old trick from the islands. It'll work, guaranteed. I don't think you're ready for it, though. Let's get this crop done, see how it goes. Maybe next year, year after, you'll be ready."

James felt his heart quicken. "No," he said, "I can't wait until next year. This has got to work, it's got to. Tell me."

"Naw, it wouldn't be right. If something went wrong, I don't want that on me."

"Twenty percent," James begged. "Twenty-five. I'll give you twenty-five percent."

"James, listen man," Colton tried to step between James and Finn.

James winked at Colton as he stepped around him. "I got this, Bro. Come on, Finn, please man. Twenty-five points."

"You sure about this?" Finn smirked, "it might cost you your soul."

"I got nothing else to lose. Tell me. I'm sure."

"Twenty-five percent? You're sure?" Finn asked.

"Hell yeah," James replied and stuck out his hand. "Twenty-five percent."

Finn shook his hand.

"What? What is it?" James demanded.

"Get your pen and paper back out," Finn told Colton. "You're gonna need to write this down."

"Damn it. man, tell me," James was nearly shouting.

"Voodoo," whispered Finn.

James grinned and turned to Colton, punching him in the shoulder. "You hear that, C-note? I told you I had this. Voodoo. That shit is real man. Voodoo. Hot damn."

8

The Back Yard

E thel Combs was tired. Tired of all the bickering about national
health care, tired of politicians in general, tired of all the idiots
in the world. She was tired of matching underwear and ankle hose,
blue-haired perms, cholesterol, high blood pressure, high sugar, TV
preachers, young doctors, Vanna White (but she still watched *Wheel
of Fortune* every night), and tired of people in general.

She wasn't tired of being old. That she enjoyed. Age provided
certain freedoms, and after eighty-two years, she exercised those
freedoms with abandon. She smoked a pack of Pall Malls every day,
dipped Tube Rose Peach snuff, and swore like a shade tree mechanic.
She liked a rum and coke while watching *Wheel*. Ethel had an opinion
on everything and happily shared it when opportunity presented
itself. They took her license away for her eightieth birthday, but every
Tuesday night, bingo night, her green '71 Dodge Dart occupied the
handicapped spot at the VFW. Thursday included a trip to the liquor
store, Food Lion for groceries, and Polly's Beauty Salon. Other days,
the post office, drugstore, doctor's appointments, the funeral home,
and the occasional Sunday afternoon leisure drive.

Her kids, two boys and a girl, never tried to intervene. All
three had secretly resented her since grade school for the same
reason—their names, but didn't dare confront her about it. It started
with Nile, the oldest, who everybody now called Niles. Ethel then
named her daughter Mississippi and everyone eventually called her
Missy. Unable and unwilling to change the theme, she hung Thames

on the baby boy, but he preferred Tim. They never phoned and only visited at Christmas, which suited Ethel just fine. Even before they moved away, Missy and Nile had gotten *sophisticated,* called their own mother . . . what was it Missy said? Quaint, that was it. Simple, Nile echoed. Thames was even worse. Same attitude as his siblings, but he still lived across the county. Fine. They'd all grown too big for their britches far as Ethel was concerned. Let them stay away. Thames' daughter, Brittany, stopped in frequently, though. Ethel liked her granddaughter well enough, but had her suspicions about the boy she sometimes brought with her. Other than Brittany, no other company ever knocked on her door.

That afternoon, when Ethel heard the rap on her front door, she snuffed out her cigarette and took her .38 revolver from the table in the hallway and snapped open the cylinder. Satisfied that a round filled each chamber, she whipped it closed, slipped it inside her apron pocket, and headed to the foyer, where she peeped out the window. The man was not bad looking, fifty-ish and tanned. Had a nice chin. He didn't have that mealy, desperate look of the Jesus freaks who knocked several times before giving up and leaving a pamphlet stuck in the door jamb telling her she was going to hell and the only avenue to avoid it would be coming to their church and asking Jesus himself for forgiveness. Or mail a donation in the enclosed envelope.

"Who the hell are you?" she yelled through the door.

"Salvador Hinson, ma'am. Folks call me Sally. I'd like to talk with you a minute."

"I already got one of whatever you're selling and if I ain't, I don't need one. Got no worries about my soul or eternal damnation and I don't give two turkey shits for whatever cause you're collecting for. Now get off my damn porch, Salvador Hinson."

"It's nothing like that, ma'am. I'm looking for some information, that's all. It'll only take a minute, if you'll just open the door."

"You some kind of pervert serial killer? I seen the likes of you on that TV show."

"No ma'am. I live in Mason, lived here all my life. I'm trying to find out who owns the land behind your house."

"I used to know a Hinson. Who's your momma and daddy?"

"Ruth and Montford, ma'am, but Daddy went by Juice."

"Juice Hinson—used to run moonshine?"

"That's him."

Ethel opened the door, but kept one hand in her apron pocket on the pistol, just in case. "Your daddy was a conniving bastard, but he always had good shine. Nice and clean."

"Can I come in?"

"Hell no, but I might come out. You sure you ain't some sicko what likes to rape old women? I ain't got no issue with the sex part, but I don't like it rough." Ethel laughed and stepped onto the porch.

They exchanged a few standard comments about families, who knew who, who'd died, then the weather, before Sally asked again about the property.

"Don't rightly know who owns it now," Ethel told him. "Used to belong to Herschel Carr. A strange piece of work, but he's long dead now. Plane hit him, mashed his ass to smithereens."

"Have you ever noticed anyone on the property? Surveyors, maybe?"

"Nobody but my granddaughter. She wanders around back there sometimes, taking pictures. Had that no-count boyfriend with her a time or two. Wouldn't surprise me if he tried to talk Britt into taking naked pictures to put on that Inner-net thing. I find out he did, I'll fix that little son-of-a-bitch." She produced the pistol and waved it in the air. "Other than that, I ain't seen nobody back there in years."

Sally took a step back when he saw the gun. "Whoa," he said. "Be careful with that thing."

Ethel raised the .38 and fired a shot toward the end of her porch. Sally jumped and a flowerpot full of geraniums shattered. "Don't you worry, I can handle this thing. Don't hit nothing I ain't aiming at." She slid the pistol back into her apron pocket.

"I can see that, and I respect a lady knows how to handle her firearm. Yes ma'am."

"You might be alright, Sally Hinson. Why don't you come in for a glass of iced tea?"

"No thank-you, ma'am, I've taken enough of your time. Much obliged, though. You sure you don't know anything else about that land?"

"Can't say as I do. How about a rum-coke?"

"I best be on my way. I'll leave you my card. Would you call me if you think of anything or see anybody?"

Ethel glanced at the card and dropped it in her pocket. "I'll do that," she told him. "You take care, now." Ethel watched him walk toward his car. That's a nice man, she thought. Like the way his dungarees fit. Broad shoulders. Got a nice ass for a man his age. "Wait," she called out, "I just thought of something. You sure you can't come in for a spell?"

"What'd you remember?"

"There was somebody, couple years back, as I recall. Strange thing. Sorry I didn't think of it earlier. Got so much shit in this head of mine sometimes it takes a bit to rattle one thing or the other loose. Come on in."

"Who was it?"

"Like I said, it was strange. Man and a woman, big woman, come strolling up out of the woods and into my backyard. I seen them and fired a shot over their heads, coming up unannounced like that. The big woman, she fell to her knees, folded her chubby fingers and went to praying, but the man just grinned. Directly, he come around to explaining they set out for a little walk in the woods and must've got lost. Course, that weren't nothing but total bullshit. Big old heifer like her don't go for no walk in the woods. As I recall, he never did offer up a believable explanation."

"Did you get either of their names?"

"His name was Phil, or Bill, something like that. I ain't positive. Her name I remember. It was Mary, *like with Jesus,* she kept telling me. She finally waddled her big ass back in the woods and I ain't thought no more about it until just now. That help?"

"Much as I hate to admit it, it certainly does. Thank you, Mrs. Combs, thanks a lot."

"Much obliged. You come on back anytime, you hear? I promise I won't shoot you."

KAT HAD A rudimentary understanding of history in general and knew even less about the economics of capitalism. Like the perpetual calendar needs an intercalary year every so often, she knew capitalism occasionally needed an adjustment to keep cogs properly lubricated, deals turning, and greed satisfied. The first adjustment of note occurred in 1773, the latest began in 2008.

First, the British East India Tea Company, deemed too big to fail, failed. Something had to be done. It served everyone's best interest—politicians, business magnets, the God-fearing Christian people of England, everyone—if the British East India Company received a bailout to keep them afloat. Three ships set sail for America, their bellies bloated with a half million pounds of tea that, per Parliament's edict, was excused from the usual excise taxes, duties, and tariffs. Let the Americans pay the taxes. Profit would be restored and the Company returned to solvency. How could it not?

Then, two hundred and thirty-five years later, starting in 2007, the gilded banks and financial behemoths of Wall Street, those deemed too big to fail, failed. Shockwaves rippled across the heartland, and in the past two years, 401Ks dwindled, the real-estate bubble burst, and honest, hard-working people found themselves homeless. Just as the Tea Party initiated a major adjustment in both politics and capitalism, it was now time for another adjustment. On February 1, 2009, an open invitation to a commemorative Tea Party protest appeared on FedUpUSA.com. The Tea Party Protest idea was born and immediately gained momentum. The movement needed a new scapegoat. Rush Limbaugh and company loudly and happily offered up the new target: intellectuals, left-wing nut jobs . . . *liberals*. Change was coming.

Groups formed. The Tea Party Patriots organized in Boston, New York, Omaha, Biloxi, Paris (Kentucky, not France), Bluefield. Somebody bought a bus and stocked it with Samuel Adams Light Beer. The show went on the road, and the next stop, only a few short months after the movement started, was scheduled at the Farmer's Market in Mason, North Carolina.

Kat didn't know about the rally when she agreed to meet Arlen Johnson in the west corner of the Farmer's Market main parking area. When she first learned of it, she tried to reschedule, but he refused to change his plans. While she didn't know details, in general, Kat knew that academia, the intellectual elite, the reading and semi-informed public had become a favorite target of the Tea Party factions, and she was nervous. Still, Johnson said he had new information. She circled once more, then drove to the overflow lot three blocks away and parked next to a Hummer with a "Protect the Smokey Mountain National Park" license tag and a "More Freedom—Less Government" bumper sticker. She locked her Prius and walked toward the Market.

By the time Kat started the last block, she'd lost hope of spotting Arlen, at least until she was closer. It was the signs—everyone had one and they blocked her view. She tried not to linger, wanted to avoid reading them, but they were everywhere.

She touched the tip of her nose, then ducked around a couple waving poster boards at the passing crowd. The woman's said "Honk for English" and the man's said "No Amnety". At least they shared a consistent theme.

More signs. More spelling, grammar, and logic errors. Kat finally saw Arlen Johnson and pushed her way through the crowd.

"There you are," he said. "Isn't this great?"

Arlen had dressed the part. In addition to the ever-present Braves cap and Khakis, he'd chosen a faded John Deere t-shirt. He'd pinned a fuzzy picture of Sarah Palin over the John Deere logo, which on second glance, Kat realized was actually a picture of Tina Fey from *Saturday Night Live* impersonating Palin.

"Yes, yes. I suppose. You said you had information?"

"I thought, you know, after the rally we could discuss it over supper. The Brown Fedora's just down the road. My treat."

"Oh, I'm not staying. And I have a prior engagement later. Ah . . . it's . . . commitments . . ." she touched her nose, "I have other plans."

"What plans? You gotta stay for the rally, you don't want to miss that."

"No, really, I'd love to, but I can't. I'm a . . . I'm a Democrat." Kat had no idea why she added that but immediately regretted it.

"You got it wrong; this ain't about Republicans or Democrats. No ma'am, not at all. This is about Americans taking back our government. We got to send a message. We the people and all that stuff. No more taxes, no more bailouts. Let the politicians know we can govern ourselves."

Kat looked around the crowd. How satisfying it'd be to skewer one of the rubes with their sign and parade them around. Instead, she asked, "Hmm. You think that's a good idea?"

"Well, hell yeah. That's what the Constitution says, and if it was good enough for George Washington, it's good enough for me."

"Perhaps. On the other hand," she stared at the crowd, "this does speak to the growing social and political dichotomy in the country."

"Political dichomometer? I thought you were different, but you ain't. You're just like all those other college eggheads. You're an elitist. Probably socialist, too."

Arlen sunk into his John Deere shirt and tugged his cap lower over his eyes. Kat didn't mean to hurt his feelings, and she worried he might not pass along whatever info he had now.

"No, it's not like that. I just . . . a discussion point, that's all it was. Open discourse."

"See, there you go again. I get it, you think you're better than me." He looked away.

"No, no. We just have different opinions. That doesn't mean one's right and the other's wrong. I'm sure there's validity to some of the Tea Party's positions. Good ones, even . . ."

Arlen looked at Kat again. "I thought we had something going, me and you. Thought we might soon be keeping time. And now this. I just don't know if I can see you again, if this is how you feel."

"Mr. Johnson, I didn't mean to create the wrong impression. We had . . ."

Arlen held up his hand to Kat. "There's no need for your apology. I'd hoped we'd be two peas in a pod, but I reckon we're just two ships in the night. Here." He took a folded piece of paper from his front pants pocket and handed it to Katherine. "That's what you wanted, all you wanted, from me."

Kat felt the urge to touch him on the forearm, even reached out, but stopped and took the paper instead. "Mr. Johnson, Arlen, thank you . . ." She unfolded the paper. "Wait, I can't read this. Is that 11 . . . 55?" She pointed to the paper.

"Lemme see. No, 22. 1122 Padgett Road."

"But . . . what is it?"

"It's what you wanted. The girl with the pictures."

"This is her address? Oh, thank you."

"It ain't *her* address. It's her grandmother's. I've seen the girl there, though. She goes out behind the house with her camera, into the woods. I started to follow her in there, but they's poison ivy all over the place."

"Where's Padgett Road?"

"Out in the county. Take the old Waxhaw Highway south, left on Rock Creek Church. Go a couple miles and you'll see Padgett on the right." He couldn't resist adding, "They ain't got MapQuest on them fancy college computers of yours?"

Kat stuck out her hand. "Thank you so much, Mr. Johnson. You've been very helpful. Very helpful indeed. This is exactly what I needed."

Arlen looked at her hand and paused. Finally, he shook it, but looked away. "Just go," he choked.

SALLY SAT ON his back porch, drinking, listening to the rain in the trees and watching lightning from the earlier storm streak across the sky. Thunder started low in the east, then built steadily as it cascaded and tumbled around the horizons for a half minute before fading. Sally smiled and took another sip of Jameson. Maybe that was it, rumble for a while, then just fade away. Wasn't that a Stones song? Close, it was *Not Fade Away*, and the Stones weren't the original. That distinction belonged to Buddy Holly. That was it, he remembered it from somewhere. Last song he ever played. God had a fucked-up sense of humor, but a pretty good grip on irony. And what about Waylon

Jennings? Gave up his seat on the plane, wrote a bunch more tunes. It all came down to choices, didn't it? One leads to another and another and another and you end up at fifty alone, with no answers, staring at another decade, or two, or three, of what? Nothing? Thunder on for a second or two and then *pffft*—done. Why bother?

He drained the glass and poured another.

He'd felt this way a lot during the two years before Bill died, the time when they weren't talking. Sally knew all his meandering over that time, all the fads and "isms" he'd tried, were only distractions. He thought he'd made his peace with it, though. All those questions of legality, of ethics, of guilt even, he'd answered. He knew some in the area thought he and Bill were shady, that they took advantage of people, were less than honest, but that no longer bothered him. If it hadn't been him, it would've been someone else. To a degree, he'd kept Bill in check all those years. Sally was a local, a native. He understood the people they made land deals with, and he really did look out for them. If Bill had partnered with somebody else, a Yankee, or a big-time developer, no telling what kind of shape some of the people would be in now. No, Sally harbored no guilt. He'd done right by people, straight through.

Instead, something about Ethel led him to this current funk. She'd called his daddy a conniving bastard. That didn't bother him so much, he'd heard him called worse. The nature of his business lent itself to rumor and Sally knew the same would be said, was said, of him. But Sally learned a lot from his old man, everything really, by watching the way he dealt with people, the way he ran his boot-legging operation, and he'd always imagined himself operating the same way. Sally turned to those memories when he had questions, when he needed a little direction.

Ethel's comment reminded him his daddy died young, younger than Sally was now. What would his old man have done had he lived longer? Would he have given up bootlegging shine? If he did, how would he have filled his time? How would his daddy and momma spend their later years together?

Ethel's comment reminded him that with his father—and now Bill—gone, he no longer had any point of reference. This latest deal, though, had sparked something familiar in Sally, something he knew. It'd be enough to quiet those questions, at least for a while. He'd figure the rest out later.

More thunder rolled. Sally refilled the glass. Another shard of lightning ran across the sky. Sally raised his glass in a toast. "What the hell," he said to the night. "This one's for you, Pop."

9

Leverage

James never considered his role or place in history, never put any stock in what lessons could be learned there, and never bothered scouring history to find future opportunities hidden there. No, he was not the type to worry about such things.

On the other hand, James sensed possibility hovering barely beyond his fingertips. He felt something, of that he was sure.

He leaned into the bed of Colton's truck and picked up the shovel. "What's with the Mexican backhoe?" he asked.

"Thought we'd need it," Colton answered.

"Not today. Today's strictly recon. Sling blade's good, though. Might need to clear out some brush."

"I like them French fried potaters," Colton tried to sound like Karl from *Sling Blade*.

"Don't start that shit, C-note. Come on, we need to pick up Britt."

"You ought not talk that way. You just a boy." Still doing Karl. He kept it up for a couple miles.

They stopped for Brittany and drove south on Old Waxhaw Highway. Brittany insisted on riding shotgun, so James hunched on the jump seat behind her. The required twelve pack of Bud sat next to him. They turned on Rock Creek Church Road, and Colton asked for a fresh beer, which James dropped as he handed it over the console. It rolled into the floorboard beneath Colton's feet and he bent down, fishing between his legs for the can. He almost had it, but it slipped away. He leaned further, his head even with the steering column, then below it as he tried to get a visual on the rogue beer. As his fingers formed around the beer, Brittany screamed.

"Car," her voice stretched toward the glass-shattering octave.

Colton sat up and jerked the wheel hard to the right. The truck swayed but settled back into the lane, nearly sideswiping a Prius coming from the other direction.

Brittany hit him on the shoulder, kept hitting him. "You idiot. You coulda got us killed. I ain't got time for that."

"Chill, Chica," Colton answered. "I got this."

Colton switched to steering with his knees so he could open the beer, and James turned to look out the back glass at the Prius as it disappeared over the hill.

"Hey," James said, "that was one of those electric hybrid toy cars. They're too quiet, you can't hear them coming."

Ethel Combs, Brittany's grandmother, came out on the porch as the trio stashed the beer and got out of the truck. James had met her several times, but couldn't decide if he liked the old woman or not. She was short and square. Standing at the top of the steps with her arms folded, she looked immoveable, like a stump. James had never seen her in anything other than a non-descript, casual dress with her hair knotted into a tight, bluish bun just below the crown of her head, and today was no different. She usually wore a stained apron over the dress and was constantly looking for her glasses, which, as far as James knew, she never located. Brittany said Memaw was legally blind, but James thought the old woman only told people that, either for sympathy or to keep them off guard. Didn't stop her from driving to the liquor store.

James didn't think she liked him, or anybody else for that matter, other than her granddaughter. Everything about her told James she was a woman capable of . . . *things,* the kind of things that made him afraid of her. But she cussed a lot, and that impressed him. He called her Granny, but she didn't seem to care much for the term.

Brittany bounded ahead of them, yelling, "Memaw" with out-stretched arms. Ethel hugged her, but kept her eyes focused on James and Colton as she did. When the two released, Ethel re-folded her arms and thrust her chin toward Colton.

"Who's the colored boy?" she asked.

"That's Colton, James' friend," Britt answered.

"Afternoon, Mrs. Combs." Colton gave her a nod as he spoke. "Pleased to meet you."

"We'll see about that shit. Who's your momma and daddy?"

"Rufus and Maggie Ratterspan, ma'am."

"Don't recollect the name. Who's your mama's people?"

"Memaw," Brittany whined. "It's just Colton. He's cool."

"If he's hanging around the likes of that one," she pointed at James, "I need to know who raised him up." She turned back to Colton. "Well?"

"Momma was a Cuthbertson. Marlin and Sarah were her folks, my grandparents."

"Un-huh. It's coming to me. I recall Marlin and Sarah had a girl run off from college with some half-breed hippie fellow. That your folks?"

"Yes ma'am."

"I don't know your daddy, but your momma comes from decent stock. Best watch yourself around old Jack-leg James there. He's more trouble than a cross-eyed copperhead."

"Memaw. Stop it."

"Don't know what you see in him, girl. Now, what you young folks aiming to do out here?"

"Thought we'd take another walk in the woods back of your place, Granny. Get some exercise. Fresh air," offered James.

"Well, that's a hairy-assed lie. Britt, honey, what these boys put you up to?" Ethel asked.

"No, that's it, Memaw. They're gonna help me take some pictures of those flowers, that's all."

Ethel eyed each of them.

James eyed her back. He saw an upside. Once they established a crop, Granny was mean enough she'd run off anybody who came snooping around and clueless enough that she'd never suspect a thing. Not a courtesy, just part of her ornery nature. Brittany said she kept a loaded pistol by the door and a shotgun in her hall closet, and James didn't doubt she'd use them. And there was no way she'd wander around back there, not at her age. It was the perfect set up. Even though it provided him some leverage, he decided it best not to rile her any further.

"Naw, Mrs. Combs," James started. "Britt showed me some of the pictures. I didn't want her off in the woods by herself like that, not without me checking it out. Thought Colton and myself would take a look. Make sure it's safe and all."

"I see." Ethel glared at James. "I hear tell of any funny business, I'll skin your sorry ass like a corn-fed possum on Thanksgiving, you hear me?"

"Yes ma'am."

She looked at Colton. "That goes for you, too." Then she turned to Brittany. "Well, alright then, honey. I expect to hear if either of these two tries any foolishness. Remember, you're my baby girl, and everybody best treat my baby girl like a lady."

"Memaw. I'm almost seventeen." She gave her grandmother a peck on the cheek and skipped down the steps toward James and Colton.

Brittany took her camera from the truck, snuck three beers into her backpack and headed toward the woods. James and Colton followed close behind. When they reached the clearing, she told the boys she wanted pictures of the plants even though she knew their yellow flowers wouldn't bloom for a few months yet, and she started down a faint path along the edge of the clearing.

The boys looked around the clearing. After a fifteen-minute rant about problems involving cut worms, rabbits and deer, poachers, low-flying planes, culling males, toting water, PH levels of the soil, and Carlos Castaneda, Finn had grudgingly given them a few pointers for growing outdoors. They needed an area with plenty of sun, especially late afternoon. Well-draining, slightly sandy soil, and preferably a tall thicket or briar bramble for cover. If they couldn't find anything tall enough, they could always bonsai the plants. If that proved too hard, and Finn assured them it would, get some red Christmas balls, the plain kind everyone used to hang on their trees. Dull the finish a bit with some four-aught steel wool and hang them on the plants, make any nosey pilots think they were tomato plants.

James forgot most of the advice before returning to his room.

"Did you remember your notebook, the one with all the notes you took from Finn?"

"You didn't say anything about bringing the notebook," Colton answered.

He scratched his head, swatted a gnat, and asked, "Okay, then where's the sun come up?"

"In the east," Colton answered.

"A+, college boy. Which way is east?"

Colton looked up. The sun glared almost directly overhead. He licked his right index finger and held it up, waiting for a breeze. Then he grabbed a clump of weeds and tossed them in the air. They floated aimlessly back to the ground. He glanced at the sun again, but it hadn't moved. Colton licked his left index finger, held it high above his head, then lowered it and pointed. "That way."

James started whacking away with both arms as he high-stepped into the broom sedge and briars, careful not to put too much weight on his bad foot as he moved in the direction Colton had pointed. "Ow." The first thorn snagged into the crook of his arm. He freed himself and dabbed at the tiny drop of blood. Another step. "Ow, damn it." Louder this time, another speck of blood on the opposite forearm. A few more steps. More swearing, more scratches. "Hey C-note, that sling blade's doing me a lot of good in the truck," he yelled.

"Some call it a sling blade, but I call it a Kaiser blade, mmm-hmmm," Colton mimicked Karl from the movie again.

"I call it freaking useless in the truck. You gotta go back and get it." James pulled another thick briar branch away from his Widespread Panic t-shirt.

"Reckon you make me some biscuits. Mmm." Still Karl.

"Well, at least get in here and help me find the right spot."

"Man, I ain't going in there." Colton shook his head. "There's probably ticks. Snakes, too. Nope, it's all you, brother."

Colton stepped back into the shade of an oak tree and sat down, cross-legged. On the other side of the clearing, Britt snapped pictures of the purple-stemmed plants. James pushed forward, cussing and keeping an eye out for snakes, until he disappeared into the knot of weeds and briars. After about twenty minutes, he re-emerged, twigs stuck in his hair, his favorite t-shirt torn in several places. "Screw it," he said, "it's too much trouble. We'll come back tomorrow or the next day, just plant around the edge." He worked one of the twigs from above his ear loose and threw it at the ground. "Brittany," he called. "Let's go."

The three of them made their way back toward Ethel's house. Brittany led, followed by Colton, who sang Steve Earl's *Copperhead Road* in time with his steps. James shuffled along behind. His face, neck, and arms looked as if he'd spent the afternoon trying to cuddle a feral cat. As he walked, he plucked what thorns he could from his skin and thought about all the money they'd make. His payday was so close he could almost smell it.

THE BROWN FEDORA had not been this crowded for lunch since the day of the Tea Party rally. Three stools were open at the far end of the lunch counter, and Sally took the first one. As he settled in, the waitress brought his tea and took out her pad.

"Hey Sally," she said. "Stew beef over rice is good today."

"That'll work. Limas and corn," he answered.

"Back in a jiff, hon." She winked at him and left.

Sally swiveled and glanced around the room. Must be court this week, he thought. The restaurant was only a few blocks down from the new courthouse, and when it was in session, the lawyers and clerks, legals and deputies, all converged on the Fedora during lunch break. The owners, George and Irene Economous, updated and expanded the place several years back, but it still had the feel of a small-town diner. Nothing like the chains out on the boulevard and not as artsy as the new places springing up downtown. It was the kind of place where lawyers sat next to farmers, bikers next to retirees, politicians next to mill workers. More than one deal had been struck over cornbread and pintos, more than one office romance sparked over soup and salad. The food was utilitarian, meat and three, nothing fancy, even the daily specials. Fish on Fridays, banana pudding or peach cobbler for dessert. The gabby regulars could spend an hour after their meals making the rounds, visiting, catching up, being nosey. But it was just as easy to melt into the patchwork and go unnoticed except by the waitresses, and Sally hoped to do just that.

He'd closed his share of deals at the Brown Fedora and when Bill was alive, they'd hashed out ideas and weighed prospects over lunch or dinner several times a week. Today he only needed home-style cooking and an hour to gird himself for the afternoon phone call to Mary.

Sally knew how to work it. He'd call, ask her to dinner, no doubt the woman liked to eat. Tell her he'd like to get to know her better.

Then, get her started on the god-squad thing, ease in a casual question for information. Put a plate of food in front of her, show her a little attention, let her talk and she'd eventually tell him what he needed to know. It hinged on the attention factor. Toss out a few compliments, pretend to listen, make eye contact, smile and nod. Once she believed he was interested, the rest was easy. It almost wasn't fair.

As Shirley brought his plate, a woman eased by him and took the last stool at the counter, leaving an empty space between them. Sally spooned a bite of corn and cast a glance in her direction. Not bad looking. No *Maxim* cover layout in her future, but she'd do. Late thirties, maybe early forties. Glasses, brownish hair twisted in a loose knot, a few stray ringlets falling past her ears and brushing against her cheek. Kind of tall, a little flat chested, but overall a nice figure as far as he could tell. No ring. Not his usual type, but there was something interesting about her.

"Here's a menu, hon," Shirley told her. "Stew beef over rice is the lunch special. Back in a jiff for your order."

The woman didn't open the menu. Instead, she began pulling papers from an oversized bag she'd placed on the floor and spread them on the countertop. Then, she briefly scanned the menu, closed it, sighed, and picked up one of the papers. When Shirley returned, the woman ordered water with lemon and a chef's salad—ranch dressing, and went back to studying her papers. When her order came, she absentmindedly picked at the salad, took an occasional sip of her drink, and focused her attention on what she was reading. Sally finished the last of his lunch.

As he went for his wallet, he noticed the woman reaching for her glass, unsuccessfully. Sally smiled. His impulse was to slide the drink within her reach but before he could, she hit the plastic glass and sent it tumbling in Sally's direction. He swiveled and only a few drops of water and ice landed on his pants, just above the knee. The rest of it surged across the counter, carrying the ice over the edge with it.

"Damn it," she muttered and grabbed a handful of napkins. Shirley rolled her eyes, picked up a dishrag and motioned for one of the kitchen help to bring a mop.

The woman dabbed at the water, moving along the counter in Sally's direction. She pulled several more napkins from the dispenser and blotched the few wet spots on Sally's pants. "I'm sorry," she said. Then, as if she realized she was touching him, she sat up, touched her index finger to her nose, and sucked in a ragged breath. "Oh. I didn't mean . . . I . . . Oh. I'm sorry. Here." She handed the napkins to Sally. Touched her nose again.

"No big deal," he waved away the napkins. "Hardly any on me."

"I was distracted," she said. "I'm so sorry. It's just . . . I don't know. Ever have one of those days?"

Sally nodded and smiled.

"I met this pill of an old woman this morning. Some teenagers in a truck nearly ran me off the road on the way here. I have all this work. Leaderlick's asinine Twelve Point Revision Plan. I just . . . I'm sorry. I'll pay for your lunch."

"No need for that. Really. Look, already dry." Sally smiled at her. "Tell you what. Sounds like you could use a bright spot." He took a twenty and a business card from his wallet. "Shirley," he held up the twenty and waved it at his plate and the woman's. "I got both of these," he said. He put the twenty with his business card hidden beneath it on the counter near the woman.

"Oh, please, no. Let me."

"Nope. My treat, I insist. Hope your day gets better."

"Well, thank you. That's very kind."

As Sally walked to his Lexus, he checked to make sure the ringer on his cell wasn't muted. She'd find the card, he didn't doubt that.

Even if she didn't, Shirley'd give it to her once she saw it. Maybe put a plug in for him. Sure, he could have introduced himself, but no. Too obvious. Better to create a little mystery. Something about her told Sally she'd appreciate that. The intrigue would smolder, her curiosity would build. She'd look at the card, put it away, look again later. And again. Once more. Hold the card *and* her phone, then put them both away. Next, she'd dial the number, but not hit send. Finally, she'd muster the courage. She'd call, Sally was certain. Like closing any other deal. And if she didn't? Nothing lost. But, she'd call. He thought about the way she gently touched the tip of her nose, as if she wasn't aware she was doing it. The act held an air of vulnerability and Sally found it oddly appealing.

10

Pictures

Livingston was nervous, more nervous than usual. He'd not even had time to adjust to the idea of being unemployed and then Trudy was pregnant. And now, according to her, turning the extra bedroom into a nursery was the first top priority. But we have nine months, he told her. Liv missed most of her reply, but he then understood there were many top priorities.

Next came the books. The titles alone disturbed him in ways he never thought possible. *Pregnancy in the New Millennium. You're Pregnant, Is It Too Late to Land a Good Preschool? Music: Emo for the Embryo. Satisfying Mommy: Sexual Positions for Each Trimester.* A full color coffee table book titled: *Delivery—A Pictorial,* which Livingston kept putting on the top shelf of the hall closet only to find it on the table yet again. It was too much.

After the third week, Trudy began removing his books from the shelves in the study, packing them in plastic containers, and storing them in the garage. She needed Liv's shelf space for the formative years and beyond books, even went as far as labeling each section.

When Livingston realized she'd made Amazon.com their homepage, he considered confronting her, but decided against it. The wounds his mental state endured from the verbal lashing following his "we still have nine months" comment had barely scabbed over, no point picking at it.

Baby clothes appeared, two of every outfit, one pink, one blue. Pamphlets, brochures, advertisements. Cloth or disposable? Lactation consultants, nannies, pediatricians.

And names. Books on names and their popularity, ancient meanings, their etymology. Potential name lists hanging from fridge magnets, taped to the bathroom mirror, the steering wheel of the Volvo. One evening, Livingston opened his copy of Percy's *The Moviegoer* to find she had replaced his favorite Shakespeare bookmark with a narrow list of middle names to consider. He felt a tightening, no a stabbing, in his chest and checked his pulse. Satisfied he was not having a heart attack, not at the moment, he switched from *The Moviegoer* to *The Thanatos Syndrome*. He'd put off reading it for years, but now the title intrigued him as never before.

Slowly, a compressing weight replaced the stabbing pains in his chest, the weight anchored by dollar signs. How did people do it? He couldn't afford the ephemera that came with pregnancy, how would he manage the bills after the baby was born? He had nightmares about the credit card bill arriving. A new tic appeared: snapping the fingers on his right hand, middle finger against thumb. At first, there was no audible pop when he did it. The action emitted a soft and sweaty thud, but once the calluses developed, it evolved into a drier scratching sound, like the faint scrape of dead winter leaves against a window screen.

The doctor showed them the grainy ultrasound pictures of their baby. Trudy bubbled all the way home. Livingston said nothing. That night, after she'd fallen asleep, he found her paperback copy of *The Cost of Raising Your Child to Adulthood,* went to the chimenea on the patio and built an elaborate pyre. He placed the text on the top, coated it all with a heavy dose of charcoal starter fluid, stood back, and tossed a kitchen match on the structure. The concussive whoosh and the heat following it made him take another step back.

He sat in the patio chair and stared into the fire, mesmerized. Knowledge didn't flicker in the flames, no epiphany rose on the smoke. He didn't want to do it, then or now. When Bill Tucker first approached him with the offer, Liv couldn't name a reason for turning him down. He didn't care about the land, had no plans for it at the time, but *something* wouldn't let him sell it. The feeling bordered on premonition. An illogical attachment. When he considered the offer, the same feeling he had about light switches, always putting his left shoe on before the right, buttoning the second button from the top on his dress shirts first, three ice cubes in his tea, rose inside him. He was reluctant to sign the right of first refusal letter, but it seemed the only way to get Bill Tucker to stop pestering him about the property.

Livingston didn't feel any better about it now, but didn't see any other options. He went inside, opened the box containing the letters, and pulled out the obituary. *Survived by his wife, Jolene Tucker.* He didn't want to, but what other options did he have?

Jolene Tucker was decidedly less than happy to see him. Probably still grieving, he thought, maybe a little delirious. Jolene cracked the door, but left the safety chain attached, and Livingston introduced himself and leaned forward to explain, directing his words at the open space provided. He told her about losing his job, spending his days at the library, Trudy being pregnant, the books, and the lists of baby names, *all* the lists of baby names.

"That don't confront me," she said. The door didn't budge.

Livingston continued. "I understand. It doesn't ... I didn't expect ... I thought ..." Finally,

he blurted it out. "I came about your husband, Bill."

"Well, you're late. He's dead. That whore, Mary Carson, murdered him."

"Murdered?" Livingston took a step back.

"That's right. Murdered. Killed him dead. She killed my Billy and nobody will do a thing about it. I know she did, that home wrecker. Her and that cult she got Bill mixed up with. They were in on it, too. Part of a big conspiracy, I'm sure."

"I don't know anything about that ma'am, but your husband and I had this sort of deal, an agreement really, in a letter about some property I own that he was interested in buying. If I decided to sell, that is."

"For all I know, you're in on it. You a part of the conspiracy? Are you? I got the law on speed dial."

"No, no. Here, look." Livingston slid the folded letter through the opening. "We had a deal. It's all there."

After a few seconds, the letter came back through the door.

"He made lots of deals, but I stayed out of his business stuff. Probably should've paid more attention. Might've caught him with that jezebel before she drowned him. Sorry, I can't help you." The door started to close, but she paused. "When did you see Billy last?"

"When we signed this letter. He came by my house with his secretary. See," he unfolded the letter and pointed to a notary seal, "she notarized it for us, made it official."

"Secretary? Billy didn't have a secretary. It was just him and Salvador. What name's on that notary seal?"

Livingston looked at the letter. Moved it closer. Farther away. "Looks like, hmm, Manny Carzoni. That can't be right."

"Mary Carson?"

The door closed, the safety chain dropped free, the door swung wide. "Get in here." Once Livingston was inside, Jolene poked her head out and looked down the street in both directions before slamming the door closed again.

She explained everything—Bill's conversion, the cult, the alleged drowning, Mary's role in it all, the altercation at the funeral home, the authority's indifference. She digressed, telling Livingston what she knew of the real-estate operation Bill and Salvador ran.

"And she was with him, this Mary Carson?" Jolene asked.

"Yes. I'm certain. We met seven times, and she was there each time," answered Livingston.

"Un-huh, I see. Well, like I said, I can't help you with the land. I mean, I could, Billy left me in good shape, but I don't know the first thing about investing in real estate. You talk to Salvador Hinson, he might be interested."

"But the estate—"

"That went to me, all of it. And I told you. Talk to Salvador."

"Thank you, Mrs. Tucker. You've been a big help. And I'm sorry about your loss." Livingston stood to leave.

"That Sally, he's shady, though, so watch him. He might be in on it. And that whore, Mary Carson . . . well, it's all part of the conspiracy. That cult wanted your land, probably for some kind of sex ritual with goats and sacrifices and stuff. If they brainwashed my Billy, they'll get in your head, too, so watch yourself, Mr. Carr. Sell it to them if you must, but don't let them poke around in that brain of yours."

Livingston sat in the Volvo, snapping his fingers. He no longer recognized the picture he once had of himself. An accountant for Orangutan Condom Company, solid and dependable husband. Predictable, stable, everything in its proper column, every column balanced. He'd work out his years with the company, take his pension, and he and Trudy would settle into a Florida retirement community, read Tim Dorsey novels, play Scrabble, and wait on the sweet release of death, just the two of them. That picture he recognized. How did it come to this? No job, no retirement, no insurance, a baby on the way, Trudy—who was normally frugal in all she did—spending money like eating M&M's (which she *was* eating, in Costco quantities). Conspiracies, scams, murder, cults.

He wanted his old picture back.

First, meeting the old woman shattered the Norman Rockwell version of a senior matriarch. Crusty: Katherine had never considered that word to describe a personality, but it fit. The woman's language leaned toward crude, and while her colorful word choice made Kat blush, she had to admit a certain appreciation for the woman's bluntness. The woman had been both suspicious and protective when it came to her granddaughter, refusing to give Kat any information other than admitting the girl did like to take pictures. No name, no contact information, but *her pictures are awful damn pretty to look at.* Despite first impressions, the brusque demeanor, the anvil-like posture, Kat detected a softness in her eyes whenever the lady spoke of her granddaughter that suggested an underlying gentleness and intelligence in contrast to the exterior. It was obvious the woman would deny such a chink in her countenance, though. Kat made a mental note to discuss the matter with Janice, her friend in the psych department. There must be a deep-seated impetus for the woman's behavior. Stay focused, Kat reminded herself.

"So, yes, I should go. Thank you for your time. Again, it'd be extremely beneficial if you'd share your granddaughter's contact info. I'd be happy to meet her here, with you present, if that would help facilitate—"

"Nope. That's not gonna happen." Ethel began closing the door, using it to usher Kat toward her car.

Kat leaned her hip into the door, buying enough time to hand Ethel her card.

"Here's all my contact info. Please, please explain everything to your granddaughter. Have her call me, email, just get in touch with me so we can come to an agreement that benefits everyone. Please."

Ethel took the card, then shoved the door closed. Kat stood on the porch for a moment, dejected, until she noticed the window curtain peel back enough for Ethel to glare at her. Kat had no choice but to drive away empty-handed and only slightly closer to her Schweinitz' sunflowers.

Kat checked her phone and text messages as she drove back toward town. Five voice messages—her mother. Delete. Four from Leaderlick. She saved the first one, just in case, and deleted the rest without listening. Seven texts, all from Leaderlick, the last three in CAPS. She knew he had meetings the next two days, there was no need to shout. She looked at the first text. "The Prospective Students Open House on Saturday." Leaderlick reminding her she was staffing the Botany information table. Oh, *please.* Delete. She scrolled to the first CAPS text. Apparently, the administration now hoped to use the Twelve Point Strategic Revision Plan as a foundational springboard for the new Mason University Pledge to Prospective Students *and* as a retention tool. Delete. Next. Leaderlick wanted her input. A nice gesture, but . . . Kat had a plan, a pledge, and a retention tool for him. She tapped to activate the mic, glanced at the road, made sure the mic was on and started speaking. "Dr. L, how's this, colon, we are no longer accepting the scholastically tired, comma, the academically challenged, comma, the intellectually stunted, period. If you are Mason material, comma, you will arrive prepared, comma, complete college level work, comma, expand your horizons, comma, and maybe, comma, if you really apply yourself and show some responsibility and a glimmer of promise in your chosen field, comma, you will eventually matriculate, period No more pampering, comma, no more coddling, comma," Kat looked at her phone, saw the typed words, and then thumbed "LMFAO."

Nope, she couldn't chance it. She erased the message. No tenure, and she needed her job. Kat looked up, saw the red truck crossing into her lane, and swerved just in time.

The morning, the messages, and the near miss unsettled her. She wasn't really hungry, but stopped at the Brown Fedora for a quick lunch, hoping the food would stave off an afternoon headache and she could review her research notes from the night before. Kat sat at the counter and absentmindedly picked at her salad, raking the carrot slivers to one side, eating an occasional cucumber slice. Just as she thought, she discovered an interesting correlation between optimal soil requirements for the Schweinitz sunflower and those in a particular section of the county, she embarrassed herself by spilling her drink on the counter and the man sitting in the next seat. She went from embarrassed to mortified when she caught herself dabbing at his pants with the napkin. She felt the heat rise up her neck and spread across her face. He was very gracious about it, even paid for *her* lunch, which made her feel even worse. When she realized he left his business card beneath the twenty-dollar bill, she originally dismissed it, but put the card in her bag anyway.

Now, curled on the couch with Oscar, her cat, and her third glass of Merlot, she let her mind wander. After suffering through two days of Leaderlick's belligerence, producing reports, revising and re-revising notes for *his* meetings, and facing the next day's Open House, the last thing she wanted to think about was work. She remembered the man's card, and leaned over and took it from her book bag. She stared at the wording, the font. Neat, but a little pretentious. Palatino Linotype, she thought. Turned the card over. Took another sip of wine, shook her head, and put the card on the table. Several minutes later, when she finished the glass, she picked up the card again.

"No, Oscar. I can't. Don't let me." She put the card on the arm of the sofa.

Oscar stretched.

"He was rather handsome, though. Strong chin. Kind eyes." She rested her glass on the end table, fingered the card, and picked up her cell. Oscar yawned and uttered a half purr, then started licking his right paw.

"You're right. I should focus on my research. No distractions. Besides, how forward of him, leaving his card." She placed her phone on the table and the card on top of it. Kat padded to the kitchen, poured the last drops of merlot in the glass and opened a bottle of cabernet. She carried the glass and the bottle back to the sofa and picked up the phone again. Maybe it wasn't being forward. Maybe this man was different. Maybe it was the opposite of forward. Leaving it up to her to call, well, for a man of his age, his era. Not forward but enlightened. Something a gentleman would do. Maybe. She dialed. Paused before hitting send. Put the phone and the card back on the table. Took a sip of wine.

She repeated the process until half the cabernet disappeared, then picked up the phone once more and entered the numbers.

She looked at Oscar. "It's only polite to properly thank Mr. Salvador Hinson for buying my lunch, Oscar, you know that." He meowed and jumped from the couch. She pressed send.

JAMES CRUSHED TWO Adderalls on the mirror and chopped them into a fine powder with the razor blade. By the time Colton arrived, he'd pushed the powder into four heaping lines.

"C-note," he said. "Just in time, blood on the tracks." James pointed at the mirror and offered Colton a length of a McDonald's drink straw.

Colton shook his head. "You know I don't mess with blow, James. Come on."

"Ain't coke. This is brain food. Shit'll make you smarter. Help you focus. And we need to focus, get shit done. Big day ahead of us."

James didn't take the straw, but leaned over the mirror. "What is it?" he asked.

"Adderall. That stuff they give kids with ADD. Zombifies them, but if you don't have ADD, the Adderall's got a nice, smooth kick to it. Lot more staying power than blow. The smarter thing's a freebie, like a real-time acid flashback."

"Un-huh. I'll pass, just the same. Stick with what I got." Colton tapped his temple.

"More for me." James hoovered two lines in succession, switched nostrils, and cleaned the last two lines. He stood up, his eyes watering. "Boy howdy, I feel some Einstein coming on all ready."

Colton shook his head and laughed. "Where's Brittany? She still going with us?"

"I'm in here. I'll be ready in like, two seconds," she yelled from the bathroom. "After that college thingy, you got to drop me at my house, though."

They piled in Colton's truck, Britt calling shotgun, and left for the Open House at Mason University. Colton was starting in the fall and had an appointment with his advisor to pick up his schedule and some other orientation materials. Brittany wanted to tag along, hoping the art department might have a table with photography information. Not for a class, she told the boys. She was thinking a tip sheet, how-to guides, pointers and suggestions, anything that might give her some ideas. James went because he needed Colton to help him cull the male plants later that afternoon, and he wanted to make sure C-note didn't spend too long talking to the eggheads. Even though the first week of June was a little late to be planting, the plants were coming along, and all of them two or three feet tall. The small pistils had appeared in the notches last week—they spotted them on the fourth before they went to the fireworks show. They couldn't wait any longer to sex the plants. Finn had told them the males had to be destroyed before the buds developed or everything would be seedy, and the THC in the females would be lower.

They found a parking place near the quad and stared at a locator map framed in Plexiglas until Colton spotted his advisor's building.

A student in a teal colored t-shirt with "Ask Me" printed on the front handed them fliers. "All the Business stuff is that way, along the left edge of the quad," she said, pointing. "Math and Sciences are in the far-left corner, Foreign Languages in the far right, and Humanities along the right edge. Fine Arts are around the corner, follow this sidewalk past that building."

"Where's P.E.?" James asked.

The girl smirked. "Oh, you're a run, jump, play, and make an A major?"

"No, I ain't coming here, I just might like Indian stuff. Not the kind that owns the hotels and 7-11s, you know, with the dot," he touched the middle of his forehead, Brittany slapped his shoulder, "the cowboy and Indian kind. Thought the P.E. folks might let me try out a bow and arrow."

The girl sighed and slid her finger along a clipboard. "You mean archery. Sport Sciences are located between the *real* Sciences and Foreign Languages, back edge."

James didn't care for her attitude, or better, her lack of one. Like he was less, almost invisible. Not one of *them*. Fine. James was used to it.

"Gee, thanks for all your help," he snipped.

The three split up, Brittany in the direction of the Art section, Colton to his advisor, and James flitting from one booth to the next, moving from right to left around the quad, stuffing giveaways in his pockets, and hanging lanyards around his neck.

James found Sports Sciences, but no archery. He noticed a variety of plants covering several tables to his left. James thought he recognized the woman behind the tables, but he couldn't place her. He moved closer, stood right in front of the table and shielded his eyes from the sun's glare, squinted at her nametag, his mind clicking through its Rolodex at warp speed. Adderall speed. Dr. Katherine

Sardofsky. Click, click, click—no, no, no. Click—that's it, the medical marijuana meeting. The hot professor chick.

He lifted a potted flower and smelled it. Took a pamphlet. The professor ignored him. Picked up another plant and studied it. Wiped his sweaty palms on the back of his pants. "You work with plants?" he asked.

"Yes, I'm a Botanist. Are you thinking of majoring in Botany?"

"Naw, don't need to. We got something in common: I work with plants, too." James grabbed another piece of paper, and when he saw it contained a schedule of fall classes, he laid it back on the table. Shifted his weight from one foot to the other, felt like the professor was sizing him up, as if his high school grades were somehow printed across his forehead.

"You work for a landscaper? A flower shop?" she asked.

"Nope. I grow 'em." James shuffled, looked over his shoulder and saw Brittany coming across the quad. She'd find him in a minute or two, he better pull it together quick.

"We buy some stock from a couple of local growers. Who do you work for?"

"I'm independent. Got my own grow operation. Me and my buddy Colton. He's going to school here in the fall."

Brittany spotted him and called out his name.

"I see. Do you specialize?"

"Yeah, you could say that. We grow weed. It's gonna be top shelf stuff."

"Wait. Weed? You mean cannabis? Marijuana? But that's illegal."

"Yeah, we gotta keep it on the down-low. You know, don't tell nobody or nothing. It's cool, it's cool." Brittany getting closer, he could see her out of the corner of his eye, now only a few feet away. "Maybe we could get together sometime and compare notes, you know, one grower to another?" Brittany at his side. The professor touched the tip of her nose, touched it again.

"No, I don't think so," the professor answered James, but stared intently at Brittany as she did.

Britt tugged at James' arm. "Come on, James. We've got to meet, Colton." She glanced at the professor. "Hey," she told her.

"Have we met?" Dr. Sardofsky asked. "Are you a student?"

"No, I'm like, seventeen. I'll be a senior this year." She faced James. "Let's go. Colton's waiting on us by now." She turned to go, dragging James with her. "Nice meeting you," she called back over her shoulder.

The boys dropped Brittany at her house, picked up a six-pack, and headed south toward Britt's grandmother's place. Colton parked off the edge of the drive and they hurried for the woods behind her house, hoping the old lady wouldn't come outside. Colton carried the notebook with the shaky drawings Finn had made to distinguish between males and females, a shovel, a rusty machete with electrical tape wrapped around the handle, and a magnifying glass. James was already twenty feet in front of him, carrying the beer and picking up speed. They skidded along, almost breaking into a trot. Ten yards after they made the tree line, they heard Granny yelling at them from her back porch. Colton stopped and looked back. "Keep going," said James. Colton readjusted his load and followed.

It was a long afternoon. Hot. James and Colton circled the clearing. At each plant, they'd stop and study the crooks of branches under the magnifying glass.

"Look at this one," James said, handing the glass to Colton. "Are those white hairs or the pistil?"

"Pistil, I think. Wait. Might be hairs. No. It's a male. Maybe."

So it went. Slow, tedious work. After several hours, they'd culled the crop by two dozen plants, downed the six-pack, accumulated thirty-four bug bites between them, but avoided the poison ivy. They talked while they worked. Discussed who'd win—Spider

Man or Iron Man, immigration reform, why Wile E. Coyote always bought from ACME, black holes, and Colton's vivid, detailed, and probably illegal infatuation with Joe Biden's wife, Jill. It took a couple hours, but they finished. All in all, a good day.

Ethel was waiting on them when they returned.

"Just what in forty hells were you boys doing back in those woods?" she asked.

"Nothing, Granny." James answered. "Just clearing out some weeds so Britt can get better pictures." He winked at Colton.

"That ain't your property; you got no business back there."

"I'm trying to do something nice for your granddaughter."

"You want to do something nice, why don't you get a job instead of raking around in those damn woods?"

"Chillax, Granny. I got plans for some income."

"Chillax my wrinkled ass. You're up to something, James Flowers. Chillax. What kind of talk is that? You sound like a shit salesman with a mouthful of samples. Well, I ain't buying, so unless you boys aim to weed my flower bed, get on down the road."

"Sure thing, Granny." James turned to leave. Colton had slipped away when Brittany's grandmother started talking and now waited in the truck, engine running. James paused before climbing in the passenger side. "I'll see you tomorrow for Sunday dinner," he yelled and closed the door.

ETHEL WATCHED THE truck turn around in her side yard and start down the drive. "Sunday dinner. You'll be damn lucky if I don't poison your sorry ass," she mumbled to the tail lights.

Naptime, but her mind was troubled and she didn't think she'd go to sleep. She sat in the rocker and stared out the window. Something was up with that boy. The colored one seemed nice enough, but not James. Brittany could do better. That girl had a good head on her shoulders. Ethel wished she wouldn't watch all those trashy reality TV shows, though. She'd tried to get her interested in *Wheel of Fortune,* but Brittany had said it was boring. Ethel had to admit there wasn't much to choose from when it came to television these days. If it wasn't a fake reality program, it was one of those crime shows, and they were just gruesome. Or, the doctor and hospital dramas. Those were even worse. Ethel finally stopped looking at those programs. Whatever symptoms the TV patients had, she'd lie awake that night trying to determine if she had the same, which usually meant she had to fix one more rum and coke to help her fall asleep. At least Brittany didn't like those shows either, which was a good thing.

But there was something more than James on her mind. It wasn't so much that he was back there in the woods, even though she knew his reasons were no good. Ethel sat and rocked, rocked and sat. Rolling things around in her head. That land seemed to be drawing a lot of attention lately. Sure, Britt walked back there to take her pictures, but she'd done that for years. But now, James and that friend of his started going back there. All of a sudden, too. It started when the man and the heavy woman came strolling up from out of the trees. They weren't a bit more lost than she was, *and I been living here since we built this house in '53,* she thought. And Salvador Hinson appearing out of the blue like he did, asking questions about the property. That fancy talking lady professor from the college. Ethel didn't doubt it would only be a matter of time before she came back and started traipsing around. Something was going on and it all circled around that piece of dirt behind her house.

Fine, she decided. Ethel Combs didn't tell the DMV where they could stick their eye exam without reason. There wasn't a thing wrong with her vision. She could see. And Ethel Combs hadn't made it this far, didn't raise three ungrateful kids on her own, without being able to figure out a thing or two along the way. She'd figure this out, too. Yes, the picture was fuzzy, but coming into focus. She'd soon have it framed and hung.

11

A New, Comfortable Spot

On a hot Memorial Day in 1925, patrons crowded into the cool confines of the Rivoli Theater to experience Willis Carrier's latest invention. Air conditioning was an instant hit. Units began to appear in the homes of genteel Southerners in the mid-Sixties. By the end of the Seventies, nearly every home and business had A/C, and the northeast exodus began. Sometime in the late Eighties, the area from Mason west to the county line turned into a bedroom community for Charlotte. A feeding frenzy started. By the nineties, the county was a boomtown and the transplants had taken over. Why can't we have world-class city stuff like we had up north, they asked? Why can't we do things in Mason the way we did them in New Jersey they wondered?

Plans were made, the re-making began.

The Crescent Moon Café was part of the downtown rebirth. Sally thought the place felt like a cave—shadowy and confining. Tables arranged at odd, unpredictable angles, high back booths at the rear near the bathrooms. Reproduction movie posters from the forties and fifties and a few Louis Icart prints hung on the brick walls. New age sounds dripped from speakers suspended in the corners. Sally hated it all. Even the façade made him weary in a way that had become too familiar. If he could give form to the existential questions plaguing him, that form would look like The Crescent Moon Café in every way.

Four people sat at the bar, two men, two women, and if they knew one another, nobody acknowledged the other. They had an air of arrogance and entitlement perceptible from where he stood just inside the door. Each drank a different designer beer. The bartender, a thin man in his late twenties, dreadlocks, full sleeve work inked on both arms and a nose ring, ignored everyone. A couple, artist types, at one table near the door. Three soccer moms at another table on the right. No sign of a waitress or hostess.

Mary waited in the last booth. She looked as comfortable as an Aztec virgin on the steps of the sacrificial pyre.

"Oh Sally," she whispered when he approached, "I'm glad you got here. This place is . . ." she looked around the room, then leaned forward. "*Different.*"

Sally slid in the booth. "Yeah. Thought it'd be a little more private. A comfortable place where we could talk."

A waitress appeared, black jeans, black Care Bears on Fire t-shirt, bottle-black hair cut in stark angles, black eyeliner, and a full-color Betty Boop tattoo on the inside of her pasty forearm. She was rail-thin, and Sally half expected to see meth-head scabs on her hands and arms when she dropped menus on the table. "Drinks?" she asked.

Sally ordered a Miller Lite, Mary asked for sweet tea. Sally picked up the menu, Mary followed suit. He'd been to the Crescent Moon a couple times, enough to know they were fashionably slow in bringing out your meal. He planned to find out what Mary knew about Bill and the land before eating. Once the food arrived, Mary'd have a hard time focusing on anything else.

"Order anything you'd like," he told Mary.

"What are you having?"

"The Macadamia Nut Goat Cheese Salad, I've got dinner plans tonight. Don't want to fill up."

"I don't know what any of this stuff is. Artichoke with Avocado Cream? Wasabi Infused Brie? Havarti Cheese Chicken? Spinach and Goat Cheese stuffed Portobello Mushrooms? Don't they have any plain old yellow American cheese? And there's nothing fried."

"Take a chance, Mary. Columbus did. Try something different."

"I don't know. The cook looks just like that . . . that . . . the one behind the bar. You think it's safe?"

The waitress returned. She placed Sally's beer on a napkin and slid Mary's unsweetened tea and two packets of NutraSweet across the table. She dropped her order pad on the table, sighed, leaned down with pen on the pad, and stared at Sally vacantly.

Sally ordered his salad. Mary stammered.

"Hmm," she said. "I think I'll have . . . the crab cake with dill sauce . . . no, wait . . . oh here's something fried. I'll have the chicken nuggets. Does that come with bread?"

The waitress sighed again and slouched toward the kitchen. Sally looked at Mary, trying to gauge his best opening. For a second, he almost felt sorry for her, but then he remembered her and Bill. And the panties. She wasn't that innocent. Mary stared at the bartender and wiped the sweat beading on the side of her glass. There was no best opening. Get to it.

"Mary, listen. I need to talk to you about something, and I need you to be straight up with me."

"Now Sally, I wouldn't be anything else." She smiled and resettled herself into the seat.

"It's about you and Bill . . ."

"Let's not talk about Bill, God rest his soul." Still eager.

"I think there's a little more to tell, Mary."

"It's Jolene, isn't it? That woman just won't let it go. What did she say to you?"

"No, I've not talked with Jolene. Bill was working on a land deal. You knew about it, didn't you?"

"I counseled Bill on his new faith, helped him to walk closer with the Lord."

"Mary."

"We had prayer vigils and Bible study. Christian fellowship, that's all."

He didn't really want to hear the explanation that would likely follow, but Sally didn't see any other choice. He reached in his pocket, and stretched the red thong to its full width above the table. "Recognize these?" He asked.

She moved quicker than Sally expected, her chubby hand darting out for the panties. He snatched them back.

"Give me those." Her lower lip trembled.

"So you do recognize them?"

She nodded and lowered her head.

"Bill had a safety deposit box. Found them in there. I don't need an explanation, it's none of my business. But I do want to know about that land."

"I don't . . ."

"I could ask Jolene about the underwear," Sally interrupted. "I can't imagine what effect that might have on a grieving widow."

"I thought you were a good man, Sally. You wouldn't."

"Good's a relative term, Mary." He dangled the panties once more. "You should know that. Now let's talk about a hundred acres out in the county, see if we can't get these drawers back in the proper lingerie chest."

Sally asked questions, Mary answered. The food came and Sally let her feed while he picked at his salad. The confrontation had little effect on her appetite. A teenage girl bounced through the door. Sally thought he recognized her, but couldn't place from where or how. She hopped on a bar stool near them, ordered a Red Bull, and took a notebook from her backpack. She was blonde and leggy, late teens, maybe early twenties, oozing a wholesome seductiveness reflective of that age when a girl is only aware of her sexuality in terms of TV shows and horny, pimply boys, and not the torture and despair her every move created in older men. Sally sighed and returned to his lunch.

By the time Mary had finished her meal, Sally had a better idea of the how. His threat produced part of what he needed—a name, Livingston Carr, and the deal—right of first refusal. It also produced far more about Mary and Bill than he needed. The fact they were doing the nasty didn't surprise Sally, the level of detail she offered did. All of it sprinkled with pleas for him not to tell Jolene, and he agreed without hesitation.

There was something more, though. Sally'd seen it so many times, let a person talk and they'd eventually tell you what you needed to know. While Mary's details turned from confession to reminiscing, she didn't say why Bill wanted the land, and Sally felt he needed that info before talking with this Livingston Carr fellow. Not knowing put him at a disadvantage. And, he felt a spark inside growing stronger, taking on an edge he'd never known when Bill was alive. Different, yes, but in a good way, a way he liked.

Mary looked spent, exhausted, unburdened when she shoved her plate to the edge of the table. Sally leaned to one edge of the booth to stretch his legs. The door swung open, casting the sun's glare on Mary, and a hefty man in an Atlanta Braves cap shuffled in, glanced around, and quickly wedged himself behind a table near the artist couple. Mary squinted and Sally waited until she opened her eyes before starting.

"Mary, you've been a big help. It felt good to get all that off your chest, didn't it?"

She nodded.

Sally told her what she needed to believe. "Your secret's safe, too. Jolene, nobody, needs to know a thing about it. Trust me."

Mary looked up, dabbed at the corner of her eye with her napkin. She stifled a belch and said, "Thank you, Sally. I appreciate that."

"There is one more thing." Her face said *yes, anything*. She believed. Sally had her and that feeling, that old confidence swelled in his chest. "Why did Bill want the land?"

Mary didn't answer. She looked at the man in the Braves cap, at the bartender, at her hands. Her face changed, the eagerness from earlier returned.

Finally, she couldn't contain herself. "Oh Sally," she bubbled, "you won't believe it. Bill did it for Preacher Mike, for the church. We were going to establish a retreat and sell memberships. Fifteen thousand a year bought use of a cabin for two weeks out of the year and your name on the prayer request list as often as you'd like. After the cabins, there'd be a prayer hall, walking trails, a community building, an interactive creation museum. We already had plans drawn. Preacher Mike came up with the idea, all of it. Oh, best of all, he planned to dig a big lake in the middle and build an ark on this island in the middle of it, bring in all kinds of animals, two each, and keep them in the ark. A year-round nativity scene next to a building for Santa's Wonderland, there'd be lights and carols and holiday tours designed around that. Then a trail leading through the woods to the other side of the land where there'd be a replica of the crucifixion. Stations along the trail to show all the big events of Jesus' life. All self-contained."

"Sounds like quite an undertaking," Sally stifled a laugh.

"Oh that's just to start. It was gonna put that Creation place in Kentucky to shame. You know the one I'm talking about."

Sally had no idea what she was talking about, but it didn't matter.

"The stations on the trail would be life-like animations, wax figures that could move and talk, all this computer stuff. At each station, you'd be able to feed a dollar in the machine, mash a button, and the figures would act out the story. Changing water to wine, the Last Supper, walking on the water. That one was a little tough, the experts said the warranty would be void if the wax Jesus got too wet, so they planned to put stones just below the surface."

"Well, that's logical. And how did Bill wanting to buy this property figure into the plan?"

"He was gonna make the deal, then donate the land to the church."

"Donate? Bill Tucker? I'm having a hard time with that, Mary. Why would he do something like that?"

"I told you. He changed, really. He talked to Preacher Mike, something about tax shelters . . . the IRS . . . but I didn't understand all that."

"Shit. The IRS?" He did not need the IRS nosing around.

"I think. I don't know. Is that bad? It can't be bad; Bill was doing it for the church. I mean, Preacher Mike was going to give him a share of the ticket sales, but they both said that was standard."

Sally calmed down. So that was it, a tax shelter. Made sense, seemed more in keeping with Bill's nature. And a share of the gate? A lifetime of tax-free mailbox income. Damn. Brilliant. That explained the whole church angle. He had what he needed.

"Maybe so, Mary." Sally slid to the edge of the seat. "I best be going. You've been a big help, I appreciate it."

"You're not gonna tell anyone, right?"

Sally winked. "Like I said, our secret. Thanks again." He left a fifty on the table and started to leave.

"Wait," Mary said, but he was already out the door.

A RED PICKUP stopped in front of the Crescent Moon Café. A blond jumped out and said something to the two guys in the Ranger before they drove away. Arlen looked at the sign on the front of the building. It wasn't Red's Pure Country Saloon, and it was a safe bet none of

Red's regulars ever came here. He looked up and down the street. No parking places offered a view of the restaurant's door. He didn't want to go inside, but without a spot where he could watch who went in and out, he didn't have much choice. Arlen drove through the light and turned into the adjacent lot.

Inside, the girl sat at the end of the bar, drinking a Red Bull and thumbing through a spiral-bound notebook. Arlen chose a table near the door, keeping the girl in his line of sight, and tried to blend in, which wasn't working. He took off his Braves cap, put it back on. Off again, on again. When the waitress finally came over, he told her to bring him a water and that he was waiting on someone else. Arlen wanted a chili cheeseburger and a Bud longneck, but from the looks of the place, that wasn't a possibility. Even if it was, what if she left before he finished eating? He'd been working up to this ever since the Tea Party rally. The plan was to talk to the girl, tell her he'd been following her and why.

Arlen checked to make sure he'd remembered Kat Sardofsky's card. He felt the card's outline in his pants pocket and tried to muster the courage to approach the girl. Finally, he stood, but a plus-sized woman in a pink sweat suit was leaving and blocked his path. He took it as a sign and decided to wait for a better opportunity.

The girl at the bar checked her phone, paid for her drink and started toward the door. Arlen tried not to make eye contact as she passed but turned to see her getting back in the same truck. He hurried out and merged a block behind the Ranger, following it away from downtown, still determined today would be the day.

They drove out of town, picking up the boulevard near the new mall, which was now the old mall since the Best Buy and Target complex opened a mile west. They passed the car lots, Lowes, the Wal-Mart Supercenter. Passed the city limits and into the short stretch of the four-lane that Mason's westward or Charlotte's eastward growth hadn't yet swallowed. Still driving west and Arlen wondered where they were going.

A gray Volvo tailgated, swerved around him, darted in and out of traffic, passed the Ranger with the blond and two guys, and scooted under the light as it turned from yellow to red.

"Speed on brother, Hell ain't half-full yet," Arlen yelled at the driver as he stopped for the light. While he waited, he looked at the cars around him, the drivers all doing the same thing. Cell phone, cell phone, cell phone, picking his nose while talking on the cell phone, and cell phone. The car in front of him edged into the right turning lane, leaving Arlen directly behind the red pickup. He tugged his Braves cap lower.

The light changed. After a few more miles, the truck turned left toward Statler. Arlen followed. When they came to the Statler town park, the Ranger slowed and signaled. He panicked, there was only one other car in the parking lot. If he pulled in behind the truck they'd spot him. But you want to talk to her, he thought, what difference will it make? He wanted to talk to her alone, though, so he wheeled into the town hall parking area across the street.

The girl got out sliding her arms into a backpack and holding a camera. She waved to the guys and when the truck was out of sight, Arlen eased across the street and nosed in two slots down from the only other vehicle. Good, the park was practically empty. The girl had settled under a shade tree and was taking pictures, facing in the opposite direction. The only other person around was at the far end of the park, near the seesaw. The man walked in circles around the seesaw, snapping his fingers on his right hand and motioning in the air with his left. It looked like he was talking to himself, but Arlen figured he probably had one of those phones that fit in your ear. Harmless, making some kind of business deal or arguing with his wife. Arlen took a deep breath and got out of his car.

Gotta do this right, he thought. Let the girl know Kat was looking for her, that the professor was interested in her pictures. If he'd only gotten more information the first time, Kat wouldn't have dismissed him. But, if he could give the girl Kat's name and number, have her call the teacher and tell her Arlen told her to . . . well, Kat would be so grateful she'd have to reconsider.

She didn't notice as Arlen walked up behind her. "Hey there," he said. The girl jumped, nearly dropping her camera as she turned to face him.

"Hey," she said and picked up her backpack.

"You taking pictures?" he asked.

The girl looked at the camera in her hand, then raised it toward him. "Duh," she said.

"Listen," he said, "I need to talk to you. I've got something for you."

"Who are you?"

"Me? I'm Arlen. I've been following you."

"You perv." She took a step back and looked around the park. The thin man circled the seesaw. A city cop car turned in across the street. Nothing else.

"No, no. Not like that, I was following you for somebody else."

The girl took a few steps to the right, easing around Arlen, moving closer to the parking lot. "There's a cop right over there," she nodded toward the building across the street.

"Easy, it's okay." Arlen held up his left hand and reached in his pocket with the other. "Here, I've got something for you."

"Ew. My boyfriend'll be back in a minute and he'll kick your fat ass. Now leave me alone."

She started toward the street and Arlen reached out and grabbed her arm. The girl hit him over the top of the head with her backpack, knocking his cap down over his eyes.

"Damn it, that hurt. What've you got in that thing?" Arlen re-situated his hat.

The girl dropped her pack and started snapping pictures of Arlen. The camera clicked four, then five shots. "Evidence," she shouted then picked up the backpack and raised it for another swing.

"Just wait a minute," Arlen cowered with both arms covering his head. "Listen to me. I ain't a perv, somebody wants your pictures."

The girl lowered the pack. "My pictures? Who?"

"I'm trying to tell you. Here." He handed her Kat's business card.

"Dr. Katherine Sardofsky. Who's she?"

"A professor at the college, something to do with plants. Flowers and stuff. A friend of mine's brother's second cousin knows your daddy. That's how I knew you took pictures. I saw a flier at the laundromat where this lady wanted to know if anybody'd seen this yellow flower. You know, like those posters for a missing dog or a criminal. I recognized it from a picture of yours my friend had."

"I got lots of flower pictures. Does she, like, want to buy some?"

"Maybe, yeah. You should call her."

She looked at the card and shrugged. "Maybe."

The red truck pulled in and blew the horn. A shaggy haired boy leaned out the passenger window and yelled, "Come on, Britt. Get a move on."

"That's my ride. See ya." She started skipping toward the truck.

"Wait," Arlen called out. "Be sure and tell her I told you to call. My name's on the back of the card. Be sure, now."

After she left, Arlen sat in his car, feeling good about his chances. The professor would appreciate his effort. You had to go the extra mile with a smart woman like her. Maybe when she called, he'd suggest they go to the Crescent Moon Café for supper. The place had the kind of atmosphere you couldn't find at Red's or the Brown Fedora, Captain Steve's, even. She'd be impressed.

He watched the man round the seesaw and smiled. "I know how you feel, buddy," he said to himself. "I was going in circles myself, but I ain't now."

LIVINGSTON THOUGHT HE smelled toast. He'd read somewhere that was a sure sign of a stroke. Now, he could add the symptom to the phantom pains radiating down his left arm, the intense throbbing pinpointed behind his right ear several times a day that surely indicated an approaching aneurism, the very real rash creeping around his ankles and wrists, and the hiccups that, for the past few weeks, appeared every morning at precisely 10:05. Liv tried several new tics and quirks to compensate for these new afflictions, but nothing helped. He snapped his fingers constantly, made rounds through his house every ten or fifteen minutes checking light switches. He sensed he was coming undone.

First, it was Trudy. The books, the endless lists of potential names. Beginner level anxiety, manageable. The food came next. Liv was prepared for the dill pickles and ice cream, not the gastronomical kaleidoscope which followed. Fried calf liver topped with blueberry cobbler, mashed potatoes mixed with strawberry jam, sliced bananas in Campbell's tomato soup. The sight and smell he learned to tolerate, but the unpredictability of it all distressed him. Their nightly meal schedule had disappeared. Livingston spent each day driving from one location to the next, unsuccessfully filling out job applications. If it was Thursday, for instance, he expected to come home to salmon patties and garlic mashed potatoes, just like always, not green beans swimming in applesauce with pineapple popsicles for dessert.

Soon after the food came the mood swings. Nobody warned him about those. They watched a comedy on the television—Trudy cried for hours. She'd cry at commercials, a compliment he gave her, a pile of laundry, the neighbor mowing the lawn. Those weren't so bad; Liv at least saw a cause and effect. The random outbursts really got to him. They could happen anytime. Once she woke him from a sound sleep—which he rarely got anymore—just to cry.

When the mood swung the other way, it frightened him. His diminutive bride, the mother of his coming child, giggled when the evening news reported a violent crime on the other side of town. One evening at dusk, he found her standing on her footstool, looking out the kitchen window into the back yard. An owl had taken up residence in the neighborhood a year or so earlier. When Livingston looked over her shoulder, he saw the owl with a rabbit pinned to the ground in its claws, picking at its flesh with its hooked beak. Trudy stared at the scene, a sinister, satisfied smile on her face. Livingston locked himself in his study until after she fell asleep.

The sex was equally disturbing and even more random than the mood swings. Morning, noon, night, odd days, strange locations, even stranger positions. Granted, given the size of her belly in proportion to her height, Trudy had become nearly perfectly round, making missionary difficult at best. She'd dog-eared every other page of her book, *Satisfying Mommy*, and Liv was convinced she intended to try every position listed, no matter how bizarre. The night he came home and found the swing fastened to the ceiling in their bedroom was almost fatal. He agreed to try, even helped Trudy into the contraption. Things got a little out of control, and Trudy started swinging at too wide of an arc. Liv stepped forward to stabilize the swing, fearing she'd fall out and hurt the baby. When he reached for it, his arm tangled in one of the supports, he lost his balance and fell from the bed, twisting his ankle as he hit the floor.

While the frequency and variety of the sex caused waves of anxiety to course through him, he worried most about hurting the baby. One night, she was on the large ottoman, on her hands and knees, Liv behind her trying to be gentle. She kept telling him, "Harder, harder," and he tried to block out her voice. He did the best he could, which must have been alright as Trudy's voice got louder and louder until she screamed, "Yes, yes, yes," and fell forward on the bench and rolled over, smiling at him. Livingston couldn't look her in the eye, lied about needing to work on his resume and excused himself to the study.

His home life settled into perfect chaos, void of all predictability, his necessary routines vanquished. His career path looked as promising as a yardstick—flat, narrow, and marked by equal and incremental lines of failure. The recession that started in '07, went full psycho in '08, and led to his getting fired in January, was still lingering on with fall approaching, and investment firms rolled bailout money into bonuses and graced them on the upper echelon while cutting positions from the lower rungs. The rich called Cayman Island financial institutions, the poor played the lottery, and nobody needed a forty-something accountant who'd spent his career balancing books for an off-brand condom manufacturer. Most places wouldn't take his application, those that did never called. The want ads left him wanting and the bleak postings on Monster.com made Livingston want to hide in the closet. Trudy spent, funds dwindled.

After one spectacularly unproductive morning of job hunting, Livingston became obsessed with Plan B, which was not a plan at all, but more a vague nagging that his solution lay in the land his father left him all those years ago. He drove aimlessly through lunch, trying to determine what troubled him about selling it. Normally, Liv was a stay in the right-hand lane, one mile an hour below the posted speed limit, check the mirrors every fifteen seconds, always use the turn signals, driver. The deeper he slipped into his mind, the more carelessly he drove, and he was soon weaving in and out of traffic, hurtling ahead with purpose but no destination. He nearly rear-ended one car, veered left, cut off a truck, and ran a red light as it turned. The truck blasted its horn, which startled Livingston. He slowed. He could see the man shouting at him in the rear-view.

After a few miles, he turned left on Statler Road, for no reason. When he came to Statler Park, he wheeled in, thinking a little time outdoors might lend some clarity. He walked around the outskirts of the park twice, snapping his fingers, weighing options. He stopped for a moment at the seesaw, then began circling the ride counterclockwise.

"What are the options?" he mumbled.

"Find this Salvador Hinson, sell all the land." The index finger on his left hand signaled *one* in the air. Right fingers snapped quicker.

"How much to ask?"

"Or lease the land. Steady income." He signaled *two*.

"But what amount? And in this economy?" He waved his left hand back and forth, erasing one and two. A young girl walked across the park, sat down, and started taking pictures of the trees and sculptured shrubs across the way.

"I wonder if we're having a girl?"

Walking. Circling.

"But if it's a boy, maybe I should keep the land for him."

Another *one* from the left hand.

"A girl might want it, too."

Erase the one and start over.

"Why can't I find a job?"

A man in a Braves cap approached the girl.

"I like baseball, the symmetry, the statistics, the order."

"Did she just hit him with her backpack? Should I do something? I shouldn't interfere. What if it were my daughter? How am I going to protect her? My God, I'm going to be a father." Fingers snapping faster, left hand waving nervously, steps quicker.

The girl left, the man left, Livingston walked, the circles around the seesaw growing tighter. Repeating words in cadence with each footfall. Father. Money. Land. Job. Daughter. Trudy. Sex. Future. Son. Future. Plan. Plan. Plan. Plan.

Livingston broke from his path and ran toward the park's lone picnic table, crawled under it, hugged his knees to his chest, rocked back and forth, and tried not to cry. After an hour, he dusted himself off, calmly walked to his Volvo and started home, his grip on reality more tenuous than ever.

Late afternoon, and the dog eased out from under the trees, wary. The animal's tail curved in a perfect fishhook over its back, nearly touching the rusty-blond fur along its spine. His head proud, the pointed ears alert, the muzzle black and flecked with gray around what appeared to be a permanent smile. Something about the dog's dark eyes suggested a calm wisdom. The body was slim but thick through the chest, medium-sized overall, probably thirty or forty pounds, much like a dingo. A few cockleburs had attached themselves to the animal's coat, but otherwise it appeared healthy.

He gingerly took a few more steps, stopping at the edge of the tree's shade, where he dropped something from his mouth and lay down, paws outstretched in front of him, head held high, watching.

The first week, he stopped at roughly the same spot, never venturing further from the protection of the woods. The second week, he advanced a few feet more, then paced back and forth, scenting, before choosing a new comfortable spot.

Ethel studied him from the kitchen window those first two weeks. Carolina Hound, she was sure of it, but couldn't recall any neighbors who owned one. Maybe someone put him out. He was a handsome animal, but she didn't need anything that ate or crapped. Still, each afternoon she found an excuse to stare out the window. Each day it was the same—the dog appeared at about the same time, paced, dropped something from its mouth, and settled down. And each day, it stayed a little longer, especially after it started moving closer. At dusk, he'd turn and go back into the woods. Once, on Tuesday of the second week, Ethel walked out in the backyard and busied herself in one of the flowerbeds, not really doing anything, but keeping an eye on the dog. When she took a few steps toward him, he bolted for the woods, but she saw him stop behind a knot of honeysuckles and peer around at her.

He came back the next day and went to the same spot. Ethel again went in the backyard. This time he stayed, but didn't come any closer. On Monday of the third week, Ethel saved scraps from breakfast and lunch. She watched the clock, and a few minutes before the dog normally appeared, she raked the scraps into an aluminum pie tin and carried them halfway between her house and the woods. She left them and walked inside without looking back.

The dog came on schedule, found his spot, and rested. Ethel wasted the afternoon at the window, but the dog didn't consider the food at all, wouldn't come any closer. Still she waited, sipping her rum and coke, missing *Wheel of Fortune*. When it was too dark to see, she gave up.

Before breakfast the next morning, she checked and found the pie tin empty. She smiled, but then reminded herself that a coon or possum could have just as easily eaten the scraps during the night. Back inside, she scrambled one more egg than usual.

12

Cowboys, Indians, and Serendipity

James believed the universe gave everybody gifts. James also believed, based on experience, the universe was like that in-law you only saw at Christmas who insisted on giving crappy gifts they made, like a poorly-carved wooden gun letter holder with a clothespin for a hammer that was supposed to hold the mail, or worse, the framed family portrait of them in stupid Christmas sweaters. Holding the pet cat. These were the gifts the universe gave him.

Still, he held onto the notion that every-so-often, the universe got it right and actually gave a decent gift, one you could really use. James had not seen it first-hand, but he'd heard about it. Like that family in Aurora, Nebraska, back in 2003. They relaxed on a typical Sunday night in Nebraska. And as is common for June in Nebraska, a thunderstorm boiled across the plains with Aurora in its sights.

KRGI out of Grand Island spun Chris Cagle's "What a Beautiful Day." No one in the family, at the radio station, the National Weather Center, or Chris Cagle imagined the serendipity the approaching storm would provide. The storm dumped hailstones on the town. The family, having heard something crash into the roof gutter, went outside to survey the damage and found a large, oddly shaped hailstone they immediately suspected as noteworthy. They carried it inside and wedged it in the freezer. "Forever and For Always" played on the radio, Shania Twain's voice as sexy as ever.

The family learned about hailstones over the coming weeks. Friends, neighbors, the authorities, everyone who was anyone, except for Chris Cagle and Shania Twain who were busy touring, were consulted. They learned large hailstorms such as the one in their freezer could fall at one hundred miles an hour, which explained the condition of the aluminum gutter. Some could contain leaves and twigs, pebbles, even insects. Theirs didn't.

Still, it was a special hailstone. The authorities determined it was indeed the largest hailstone on record, measuring a full seven inches in diameter. The family, and Aurora, had their fifteen minutes and shipped the hailstone to the National Center for Atmospheric Research in Boulder, where it, and the record, remain. The family enjoyed the gift despite the claims about the stone's origin made during the next year's UFO Festival in Roswell, New Mexico.

If it could happen to them, it could happen to James.

The universe, or the promoters, scheduled Toby Keith's American Ride Tour to play the amphitheater in Charlotte. The concert was presented by Ford F-series trucks. The economy had caused a lag in ticket sales, so Ford held a contest. Anyone who owned a Ford truck could enter to win two free passes to the show. Colton signed up on a whim. When he won the tickets, his first idea was to give them away, but he decided to force James into going with him. With college starting in the fall, he thought the country music crowd might provide a head start on the cultural and intellectual diversity he'd soon encounter.

James wanted no part of it, but finally agreed. "I'll have to get my mind right, but I'll go."

"No weed," Colton warned him.

"No problem."

They had lawn seats, which meant they settled into a likely spot on the ground. When the show started, thunderheads darkened the western sky, blanking the sun before it set. James washed down two Valiums, the blue ones, with a beer from the sixer he'd smuggled in.

The first act finished their set, James finished his third beer, and the weather held. When the last note of Trace Adkins' encore died out, the first drops fell. Most of the crowd started pushing under the covered area, or heading for the gates. James, working on his fifth beer, tried to stand up and follow Colton toward the cover. "Think I'll just sit it out right here, C-note," he mumbled.

Toby Keith took the stage, played through his set. The wind picked up but the rain halted briefly, replaced by a quick burst of hail. By this time, James lay sprawled on his back, arms outstretched, a smile on his face, his eyes closed. Breathing, but not moving. Keith chording through the oldies-but-goodies part of his show. There were no record setting hailstones, but the largest of the storm, one roughly the size of a quarter, hurtled earthward.

Keith sang about going west.

The hailstone smacked James in the forehead. "Ouch," he mumbled as he sat up and looked around, bewildered.

From the speakers, promises of women, whiskey, and riches out in California.

"Yeah it is," James grinned and rubbed the robin's egg knot rising above his eyebrows. He looked around again, still rubbing his head. He checked his fingers and saw a faint drop of blood. As quickly as it started, the hail stopped.

Keith rolled into the chorus, wishing he had been a cowboy.

The words slowly washed over James, swimming upstream against the valium and beers. James felt the waters clear, if only for an instant. Maybe that was the problem with Britt, with lots of things. Doing something didn't matter, he had to *be* something, something different. He looked down at the stage, studied the singer's cowboy hat. The hat, the words . . . "I know exactly what you're talking about," James mumbled.

The show ended, the air hung in steamy curtains around James as he walked toward the parking lot, looking for Colton's truck, the chorus of Keith's song stuck in his head.

He found the truck, Colton sitting inside listening to a Steely Dan CD.

"Turn it down," James pleaded as he slumped into the passenger seat. He was beginning to feel his heart thumping behind his temples.

"Couple more tunes. Need to get that country shit out of my head. I swear my IQ dropped fifty points tonight."

"Naw, that Koby Teeth fellow, he gave me an idea."

"Toby Keith. And what idea was that, chasing Valium with beer doesn't improve your line dancing abilities?"

"Four beers, that's the ticket. If I'd stopped at four, I would've been golden. But listen, he *spoke* to me, C-note. All that *should've been a cowboy* stuff. That's me."

"Wrong place, wrong time, for starters. And I don't think you're cowboy material."

"No, for real. You know how Britt's always telling me I need some outside interests, you know, stuff besides growing weed and drinking beer?"

"I did not know she told you that."

"Well, she does, and the cowboy hat guy helped me figure it out. You know that museum, the one out past the grow site?"

"The one in Waxhaw?"

"That's it. Did you know Waxhaw is named after the Waxhaw Indians? I remember something from school, some dude came and talked about it. I'm gonna learn about those Indians. Maybe start collecting arrowheads or something. See what Britt thinks about that. I've got to *be* somebody more interesting."

"Un-huh. And how does being somebody who collects arrowheads fit in your master plan?"

"It doesn't, that's why it's an *outside* interest."

Colton shook his head. The glow from the dashboard lights reflected in his grin. He turned up the volume, Fagen's smooth voice calling out *hey nineteen*. James looked out the passenger window, listening to the lyrics, his brain drawing fuzzy pictures of Indians lurking in the trees, his thoughts trying to catch up with the world passing by outside, everything still draped in the soft cottony gauze of the fading Valium. He didn't know where this latest idea came from, but it didn't matter, it felt right. He needed that. Brittany would be a senior when school started, then graduating. Colton would be busy at college, studying, making new college friends. Everybody around him seemed to be in motion. The weed crop would be ready soon, but what then? Indians? Indians. Why not? It was meant to be; a gift from the universe.

"I BELIEVE, BASED on my research, if I can locate the sunflowers there is a chance of re-establishing the species in the area."

At this point, Sally normally would have been contemplating the shortest distance to the bedroom or his quickest exit. But this girl, this lady, was different. For some reason, he found all the talk about the sunflowers fascinating. The sound of her voice, how her face radiated a different light as she talked about them, something held his interest in a way he'd never imagined. It made him a little nervous, but he didn't want her to stop.

"Why do you think it's important to re-establish the flowers? What's the benefit?" he asked.

"The flowers have a tuberous root that's edible. For Native Americans in the area, it was once a primary food source. The Wisacky Indians, most people know them as the Waxhaws, cultivated the flowers through the 1600s. If the soil conditions are still favorable, they could become a cash crop to supplement soybeans and corn. At the least, organic farmers could produce them on a smaller scale. I think they'd be popular, given the recent locavore movement."

She made even the boring details fascinating. Sally took a sip of wine. The waiter cleared the appetizers. "I remember something about them from grade school," he offered.

"They were a branch of the Sugeree." A vibration sounded in Kat's pocketbook. She quickly glanced at her phone, then continued. "The tribe fought the English in the Yemasee War of 1715. Their numbers were decimated, and of course, small pox didn't help." She stopped. "I'm boring you."

"No, not at all. Go on, please." The waiter brought the main course. "So, are there any descendants left or just the flowers?"

"I doubt it. The descendants, anyway. What few were left of them were absorbed into the Sugeree Tribe. But I'm certain there are a few flowers left, I just have to find them." Her phone sounded again. "I'm sorry. I should've turned this thing off." She checked the display, a puzzled look on her face. She shook her head and slipped the phone back in her bag. "No more interruptions."

"Maybe somebody should research the descendants, the way you're working on the flowers?"

She nodded and fell quiet. He watched her eat, noticing the concentration wrinkling around her eyes. Her intensity both frightened and intrigued him. A woman like her, she'd see through him in no time. He changed the subject, made small talk. Her interests: her cat, Impressionist art. Wine, plants, of course. Shakespeare—the sonnets, not the plays. Favorite twentieth century authors: Faulkner and O'Connor, for starters. She listened to some classical music but preferred Americana, especially James McMurtry and Jason Isbell. Sally hadn't heard of any of them. "I'll burn you a sampler disc," she told him.

She touched the tip of her nose again. "And I'll quit babbling. Tell me more about Salvador Hinson." She smiled and finished her wine. Sally signaled for a refill.

"Not much to tell. Grew up here, lived here most of my life. The usual." Sally shrugged. He wanted to tell her more, tell her he understood why she was so interested in the flowers, explain how much it was like putting together the land deal. Well, not like it specifically, but the feeling she had for it, the passion. But he couldn't tell her that, not yet. He liked this girl, best to move carefully.

"You said you were in real estate? That must be interesting."

"Sort of, but it's hardly interesting. Dirt's dirt, you know? Land deals, speculation, investments, that sort of thing. It's not brain surgery," he smiled. "Or scientific research."

She laughed, then lightly touched the back of his hand, let her fingertips linger before quickly touching her nose and blushing.

"Don't be so dismissive. It's honest work."

Sally mentally flinched. He thought of Bill, some of the deals. "I suppose. Buy low, sell high. That's all there is to it."

She leaned forward. "No, I think there's a certain exotic air to it all. Are you working on any big transactions now?"

"Maybe. I guess I'm in a similar spot to what you're doing."

"Really? How's that?"

Careful. You don't know her, don't know who she knows. People talk. "Well, you're doing research on those flowers, trying to find the location, the property where the girl took the pictures. I'm doing research to track down the owner of a particular piece of property I might be interested in purchasing."

"Where?"

Sally laughed. "Well, I don't exactly know where mine is, either. I do, I'm pretty sure, but . . . it's complicated. If I can track down the owner, then we'll see."

"I understand. Yes, I'm trying to find the girl with the pictures, and the flowers, but there's all this pressure from the University complicating everything. My boss's unnatural infatuation with the administration's Twelve Point Strategic Revision Plan, funding issues, and with the economy, all you hear in meetings is retention, retention, retention. All I want is to find those flowers, conduct my research, reestablish the species."

"Tell you what, if I run across those sunflowers while I'm sorting out this land deal, I'll let you know." Why did he say *that*?

More small talk. Another glass of wine. Sally noticed that, as the evening glided along, she touched her nose less and less. Whether it was the wine or the company, he couldn't be sure. A good sign either way, he decided. It made him relax, whatever the reason.

Outside, the moon hung low in the sky, the summer air sultry. Sally walked Kat to her car, where she turned to him.

"Thank you for dinner." She blushed. "And lunch."

"My pleasure. Both times."

She paused. Sally debated. It had been a long time since . . . She touched her nose once more, then let her hand fall onto Sally's forearm. She leaned forward, lifted up on her toes, and breezed a kiss across his cheek. "I had a really nice time," she whispered.

"Me too."

She smiled as she reached for the door of her Prius. "Good. I'm glad. Next time, I'll bring you that sampler CD." She opened the door, but stopped. "And it's okay for you to call me. I don't think you're too dangerous." She started the car and rolled down the window. "Nice touch, though," she said. "A very gentlemanly introduction."

When her car disappeared, Sally reminded himself, "Careful, Sally. You're edging toward the deep end of the pool." His mind lingered on her words. *Next time.* If he believed in luck.

13

Cash Flow Mojo

White parking stripes lined the street in front of Mason City Bank, but all were filled. Ethel sneered at the cars and wheeled her Dodge toward the small lot behind the building. She swung in a bit too wide and barely nicked the P.O. drop box on the corner. She surveyed the spots, looking for something close to the door. Five cars sat in the lot. Two late-model Civics, both silver, and a burgundy Camry, with a McCain/Palin bumper sticker, parked on the west side of the lot. Boot Jackson's black Lexus was parked near the back entrance. The vehicle gleamed, radiating opulence. Tinted windows, spotless finish, and a parking place open right beside it. Ethel aimed for the open space, miscalculated the approach, and thudded to a stop against the rear bumper on the driver's side. She shifted to reverse and eased her car back, the red glass and plastic from Jackson's taillight crackling to the pavement as she did. Her aim improved on the second try. She took the handicap placard from the glove box, hung it on the rear-view, and slid out, slinging her purse onto her shoulder as she stood.

Inside, she bypassed the tellers and went straight to the assistant's desk in front of Jackson's office.

"Boot in?" she asked.

"Yes ma'am," the assistant answered, "but he's busy at the moment. If you'll have a seat," she pointed toward the leather chairs behind Ethel, "I'll let him know you're here, Mrs. Combs."

Ethel looked toward Boot's office, noticed the door was cracked open, and said, "No thank you, honey, I'll show myself in."

Before the assistant could react, Ethel barraged around her desk and into Boot's office, closing his door on the assistant's pleas to "wait." Boot looked up, briefly startled, then closed the latest copy of Guns and Ammo he'd been reading, and stood to greet her.

"Mrs. Combs, always a pleasure." He shook her hand, taking it in both of his. "Have a seat, tell me what we can do for you?"

"Don't you start with that *Mrs.* shit, Boot Jackson. You ain't that young."

He chuckled as they both sat down. "Well, you're right about that. How've you been? How's your family?"

"I'm right as rain. Family's still ingrates."

"Now Ethel, at least one of them was nice enough to bring you to town."

"Ha. You keep on thinking as much. I drove my damn self here."

He winced. "I see. Well, what can I do for you?"

"I came to check on my money. I'm thinking on spending some of it."

"Your money's fine, Ethel."

"Can I see it? My money?"

"You never get tired of that one, do you? You know how it works, we have your money, just not in cash, not all of it. Tell me what you have in mind, and I'll take care of it."

"And you tell me that every time, but this time I'd like to see it, every damn cent of it, all at once. Come on, bring it out and blow the dust off. Stack it up, let me take a gander at how high the stack reaches. I'm thinking I need to get my cash flow mojo working."

"Now Ethel . . ."

She chuckled. "Boot, you oughta know by now I'm just poking fun at you. I *am* thinking on turning loose of some of it, though."

"Well, you know what they say, you can't take it with you."

"I ain't planning on going anytime soon." Ethel leaned forward, "but you're right, I ain't never seen a hearse pulling a U-Haul."

He laughed. "So—what? It can't be time for a new car, can it?"

The detached, framed garage at Ethel's house contained a Cadillac, not yet two years old, with three hundred and forty-seven miles showing on the odometer. Every two years Ethel traded the old one on a new model, had done for decades. Her Dodge, a green '71 Dart, served as her everyday car. The Caddy was for the weekly trip to the cemetery to visit her husband's grave. Ethel was always careful and reasonably sober on those trips. And when driving the Caddy, Ethel always wore her prescription glasses and never pushed the speedometer above thirty, there or back. When the horns blew, she gave them the one finger salute and then plodded on down the road, her head not visible over the headrest to the cars that raced up behind her.

She planned the trips around visits from Brittany. Britt didn't go with her, but each time when she returned, Britt would wash the car for her, Ethel supervising, before pulling it back into the garage. It was their secret. And every two years, the folks at the dealership shook their heads and completed the paperwork. She knew it made no sense, and she didn't care. Knowing the new car was in her garage, having it, was enough. But Ethel had six more months before time to trade. A car was not what she had in mind.

"I'm of a mind to purchase me some real estate," she told him.

"Real estate? Where? Why?"

"Some property next to mine. The why don't matter."

"What are they asking?"

"I don't rightly know. Ain't exactly for sale, as I know of. I ain't talked to the owners yet. Thought I might, though."

"Well, Ethel, you work out the details, get me the info. I'll be happy to work out the financing, get you the best rates."

"The hell with that. At my age, you don't buy green bananas nor magazine subscriptions. I'll pay cash. I just need to know there won't be any problems getting my money when the time comes."

"I can't imagine any property out your way costing more than what your account can cover. There won't be any problems. I wish you'd let me help you with it, though. I'd feel better."

"I guess you would. Tell me, is there anybody got more money than me in your little old bank?"

Jackson stammered. "Well. I can't, you know that's private information, Ethel. Let's just say you're definitely on our preferred customer list."

"Thought so. I can handle my finances just fine, Boot. Don't you worry." She stood up and winked. "Now I'll let you get back to dusting my money. I'll be in touch."

"Always a pleasure, Ethel. Drive safe."

"Always do."

ENTERTAINMENT TONIGHT BLARED from the TV. Brittany sat on the bed in room 115 of the Budget-Tel Motel, her back against the wall. Her notebook rested in her lap, pen in her right hand, her left hand twirling a swirl of hair. Other than the reality shows, *Entertainment Tonight* topped her favorite programs list. It was educational. She made notes as she watched, career planning.

James lay on the floor between the bed and the air conditioning unit. His fingers interlocked on top of his stomach, his legs crossed at the ankles. A concrete paver he'd stolen from the common area behind the motel balanced on his forehead. A plastic Food Lion bag held a partially clothed, one-armed Ken doll he bought for a nickel at a yard sale. The bloodstained Converse with a ragged bullet hole through the sole and canvas upper sat on the floor next to him.

They waited on Colton. When they heard the knock at the door, neither Britt nor James moved.

"It's open, C-note." James said.

It wasn't Colton.

Gajendranath, the motel's owner, stepped inside and surveyed the scene. He cleared his throat. "Mr. Flowers," he said, "have you received the notifications I am leaving for you?"

James raised his right hand, careful not to upset the paver, and pointed toward the chest of drawers. "Yeah, top right-hand drawer, the one beneath the TV. Top right," he repeated, "you don't want to open the one on the left."

"You have not responded appropriately. You read the notifications, I presume?"

"Skimmed. Got the gist of it. No, not really. What'd I miss?"

Brittany sighed and turned up the volume on the TV. The *Survivor* recap segment was next, she didn't want to miss it.

"You have not paid for three weeks. This is unacceptable."

"About that, I've got some cash flow issues at the moment. Economy's in the shitter, Gaj, haven't you heard?"

"This may be true; it does not relieve you of your obligation for the room."

"What is it you're trying to say, Gaj?"

"If your bill is not made current by next week, you will no longer be allowed to stay. You will be evicted, removed forcibly if necessary."

"Dude, don't be that guy." The paver wobbled. James slowly reached to steady it.

"I will contact the proper authorities if necessary. One week, Mr. Flowers." Gajendranath turned to leave.

"Hang on, Gaj. Let's think this through. How would you feel if *I* went to the authorities? Every Friday the Mexicans bring a goat in the room down the hall, every Saturday they have a barbecue. The meth lab in 208 could blow any minute. Cherry, Jasmine, and Desiree seem to have *a lot* of company. You sent them notifications?"

"They pay their bills on time. You, Mr. Flowers, do not."

"So, it's like that? Where's the love, Gaj? Okay, here's the deal. You're a businessman. You give me four, six weeks tops, grace period. I got a big payday coming about then. After that, I'll pay my back rent, all of it. Twice over."

"I don't understand."

"Say my note's five hundred dollars . . ."

"You will owe four hundred and twenty next week . . ."

"Whatever, don't get caught up in the details, Gaj, stay with me. Say it's five hundred. Give me the time and I'll pay you the five Benjamins, *plus* another five hundred."

Gajendranath considered the offer. "Four weeks, Mr. Flowers. Four weeks." He started out the door, but hesitated. "And I expect you to place the paver back in the walkway, just as you found it."

"Got it covered. I'm feeling the love, now, Gaj. You won't regret it."

Entertainment Tonight ended, *Inside Edition* began. Brittany put down her notebook, took a business card from her backpack, and made a phone call. No answer, she didn't leave a message. When Colton arrived ten minutes later, James removed the paver and checked his forehead in the mirror, first straight on, then both profiles, before picking up the Food Lion bag and handing it to Colton. "You got all the stuff?"

"In the truck."

"Bring it up here, we've gotta run the checklist. Finn told us, once we set this in motion, we've gotta see it through, no interruptions. We can't forget anything. Chop-chop."

Britt picked up her phone again and hit send. Still no answer. She hopped off the bed as the voice played, walked into the bathroom, and closed the door. This time, when the voice finished, she left a message. James could hear her through the wall, but couldn't make out what she was saying.

Colton returned wearing a leather tool belt and carrying two large bags. After spreading the items on the bed, James handed

Colton a wrinkled piece of paper and they started the inventory. The essentials: doll, discarded shoe, two raw chicken gizzards, an empty pack of ZigZag rolling papers, an arm's length of red ribbon, a handful of fresh cut human hair (which originally posed a problem until Colton realized he could get it from a beauty salon), four small white pebbles, and one uncooked pinto bean. The tools: hammer, sixteen penny nails painted green, compass, and a flashlight. The necessities: twelve pack of Bud. Check, check, and check.

"Brittany, turn it off and let's go," James said, putting everything back in the bags.

"I'm not going, its *Survivor* night."

"C'mon Britt. I want you to go," James whined. He started to tell her what he had planned, that when the money rolled in, he'd help her cover all the *Survivor* expenses, but he didn't. She'd be more impressed when he surprised her with it.

"It's, like, stupid. I got better things to do, *I'm* working on my life plan." The volume bar on the TV inched to the right. She didn't look at James.

"Aw Britt, we never do anything anymore. Come with."

"No. I do plenty, it's you not doing anything. You go on, and don't park at Memaw's. Go in the other way."

"Fine then. C-note, let's roll."

In the truck, James popped the top on two beers and handed one to Colton. Britt was sure acting weird, had been for a while. Finding excuses not to hang out, bitching about everything. The only reason she was there tonight was because her mother was having friends over and wouldn't let Britt watch TV. And the phone call bothered him. Who could she be talking to, and why not send a text? Sure, she was a part-time thing, sort of, but it was steady, and lately James noticed he missed her when she wasn't around. He didn't want to admit it, but he figured giving her the money from the weed would be enough that she knew they were, well, together. He must've thought about her too long, Colton kept glancing at him.

"What?" James asked. "What're you looking at?"

"Checking to see if that rock thing is working, that's all."

James turned the rearview mirror and looked at his forehead. "Whatta you think?"

"I think you might've started too late."

"That's why I'm using the paver stones. They're heavier. It'll work, I just gotta stick to it. Britt says I have no ambition, that I never finish anything." James checked the mirror once more.

"And all this Indian stuff will show her different?"

"Yeah. Plus, I've been reading a bunch of other stuff about the Waxhaws and other Indians. Pretty cool. I got some other plans, too."

"Wait. Reading? You? And I thought Britt was just a thing."

"Yeah. Maybe."

James didn't say anything more, neither did Colton. The moon rose above the trees, saucered full against the night sky. They drove to the opposite side of the land behind Britt's grandmother's house. Colton slowed, looking for the overgrown fire road into the property. The car behind them was considerate, didn't blow the horn, but didn't pass either. When he found the path, he eased the truck in and they bumped along at a crawl as far as they could. When they stopped, patches of the clearing were visible in the high beams. Colton switched off the truck, leaving nothing but B-movie shadows casting around them from the moonlight. They took the supplies and followed the flashlight to the edge of the clearing. James swung the light in both directions, pausing on the pot plants, most of them now head high. Satisfied, he handed Colton the compass and started around the edge of the clearing, flashing the light on the trees.

"There, that one's the biggest, so it must be the oldest, James said. Figure out which way is north." He shined the light on the compass, watching the red end of the needle. It settled and they walked to the north side of the tree trunk, dropped the bags on the ground.

Colton took the hammer and a few nails from his tool belt. "What now?"

"Well, Finn said we have to read this incantation thing first. It's some kind of prayer to Cousin Zaka. Then we put the offering together and read the rest of it. Easy-peasy."

"Who's this Cousin Zaka dude?"

"I told you, the agriculture spirit, brings good crops and stuff. He's a Loa, a lesser deity. Hand me the baggie of hair, we're supposed to mix the stuff in there."

"And we need to do this why?" Colton looked around the woods. The September night was thick and humid, but he felt a hint of the coming fall chill all the same.

"Frosty buds. The ritual started in Haiti, then some cats in Jamaica picked it up. Finn says it'll guarantee high potency. You know how heads will say *smoke this, it's the shit that killed Elvis?* Well, according to Finn, if we do this right, we'll get the kind of shit Elvis *came back* for. That's what I'm talking about. Now let's get started."

James took another look at the instructions and began. He put both chicken gizzards in his mouth, circled the tree trunk three times, clockwise, opened his mouth and let the organs fall into the bag of hair. He spaced the four pebbles in the palm of his left hand, pressed them to his chest, then held them under the moonlight and counted to ten before dropping them in the bag. Next he took the single uncooked pinto bean, folded it inside the ZigZag pack and slid them into the baggie and shoved the baggie into the toe of the tennis shoe. "Now, give me the poppet," he told Colton.

"Oh shit, we didn't get a poppet."

"It's the doll. That's what the voodoo people call it."

"Oh." Colton handed James the disfigured Ken doll. "Does it matter he's only got one arm?"

"I asked Finn about that. He said it shouldn't be a problem. Since he's missing his right arm, Finn thinks this weed'll probably make you lean to the left once you get stoned. That's all."

James stuck the doll into the shoe's opening, wrapped the red ribbon around the offering, and tied it into a square knot. "Get the hammer and nails ready, I'll read the first part."

"Cousin Zaka, take this offering and bless our buds. Keep it safe from feds and poachers. Send the psychedelic powers from the otherworld to this ganja and make it kind and trippy with no couch lock."

"That doesn't sound anything like how I thought a voodoo incantation would sound," said Colton.

"Well, it's been translated. This is the American version, that's why. Now nail the offering to the north side of the tree."

James read the closing poem:

> *"For Cheech and Chong and Jerry Garcia,*
> *We leave this poppet on this tree.*
> *For Bob Marley and Jimmy Buffet,*
> *May this potion bring us THC.*
> *For all the heads in all the world,*
> *Even you and me,*
> *Bless this crop, and all these buds,*
> *And may they set us free."*

"We supposed to say amen or sing a song or something?" Colton asked.

James shined the flashlight on his notes. Turned the page over and checked the back. "Nope. Now let's get out of here, this shit's a little creepy."

Once in the truck, Colton flipped through his CD case and found a copy of *Natty Dread,* had it spinning as they drove back toward the motel, windows down, heads nodding in time to *Lively Up Yourself.* When the track ended and *No Woman, No Cry* came on, James looked out the window at the moon, climbing higher. He watched as they rode, still nodding, listening to the lyrics, wondering why the moon, bright as it was, looked so damn sad.

14

A Job's A Job

As a scientist, Kat knew everything—*everything*—was connected and followed a certain order. She knew around thirteen or fourteen billion years ago, a mass heated and then exploded. Bang. The blast created density and provided motion, birthing a universe. It expanded, stretching, spinning around itself. Substances gathered and cooled, as orbits were established. On one of the masses, ice melted, water formed, then oceans, seas, rivers. Conditions improved, life grew. About four hundred million years ago on that same mass, she imagined a colony of college-age tetrapods got freaky one weekend and invited a few fish to their party. A few months later a strange new breed, part fish, part tetrapod, crawled from the primordial slime. It wasn't perfect and it wasn't quick, but evolution had begun.

And evolve they did. Amphibians, reptiles, mammals, birds. Two and a half million years ago—*Homo Habilis,* which led to *Homo Erectus* then *Homo Sapiens.*

Uh-oh.

Fire, wheel, Buddha, Jesus, Mohammed, Darwin, motion pictures, hydrogen bomb, atom bomb, TV, Elvis, The Beatles, Reagan, Internet, Limbaugh, Bush-Bush, and a black president.

The universe kept expanding, stretching, evolving, everything connected. And one day, the universe will reach its thinnest point, can't stretch any further, and inevitably, it'll implode on itself. And the process starts all over.

But while Kat understood the process and accepted the connections, she also believed occasionally, every once in a great while, the universe offered a random smile. Two in the same day rarely happened, and when it did, it made her giddy.

The date was almost perfect. She felt a calming sensibility in Sally. He was nothing like the men from the University. None of the pretention, none of the insecurities. He listened. She assumed he didn't have much formal education, at least not any advanced degrees, but she considered him an equal intellectually. He *knew* things. Earning a PhD really meant one was stubborn enough to stick with one subject and endure a multitude of humilities at the hands of professors. Sally had a wisdom she seldom sensed in her colleagues.

Their conversation was lovely, entertaining, even though she thought she'd talked too much. But mostly, he listened. The meal tasted delicious, and the slow service allowed time for them to get to know one another. He *was* a gentleman, kind and honest. Maybe it was his age, she suspected he was ten or twelve years older than her, at least. And quite attractive, regardless. By the time she arrived home, she was already wondering when he'd call, where he'd take her next.

She couldn't believe she'd forgotten to turn off her cell, or at least put it on vibrate. It was rude. Sally didn't seem to mind, though.

The number on the screen puzzled her. When she landed her first teaching job as an adjunct, she made the mistake of putting her number on the syllabus. Students kept odd hours and obviously had no sense of protocol or decorum when it came to contacting their professors. Since that semester, she'd been particular about giving out her number.

The date went so well she forgot about the call until she was back in her apartment. When she first listened to the message, she danced around and around her living room before replaying it and jotting down the name and number.

It was late, she'd return the call in the morning. It took forever to fall asleep. She replayed the message on her phone, she replayed the date in her mind even more. One day, she knew the universe would implode, but not now. Now was serendipity.

The Schweinitz Sunflower did still exist, and she had it.

LATE AFTERNOON, AND the hot air had a metallic smell. Towers of cumulus climbed higher in the hazy southwestern sky, signaling thunderstorms. No birds flew, no breeze stirred. Earlier, a mourning dove had called, and its mate had answered, but now, only thick and oppressive silence. The dog days. The time of year when the under-medicated and unstable crossed the thin line into madness, the mad became serial killers or ran for office, and the serial killers took vacations in cooler climates. Kids actually longed for school to start. Stay at home soccer moms doubled up on Xanax washed down with fruity Chardonnays and loathed the sound of their husbands brushing their teeth. Husbands contemplated suicide and solitary road trips through the desert of New Mexico.

It was Ethel's favorite time of the year.

She woke at dawn, enjoyed her coffee and the day's first Pall Mall on her porch without interruption, the tiniest beads of sweat already trickling between her shoulder blades. The RC Cola thermometer read seventy-eight degrees at seven o'clock. She had a leisurely breakfast and another cigarette before going to the flowerbed and plucking three ripe tomatoes from the vine. She showered, patted lilac powder on her lower neck and chest, then slipped on her favorite dress, the one she planned to wear when she was buried. She gathered her purse, fetched a fresh pack of smokes from the carton, and started the Dodge.

Ethel made two wrong turns, over-shot three more, and side-swiped a green recycling bin at the end of someone's drive, scattering

Diet Coke cans, milk cartons, and wine bottles along the sidewalk. She found the address, parked on the street out front, and gathered herself before approaching.

The neighborhood was pleasant, and the house appeared practical—a brick two-story Georgian near the cul-de-sac. A bit fancy for her taste, but she didn't have to live there. The yard was composed: the grass manicured and too green for this time of year; no trees in front, but a neat collection of azaleas, camellias, boxwoods, and monkey grass formed a uniform border between the walk and the front porch. Two whitewashed rockers sat on the porch, turned just so. From the street, the residence suggested a snapshot of neat, well-planned order and control. This guy must be wrapped tighter than Dick's hatband, she thought.

She rang the doorbell. Shuffling, footfalls, but no answer. She rang again. This time, a head popped up behind the arched, beveled glass window near the top of the door. A man peered down at her, but said nothing. The door didn't open. She rang again. The head disappeared, more shuffling, the head reemerged.

"Yes?" A muffled voice from behind the door.

"You Livingston Carr?" asked Ethel.

"Well ... I could ... but ... yes. Yes, that's me."

"Then open the door, you're the man I need to talk to." Ethel took a step back to allow room.

The head vanished again. She heard movement. It reappeared.

"Trudy's not home. She has a doctor's appointment. I should have gone with her, but I couldn't ... I just ... She'll be back soon. Thank you."

"I need to talk to you, I don't know any Trudy." Ethel punched the doorbell five times in quick succession. When the chimes stopped, she tried a new approach. "I knew your daddy," she shouted, "I just want to talk a minute ..." Under her breath—"you damn lunatic."

The door cracked and she saw half the man's face wedged against the opening, one eye shining at her. "Who are you?" he asked.

"I'm Ethel Combs. Now let's chat a bit, I ain't gonna bite."

After a few more seconds, the door eased open. Livingston invited her inside and they sat in his living room. Ethel ran her fingers along the toile on the side of the wingback and took stock of the room, trying to quickly get a feel for the man. Looked normal, for the most part. Nice lamps, standard bric-a-brac, lots of books, most of them about pregnancy or raising children. Must be his first, house is too organized for kids. She surveyed the walls. Vacation scene picture, store-bought picture, wedding picture . . . damn, his wife's a midget, wonder how that works? She wanted to ask, but decided against it.

"I'll get right to the point," she told him. "Your daddy had a hundred acres of land out in the county. Turns out, it butts up against my property. I figured he left it to you, I never heard of him having no more kids, and I wanted to see if you might consider selling it?"

The finger snapping increased in speed and intensity.

"I don't know. I haven't . . . I lost my job. Yes, I will consider it."

This man was one strange bird. Real squirrelly type and Ethel couldn't get a clear read of him. That part about losing his job was interesting and with a baby on the way, it provided her some leverage.

"Well, what do you want for it?" she asked.

"The land? I . . . I don't know. How much do *you* think it's worth?"

This might be easier than she thought. "Oh, I wouldn't know. I'm just an old widow woman, I don't have no experience in things like that. How's two thousand an acre?"

Snap-snap-snap. "Oh my, no. The tax office has it valued at ten thousand, two hundred an acre."

"Let's see, that's . . . oh, my mind's not sharp like it used to be, I'm eighty-two, you know. I might be catching old-timer's disease. It's a wonder they haven't found me wandering around the Wal-Mart parking lot in my housecoat in the pouring rain, talking to myself. One million, two hundred thousand, that sound about right? I can pay cash."

The snapping stopped.

"Yes, that's exactly right. That's . . . No, I can't. My wife's having, we're having a baby. My father left it to me, I should do the same thing for my child one day. That's how it works, isn't it? A child needs an inheritance. And besides, I already have . . ."

"What?"

"Nothing."

"Well, an inheritance can be a good thing, that's right. In fact, that's how I come into my money. We have that in common, you and me."

Livingston nodded slowly. "But . . . the inheritance. What about for my child?"

"Well, you know an inheritance can be a curse, too. What if there's more than one child, what'll you do? What if there's three or four? They'd end up fighting over your estate. They always do."

"Oh, there's no danger of that. We're not planning any more pregnancies. No, this is the only one."

"It could be twins, maybe triplets. Mine weren't triples, but raising three 'bout sent me to the poorhouse, and that was years ago. I'd hate to think what it might cost raising triplets this day and time."

Snap-snap-snap-snap.

Ethel thought Livingston might throw up. His face drained to the color of spent charcoal, pinpricks of sweat beaded on his upper lip.

"Twins n-n-n-never occurred to me."

"You got to consider everything, every possibility you can think of and some you can't. You're gonna be a daddy. Their future, that's what's important now."

"Perhaps you're right. I have considered selling, even before you came. I've only been there once in my entire life. Caught the worst case of poison ivy imaginable, it was horrendous."

"Camphor oil's good for that." Ethel reached in her purse. "I wrote up this agreement, just in case you were interested. All we need to do is fill in the numbers. Then I'll take it to my banker, he'll get somebody to draw up a formal real-estate contract and you'll get your money."

"No. I mean, yes, but I already have—" he stopped.

"Have what?" Ethel asked.

"Um . . . nothing. It's nothing. I meant to say I have to talk to my wife. Think it over."

"You should. A woman likes to feel she's included in the important family decisions. I understand, being a woman myself, and I took it into account. This agreement is good for sixty days. Let's go ahead and sign it, and I'll just hold onto it until you give the okay."

Ethel moved to the couch beside Livingston, took out a pen, and held it and the papers in front of him. "This is your kid's future," she whispered.

Ethel made all the turns on the way back home and only clipped one paper box in the process. She didn't hit the post, only the box, and since it was plastic, it didn't do any damage to the Dodge. They could replace the box.

She looked at the thunderheads billowing in the southwestern sky and smiled. Jesse always enjoyed an approaching storm. How many times he'd called her outside where they'd sit under the pin oak, the smell of coming rain sharp in the stillness. How he'd take her hand as the wind rose and the first drops fell. How many times? Not nearly enough.

After putting the plateful of scraps at the foot of her back steps, she took her dentures out with her right hand. Ethel put the pinky and index finger of her left hand in the corner of her mouth, whistled twice, and waited. The dog bounded from the woods on the backside of her property, carrying a bone in its teeth. It slowed to a trot as it got closer. It stopped a few feet from the plate, and laid down with its front paws outstretched, its tail curled perfectly up and over its back, the bone still in its mouth. Ethel stared at the dog. The dog stared back. "I love this time of year, don't you? Fall coming on, a cool night ever now and again, them flowers Britt likes blooming." She paused, caught by something about the dog—it's appearance, maybe, the glint of light off its coat, that reminded her of her late husband, Jesse. "If Jesse were alive, he'd take you in in a minute," she told the dog. "Hell-fire, I bet he'd call you Sunflower." she told him. Ethel scanned the horizon, drew in a deep breath, smelled the hint of the coming rain. "This kind of weather sure clears your mind, don't it?"

When she went inside, the dog ran the few feet to the scraps, which he gulped down in four bites. He forgot all about the bone.

SUMMER BREAK ENDED too soon. Starting a new semester always brought the same complications. First came the eager anticipation. Budgets would increase, all of her students would be bright and engaged in the material. This semester, her research would be fruitful, she'd publish, she'd receive tenure. Then the meetings began. Economic and academic reality reared its head, and deep down, she knew she'd be lucky if one or two students demonstrated an above average intellect. Her anticipation put on a cloak of dread and pulled the collar high.

Kat had not accomplished nearly as much as she'd hoped over the break, and as she faced the fall session, her research was not much further along than when she'd left in the spring, which meant enduring more of Leaderlick's snide comments, innuendo, and veiled threats. She'd spoken with Brittany twice, and both times could have been more productive. The girl admitted she'd taken the pictures of the Schweinitz sunflowers but wouldn't tell her where. She offered to take Kat, for a price. Said she needed twenty thousand dollars, five thousand of which she demanded from Kat. Something about trying to raise money for an audition video for a TV show called *Survivor*, which Kat knew nothing about. The subtle extortion didn't bother Kat; trying to find the money did.

She halfheartedly reviewed her syllabi for the term's classes and scanned emails between faculty workshops and departmental meetings. The workshops were infantile, filled with buzzwords and breakout sessions that were a delight compared to the departmental meetings. Kat suffered through Leaderlick's pounding of how the Twelve Point Strategic Revision Plan should be reflected in their pedagogy and classroom delivery, and why it was important that those efforts also increase retention. Leaderlick droned, Kat sketched flowers on her notepad. When Leaderlick reminded them the research budgets would not increase, that they, in fact, had been cut by ten percent, she scribbled a line of question marks across the top of the page. At the end of that line, she wrote *flowers* and a dollar sign. Still, at least she had a job, Leaderlick reminded her.

The science department meeting finally ended, and Kat managed to escape without getting caught one-on-one with her boss. She didn't want to answer any direct questions about her project, at least not until she had some idea of what came next. Leaderlick left for a meeting of all department chairs at the local country club and Kat decided to go to faculty lunch.

LaSeur Dining Hall was nearly full. She saw a seat open at a small table near the windows on the west side of the room. Dr. Aldus Culpepper was in the opposite chair, dumping packets of Sweet-n-Low in his tea. He was an anthropologist, but in the "real" sciences branch—archeology, not cultural anthro. Everybody wanted to like him, but nobody *knew* him. When approached, he was warm and conversant, but most faculty and students seemed to avoid him. Everyone agreed — great mind — but his mattock swung just a little off center.

Aldus was in his late sixties, had been at Mason University for decades. His hair was nearly to his shoulders and fell in a wild tangle of grayish-brown sprouts, wisps, and clumps fighting for their independence. His perpetual uniform — slogan t-shirt, tan cargo pants, wool socks and Teva sandals, pipe either clenched between his teeth or used as a pointer in his left hand. His publication credits were extensive. Museums and government agencies, even the occasional TV program, frequently hired him as a consultant on special cases. What Kat admired most about him was his knack for avoiding committee appointments and maintaining a completely oblivious attitude when it came to the political and administrative gyrations of a college campus.

"Hello, Al. Mind if I join you?" she asked.

"By all means." He nodded toward the vacant seat as he opened two more packs of sweetener.

"How was your break?"

"Phenomenal. Went to Tibet. You ever been?" He unfolded his napkin and spread the utensils. "Hmm. No knife," he said, and speared his chicken breast with his fork and brought it whole to his mouth.

"I haven't been. Working on anything in particular?"

He waved his fork in the air, the speared chicken still on it. "Completely out of my wheelhouse. Attached myself to a group of bio-anthros. We discovered 10 unique oxygen-processing alleles in Tibetan highlanders. Lungs like fifty-five-gallon drums, those people. Amazing culture. You gotta go sometime."

"Sounds interesting."

"Unbelievable scenery. Base camp on the flank of Shishapangma, very remote, had to get special access permits from the Chinese. It's the fourteenth highest in the world, but the lowest of the eight-thousanders. These alleles, the genes, prevent edema. May lead to helpful developments in asthma, bronchial constriction and the like. Fascinating stuff, especially for a bone-duster like me. I don't usually study 'em while they're still breathing, you know." Al took another bite of chicken, washed it down with tea, then poured two more Sweet-n-Lows in the glass.

"Well, with summers like that, I don't suppose you're worried about the funding cuts."

"Damn bean counters, what do they know about academia? You're right, though, I can't complain. Since the *Sixty Minutes* interview, funding issues are not an issue. Of course, the University prostitutes me to the fullest. Have you seen the website? It's embarrassing, but the money's good. Sometimes it's a chore to spend it all."

An idea began taking shape for Kat. She'd forgotten Anderson Cooper had interviewed Aldus two years earlier about the *Lucy* fossil. Granted, it wasn't Morley Safer, or Scott Pelley, but it was national exposure, and the University made the most of it. Moreover, while the entire faculty *liked* Aldus, the benefits of his celebrity fueled their professional jealousy, which they compared in hushed tones whenever they had the chance. Kat had heard the talk regarding the size of his budget.

"Are you still working on the project? With the Tibetans?" she asked.

"No, no. A working vacation, nothing more. I'm scheduled to return to the Moche Valley dig after first of the year. Finishing touches through the spring and summer on that project. Teaching two classes this semester. But I'm monopolizing. What about you? Your research?"

Kat made initial forays about her work on the Schweinitz Sunflower, but didn't mention her current dilemma, not yet. Aldus finished his lunch while she explained, and once she felt she had his attention, she moved toward her idea. "There is something about the sunflower you might find interesting."

"How's that?" He stuck his pipe between his teeth, leaned back in his chair.

"The roots of the plant provided a food staple for the local indigenous peoples, the Sugeree, the Waxhaws, probably the Catawbas, as well."

He leaned forward, pointed at Kat with the stem of his pipe. "Ah yes, the Waxhaws. Right here in our county. Not many folks know about them. It's a shame."

"Exactly. I have documentation, I know there are Schweinitz sunflowers growing wild in the county—"

"Lederer and Lawson both wrote about them," Aldus interrupted. "A tall people, lived in pole huts covered with bark. Unusual. They disfigured their infants by placing river stones on their foreheads while they slept or were lying down. Believed flattened foreheads to be a sign of wealth and intelligence."

"I didn't realize that."

"Most don't," Aldus said, excited now. He took a pouch of tobacco from his backpack, started packing the carved bowl of his pipe. Kat breathed in the cherry scent and briefly thought of her grandfather. "You know, there's no concrete evidence of the flattened heads, only what Lawson wrote. I'd be interested in seeing these flowers of yours, Katherine. Not the flowers specifically, but the land where they're growing. Very interested, indeed." He scratched his temple with the tip of his pipe, but didn't light it.

"That's wonderful, but . . ."

"Yes. Definite potential. When can we go?"

"Well," Kat touched her fingertip to her nose, "I don't know exactly where the flowers are located. I've seen the pictures, know the girl who took them, but she didn't tell me where. She wants . . . oh, I'm embarrassed."

"What? She wants what?"

Kat touched her nose again, hesitated. "She wants five thousand dollars. I don't . . . my budget . . ."

Aldus waved his pipe. "Bring me copies of the pics. Bribing locals is standard procedure in my field. Of course, it's my budget line, so my party. We'll say I'm looking for artifacts, mounds, whatever. You tag along and conduct your research independent of me, the suits in administration don't need to know more. If the Waxhaws cultivated these flowers, I can justify initial research on the site. No excavation or anything such as that, just a look-see, a little recon."

"Thank you, Aldus. That's very kind."

"Think nothing of it, always glad to help a colleague, especially when there might be something in it for me." He stood to leave. "Bring the pics by my office along with the info on the girl. I'll have the check drawn and we'll get things moving."

"I'll be over this afternoon."

"Make it tomorrow. I'm getting a new tattoo this afternoon, patterned after an intricate line drawing one of the Tibetan artists gave me this summer. I'll be in by eleven, see you then."

"Eleven it is." Kat smiled. Her anticipation returned.

AT EIGHTEEN, LIFE had been fill-in-the-blank, and Sally had had all the answers. Everything was absolute. At thirty-five, it became multiple choice, which meant narrow it to the best two and pick. Not exact, but still reasonably clear. Now, at fifty, each question only led to more questions. Something his father had once said was the only thing close to an absolute that Sally knew, and even *that* he didn't figure out until after his father was dead.

Juice Hinson, Sally's father, had been a moonshiner and a natural salesman. Sally remembered walking down the street with him when he was a boy. It seemed everyone they passed knew his father. *Hey Juice, how you doing; good to see you, Juice,* they'd say. Everyone, men, women, teachers, businessmen, farmers, even the local preacher would nod when he passed, and they never went to church.

Know your customer, was the advice, and apparently, Juice did. It didn't dawn on Sally what it really meant until the first big real-estate deal he attempted blew up around him. Juice had been dead for several years, Sally and Bill had bought a few properties, rental houses, and remodeled them. They had an opportunity on twenty-two acres of land, just off one of the main roads in the western part of the county. Sally and Bill heard rumors that a new school was planned on the adjacent property and wanted to scoop up the property and flip it to a developer. Time to move up a level.

An old man, Stafford Mills, owned the land. His wife had died a few years earlier and his kids, who lived out of state, were pestering him to move into a retirement home near them. In addition to the acreage, there was a three-bedroom brick house and several wood-framed shops on the property that Mills had used for his plumbing business. Perfect for development.

It only took one meeting. Sally sat on one side of Mills, Bill on the other, shooting rapid-fire reasons at the old man. The neighborhood's changing, you should be close to your family, hard to sell a piece of land this size, nobody farms anymore, you can watch your grandkids grow, we heard they might widen the road, traffic, you know. Sign here. Two hours later, they left with Mills' land under contract for half of market value.

Bill leveraged the purchase cash through a series of handshake deals and a good faith offer from Boot Jackson. Sally had lined up a developer before they met with Mills, who agreed in principle to buy the land from them at seventy-five percent of market value. What Sally didn't know was the developer's brother-in-law drove a refill tanker for Roberts Oil and Gas. The brother-in-law mentioned to the developer something about the underground storage tanks on the property. Mills had used the four one-thousand-gallon tanks to store fuel for the back hoes and trenchers he used in his plumbing business, but failed to mention it to Sally or Bill, and they never thought to ask. When he heard, the developer bailed, but not before making an anonymous call to the EPA. By then, Mills was in Georgia, watching his grandkids play soccer, chasing widows at the home, and letting his kids siphon off his money. Sally and Bill were on the hook to the bank for just over a hundred thousand and another hundred grand to the EPA for cleaning the soil contamination on the land they now owned.

Know your customers. So that's what Juice meant.

They eventually sold the property and considered the loss as paying for their education. Sally had his absolute. They'd not made that mistake again, and Sally didn't intend to now.

He knew Livingston Carr. Nervous, quirky, unemployed, only child, married with one on the way, about a month, maybe two from foreclosure. He had to be feeling the pressure and getting more than a little desperate. And Sally knew all about the right of first refusal agreement Carr had signed with Bill. Perfect.

Sally knew the developer he'd lined up, Southern Exposure, LLC. He'd done a couple of deals with them in the past. They were between major projects. Their last, a golf course community on the north side of the county, would be built out in a month, their profit long since made. They were liquid. Not only liquid, but fluid. And eager. And on cue, Southern Exposure, LLC loved it; the price—thirty thousand an acre, the aerial shots, the topography maps, access, and in general, the location. Sally knew better than to give them a specific address even though he knew, based on past dealings, they'd not try and backdoor him on the deal. Giving them the general area caused the expected Pavlovian response—their drool spilled all over the conference table.

Sally knew the land. The deed was clean, no restrictions, no encumbrances. Hard top access on the southeast side, possible easement access on the northeast side if the Combs lady could be convinced. The piece had never been developed in any way—no danger of leaking underground storage tanks, no buildings to knock down. One hundred acres of prime real estate, aching for a two hundred and fifty home development in the five hundred to one million dollar per-unit range gathered around a nice little common area slash park in the center.

One last deal. The homerun, the whole enchilada. Sally felt sure he could get the piece at a million, maybe less. The Southern Exposure guys were in at three million total. Two mill profit. Not a bad day's work. Even after taxes, that'd be enough to see him through in comfort until he checked out for good. And he'd put it all together himself. Life's validation.

Almost. What next? What about all the other nagging questions? It might be enough to make him forget about the questions. He doubted it. Sure, he could go anywhere, do just about anything he wanted with the money, but what point is there in taking tourist pictures if there's no one to show them to, no one to share the experience? He knew the typical move would be to rent arm-candy, a mid-life crisis companion. But there was one other thing Sally remembered about his father. Despite what Juice did for a living, how he did it, or what other people thought and said about him, he always seemed happiest around Sally's mother. Sally remembered the way they'd looked at each other, the way they'd laughed. His father was somehow *different* around her. She made him better.

He had some ideas on what to do with the money. And what about this Katherine Sardofsky? Sally smiled.

Time to pay Livingston Carr a visit.

GREEN-POUR FILTRATION'S HOMEPAGE pictured lush flora, palm fronds, ferns, and other greenery with what appeared to be a waterfall spouting near the top of the page and cascading down the screen. Every five seconds, the word ENTER appeared and seemed to surf the tumbling water downward. It took Livingston nine tries to time his click properly.

Once he surmounted that obstacle, an array of confusing choices and potential problems appeared. A series of pop-ups kept obscuring the navigation bar. The pop-ups were unimaginative starbursts with phrases like *Go Organic, Green is Lean, Partner Opportunities, Cool- Clear-Water* stenciled in the center. They finally stopped and Livingston searched the tabs hoping to find something about the company's financials, sales figures, CEO or management team, pricing information. Instead, he found articles describing the health benefits of drinking purified water. Plenty of charts and graphs ranking Green-Pour's water filters as the best on the market, but nothing that helped him weigh the job potential. He scrolled through an endless list of testimonials, all glowing. Proven track record, at least that was good.

The FAQ section didn't provide any real help, either.

Q: *How much does a filter system cost?*

A: *The body is 97% water. We cannot live without water. How can you put a price on a life? The Green-Pour Water Filtration System provides healthy, pure water for pennies a day.*

Q: *Is the system safe?*

A: *Europeans have enjoyed Green-Pour Water Filtration System's benefits for years. The US politicians are trying to keep these benefits from* the public, but the Eastern-European Water Filter Association gives the Green-Pour Water Filtration System a five-star, three-sickle rating, the best a system can receive.

After Q&A number sixteen, Livingston returned to the homepage, chose another tab. Then another, and another. More of the same. He would have become skeptical, but the graphics were excellent and the pages loaded quickly. And he really needed a job. Before Trudy came home from her doctor's appointment, if possible.

He clicked the "Become a Partner" link. A short paragraph: *No sales experience needed to become a top selling partner at Green-Pour Water Filtration Systems. Simply use our lab-tested sales techniques, and then the systems sell themselves. You are one step away from financial independence. Click on the links below, either Salesperson or Partner, and get started today.*

Livingston tried the "Salesperson" link. Not Found. Again. Not Found. Refresh. The "Partner" button took him to a lengthy description of how to become a distributor and parlay that into big money and eventual partner status by supplying the salespeople with product, the goal being to sign up as many salespeople under you as possible and encourage them to sign up as many under them as possible. Then sit back and count the profits. The last page gave Livingston all the information he needed to enroll, today—send credit card info, a money order or certified funds totaling seven thousand, two hundred and thirteen dollars for the starter kit and sales product. A representative would be in touch in the near future.

He was snapping his fingers and calculating break-even points when the doorbell rang.

Livingston peered through the glass in his front door. The lady looked like a church solicitor. He ignored her and returned to the computer, hoping she'd leave. She rang again. He looked again. What if something had happened to Trudy? What if she'd gone into labor?

"Yes?" he asked through the door. The lady asked for him by name. Liv considered his response before returning to the door.

"Trudy's not home," he told her, but the lady was persistent. He should've gone with Trudy, even though she'd told him it wasn't necessary. The lady rang the bell again. He counted five times in a row. Liv covered both ears with his hands, but heard her say she knew his father. He cracked open the door. "Who are you?" he asked.

She told him, but he didn't recognize the name. Still, she knew his father and against his better judgment, he decided that was reason enough to let her in, hear what she had to say.

By the time she'd left, Livingston couldn't catch his breath and was sweating through his t-shirt. Twins? Or triplets? It was too much. He raced through the house, fingers snapping, light switches up, reversed course, light switches down. He looked at the paperwork she'd left, felt the grilled cheese on wheat from lunch rising in a gooey knot. What had he done? What could he do? Why were people so interested in that land? Maybe he should keep it. No, that might mean going out there again. Even the thought made his legs itch. What if Bill Tucker's heirs found out? He'd promised Tucker first shot. Now he'd told Ethel Combs she could buy it.

No he hadn't. He told her he needed time. Trudy could get him out of this. No, no, no, he couldn't tell Trudy, what would she think? But he'd signed this paper, too, just like the one with Bill Tucker. Still, a million dollars. Trudy'd certainly understand. No, he couldn't, he had to find another way, he had to find a job. His father left the land to him. He should leave it to his son or daughter. Sons or daughters.

After the grilled cheesed reappeared, Livingston rinsed his mouth, stumbled to the bedroom and fell across his bed, hugging his knees to his chest, arms wrapped so tightly around them that he soon lost feeling in his fingers. He stared at the wall, unable to focus, unable to blink. His lips moved, repeating something, but no sound could be heard.

Finally, he fell asleep. When he awoke an hour later, Livingston checked all the light switches and sat on the sofa, snapping his fingers and waiting for Trudy to come home. He had no idea what he'd say when she arrived.

15

Ambition, Education—Bingo!

James sat in the plastic chair outside his motel room, watching traffic pass and contemplating options. He needed wheels. Brittany's mom let her drive her car to school and for errands, but that was it. Didn't matter: Britt wasn't talking to him at the moment. Again. Said she needed to concentrate on schoolwork during her senior year, just in case the *Survivor* gig didn't come through. James didn't buy it, but what could he do? He sent her texts, left her messages, posted on her Facebook wall. For two weeks, she'd ignored them all. It had become a distraction he couldn't keep from his mind. It didn't help that he was hornier than a two-headed billy goat. Worse yet, he'd begged Gaj into a little more time on the rent, but with Gaj's *October 5, no more or I call policemens* deadline only a couple weeks out, homeless was on his immediate horizon.

Since Colton had moved into the dorm at Mason University, he didn't come around as much, either. He told James he'd drive him out to the grow site on Saturday, but James couldn't wait. The plants were at a critical stage. Finn had warned him, dove season started in September and the game wardens would fly around looking for hunters in baited fields. The chance of them spotting the plants, even by accident, increased. Last time he checked, the buds had fattened and several of the main colas were five or six inches long. He sure didn't need complications now, payday loomed. James bought ten dozen red Christmas balls at the flea market and dulled the sheen with steel wool. He had them wrapped in paper towels and loaded in paper grocery bags, but with no ride to the grow site, there was no way to get the camouflage on the weed.

Bicycle Bob rode past. He stopped at the corner, leaned his bike against the light post, kneeled down on the concrete, and started praying. Out loud.

James leaned the chair forward, balancing on its front two legs, and studied Bob's bike. It was a two-toned, blue and white beach cruiser model with an aftermarket banana sea. A miniature license plate, the type cheap gift shops sold, hung from the rear of the seat. It said BOB in red letters. Stickers covered most of the handlebars, which also had red, white, and blue streamers at the grips, horn on the left side and a bell on the right. A large basket hung from the front of the handlebars. On it, Bob had mounted deer antlers, an impressive eight-point rack. Wire saddlebags flanked the rear tire. Duct tape held two clothespins to the front forks, the clothespins each gripped playing cards—the suicide king and the jack of hearts, which poked through the spokes.

A little obvious, but it'd work. James took two Bud Lights from the mini-fridge, a couple of Adderalls, and a few Advil from the dresser drawer and went to proposition Bicycle Bob.

He approached and waited for an opening.

Bicycle Bob prayed. "... and please cast the holy gamma tentacles toward the bingo parlor. Use the high beams to show them that the evil forces gain access through the free space." He took a breath.

"Bicycle Bob, s'up?" James interrupted.

Bob opened one eye toward James. "Can't talk, Brother James. Prayer time."

"How is Mr. Checkers?"

Bob frowned. "Almighty *Father* Checkers, James. Don't blaspheme. And he's fine. Needs to insufflate the spirit into the folks at the bingo parlor, though. It's bad, James. Two hundred and thirty-seven games, not even close to a bingo. No G-64, that's how it starts. Next thing you know, it's in the water, the day care centers, Congress. Then—mind control, the whole world. Otosclerosis is a symptom, often the first sign the bad forces are calling the shots."

"Huh?"

"See what I mean, hearing's gone. When did they get to you? Kneel down here with me, I'll be Father Checkers' instrument, heal you through touch."

Why not, James figured, he needed the bike. He looked up and down the street, then knelt on the sidewalk beside Bob. Bob knee-walked around in front of James and put both elbows over James' ears.

"Father Checkers," Bob started, "let the bad forces pass from this boy's ears, take the evil empire from his brain regions, send it out through me." He removed his elbows and held both fists in front of James' eyes. "Now watch." He opened his fists and thrust them, palms up, toward the sky. "See." He pointed. "There they go. Feel better?"

"Yeah, lots better. Thanks. Bicycle Bob, I need your bike. Got somewhere I gotta be."

"Well, everybody's gotta be somewhere, James. Duh. If you're not, you're vaporized. And let me tell you, being vaporized is a bitch. They won't even give you a card at the bingo parlor if you've been vaporized. But if you take my bike, I won't be Bicycle Bob. Then I'd be Just Bob."

"It's only for the afternoon. I'll give you two beers and these pills." James sat the Buds on the sidewalk and held the Adderall and Advil out toward Bob.

Bob looked at the beers. "You don't have any Coors Light?"

"It's all I got, buddy."

"Well okay then. I'll be Just Bob until you get back."

James went for the bike.

"Wait, wait," Bob stopped him. He dug into his garbage bag and pulled out a roll of Duct tape and a red Sharpie. He put a strip of tape over the license plate and wrote JAMES across it. "It don't matter what you are, long as you know who you are," he said. Bob stood and raised his right arm SS style. "May Father Checkers ride with you and may all your jumps be doubles."

James loaded his Christmas balls in the baskets and waved as he pedaled away.

He thought he'd die on the ride out. Climbing the hill in front of The Brown Fedora was torture. His thighs screamed and his lungs ached, but he made it. It took him a couple hours to hang the Christmas balls on the pot plants. He kept placing and replacing them, trying to find the right spots to make them look like tomatoes from the air. He considered climbing a tree for an overhead check, but after a couple of tries decided against it. Instead, he found the voodoo trinket he and Colton had nailed to the tree and rubbed it for luck. He checked several of the buds. Nice and sticky, another week or two and it would be harvest time. They were heavy, too, plenty of yield. Forty-two plants had survived and Finn told them to expect between one and three ounces per plant. James thought it looked like there'd be more than that. If he harvested at just the right time and had good luck curing the bud, this strain should sell for around three hundred bucks an ounce. James did the math as he pedaled back toward town. By the time Just Bob came into sight, James had not only counted his future earnings, he'd spent most of it, too. A used truck . . . no, a motorcycle *and* a truck. An Xbox, a new pair of Chucks. Oh, and a bow and arrow set, had to have a bow and arrow. And something for Britt, something nice. Jewelry, maybe. A little token to get her attention, show her she was wrong about him, that he did have ambition. And cash. She'd talk to him then.

SALLY WALKED THROUGH the doors at the Brown Fedora and looked around the room. Average crowd for that time of day. Four men sat alone at separate tables scattered throughout the dining area. Sally headed toward the bar.

"Hey Shirley. Anybody come in looking for me, a guy, forty-ish?"

"Nut job in the corner." She nodded at a table near the kitchen.

"Yeah, I got that impression from the phone call. Bad, huh?"

"Certifiable, if you ask me. You keep some strange company, Salvador Hinson."

"Takes all kinds, Shirley, takes all kinds. Can I get a beer when you get a second?"

Sally watched the man while he waited on his drink. It wasn't a pretty sight. The man's shirttail was half untucked and thoroughly wrinkled. He had dark, baggy circles beneath both eyes, his face looked drawn, gaunt. The vision reminded Sally of those old shadowy daguerreotype photos, maybe of Lincoln in the later years, just before attending the play. The man turned his glass of tea in a continuous circle with one hand, snapped his fingers on the other hand in rhythm with each revolution. It looked as if he was carrying on a detailed conversation with himself, mouthing words and shaking his head, sometimes in agreement, other times disagreeing. Beneath the table, one leg hammered up and down like a rocker arm on a high revving V-8.

Shirley brought his Miller and Sally gulped half of it in one swallow. "Well," he told her, "let's see if this dog'll hunt."

"Good luck," she smiled. "You need one of them jackets that fasten in the back, give me a nod and I'll make the call."

He approached the table. "Mr. Carr?" he said as he pulled out the chair. The man jumped when Sally spoke, then nodded and stuck out his hand. "Everything okay? You look a little nervous."

"My wife. Pregnant. Next month. It's . . . it's . . ." Livingston's breaths made a sucking sound, hyperventilating. He picked up his napkin and breathed into it for a moment. "Yes. Nervous."

"First one?" Sally asked. Livingston nodded.

"You'll do fine, I'm sure. Listen, I know you've got a lot going on, so I'll get right to it." He slid the aerial photo of the land toward Livingston. "Do you recognize this property?"

Livingston started snapping his fingers again and shook his head "no."

"How about this?" Sally turned the picture over, revealing the words Bill had scribbled on the back. He pointed to the initials. "LC," he said. "Livingston Carr. Recognize it now?"

Before, Livingston had been an electrical current, a blur or motion, tics, and twitches. When he saw the handwriting, he froze. Sally noticed Livingston was holding his breath. He waited. The waitress refilled Livingston's glass, asked Sally if he wanted another beer. Still, no movement from Livingston. When Sally saw his eyes flutter and begin rolling back in his head, he shook Livingston's arm. "Mr. Carr. Livingston. Are you . . ."

Livingston finally drew in a long, deep breath and released it in a protracted sigh. "I can't, I can't," he mumbled. "It's too much . . . Bill Tucker . . . my father left it to me . . . nobody's buying condoms . . . economy, bad, no sex. Trudy, too much sex . . . scary sex. I don't . . . salmon patty Thursdays . . . library closings . . . accruals . . . accounts receivable . . ."

"Whoa, slow down. Take a drink of tea. Let's try and focus." Sally tapped the photograph.

Livingston took another long breath. He rubbed his eyes with the heels of his hands, then shook his head like a dog that had just come out of the water. When he finished, he stared at Sally, his eyes flat, his face expressionless. He turned his gaze downward, toward the tabletop and said, "I should go, I'm not feeling well."

"No, you're not going anywhere until we straighten this out. Now, you own this property, right?"

Livingston nodded but didn't look up.

"And you gave Bill Tucker a right of first refusal contract, didn't you?"

More nodding, accompanied by a quiver in Livingston's lower lip and chin.

"Well, Bill's dead, and he assigned the contract to me."

More quivering. Fingers snapping. A faint, humming moan started.

"Livingston," Sally's voice softened, as if he were talking to a lost child. "Listen, it's alright. I can help you. We're like partners now, and partners look out for each other. I know things are tough—baby on the way, the lay-off, and the job market's for shit—but it'll all work out. That's what you want, right? Everything back to normal?"

Livingston raised his head and stared at Sally. Sally couldn't remember ever seeing such a defeated look on a man's face, such desperation in his eyes. Hidden in the despair, though, Sally saw the last small flicker of hope and he could see how tightly Livingston now clung to it. That was all he needed. Livingston believed and Sally closed. "Let me help you," he whispered.

The humming and finger popping stopped. "You can't," Livingston mumbled.

Damn. What had he missed? Too quick? Maybe he needed one more nudge.

"Sure I can. The land's not doing you a bit of good. It's part of the problem now; it can be the solution. It's only an asset if it's working *for* you. You've got a baby on the way, a mortgage. The state's already running out of unemployment funds, how long before yours are gone? I can pay you cash money for the property, enough so you don't have to worry about finding a job for quite a while. You can ride out this recession. Enough you can start a helluva college fund for the baby. Make all your worries disappear. It's the right thing to do for your family, Livingston. Show a little ambition, here."

Livingston shook his head. "You don't understand. I knew Mr. Tucker died. It's too late, I signed the papers."

"No, it's alright. Bill took care of the paperwork. It's the same deal. Me and him were partners, sort of like me and you are now. Signing with Bill is the same as if you'd signed with me."

"No. The other papers, I signed them just last week. Tucker was dead, I didn't think . . ."

"Other papers?" Sally slammed a fist down on the table. Livingston jumped, nearly spilling his drink. "Son-of-a-bitch. Those bastards at Southern Exposure. After all these years and now those shitheads backdoor me. We'll fight it, Livingston, I'll take their sorry asses to court. What'd they offer?"

"Who's Southern Exposure?" Livingston looked even more confused.

"But they're the only ones who knew," Sally was talking to himself. "They must've figured out where . . . oh shit. Mary and Preacher Mike. It's that damn church carnival freak show they want to build. I should've known. Damn it to hell. No, no, I'm still okay. I've got the right of first refusal. I'll fight them too."

"You're frightening me. Southern Exposure, Preacher Mike—I don't know those people . . . and what did I do to them? What do they want? Am I in danger? Trudy . . . the baby . . . I didn't mean anything, I had to sign . . . so much money . . . the hospital bills . . . she said she'd pay cash . . . pediatrician . . . she knew my father . . . the books, all the books . . . bills . . ." The moaning started again, the finger snapping followed right behind. Livingston began drumming the fingers of his unoccupied hand against his forehead.

"Wait. She? You said *she*. She who?"

"Mrs. Combs. Ethel Combs. I'm sorry, Mr. Hinson. She had the paperwork. I needed . . . I didn't know . . . I had to."

"Ethel Combs? The old woman? Well I'll be damned. Do you have the contract?"

"Not with me, but it's practically the same as the one I signed with Mr. Tucker." Livingston started rocking back and forth with his arms folded across his chest, his hands tucked tightly in his armpits.

"A right of first refusal, not a purchase contract? That's what you signed?"

Livingston nodded yes. "I think."

"Well hell, we're back in business. Come on."

"I can't . . ."

"Yes you can. We're going to pay Mrs. Ethel Combs a visit, right now."

Sally stood and gently took Livingston's left arm and guided him out of his seat. Once he was upright, he put his arm around his shoulder, led him out the door, and buckled him into the passenger side of the Lexus. As he started the car, Sally switched on the child safety locks, just in case. He had to wait before pulling into the street. A teenage boy on a bicycle decorated with deer antlers, garland draped baskets, and Christmas balls struggled up the hill, blocking the exit. "Must be a full moon," Sally muttered under his breath, "they're everywhere."

THE DOORBELL CHIMED. Ethel snuffed out her cigarette, cut the TV off, and peeked out the window. Shit fire, she thought, they figured it out quicker than I expected. Together. She never doubted Salvador Hinson would eventually find his way to Livingston. That was why she'd been in such a hurry to get something on paper with him. But Sally she could deal with, he seemed to be a logical man. She knew all about his business, about his dead partner. Ethel went to the cabinet, found the paperwork she'd drawn up, and put it in the top drawer. She knew these two would show up eventually. And she respected Sally—knew he'd appreciate the fact that she took the initiative in drawing up this new agreement. Livingston Carr, though, his crazy button had a hair trigger and he already had his twitchy finger wrapped around it. The slightest squeeze and he'd be making macaroni art at the nuthouse.

She opened the door.

"Salvador. Livingston. What brings you boys out?"

"Afternoon, ma'am," Sally answered. "Me and Livingston here were having a conversation and your name came up. Ain't that right, Livingston?"

Livingston nodded.

"Salvador Hinson, I didn't take you as one to gossip. I know your mama raised you up better than that, so what the hell is it you want?"

"I'm doing Livingston a favor, helping him out a bit." Sally slapped Liv on the back. Livingston stumbled forward, then righted himself. "Thought we might talk to you about a mutual interest."

"Mutual interest? What kind of talk is that? I'm a busy woman, don't be wasting my time with no *mutual interest.* Say what's on your mind."

"Alright, then. It's about this contract you made Livingston sign."

"I don't see how that's any of your business. That's between me and him, right Mr. Carr?"

Livingston looked at Ethel, then Sally. Panic gripped him. "I suppose, yes. Technically, since both our names are on it, that makes it between you and me, but I... see, there was... it's... it's... mmm..." The humming started.

"What he's trying to say is the contract's void. I already had a written agreement with him, had it for years," Sally explained.

"Huh. Now I'm an old woman. I got more cobwebs in my brain than Catholics got communion wafers. But if I recollect correctly, you came snooping around asking questions about who'd been on the property and the like just a few months back. By my calculations, that don't add up just right. If you had an agreement for years, wouldn't have been no call for you to come asking me such questions. Now I got things to do."

"Hear me out. You know me and Bill Tucker had the real-estate company. Before he died, Bill made an agreement with Livingston, made it in the company name. Now, I didn't know anything about it beforehand, but Livingston says the contract was on our company form. That means it's our company deal, it reverted to me when he died. Livingston's got the copies. Your deal's no good."

"That true, Livingston?"

Livingston nodded. The hum changed to a whimper. Sally shifted his weight and stared at Ethel. Ethel smiled. She was right, there *was* something about that piece of land. Salvador Hinson standing in her front yard proved it. He wouldn't be involved if he didn't have some sort of deal working, probably already had a buyer. She'd been working, too. Sure, she planned on a solitary operation, but with this much interest in that piece of dirt there was no point being greedy. Better to take on a couple of partners than let everything slip away on a paperwork technicality.

"I see," she said. "Why don't you boys come in out of the heat, let's see if we can't find an agreement to suit everybody."

Once inside, Ethel offered them both drinks. Livingston had an iced tea, she and Sally each a rum and coke. Ethel sat down, ready to explain her idea, but Sally started first.

"Mrs. Combs, I have one question. Livingston told me what you offered. No offense," he looked around the outdated kitchen: funeral home calendar, quaint homemade curtains, worn out Seventies era dinette set. Best not judge by appearance, he'd long since learned to avoid that mistake, but the evidence before him spoke pretty strongly. He continued, "but where are you gonna get that kind of money?"

She hesitated. "Not that it's any of your damn business, but since God and everybody else knows you can afford it, I reckon it's only fair I pony up. How old are you, Sally?"

"I'll be fifty next month."

"Too young to remember. This would've been six, seven years before you were even born. 1953, it was." Ethel laughed. "First couple of years we were married, I was barefoot and pregnant. Anyway, my husband, Jesse, he worked at the Chevy dealership in town. He was a fine mechanic, too. We'd just built this place, and the three kids, we made ends meet, but there wasn't much extra."

She paused to finish her drink, then poured another and continued.

"Jesse took a part time job as a machinist's helper. His crew mostly did maintenance jobs, repairing equipment for other companies, service work, and the like. Jesse was a good man, none better. He wanted to buy me a river or lake lot one day, more than anything, he did. But, it's only a thin veil that separates ambition from pipe dreams."

Ethel looked out the window, and for a moment, she was on the dock of the honeymoon cabin she and Jesse rented at Fontana Lake. Her feet dangling in the cold blue-green water, the June bugs droning from the locust trees while Jesse cast for smallmouth. She sighed.

"One weekend he was working in Charlotte. Me and the kids went to visit my mother, so Jesse went sight-seeing. He wandered into the coliseum they'd just built. I reckon he got tired or something. They told me he must've laid down on the floor. Anyway, the light fixture and scoreboard fell on him. Killed him, just like that. No explaining it."

"That must've been terrible," Sally said.

Livingston nodded. His whimpering returned to a low hum.

Ethel looked down, straightened her apron. "They don't know how he got in to start with. Then they said the hardware could've possibly failed, that's what caused the thing to fall. Who knows? The city, the hardware manufacturer, the architect, they fell all over themselves pointing the blame at each other. Afraid I might sue."

"So that's how you got your money?" Sally asked.

"Led to it. Like I said, they were afraid I'd sue. They offered me 1.7 million if I agreed not to. Put it in the bank and it's been drawing interest ever since." She leaned forward, looked at Livingston, then Sally. "So don't you boys worry about my money, they's plenty."

The humming stopped. For once, Livingston sat perfectly still. "My mother told me that story once, when I was a kid," he whispered. "Not about you, about the scoreboard falling. I never knew someone was . . . was . . . I'm sorry for you."

"That's kind of you, Livingston. Now, how is it you think Sally's money is better than mine? Huh?"

The finger snapping started and Livingston bowed his head. Ethel shook hers. At least he wasn't humming.

"Sally," she said, "we can back and forth this thing from here to the Supreme Court. I got a notion that might suit us better."

"I'm listening."

"I figure you already have something lined up for flipping that piece of land. That's your line of work and I don't blame you for it. What you're missing is competition."

"Apparently not, I'm competing with you right now."

"That's what I mean. Me and you both want it. You've already got somebody else interested, and at a profit. I figure you offered about the same as me, or else you wouldn't be here, right?"

Sally shrugged and nodded. "Pretty much."

"Well, I've talked to somebody says he might know three or four more that'd be interested. You know Rick Landon?"

"With Landon Auction and Realty? Me and Bill bought a tract of farm land at one of his auctions several years back. Paid twenty percent more than we'd planned. Got all caught up in the bidding and couldn't stop, figured hell, if the other bidders were willing to pay more, maybe we'd undervalued the piece. Still made . . ." Sally stopped and smiled. "Damn, Ethel, I like the way you're thinking. I see it now."

"Thought you would. Landon says he'll do the auction. Won't charge us a commission, he charges the buyer instead."

"Oh yeah, the buyer's premium, I remember now."

"We'll pay the advertising cost up front, though. Five grand. I figure we'd split that."

"I could do that. What's he think it'll bring?"

"Neighborhood of four million."

"That's better than what I had. I got another question. If you're sitting on all that money, why are you so interested in this deal. I mean, at your age, how much more do you need?"

Ethel grinned. "Like Mr. Rockefeller once said, just a little bit more."

"I heard that. The idea's growing on me, what's the next step?"

"I'll call Landon this afternoon. Then we sign the contracts and he'll start advertising. Said he'd like to hold an open house preview soon, make it a big to-do, get people excited. Hold the auction soon after. We could close in less than sixty days, cash in hand."

"Make the call. I'm in."

"Good. Now this might sound like picking the fly shit out of black pepper, but there is one little thing we need to get around. Me and you don't own the property, so we can't sign the auction contracts."

They both turned toward Livingston. The humming was back, the finger popping increased and he was rocking back and forth in the chair. Ethel went to the cabinet and came back with a piece of paper and another glass. She poured her and Sally another drink, then poured a third and slid it and the paper toward Livingston.

"That says we're partners on this deal, we split the profit three ways. I figure we all sign and we'll seal it with a toast."

"He's in a bad way, Ethel. I don't know. You think he's competent?" Sally asked.

Ethel scooted her chair beside Livingston and put her arm around his shoulder. "Mr. Carr. Livingston. You remember what we talked about that day at your house? Selling's the best thing for you and your family. You understand that, don't you?"

He sniffled and mumbled yes.

"Mr. Hinson here told you the same thing, didn't he?"

Nodding.

"Me and him are only trying to help you with this. You trust us. Think how happy your wife will be . . ."

Livingston whimpered.

". . . think what all this money can do for your family, for your baby. Four million divided three ways will give you three hundred thousand more than me or Sally offered. You need this. What else are you going to do?"

Livingston picked up the pen and scrawled his shaky signature at the bottom of the page. They all raised their glasses. Livingston held his with both hands.

"To profit," Sally said.

"It's the American way," answered Ethel.

Glasses clinked. Ethel and Sally downed their drinks, Livingston took one last sip of tea.

Ethel watched them drive away then carried the lunch and break-fast scraps out back. The dog lounging in the shade of her oak tree dropped the bone he was gnawing and trotted over to the bowl. A small yellow flower clung to his fur just behind his ear. Ethel pulled it free and admired it for a moment before tossing it in the yard. She then leaned down and scratched his chin. "We gonna hit a lick on this one, Sunflower. You wait and see," she told the animal.

She laughed and went back inside. The dog finished his meal, belched, and returned to his bone for dessert.

16

Growing Up, Growing Old, and Dying

Saturday morning and Ethel was tired. It had been a busy week, but the weekend was starting nicely. Britt called and said she planned to stop by, and when Ethel finished cleaning the breakfast dishes, she decided to wait for her on the front porch. The dog heard the screen door slam and bounded around the corner of the house and up the steps where he nuzzled against Ethel's leg. When she sat in the rocker, he stretched on the porch beside her.

She lit a Pall Mall, exhaled, and watched the haze of smoke hover, then disappear. Ashes to ashes, she thought. Here, then gone, like the smoke. You did what you could. You suffered, you endured, and you wondered why. There was no answer, but somewhere along the way, she realized she no longer needed one. Her husband wandered into that building all those years ago. Out of the blue, a lighting fixture falls and kills him. Nothing could explain it, and nothing eased the longing she'd felt all these years. No, she didn't need any answers because she knew any answer was really a lie. She fooled herself, everyone did if they lived to her age. Always reaching, creating reasons, perceptions of forward motion. For what?

Raise three kids, give them what they needed, and in return she lived ignored and forgotten. From time to time, she wondered if she should have told them about the money, lavished it on them, but that would've only made things worse. They thought they were better than her as it was, with all their fancy gadgets and big houses. It was never enough with them, and they didn't appreciate what they had now. They'd remember her when she left it all to Brittany, though. Or the dog.

It would be nice to hang on for another year, until after Britt turned eighteen. Ethel hadn't told her, but she planned on giving a couple thousand or so toward that *Survivor* thing. For the rest of it, she'd set up a trust, but she'd rest easier knowing Britt was of legal age to receive the money. Boot Jackson, at the bank, told her to put it in writing Britt had to wait until she was older, twenty-five or twenty-six, before she could actually get the cash. Eighteen's just too young, he said, but Ethel didn't care. For the most part, Britt had a good head on her shoulders, and besides, Ethel had been a widow by twenty-five. Anything could happen. She intended to give her granddaughter every opportunity possible, and if nothing else, money created opportunity.

Yes, she was tired, but she didn't mind the feeling. It reminded her she was still alive. When she noticed all the attention surrounding the piece of dirt behind her house, it filled her with an excitement she'd not felt in a long, long time. She certainly didn't *want* the land and from the start she'd planned on having Landon auction the property. That damn Livingston almost ruined it, but what could she expect, the man was squirrel-shit nutty. Sally was right, she didn't need any more money, she already had enough that Brittany would be set for life. Chasing this deal gave her a reason to get out of bed every morning; a person needs that. If she could make a little more profit along the way, all the better. Better to partner with them than hope to outlive a court battle.

Britt pulled in the drive, and another car Ethel didn't recognize pulled in behind her. A man and woman got out and followed Brittany toward the house. Ethel thought she recognized the lady, but the man was unfamiliar. When they came closer, Ethel remembered. The woman was the one asking about Brittany's pictures.

"Hey, Memaw." Hugs and a kiss on the cheek.

"Who's your company?" Ethel asked.

"That's Dr. Sardofsky, she's into, like, plants and stuff. And that's Dr . . . Dr . . ."

"Dr. Aldus Culpepper." The man volunteered. He took his pipe from his mouth and stepped forward to shake Ethel's hand. When he did, the dog sat up, then moved himself between Ethel and the two professors. "Pleasure to meet you, Mrs. Combs," he said, but looked at the dog and decided against shaking hands.

Ethel nodded, but didn't take her eyes off Kat.

"And I'm Dr. Sardofsky. Katherine. My friends call me Kat. We've met."

"I see you found her."

"Yes ma'am. Well, she found me, actually. And you were right, your granddaughter is a fabulous photographer. So much raw talent and potential."

"Potential, huh? If you got the pictures, what brings you and your friend here out my way?"

"Memaw," Britt whined. "She came by earlier and you didn't tell me?"

"I'm an old woman, Britt. I forget things." Ethel apologized. "Now what are you two after?"

"They want to see those flowers, and, like, where they're growing and all. I told them it'd be cool to park here," Britt answered for them.

"I see." Ethel looked from Kat to Dr. Culpepper and back again. "That land's private property."

"Oh, we'll be cognizant of the fact," said Dr. Culpepper. "Just going for a little walk in the woods. Take a few pictures, nothing more. We'll disturb nothing in the process. If the land was posted no trespassing, surely your granddaughter would not have been taking pictures there."

"You already saw Britt's pictures, what the hell you need with more?"

Kat touched her nose. Aldus relit his pipe with a wet sucking sound. "Brittany's photographs were taken from an aesthetic point of view," Kat offered. "Those flowers are extremely rare, nearly extinct. I'd like some close-up shots for academic purposes, that's all. I'm a botanist. I'm researching the Schweinitz sunflower, the ones your granddaughter photographed on the property."

Ethel jutted her chin toward Aldus. "You one of them botanists, too?" she asked.

"Oh no, I'm an archeologist. I'm only tagging along, so to speak. Keeping Dr. Sardofsky company."

Ethel didn't believe him. Still, they were only college teachers. Not the type to have any designs on the land. Maybe Britt's being around intellectual types would prove a good influence. What was the harm?

"Well, I suppose there's no harm in going for a walk and taking a few pictures. Cut through the back yard and head for the trees, you'll find your way from there."

"We appreciate that, Mrs. Combs," Kat told her. "We won't be long."

Ethel looked at the man as the two of them started around her house. He wore shorts with lots of pockets, like a kid, and socks with sandals. "Culpepper," she called out. "Best keep an eye out, there's a bunch of poison ivy back in there."

"Thanks for the warning." He waved. "But I'm not allergic. Strolled through it numerous times, never the first sign of a reaction."

"I'm not allergic," Ethel said when they were out of sight. "You pompous ass." She turned to Britt. "Let's go inside, honey. I made you some blueberry muffins."

They had a nice visit. Britt bubbled about making some kind of audition video for that *Survivors* show, but Ethel didn't understand much of what the girl tried to explain. Seeing her granddaughter so excited was enough. An hour later, Ethel heard the dog bark and looked out the kitchen window to see the two professors coming out of the woods.

"Your two college friends are back," Ethel told Brittany.

"They're not friends, Memaw. They're just, like, people."

"All the same, it's good to know them. They might could help you. You could go to college and study photography, you know."

"Yeah, I know, but college costs money. Daddy says I'd need lots of scholarships. Besides, I'm gonna be on *Survivor*, I just know it."

"You oughta think of a backup plan, I'm just saying. I'd be mighty proud if you got a college degree."

"Okay, Memaw. It'll be my plan B, just in case. If I don't get on *Survivor*, but I know I will, and I'll apply for those scholarships. If I get them, then I'll go."

"That's my girl. Now let's go see these two eggheads off."

They waited under the shade of the pin oak in Ethel's back yard. The dog sprawled at their feet, worrying another one of his bones.

"Y'all find what you were looking for?" Ethel asked when they neared.

"Oh, yes ma'am. Unbelievable. They're Schweinitz, alright. Remarkable specimens. Hardy, too, and more than I expected." Kat said.

"Yes, very interesting. Very interesting indeed," Dr. Culpepper said. He looked as if he were going to say something more, but he suddenly focused on the dog. "Did you give your dog those bones?"

Ethel looked toward the dog. Over the past few months, he'd drug several of the bones into her back yard and now had a nice pile to choose from. "No," she told him. "I don't know where he gets them, just drags them up and drops them."

"Mind if I take one with me?" he asked.

"What? Take one with you? It's probably from a deer or something. People hit them on the roads all the time out here. What in the name of Sam Hill would you want with one of those?"

"Professional curiosity. As an archeologist, you know."

"Hell, I ain't never heard the like, but if you think you can get one of them, help yourself." She grinned.

Dr. Culpepper started toward the dog. The dog cut his eyes toward him as he approached then inched backward with the bone in his mouth. The doctor took another step and the dog growled. Aldus stopped. He lifted his right leg and scratched his left shin with his sandal. "I see what you mean," he said and turned toward Ethel with a perplexed look on his face. "I'd really like to have one," he said then bent and scratched his shin with his fingernails.

Ethel walked over and rubbed the scruff of the dog's neck, then picked up another bone from the pile nearby. "I don't believe he much cares to part with the one in his mouth. This one work?" she asked. Culpepper nodded.

Dr. Culpepper grinned when Ethel handed him the bone. Eighty-two years, she thought, and I've never seen a grown man get so excited about a dead deer's bone. The woman and her flowers she understood. She watched the man scratch his leg again, this time with focused intensity. Reckon there's a first time for everything, she thought.

THE SCHWEINITZ SUNFLOWER blooms had appeared to bow as Kat approached. She felt her heart quicken, her palms begin to sweat. She didn't see them when she first entered the clearing, but as she rounded a corner, the stark blaze of yellow greeted her. It was a substantial cluster, and she soon found several other stands scattered around the edges of the open area.

They were perfect. The purple pubescent stems rising proudly, the lower regions containing larger leaves thick and stiff in texture. Higher, the flowers burst from the stalks. Brilliant yellow petals with two or three channels running along their length gathered around small, beady heads. The vision overwhelmed Kat. While Brittany's pictures were good, seeing the flowers in person filled her with . . . with . . . something powerful and moving she couldn't name. In that moment, she was no longer a scientist. Emotion and veneration replaced reason and logic. Nothing else existed—the years of research, her job, Leaderlick, student retention, the Twelve Point Strategic Revision Plan—all fell away. Kat was transported. Free falling to another time and place when vast prairies stretched uninterrupted across the Piedmont plains, when tall Indians with flat foreheads nurtured the plentiful flowers, dug their roots for nourishment.

She allowed herself to linger a few moments longer before snapping pictures and making notes.

The flowers did not have the same effect on Aldus. "Hmm. Nice. Look kinda like yellow daisies, no, black-eyed susans without the black eye," he said before wandering in the other direction. While Kat was absorbed in the flowers, he circled the open area in the center of the woods, eyes trained on the ground at first, hoping to find an arrowhead, maybe a tool or shard of bowl, but the groundcover prevented him from seeing what might lie in the dirt beneath. He began crisscrossing the clearing, tramping through the weeds and undergrowth, stopping at various points and looking in all directions. Kat spotted him once as he stood at the center of the open area, turning his head this way and that, then extending his right arm forward at a ninety-degree angle to his torso, sighting along his outstretched fingertips. He then moved to the tree line and did the same thing, this time pointing back over the clearing.

Occasionally, he knelt and pawed through the weeds and poked around in the top layer of dirt, then made a few notes. After a while, he ambled back to find Kat finishing a free-hand sketch of a larger sunflower. He looked over her shoulder. "Ah," he said. "Reminiscent of Bartram."

"You know Bartram's work?" Kat asked.

"Certainly. His work has an indirect appeal to some archeologists, myself included. His notes have provided insight and clarification into 18th century life in this region." He lit his pipe and exhaled skyward. "Are you ready to go?"

They spoke briefly with Ethel and thanked Brittany again. As she waited for Aldus to load his equipment in the trunk, Kat reviewed her notes, then tabbed through the photos she'd taken. Satisfied, she put them in her backpack.

"So," she started, "what's with the bone?"

"Oh, just curious. I doubt it's anything. The old woman's probably right—a deer. Hard to tell, the dog damaged the integrity. I'll run some tests."

"And what did you think of the land? You told Mrs. Combs it was interesting." Kat leaned her head on the headrest.

"Possibly. The clearing is elevated, but with the undergrowth," he glanced at Kat and smiled, "and your flowers, it's hard to tell. I'd like to come back with a wye and level rod, calculate the elevation change, establish circumference, and do some research based on the information."

Kat sat upright. "Do you think it could be a mound?"

"I can't imagine it would be, not right here in the county. Someone would have found it long ago. The rise I noted is due to the natural contour of the land, most likely. Did you notice the holes?"

"Yes, what was that?"

"I don't know. There were quite a few, and they appeared to have been dug with a shovel. Recently, too."

"You don't think Mrs. Comb's dog could have done it?"

"Oh no, definitely a shovel. I did find one other spot near the crest of the hill that looked as if some animal had been digging. There was fresh dirt at one edge of a honeysuckle thicket. I couldn't see a hole or anything due to the thickness of the undergrowth and I didn't want to disturb it much, may have been coyotes, a den possibly. A fox even."

"I could ask the girl, she's out here a lot."

"There's no need. I'm sure it was animals, and the other holes, well, around the edge of the opening as they were, someone may have found saplings to transplant, dogwoods, pines, something like that." Aldus turned into the campus faculty lot and parked.

"Makes sense. Thanks for coming along, and, well, everything. I hope it wasn't a waste of your time," Kat paused, "and money."

"Don't mention it. I'll take a look at some topography maps, evaluate the elevations. If they warrant it, I may contact you about arranging another visit to take actual measurements. Even if it's not a mound, and I don't think it is, that'll be enough to justify the expenditure." He bent down and scratched both shins. "I'll let you know."

Kat went to her office and attempted transcribing her notes to the computer. She couldn't concentrate and soon abandoned the transcription and returned to the photos. She downloaded them to her desktop and then paged back through them again and again. It was almost impossible to choose, but finally, she picked her favorite and made it her screen saver. She went through the same process with her laptop. When she finished, she thumbed through her notes once more, settling on the pencil sketch.

She studied the drawing, then scanned it. In her desk, she found a ruler and drew a faint line near the bottom of the page, and another two inches above the first. Between the lines, she neatly printed Schweinitz Sunflower in large letters. Beneath it, she penciled *Helianthus schweinitzii* in italics. In the lower right-hand corner, she signed her name and the date. She'd give the original to Sally that night when he picked her up for dinner. She looked at the drawing again, and for the first time in her life, she felt like an adult.

For a Saturday afternoon, traffic was a little heavier than usual. Colton picked James up at the motel and headed to the grow site. They drove through town, turned on Johnson. The light at the end of Johnson caught them. In the right-hand turn lane: a farm truck, a van with an elaborate Los Amigos stencil on the back window, followed by a Volvo. The driver of the Volvo rocked back and forth, apparently talking to himself. The other two drivers talked on cell phones.

In the middle lane, the only lane that continued straight, a red Audi, driver also on the phone, followed by a family in an SUV, and then a couple in a Camry.

In the left turn lane, directly in front of James and Colton, a biker on a Harley Road King, lots of chrome. Plenty loud. The biker had full sleeve work inked on both thick arms, a toothpick in the corner of his mouth. James and Colton waited behind him, windows down. The biker twitched the throttle. James studied the bike.

"Turn the radio down, I want to hear it," he told Colton.

Potato, potato, potato, the patented Harley sound rumbled, the cam loping.

"That's what I'm talking about, C-note. We get this crop sold, I'm getting me one of those."

"Yeah, road rash'll look good on you."

The light turned. The driver in the center lane, still on the phone, cut left across traffic. Colton slammed on the brakes, the guy on the bike locked it up, nearly dropping the motorcycle before he got his foot down. The bike stalled.

"Did you see that?" James shouted. "That Audi prick almost hit the Harley dude. Shit."

The biker restarted the bike and eased forward. It was only a short block to the next red light. The biker pulled in behind the Audi, dropped the kickstand, and switched off the engine. James punched Colton in the arm. "Watch this. Shit, it's on now." Soccer moms rolled windows up, others rolled theirs down.

The biker strolled to the driver's side of the Audi. The driver oblivious, still gabbing. In one motion, the biker snatched the phone from Audi's ear, slammed it on the pavement, and stomped it with the heel of his boot. Drivers cheered, others looked the other way. James banged on the roof of the truck.

Audi guy leaned his head out, looking down at the pieces of his phone crumbled on the pavement, and yelled, "Hey, that's my new Droid. What the hell are you doing?"

"Hang up and drive, bitch."

"You can't do that," screamed the driver. "I need that phone, I'm a commodities broker."

"Yeah, I hate it for you." The biker then leaned down, picked up the phone's remains and hurled them over three lanes of traffic and into the bank parking lot. "I'm a dentist," he said. He reached into the pocket of his leather vest and threw what looked like a business card at the driver. "That's my card. You give me a call Monday morning and I'll be happy to fix what I'm about to do to your teeth." He reached for the door handle but the light changed. The Audi squealed away. The crowd cheered and the biker waved to everyone before he started his motorcycle.

"Now that's class, right there," James told Colton. "I gotta tell Britt about this." He left the whole story on her voicemail.

"Still not talking to you?" Colton asked.

"Aw, she'll come around once she hears I'm rolling in cash. It'll impress her when I cruise up on my Harley. She'll talk to me then. Now let's roll. Harvest time, C-note, there's money growing on trees."

They came in from the backside of the property, opposite of Britt's grandmother's, and pulled as close as they could to the clearing. James planned to chop down the plants, load them into the bed of the truck, and carry them back to the motel to gather the buds, like Finn suggested. Colton hesitated as James rolled back the tarp and grabbed the two rusty machetes.

"I'm not sure about this," he told James.

"Weed can do a lot of things, but it ain't gonna harvest itself," James answered. "Come on."

"Seems like I'm taking all the risk."

"How do you figure? It's my pot. I'll clean it, package it. Hell, I'll even sell it. All you gotta do is help me get it out of here. And set me up with some of those college potheads for customers. No problem."

"It's my truck. I'm driving. Back through the middle of town, with a load of full-grown marijuana plants in the back."

"We got the tarp."

"Say we do make it back to your motel, you gonna drag the things across the parking lot to your room? You know Gajendranath is watching you."

"Hmm." James leaned against the side of the truck. "I hadn't thought about that." He paused. "But Finn said—"

"Finn might not have your best interest in mind, ever think of that? You did wreck his grow operation at the motel, *and* you killed the first batch of clones he gave you. Not to mention the competition."

"Naw, Finn's cool, C-note. Besides, we're colleagues now. There's rules, honor, between growers. And once they pass the medical pot law in November, there'll be more business than me and Finn both can handle. We'll wait until it gets dark to move them into the room."

"I'm not doing it. I said I'd help, but you gotta come up with a better plan."

"C-note. Colton. My brother. Come on. If anything happens, I'll tell po-po it's my weed. I need you man."

"Nope." Colton shook his head and folded his arms across his chest.

Colton had been his best friend for as long as he could remember and he'd never once let him down. That college crap was already changing him. "Well alright, frat boy, you gonna offer some high education suggestion or just stand there and bitch like a girl?"

"Oh, I'm gonna bitch, you can count on it." Colton leaned into the truck, reached behind the driver's seat and came out with a box of plastic freezer bags, one-gallon size. He tossed the box toward James. It bounced against the door. "Put the buds in there," Colton said. "Then we can chop down the plants and either burn them or hide the stalks in the woods. Easier to transport."

James picked up the box and grinned. "I reckon we could vary from the plan a little bit."

"We'll put the baggies in garbage bags," Colton reached into the truck once again, "and put the garbage bags in these suitcases."

"I knew I let you hang around with me for a reason. Let's go."

They walked out of the trees and into the bright sun of the clearing. James shaded his eyes with his hand, visor style. He looked left, right, left and right again, then at Colton. "I thought we planted some close by?" he said.

Colton shrugged. "We came in from Granny's house when we planted, didn't we? Maybe your direction's off." He pointed his machete to the right. "Check that way, around the bend."

James started in that direction, Colton following a few steps behind. James stopped so suddenly that Colton bumped into him. A bare stalk, only four or five inches tall, poked from the ground at

James' feet. The top end of the stalk was white and pulpy, slanted at a sharp, forty-five-degree angle as if it had been cut. James lifted his machete, looked at the blade, then at the stem sticking out of the earth. There were a couple of narrow hack marks in the ground on one side of the stalk. "This ain't good, C-note," James mumbled.

They walked a few yards further and found the same scene repeated—the short stalk and hack marks in the dirt beside it. James bent down and placed the blade of his machete over the angled cut, then slowly lowered it to the ground, extending the line until the knife blade slipped neatly into the gash that already existed. "Shit, this ain't good at all," he repeated.

Colton stared at the stalk, then cast nervous glances into the trees in all directions. "What if the cops are hiding somewhere, waiting on us?"

James looked around. Heat waves shimmered above the weeds and thickets. Cicadas screamed from the surrounding trees. The air hung thick and humid, smelled like rust. No cop would sit out in this shit getting eat up by gnats and chiggers over a little weed. "Come on," he said. "Maybe they only found these."

"I think maybe I'll wait in the truck."

"No you won't." James hurried forward to where the next stalk should've been. Colton hesitated, then followed him slowly, his eyes scanning every bush and tree.

James looked down, but saw no plant. He didn't see a slashed stalk, either. Before him, a freshly dug hole had caved in on itself. James ran forward with Colton close behind now. When James stopped, Colton bumped into him again. James turned to face him, tapping the blade of the machete against his thigh.

"Look. Just look." James pointed the machete at another hole in the ground.

"Dude."

"Somebody jacked my weed, C-note." His body, everything about him beginning to deflate as his dream withered in the heat. "Jacked every damn bit of it."

Colton shook his head. "We gotta get out of here, James. I'm telling you, it's the cops. They're watching us, I can feel it. Probably going through the truck right now. They'll kick me out of school. My folks'll freak." He sucked in a shaky breath. "I could go to jail."

James shook his head, not believing what he saw, or what he *didn't* see. "Cops wouldn't steal weed. But somebody did, and I'll—"

"Steal it? Are you crazy?" Colton was yelling now. "This shit's illegal. A felony. Of course they wouldn't steal it, it's evidence."

James stared at Colton. It was obvious Colton was losing it. His eyes were wide, plenty of white showing. Breathing hard, chest heaving, panicked. "Damn it, C-note, you're gonna give yourself a coronary. They can't prove it's ours. And what difference does it make if they could? I got nothing. Nothing." He turned around in a slow, sarcastic circle, both arms outstretched. "Okay, po-po, you got me," he hollered to the trees, "come on out, now, you're scaring C-note. Finish me off. Come on."

James sank to his knees, rubbed his eyes with the heels of both hands, then shook his head slowly.

"Look," James' voice was calmer now. "There's no cops. We've been ripped off, I'm telling you. If it'll make you feel better, go on back to the truck. I'll check the rest of the spots just to make sure. Then we'll figure this out."

Colton nodded and turned back toward the truck. James made his way around the rest of the clearing. At each spot, he found the same thing and each time he felt the swirling dejection sucking him downward. What would he do? Gaj would throw him out of the motel in another week or two. He couldn't go back to his parents, they'd made that clear, and his money was gone. No Harley, no Xbox, no nothing. Not a dime to give Britt for *Survivor,* which meant no Brittany.

He completed the circle and was about to go down the path to the truck when he saw it—the voodoo tree. In a neat, organized circle around the base of the tree were all the Christmas balls. He walked over. The ornaments balanced in ascending rows, wider at the base and sloping up to the tree trunk. Cops wouldn't have done something like that. But who would have, who could've known? Was it a sign? He stared from the pile of decorations to the poppet they'd nailed to the tree and back again. What if they did it wrong, maybe he'd unleashed some sort of voodoo spell. He looked deeper into the woods. Late afternoon and the shade slipped toward darkness. Voodoo spells, that was just stupid. It didn't matter, the weed was gone and with it, his options. James raised the machete above his head in both hands and slammed it down on the Christmas decorations, over and over and over until the tiny pieces of red shards looked like a sacrament of glitter sprinkled around the base of the tree. It made him feel some better.

He dropped the machete in the bed of the truck and climbed in the passenger side.

"Well?" Colton asked as he started the truck.

"Got it all, every fucking plant."

"So, what's next?"

James closed his eyes and let his head fall back against the seat rest. What was next? He'd run out of options, really, there wasn't much he could do. He felt his stomach lurching, but fought the urge to throw up. Finally, he looked at Colton. He started to admit he didn't know, but no words sounded. He shrugged and sank deeper into the seat. "Just drive," he mumbled. "Take me back to the motel."

They rode in silence. Colton turned into the motel lot and parked. James eased out of the truck, slammed the door, and half-smiled back at Colton. "You okay?" Colton asked.

James shrugged. "All a part of growing up, you know? It's just . . . well, it's like that song you told me about, growing up means growing old, means dying. Ain't none of it fun."

James looked away, across the parking lot, beyond the glow of the traffic lights, off into the black distance. Why did everything, *everything*, have to be so damn hard? Every door he opened led to another brick wall. Was this it? Was this gonna be his life? If he could just catch a break, any break. After a minute he turned back to Colton and offered a weak smile. "Naw, I'm good, man. But hey, thanks, you know, for today and stuff."

"Listen, there's this big board at school, near the dorm. People post jobs on it, help wanted, day labor. Kinda like an old-school Craigslist. You could generate some cash, keep the motel room a while longer. Some of the professors even post ads looking for help with projects they're working on, might find something interesting. I'll take a look for you."

"Sure. I got beer in the cooler. Wanna hang?"

"Not tonight. There's a . . . a thing on campus. You gonna tell Finn?"

James sighed. "Yeah, guess I got to."

"Want me to come with?" Colton asked.

"Naw. Thanks, but I got it."

"Alright, then. See you, buddy."

James half-waved as Colton drove away. A *thing*. Sure.

James trudged up the stairs, paused in front of Finn's door, took a deep breath, blew it out in a long sigh, then knocked. The door eased open from the weight of his knock and James' heart sunk. Finn's entire grow operation: the lights, the hydroponics, nutrient tubes, timers, fans, weed—all of it, was gone. The room looked like any other room in the extended stay hotel. The beds were back and the nightstand sat neatly between them. Two thread-bare upholstered chairs—one wedged in the corner, the other at the small desk—had replaced the plastic pool chairs from before. The trash was gone, the room quiet except for the air-conditioning unit humming beneath the window. Finn, too, had disappeared: no sign, no trace, nothing.

James noticed a piece of paper taped to the mirror and limped to it, the barely healed wound in his foot suddenly aching again. On the paper, printed in left-leaning caps, was a note from Finn:

SORRY KID, NOTHING PERSONAL, JUST BUSINESS. BETTER JU-JU NEXT TIME—FINN

James left the note taped to the glass, left the door standing open, and sulked back to his room, went inside, opened his last Bud Lite, and sent Britt a text. *911—Please Call.* He flipped through the TV channels, nothing interesting. Another text. More channels. Left her a voice mail. Where could she be on a Saturday night? He walked outside. Cars scattered through the parking lot, but no activity. He heard music and followed the sound around the corner and into the courtyard. The Mexicans were finishing their barbecue, drinking bootleg Barrilito beer, laughing and talking. They didn't notice James. Back in his room, he sent Brittany one last text, turned off the TV and the lights, and stretched out on the bed. The room felt even smaller than usual.

17

Over the Moon

It could be any day now. The doctor told Trudy to limit her activity, stay close to home, get plenty of rest, which she did. She was propped in the bed, watching *Entertainment Tonight*. Livingston took her a grilled cheese sandwich and the peanut butter and banana milkshake he'd picked up on the way home.

She patted the bed. "Sit with me," she said.

"Maybe later," Livingston answered. "I should do the dishes."

"They'll wait. Come on."

"No. I need . . . I thought . . . maybe later."

Trudy stared. It made Livingston uneasy, but no tics or twitches appeared. In fact, there'd been none all day. He'd been staying in the spare bedroom the past two weeks. Trudy had complained about his tossing, turning, and mumbling all night long, and he wanted her to be comfortable. It didn't help, not for Livingston anyway. The past two nights, he'd not slept at all. Instead, he lay on the bed, rigid, arms at his side, both palms flattened against his thighs, listening to the sounds inside and outside of his head. They were random, disconnected, and unexplainable: the occasional jingling of a bell that sounded like the one on his bike as a child; a monotone beep that lasted eighteen seconds—D sharp, he determined; bits of conversations. And there were voices: The Lion from the Wizard of Oz, Ed Sullivan. John Wayne, and early Barbara Walters, from when she struggled with *r*'s. Other voices he didn't recognize. Sometimes, they talked among themselves; other times they made suggestions, offered advice. Once in a while, they'd ask him questions. Sometimes he answered, sometimes he didn't. When he tried to join the conversations, sometimes they'd let him, other times they'd ignore him. Once when he tried, Barbara Walters told him it was "wude to intewwupt." Completely unpredictable, and even though they kept him awake, he found the sounds and voices, all of them, strangely calming.

That morning, just after sunrise, John Wayne said, "I think you should lose the tics, partner, that little buckaroo will be here any day now," and Livingston did. He'd kept his hands firmly at his sides all day and had only checked the light switches seven times.

"You feeling okay?" Trudy asked. "You've been, I don't know, different today."

"Fine, I'm fine. Excellent. Thinking, lots of thinking. That's all."

"I mean, you've been so nervous and jumpy. From the start, with the pregnancy and all." She rubbed her belly and smiled. "And, well, it seemed like the further along I was, the more it bothered you. You gotta admit, you've been acting kind of . . . well, nutty. I was worried you didn't want this baby. Our child."

The Lion said, "Sneaking up on me, eh?"

Livingston nodded. "I wasn't prepared, not at first. Nervous, very nervous. Yes."

"I know, Liv, I know. You're worried about a job, about money. We'll be fine. Something'll turn up soon, I know it. And I've been such a pill, but you've been great. Really great, Liv. You've taken such good care of me in spite of . . . you know, the flaky stuff. You're going to be the best father, a great dad."

Barbara Walters said, "A man cannot be made comfowtable without his own appwoval."

Livingston sighed. "Thank you, Trudy. I think I will go outside and sit on the porch for a while now."

"Okay, Liv. You know, you could try sleeping in here tonight. I won't mind."

"Yes, perhaps." Livingston kissed the top of her forehead, then went outside and settled into the porch rocker.

Darkness crept upward, first the color of grapes, then of plums, nibbling the light from the eastern sky, as it tugged a curtain of blue-black nightfall along with it. The day had been hot for September, but as night fell, its coolness hinted of turning leaves and ripening pumpkins. The moonflowers Trudy planted in the spring scented the air. Soon, the moon edged the horizon, blooming bright, its fullness both imposing and imperative. Livingston traced the rising arc, and for an instant, the only sounds he heard came from the world outside his brain, the sudden clarity opening a space for reflection, both forward and back.

Two hundred, thirty-nine thousand, two hundred and twenty-seven miles away and receding slightly each year. One day it would be gone, spinning into oblivion, but in July of '69, Armstrong and Aldrin walked there, making it real, vicariously attainable. Livingston saw no man in the moon now. The Sea of Tranquility, though, he saw that. They walked there, their footsteps remained, testament, marking the event. Something tangible saying yes, they *had* been there. Livingston imagined what Armstrong and Aldrin must have felt. Briefly felt it himself, even. They must have been terrified, so far away from home.

What had he done? Who had he become? Who might he one day be? Son. Husband? Father? Such vague notions. He understood the biology, but nothing more. Once, he knew, but somehow that knowledge had spiraled away from him.

And now? Now the baby was almost here. Now he'd agreed to sell the land, the land he never told Trudy about, the land his father left to him, the last thing connecting Livingston to the man he never really knew, the only real and concrete thing he might one day leave for his coming child. And for what? Hope? Opportunity? Security? A future for his family, his child? Those were only more abstractions. What then? Money? It certainly made those abstractions possible, probable even. Wasn't that a more important thing than a piece of land for his child? Then why had *his* father left it to him? What did it mean? Could it be the giving itself? Or was it in the dirt, the earth itself? Evidence that yes, someone *had* been here. A link to the past, maybe? Something in his father felt it important, necessary that Livingston have the land. Livingston couldn't find the answers he so wanted and it frightened him, not so much for himself, but for his child. What could he offer a child? A good father, a great dad, Trudy had said. What did that even mean? There were no owner's manuals, no directions, no neat columns in balance sheets for recording the credits and debits from a parent to a child. No finite accruals, no amortization table, no profit and loss statement to measure whatever he might give his child.

A thin cloud floated by, halving the moon and blocking the Sea of Tranquility from Livingston's view. Another followed, this one larger, blanking the moon completely, the only reminder of its presence the faint glow around the fringes of the cloud.

The sounds returned, then the voices. A jumble at first, bits and pieces, a word here, a phrase there. Livingston pulled at his ear, shook his head. One voice rose above the din, and Livingston heard it clearly—John Wayne again. "Well partner," he drawled, "courage is being scared to death but saddling up anyway."

Livingston went inside and looked in on Trudy, who was sleeping. He undressed and stood beside the bed for a moment, watching the rise and fall of her breathing, of her belly, then padded through the house checking the light switches. In the spare bedroom, he lay on the bed, hands at his side, eavesdropping.

Sally liked the drawing, but he wasn't sure what it meant, or what, exactly, he should do with it. Obviously, it meant *something*. Kat was certainly excited about it, about finding her flowers. He had never really been a flower guy. Not an art guy, either. Sure, pictures hung on his walls, but only because the decorator put them there. He was pretty sure one or two of them were of flowers, or at least had flowers in the print. Picking up tones of the paint scheme, accenting a hue in the sofa's fabric, the decorator said, but they didn't mean anything. Kat's drawing was personal, intimate even, and she gave the original to him. That made him uneasy. He sensed the gift was Kat's way of letting him know it was, indeed, a relationship. That meant he probably should take more interest, ask more questions. But, whenever they were together, it never occurred to him that he should ask those types of questions. He'd learned long ago not to talk about his work, so out of habit, he assumed she wouldn't want to talk much about hers either. He'd try to find some balance.

When he came home from dinner, he left the drawing on the counter. The next morning after breakfast, he stuck it to the fridge with a magnet, but then, each time he passed through the kitchen, he found himself stopping to look. Finally, he figured it out. The fridge was all wrong—hanging the drawing there reminded him Kat was younger than him. There wasn't that much difference in their age, but hanging the drawing on the fridge made him uneasy all the same. He took it down and promised himself he'd buy a frame on the way back from meeting the auctioneer.

The building that housed Landon Auction and Realty was one hundred and two years old. It sat beside the railroad tracks, a tin roof-covered porch ran the length of the building. Every Fourth of July, the patriotic leaned over the porch railing for a view of the passing parade. The building's original handmade bricks were intact but deteriorating. On the wall nearest the railroad tracks, traces of red dust floated to the floor each time a train passed. It had a rustic appeal.

Inside, the building had been divided into three sections: a large open area where they held everything from general merchandise auctions to antique sales once a month; a second, smaller room for storage piled high with what looked like junk to Sally; and beyond that, the office area. The door was cracked open, and Sally rapped with his knuckle. "Anybody home?"

"Salvador Hinson. Come on in." Rick Landon swung open the door.

Landon was a salesman, a good one. Sally appreciated that about him. Reasonably honest, too, as auctioneers go. Sure, he'd take the occasional bid that wasn't really there and he had a tendency to talk too much between lots, but that was because he looked out for his clients. He made sure he got the highest bid possible, whether it was a family heirloom, a forty-year-old set of worn out pots and pans, or a tract of land. And when it came to selling real estate at auction, Landon was the only choice.

"Nice building you got here," Sally said as he settled into a chair. "What is it, seven, eight-thousand square feet?"

"Seventy-four hundred. Yeah, it works. Town's on me every week to spruce it up, though. Hell, every time the train comes by, it feels like the thing's gonna cave in on me. Ain't worth what it'd cost to fix it the way they want."

"Come on. Right here on the main road, lots of through traffic, this place is worth plenty."

"On the tax records, maybe."

"Ever thought of selling?" Sally asked.

"Love to, but you can't get financing. Nothing's up to code, wiring's bad, roof leaks, no heat and the AC sucks. God knows what all's buried underneath the parking lot out back." Landon turned to the wall behind him and pinched the bricks, then let the dust crumble on his desk. "Train comes by, this shit flakes off on the floor. Every time, six times a day. Don't know how many during the night. One day it'll fall, then I'll sell the lot."

"Least you got a plan."

"Speaking of plans, we're auction ready. Advertising's done, I've already sent my mailers. Got it on the website, too." Landon opened a file folder and slid a list of names and phone numbers toward Sally. "That's my hot list. Seven buyers with good money, all of 'em qualified already. Yes sir, we got us an auction."

Sally looked over the list. Southern Exposure, his guy, was the second name. "Seven, huh? My lucky number."

"The economy's weeded out a lot—tire-kickers mostly. But they's still plenty of money around. Seven don't sound like many, but when you're offering a prime piece of property like yours, you only need two." Landon winked. "One if you know what you're doing, and trust me Sally, I know what I'm doing. I can sell pig shit to a hog farmer."

"Yeah, I remember. You got in my pocket a few years back."

"That's right. How'd that deal work out for you?"

"We did alright."

"Good, good. I like for everybody to make money. Keeps it circulating."

Sally glanced at the list again, then handed it to Landon. "Who's number six? S-I-N?"

"Sugeree Indian Nation. They just got official status, and they're looking for land. Wanna build a casino. They're my top player. I like getting in the government's pocket and the Indians like spending it."

"Ethel will love a casino in her back yard."

"That woman's a pistol, ain't she?"

"Yeah she is. Well," Sally leaned forward, "anything I can do?"

"I think we've got everything covered, just waiting on the twenty-first. My crew'll come out the day before, set up a tent, some tables for the buyer's packets, bidder registration, all the official stuff. I made up poster boards with plat maps and topos, refreshments, even hired a band to play. Hell, far as I'm concerned, it's a done deal. The property's sold, the auction's just to decide who owns it."

"You doing this on the property?"

"Naw, Ethel's backyard. It's easy to find, nice and open, and well . . . Ethel told me to. Said she wanted to keep an eye on things." Landon shook his head. "How'd you hook up with her?"

"Long story. Let's just say me, her, and Livingston Carr found ourselves in kind of a Mexican standoff. Figured it was in everybody's best interest if we partnered up to get this dirt moved."

"Carr. I've done my share of howling at the moon, you know? But damn, is that feller a nut case, or what? I meet all kinds in this business. Did an auction once for this little man two counties over who was trying to raise money for a penile implant. Sold for grieving widows and heart broke divorcees, shady lawyers, sold the personal property for a retired pro wrestler a couple years back. Nothing beats Livingston Carr. Nothing." Landon paused, looking thoughtful. "You don't think he might cause any problems with this do you? You know, signing the deed or anything?"

"He'll be alright. Me and Ethel will make sure of it."

"That's all you had to say. That I can handle."

"So we're set then, the twenty-first. Do you need us there?"

"Yeah, you'll need to sign some paperwork. And Carr will need to sign the Offer to Purchase contract to make it official. You know, binding. And if you could keep an eye on him just in case, it'd be great."

"No problem. We'll see you then."

Sally picked up three frames on the way home. He didn't write down the measurements for the drawing, so he had to estimate. It took him an hour to get the drawing centered in the matting and a few minutes more to attach the hanging wire. He spent the rest of the afternoon trying different locations around his house before settling on the wall facing his front door. If—when he had Kat over, it'd be the first thing she saw as she entered the room. That'd make her happy. Now that it was framed and in the front room instead of on the fridge, it only reminded him of Kat, not of her, or his, age.

Working on the picture occupied his hands, but Sally's mind kept returning to what Landon said about Livingston. He would be okay, wouldn't he? Know your customer, Sally kept thinking. Technically, Livingston was a partner, not a customer, but that only made knowing him more critical. Sally didn't know as much about Livingston as he should, but it'd have to do. Livingston was odd, had more tics than a watchmaker's cabinet, but he wasn't stupid. No, he'd be fine. Sally believed it. He had to at this point.

Kᴀᴛ sᴀᴛ ᴀᴛ her desk, surrounded. A cluttered path lead from her door to her chair. Since finding the flowers, the mess in her office had expanded exponentially. Essays, journals, a heavily dog-eared copy of *Bartram's Travels,* other reference books, rested on every surface. Her notes lay scattered in piles on her desk, the floor, the credenza, and she'd taped more notes and drawings to the walls. There was order in the chaos. She could find whatever she might be looking for in a moment, each stack of ephemera represented a thread with specific, related meaning, the notes now followed a logical, linear path only she could recognize, all sufficiently highlighted, all meticulously documented with footnotes and citation information. A sure sign of progress.

But Kat wasn't making any progress. Too many distractions. Her classes had become an annoyance, her students petty and needy. Leaderlick kept pressuring her for a summary, at least an abstract, of her research for an upcoming presentation he had with the Academic

Council and Board of Trustees, one that delineated how her research supported and advanced the Twelve Point Strategic Revision Plan. Aldus Culpepper, whom she rarely talked with before, now found it necessary to drop by her office to *chat* almost daily. At first, she appreciated his interest, and the scent of cherry blend pipe tobacco that floated around him, but she soon realized he wasn't really interested in her research so much as using the visits as an excuse to avoid *his* students. If he came by at regular intervals, she could have planned for it, scheduled a trip to the bathroom, to the copy room, or on a short walk—anything to avoid him, but she detected no predictability in his appearances. She suspected an emerging allergy to the pipe tobacco.

These things she could work around, all part of the academic routine. Her biggest distraction had nothing to do with her research. Well, it did, but only indirectly. Frequently, she found herself staring at her notes, reading and rereading the same sentence. When one of the other interruptions occurred, she had to force herself back to the same sentence. It was sophomoric, bordering on silly. She couldn't stop thinking about Sally. Something he said, the strength of his chin, the color of his eyes. But why? She wondered. Why him? Why now? He wasn't her type—older, not an academic—but then again, she didn't really have a type. She didn't have much experience in the relationship area, none really, but she was no school-girl, either. Could it be because the marriage questions from her mom and sister had increased so much the past couple years? Maybe. It shouldn't, but she wasn't getting any younger and she'd always assumed she would marry at some point, hadn't she? Was that where this was going? Had Sally even thought anything like that? They'd been seeing each other for a while now, but Kat didn't know what was next, or even if there was a next. She trusted research, books, academics; those things she knew. She liked spending time with Sally, and no matter how much she tried to push it from her mind, she thought about him, about *them,* a lot. But unlike her research—methodical steps, controlled variables, observed reactions, then analyzing the results—Kat had no methodology for whatever this thing with Sally was, and the lack of control fed her uncertainties.

Those uncertainties distracted her while she tried to work, and now the two areas of her life had started to overlap, which made her question herself even more. The drawing she made of the flowers, for instance. Had giving it to Sally been a mistake? Too soon? A copy would have been better, safer. The original, the way she'd signed it, made such a production out of it, as if it were art, was too personal at this point. Or maybe not. How could you tell, how did people negotiate these... these... *things*? She didn't really have a solid point of reference. They'd been out fifteen, maybe twenty times over the summer. Should she consider quantity or quality? The quality was there, even the first time Sally bought her lunch after she spilled tea on him. It had only gotten better.

Still, she lacked any real point of comparison, had no control group for reference. There was Maxwell, during grad school, but Kat knew that hardly constituted a relationship. They were, what did the students call it? Friends with benefits, a hookup. Necessity sex, something to relieve the pressure of homework, projects, research, theses. A lack of any meaningful social interaction outside of the academic work. She and Max never *did* anything together, never went on an actual date, no dinners, no movies, no walks in the park. No feelings other than biological urges, and she was always in complete control of the situation. How was she to know where this thing with Sally was going?

Kat knew where she wanted it to go, at least the next, more-immediate step, but Sally'd been the perfect gentleman so far. Damn it. It had to be the drawing. Made him feel things were moving too fast. Sure, they'd kissed, and kissed passionately. She'd rarely kissed Maxwell at all, the thought of it made her shudder. But when she and Sally kissed, she felt . . . *things*. It was like she was there, in the moment, and at the same time she wasn't. The feel of his arms around her, his hand in the small of her back, drawing her to him, the touch of his lips to hers, gentle yet confident. So confident. But her mind . . . when Sally kissed her, her mind blanked. Completely. She couldn't *think*. When the kisses ended, she had to remind herself to breathe. She held no misconceptions that Sally was anything close to perfect. She didn't think he'd hung the moon or anything as foolish, but she'd never felt this way before either.

Kat shook her head and a shiver transcended her body. She blushed, felt the warmth spreading up her neck to her cheeks. Get back to work, she told herself. She picked up the nearest essay and skimmed to the last highlighted section. As she opened a file on the computer, Culpepper bounded into her office.

"Katherine. Good, you're in."

She sighed. "Aldus, I'm really busy." At least he didn't plop down in the chair as usual.

"When are you going back to that property?" He was more purposeful than usual.

"Where we found the flowers?"

"Yes, of course, of course. You must take me with you. I need soil samples."

Aldus pulled on his pipe, which he clenched so tightly Kat could see the muscles along his jaw flexing. It wasn't lit and it made a series of sucking sounds.

"It'll be next week at the earliest. I need to compile my notes. But . . ."

"What day?"

"I don't know what day. Dr. Culpepper, I have to . . ."

"It was my budget money, you remember. You must take me with you. I insist."

Kat rolled her eyes, but Culpepper didn't seem to notice. She wondered if being an ass was part of his nature, or if it came with tenure. Either way, she knew he had a point about the money, and since she didn't have tenure, and she'd seen Culpepper and Leaderlick having lunch together several times, she didn't have much choice. Still, it was her project.

"What interest do you have—"

"I don't know yet," he interrupted. "I can't be certain until lab reports come back and I get those soil samples."

"I took a small soil sample on our first visit. If that's all you need . . ." Kat shrugged, then reached for a pile of notes and reports at the far right of her desk. ". . . I have the report with pH numbers right here."

"No, no. I need a core sample, not surface soil. Something several feet down. The topography measurements indicate—" Aldus cleared his throat, "—are interesting. I need those samples. I'm free this afternoon. Tomorrow as well."

"I have class." Kat gathered herself. "No. I'm going next week. I'll let you know."

"I could go on my own."

"I wouldn't. The girl said her grandmother fired shots at some folks she saw on that property a couple years back. I don't think the woman is overly fond of you to begin with."

Aldus paused. "I see. Well, the lab results from that bone won't be in for a few more days. I suppose I can wait."

"Good. I'll send you an email once I know the date."

"I prefer we establish something specific." He moved a stack of papers from the chair beside Kat's desk, sat down and pulled his phone from his pocket. "Yes. My calendar's clear next week. Of course, I have my classes, but I can cancel those. What works?"

Kat sighed and brought her calendar up on the screen. "Let's see . . . I have the twenty-first open."

"Excellent. I'll meet you in the faculty lot at nine sharp."

"Make it eleven-thirty. I have a morning class, too."

Culpepper flashed her a look of disdain, then entered the date and time in his phone. "Very well, eleven-thirty."

He left without saying good-bye, or thanking her, and Kat returned to the essay. She found the section, but couldn't concentrate. Instead, she picked up the PDF copy of the Schweinitz sunflower drawing and wondered what Sally would think of Culpepper. Wouldn't be impressed. In fact, unlike others she'd noticed, nothing about academia impressed Sally very much. When she told him about Leaderlick's devotion to the Twelve Point Strategic Plan, Sally called it a Twelve Step Program. No, Sally had another kind of intelligence, one she found much more intriguing than anyone she knew in academia. Seductive, in a way. Sexy, even. A sly smile etched its way across Kat's face. Culpepper or his insistent behavior wasn't worth mentioning to Sally. She had other, more important things to bring up next time she saw him.

18

A Job to Do

Images flickered on the TV screen, but no sound. *CSI, Toddlers and Tiaras.* Boring, hard to follow, stupid. *Dancing with the Stars.* Please. PBS and the chick channel. No way. James ate the last Pop Tart from the box, flipped the channel to TruTV then banged on the side of the set. Still no sound.

"I'm dying here," he said to the walls, but they didn't offer any suggestions. He checked his phone for messages, but found none. Didn't matter, they'd probably cut it off any day now, it'd been two months since he sent a payment. He'd paid it more recently than anything else—priorities mattered—but he was down to less than a hundred bucks.

More channels—ESPN, Versus, TNT . . . James threw the remote at the screen. When it hit, the sound came in, but the channel switched to CNN. He retrieved the remote, but it no longer worked so he turned the TV off and fell back on the bed. He checked his phone again. Since he'd started classes at the college, Colton would sometimes take hours before responding to a text, days to a call. When James did talk to him, Colton always sounded busy or distracted. Nothing from Britt, either, but James didn't expect anything from her. She'd told him not to call or text again until he had a job and could take her someplace nice to eat, Applebee's or Golden Corral, not McDonalds or the taco-burrito truck in the far corner of the Wal-Mart parking lot. After a half dozen more calls and twice as many texts, James got the point.

He looked at the pile of fliers and index cards on the nightstand. Colton had collected them from information boards at the college and had brought them over a few days earlier, but James hadn't bothered to sort through them. Why not, he thought now, I'm too fat to fly and the truck won't start . . . hell, I don't even have a truck. He shuffled through the fliers first. *Need Gutters Cleaned, contact Prof Nathan.* Nope, didn't like heights. *Chemistry Lab Custodian—Be A Beaker Bather!* Had potential. A chemistry lab would have chemicals, right? Could be fun. But what's a beaker? James sat it to the side. The rest of the fliers only produced one more possibility—dog walker. He thought he was overqualified, but held out the ad all the same.

The index cards didn't offer much, either. James figured if they wouldn't spring for a color flier, any job they had probably wouldn't pay much. He was right. Most of them were from students, free math tutoring for help with a psychology class, wanting rides home for fall break, a request for someone, anyone to write four papers for English 110 this semester in exchange for *World of Warcraft* lessons. The last index card had way too much writing on it, but something caught James' eye before he threw it away. At the bottom of the card, in neat letters: Native American Site. He read the rest of the message, then reached for his phone.

"Hey, I'm calling about this ad for a research laborer.

"Shovel? Oh yeah, Mexican backhoe, I know how to operate one of those.

"No, I'm not racist. Why?

"Dig a hole? How much experience do I need?

"Oh. Naw, I'm kinda between jobs right now. I worked with . . . uh . . . plants before.

"Physical ailments? What kind of question is that?

"Oh, no, I'm good. I got shot in the foot a couple months back, but it's all healed up, now. Just got a little puckered scar where the bullet went through, that's all.

"Uh, about that . . . is there any way you can pick me up? I've got my license, but I'm having some transportation issues right now.

"Yeah, in Mason. At the Budget-Tel Motel.

"I'm James. James Flowers. I'll be out front, near the lobby.

"Yeah, I got a question. It says Native American Site on your card. Like Indians and shit . . . sorry, Indians and stuff?

"Un-huh. I see. I just thought . . . naw, it's no big deal. I'll see you on the twenty-first."

As soon as he hung up, James sent Brittany a text, telling her the good news. He still didn't expect any response, even told her not to worry about it, that he'd get in touch once he got paid.

He grabbed a beer and the plastic chair and went outside. It was a nice night, the air cooling, and a sliver of moon tilted in the sky that reminded James of the white part under his fingernails, next to the skin. After a few minutes, Bicycle Bob rode into the parking lot and rang his bell when he saw James.

"Bicycle Bob, what's shaking?" James asked. "You're out and about kinda late, aren't you?"

"Bingo night, but they wouldn't let me play." He shrugged. "I felt lucky, too."

"Hate to hear that for you. Know what you mean, though. Had a little luck tonight myself." James winked. Bicycle Bob bounced his bike from side to side between his legs.

"Luck's good. Wanna go to bingo? We can ride double."

"Naw, not that kind of luck. I got a job."

"You working right now?"

"Un-uh. Next week. It ain't much, digging some holes and wheel barrowing dirt for this dude at the college, but it's a start."

"That's honest. Important, too. I could retire myself, but I like to contribute. Like to keep something in front of me, keep me going. When I was about this high—" Bicycle Bob leaned over and held his hand a few feet above the pavement, "—my daddy told me I could be anything I wanted, could grow up to be president even, if I worked hard. That's the American way. I believed him, too, that's why I keep working."

"You think you might be president one day? I'd vote for you."

Bob looked at the ground for a full minute, then slowly raised his eyes to meet James'. "I think my daddy might've lied about that part, James, but I don't hold it against him. I've studied on it a great deal. He didn't mean to lie, not on purpose. In the old days, maybe, and my daddy was old, but no, not everybody can grow up to be president. What my daddy meant was just grow up to be who you are. Trying to be somebody else, well, that'll make you crazy. So, I'm Bicycle Bob. See?"

"Yeah, I kinda do, Bob. Say, you want a beer?"

"No thank you. I have work to do." He climbed back on the seat and paused. "Congratulations about the job. Just be careful around those college types. Some of them get in those books and disappear."

"I will," James shouted as Bob pedaled away.

He went inside and started to open another beer, but didn't. Get some sleep, he decided. Bicycle Bob was good people, he thought as he peeled off his T-shirt, and smarter than folks gave credit. *Disappear,* he was right and James knew exactly what he meant. It wasn't just in college, though. It could happen to anybody. Walking around like zombies, there and not there. Hell, most people around town didn't *see* Bicycle Bob, or anybody else like him. *Like him . . .* James stopped before turning out the light and looked at his reflection in the mirror. *Like me,* he suddenly realized.

It took him a long time to fall asleep.

NOTHING SIGNIFICANT EVER happened in Mason, or the surrounding county, which either contributed to or detracted from its appeal, depending on point of view. Because of that, Ethel knew it didn't take much to draw a crowd, all you needed was to create an event.

When Rick Landon had an auction, he made sure it was an event. And this auction, *her* auction, would be *the* event of the year, possibly the decade, in Mason. Something significant. People would talk about it for years, long after she was in the ground. The last large tract of land in the western part of the county and Ethel Combs had it auctioned, they'd say. Never thought she had it in her to pull off something like that. The sale would pad her bank accounts, sure, and make a nice parting gift for Brittany, one that would see her through her life, too. But it was more than that to Ethel. Call it a legacy, call it one last thumbing of her nose at everyone—her kids, her nosey neighbors, the assholes at the DMV for taking her driver's license—and they'd remember her when she was gone.

Yes, Landon's name was out front, but she'd been plenty involved behind the scenes. She made him give her his "hot list," the seven buyers most interested in the property, and she did her homework. Southern Exposure, they were Sally's buyers. Their money was good and they had already sketched preliminary plans for a development on the property. The Sugeree Nation wanted to start a casino, bingo parlor at the least. Ethel didn't care, she'd be dead before it opened. They had a pocketful of government money, and that was all that mattered.

The big mega-church near Statler wanted it for some cock-eyed religious theme park. She didn't trust them at all, but that church had nearly five thousand members and a fat bank account. Their head pastor, the one they called Preacher Mike, had been over several times. Ethel suggested his church handle the concessions for the sale, offered to let them keep the profit. Landon thought it was a great idea. Having the church involved would bring out a lot of tire-kickers as he called them, the curious. Which was fine, the big money players didn't like for others at the auction to know they were bidding, a big crowd made discretion possible.

Three of the four remaining groups, Landon referred to as minor players. They'd push the bid, keep everyone honest, but would probably get weak when the numbers climbed. Two business partners with 1031 exchange funds to burn, a family itching to invest a recent inheritance, a young developer who came on the Mason building scene late and wanted to catch up but wouldn't be able to leverage enough money to win.

As auction day neared, Ethel felt good, better than she'd felt in years. She hired two young men from the Home Depot parking lot and had them spend two full days working in her yard, making sure everything looked just right. She stood beneath the pin oak in the back and gazed over everything while she sipped her rum and coke. The dog sprawled at her feet, gnawing his bone. She leaned down to scratch his ears and he craned his neck upward, then to the left so she could reach beneath his right ear.

"It's a beautiful thing, pooch," she told him. "After this, I can die a happy woman." The dog wagged its tail and tilted his head in the other direction, but Ethel stopped scratching and started toward the house. The dog followed. When she opened the screen door, he whimpered. "I don't allow dogs in my house," she scolded.

The dog hung its head for a moment, then raised it to look in the direction of the trees. He whimpered again and turned back to Ethel. Suddenly, Ethel thought she knew what the dog meant. "You know, don't you?" She looked at the woods, then at the dog. "Those woods are your home, is that it? You know something's about to happen." She rubbed his head, then laughed. "Hell-fire, listen at me. I'm a senile old woman. Getting soft in my old age. You don't think no such a thing, do you? You're just a mutt." The dog's tail wagged. "Well, shit. Come on." She climbed the last step, then held the screen door open for the dog. He hesitated at first, then bounded over the threshold. "I guess you *can* teach an old dog a new trick." Ethel laughed.

SALLY QUIT DEER hunting years ago. He could name several reasons: getting up in the dead of night, leaving a warm bed to sit for hour after freezing hour in a tree stand, then if he did kill one, dragging it out of the woods, field dressing, taking it to be processed . . . not worth the effort. But really, it boiled down to only two things. First, all the development in the county had swallowed the best spots and he refused to get up any earlier and drive for miles just to hunt. Maybe that reason led to the other, maybe it didn't, but at one point the kill, even the hunting, no longer held his interest. The challenge didn't work for him any longer.

He'd been just a kid, thirteen, the first time his uncle rousted him for the morning's hunt. Sally grumbled, half asleep as he layered on thermals and wool socks, heavy corduroys and flannel. His excitement rose as he lumbered down the hall, his arms and legs stiff and awkward under the weight of his hunting clothes. When he reached the kitchen, it reminded him a little of Christmas morning—still dark outside and the light above the sink bathing the room in an inviting light, the sizzle and pop of pork frying, the smell of coffee brewing thick in the room. His father sat in his usual spot, wearing only unbuttoned work pants and his worn T-shirt, his usual neat hair unkempt from sleep. His uncle stood at the stove. They both nodded when he came in, but didn't say anything; the way men do, Sally thought. His uncle spooned grits, sausage, and scrambled eggs into a plate and sat it steaming in front of him, then poured him his first cup of black coffee. The coffee was bitter, tasted awful, but the food, which was the same thing he had most mornings, was somehow better than ever before.

They ate in silence and with economy, only the sounds of forks clinking against the plates. When they finished, his father cleared the dishes to the sink. "Wish I could go with you, Sally," he said, "but I got business to tend to later this morning. Good luck. Try not to shoot your uncle. Now I'm going back to bed." Sally answered yes sir and followed his uncle, who had already gathered their rifles and hunting vests, to the truck.

They used flashlights to find their way to the tree stands. At the first one, his uncle cast the beam up the ladder steps and onto the small, homemade platform twenty feet above. "I'll shine the light for you. When you get settled in, haul your rifle up with the rope like I showed you. Now I'll be a couple hundred yards that way." He pointed to the right with the barrel of his gun. "Know what you're shooting at before you pull the trigger." He looked to the east, then at Sally. "Sun'll be up in another hour or so, you ready? You awake?"

Sally nodded and started up the ladder. He had a little trouble climbing from the ladder onto the platform, but managed to slide around and get comfortable, his back resting against the tree and his feet dangling below him. He pulled the rope hand over hand until he could grab his rifle.

"All set?" his uncle called.

"Yep."

"Go ahead and load up, then. If you fall asleep, your ass'll end up on the ground with a broke neck, or worse, so don't. And stay in the stand until I come back for you. It'll be a couple hours after daybreak."

"What if I gotta pee?" Sally asked.

"Don't think about it. Unload, lower the rifle first and climb down if you gotta go. But don't think about it. Now, I'll be back later. Happy hunting."

It was all Sally could think about, but he waited until the light from his uncle's flashlight disappeared before climbing down, relieving himself, then back up again.

The world around him began to gray, then lighten to a gauzy white. The clatter of the birds and smaller animals pinged from every direction, unafraid of Sally's being there among them. A squirrel perched only a few feet from him on the next branch, birds flitted so close he could have touched them had he only reached out his hand. Sally was lost in it, a part of it, so much so that for several minutes he didn't notice the five does grazing in the small clearing eighty yards in front of him. When he did, he nearly dropped his rifle. It's early in the season, his uncle had told him the night before, let the does pass. There'll be a buck close by, be patient.

Sally raised the rifle and scanned the brush around the clearing through the gun's scope, but saw nothing. He waited, staring at the female deer as they worked their way across the opening. The squirrel started barking and Sally found a few nuts and a stick on the platform, which he threw at the squirrel until it jumped to another branch. When he looked back at the clearing, his breath caught in his throat. Antlers. He trained the scope on the spot to be certain. A six pointer, taking cautious steps closer to the edge of the clearing, eyeing the does, its nostrils flaring as it scented the air. Sally waited with the butt of the rifle against his shoulder, the scope's crosshairs locked on the buck. He could hear his own heart thumping, feel it in his temples. A few more steps, come on . . . come on. The sweat on his palms made his gloves damp and uncomfortable. He readjusted his grip, sighted again. The buck's head and neck poked from the brush, looking left, then right. Another step. One, two more and he'd have a shot.

The animal made a small jump, then four or five quick steps and he was in full view, nothing between him and Sally. Sally's gun barrel wavered, the crosshairs jerking back and forth across the buck, below him, above him, too far in front, then behind. Sally forced himself to take a deep breath, focus, but the gun felt as if it weighed a hundred pounds or more. Finally, he steadied the sights on a spot just behind the deer's shoulder and squeezed.

The force of the gun's kick startled Sally, bruised his shoulder. The sounds of the forest stopped, only the echo of the rifle blast rolled through the trees. The buck and the does, white tails flagging, disappeared into the brush unharmed, his shot high and right. Sally didn't care. He'd never felt more excited in his life, never imagined he could feel the way he did when he first saw the deer, when he pulled the trigger. The animals were gone, but his hands still shook, his heart still pounded.

For years, the same feeling engulfed him when he hunted. His hand grew steadier, his patience stronger, and his shot more true, but the exhilaration remained. Then, without explanation, the feeling left him. He found himself making excuses not to go, and his trips dwindled to only a few times a season. The last time he'd hunted, he'd seen the biggest buck ever, twelve points, well over two hundred pounds. The shot couldn't have been easier, only about sixty yards, no brush, no obstacles, no wind. Sally never shouldered his rifle, content to watch through his field glasses as the deer grazed. His rifle had not been out of the gun case since that trip.

It wasn't that he'd lost the heart for killing, it was never that in the first place, and he still loved being outdoors. The excitement, the intensity of that one moment, had disappeared. He and Bill had hunted together when they first started their business. He missed that, missed Bill, but not the hunting itself. They'd both stopped at about the same time. At first, business was spotty, the real-estate deals small, which allowed more time to hunt. As the deals grew, Sally noticed he'd get the same sort of feeling when he first scouted a potential real-estate deal, the same excitement, the same anticipation hunting once provided. The stakes were higher, the prey more elusive, the chance of loss, even if it was only financial, was real. A full bank account was a lot more satisfying than a full freezer, and his time in the woods began to dwindle. When he thought back about the big buck he'd let pass, Sally had no regrets. He'd not really *quit* hunting, he'd just found something that challenged him more, fulfilled him more, to replace it.

So what now? Why didn't this deal, the auction with Ethel and Livingston, feel just like that day he sat in the stand and watched the trophy buck meander away? He should have been more eager, more excited, it held the potential of being one of the biggest deals he'd made. Sure, at first, he felt the thrill of the hunt, clichéd as it was, but at least he felt it. But once he *had* it, it just didn't seem that important anymore.

The feeling seemed to invade everything, not just the real-estate deals. What *was* it, why couldn't he name it? If he only could, then he could fix it, just like he'd always done. Something didn't work, something wasn't right, he could study it, locate the cause and *fix* it. Was it boredom, apathy? No, not really. Something more pervasive. A dull ache had draped itself around him and Sally couldn't figure out how to shake it. Maybe he just missed Bill. They'd been best friends for years, really Sally's only friend. They talked about anything, everything, and nothing. Mostly nothing. Like his uncle and father that morning at breakfast before his first deer hunt, him and Bill didn't *need* to talk.

And now? He enjoyed spending time with Kat, liked listening to her talk. When they were together those feelings of . . . of . . . *malaise* seemed to disappear. And too, when he caught himself thinking about her, he had to admit he actually felt happy. Was that it? Was this . . . this . . . thing, were all of these things telling him Kat held all the answers to the questions plaguing him? That Kat was the answer? Maybe? No, that couldn't be it, could it? What if it was? What next?

And what did she want, what did she expect? Sally never thought of himself as the marrying type, if that's what she had in mind. Christ, they'd only been dating a few months, why would he even think marriage? How long should it be? Besides, even if they were a . . . a . . . couple, did that mean they were friends? Was that even possible? He felt close to her, close in an unfamiliar way. He wanted to compare it to Bill, to whatever it was they had, but that made him uneasy. It wasn't like that, with Bill. No, this thing with Kat was more, much more. And it scared him. No, not scared, challenged was the better word. Wasn't it? With her, he finally felt a *reason* again, a purpose, scared or not. Maybe it wasn't Bill he missed, not physically. Maybe he missed all the intangibles. He'd never voiced it before, but now, well now he could admit it. He cared about Bill, needed him in an odd way and even without the words, he knew Bill had cared about him, too. At least he did before finding Jesus, or whatever it was. It made sense. He needed Kat.

Still, he couldn't be certain. Did she feel the same way? Maybe. What he knew for certain was that the preview was coming up in a couple of days, the auction a week later. It had been a long time since he'd scored a big deal, maybe best not to define anything, not about him and Kat, not about this feeling until he saw how that went. Make sure he could provide for her, if things went any farther. Like a hunter dragging a kill back to the cave. And like the old saying went—money might not buy happiness, but it'd sure rent it for a while. And if Landon was right, if the buyers fell in line, he was about to make enough to rent for a nice, long while. Sally decided it best not to spend any more time thinking about all those ifs. He decided to call Kat instead, invite her to a fancy dinner in Charlotte Saturday. A little post-preview, pre-auction celebration. She'd like that. Maybe he'd even suggest they come back to his house for a night cap, let her see how he framed the drawing.

Where could it be? There were three, he *knew* there were three, but now he only found two. Livingston flipped the pages, flipped them again. Clutched the front and back hard covers of the book, held it above his head and shook it violently. Nothing. He flipped the pages once more, slower this time. Pictures of red-tiled roofs, canals and gondolas, Saint Marks Square and Cathedral rifled past, but not the third auction flier.

The voices in his head grew louder. Ed Sullivan shouting, "And now . . . I told you so," at Barbara Walters. Walters telling Sullivan to "kiss my wosy ass." Livingston gritted his teeth, trying to keep his fingers from snapping. He dropped the book to the floor and turned around once, trying to retrace his steps and actions in his mind. Snap, snap, snap.

A few weeks earlier, at the post office, Landon had handed him a stack of auction fliers, but Liv gave them back. "Three. I only want three," Liv told him.

"Give 'em to your friends, pass 'em around. Think of it as your job. We want everybody to know about it, lots of people there. Here, you've got work to do." Landon shoved the fliers toward Livingston again.

Livingston folded his hands behind his back and shook his head. "No. Three's perfect, the perfect number. Only three."

Landon insisted but Liv continued to refuse until the auctioneer finally shrugged his shoulders in defeat and counted out three fliers and handed them to Livingston, who recounted them twice before walking away.

He drove home with the fliers on the seat. He recounted them at each stop light and again before going into the house. Trudy was in the bedroom, at the back of the house. He slipped off his shoes and padded down the hall, Ed Sullivan and Barbara Walters arguing about the best hiding spot as he went. Liv finally decided to go with

Barbara's suggestion. She had the better perspective, being female. He hid the three fliers inside a coffee table book, *Venice by Air*, pages thirty-seven, sixty-two, and ninety-one. The book no longer rested on their coffee table but in his study, replaced by *And Baby Makes Three* months ago. He kept it on the lower shelf, directly behind his desk.

He checked the book daily, verifying the fliers were safe, at ten, twelve, two, four, six, and again before going to bed each night. So far, everything had been fine. That morning, all three fliers were accounted for at ten and twelve, but now only the ones on page sixty-two and ninety-one remained.

Did he move it? Why move only one? What happened between noon and two? He ate lunch—grilled cheese on wheat with a Kosher dill pickle, checked Monster.com for job listings, updated his resume, but couldn't remember looking at the fliers. He couldn't have, checking before two o'clock would have ruined the schedule. Why did he take the fliers from Landon in the first place? Too much responsibility, too much risk. Why, why, why? If he'd only told Trudy about the land, about Bill Tucker, about Ethel and Sally, he could have told her about the auction. She'd be happy about it, right? But if he told her about the auction, he'd have to tell her the rest, and she'd think it all a lie . . . and after all these years. No, she didn't need that, not now, not with the baby so close. It wasn't a lie, not really. Then why hide the fliers, hide everything? He did it to protect her, that was it, yes. He did it for Trudy.

Sullivan and Walters continued to argue, John Wayne offered an off-key rendition of *Happy Trails* in the background. Snap, snap, snap. A new tic—Livingston began flicking his left thumb against his fingernails, pinky to index and back again, in rhythm with the snapping from his right hand. The Lion whispered, "What makes the muskrat guard his musk?"

Trudy . . . No, no, no, NO. Had he left the room unguarded?

She was in the shower at ten, fixing his lunch at noon, and left for her doctor's appointment at one-thirty. What did *she* do between noon and leaving? Livingston tried to concentrate. "Please lower your voices," he asked, and for a moment, they did, but his snapping and flicking continued. Think, think, think. Brought lunch into the study. Went to the bathroom, changed her top, made a phone call, went to the bathroom again. Put away the dishes, looked for her keys, went to the bathroom, changed shoes, put the original top on again. Then what?

When she put the top back on, Livingston remembered her coming into the study and asking him if he thought it looked okay. He knew that was at one-twenty-five, because he'd noticed the time as he signed off the computer. The next thing her remembered was her kissing him on the forehead and telling him good-bye at one-fifty. She went to the bathroom again and left for her doctor's appointment. Everything in between was blank.

Livingston dropped into the chair behind his desk. One job to do, one simple thing, and he couldn't even complete that. He knew why—it had happened again. He'd not slept at night for over a week now, almost two, and the past few days, he'd lose small blocks of time. He assumed he was dozing off but didn't want his insomnia to worry Trudy. Liv then tried to cultivate the moments by employing the same method he'd once read John Kennedy used when he was in office. Livingston would hold his keys in his hand, sit back, and close his eyes, hoping he'd nod to sleep and drop the keys, waking him before Trudy or anyone else noticed. It worked, too, but the naps were short—four minutes here, seven there, but never as long, not twenty-five minutes.

Then it hit him. He'd forgotten the keys. And the book, where was the book? When he checked at twelve, he remembered leaving it on the left front corner of his desk. He knew that was right, because he'd rested his lunch plate on it as he worked on his resume. But when he checked at two, the book was shelved in its usual slot, not on the desk. Trudy must've replaced it when she came in to tell him good-bye, before waking him. That was it, she picked it up and found the flier. How could he have let this happen? His head dropped to the desk. He heard John Wayne tell him, "talk low, talk slow, and don't say too much." Livingston sat up and took one of the remaining fliers from the book.

It's okay, he thought. "You're right, Mr. Wayne." There was nothing on the flier to make Trudy believe the auction property belonged to him, nothing at all. Just don't say anything. Only the sale information was printed there, date, time, and location of the auction. Nothing about who owned the property. The only name on the page was Landon's and the auction company. Worried over nothing. The right corner of Livingston's mouth tilted upward, hinting at a smile. Back to normal. He took his keys from his pocket, bounced them three times in his right hand, then leaned back in his chair and closed his eyes. Sleep washed over him so quickly he didn't have time to wonder what made Trudy take the flier with her and when the keys clanged against the floor fifteen minutes later, he felt more refreshed than he had in days. As he rose from the chair, the voices were at a whisper.

19

Flatheads

People milled about everywhere, Ethel's back yard, the front, wandered along the path mowed between her place and the property. One large group gathered around and under Landon's information tent, another stood in line at the church's concession table. The Ladies Auxiliary had gone a little overboard. There was barbecue—chopped, sliced, and pulled; hamburgers and hotdogs, pimiento cheese and egg salad sandwiches, four dozen cakes and three dozen pies, but even with the size of the crowd, they'd never sell it all. Landon had brought two of his flatbed trailers and situated one near the path leading to the property for conducting the auction and the other at the far edge of Ethel's property for the band. Landon had scanned their song list and told them if they'd wanted to get paid, he only had two rules—take out the slow stuff and the blues numbers, play everything up tempo, and keep the volume low. They'd done as he asked, and were working through the new set list at background music volume. Everybody ignored them.

Brittany had convinced Landon to hire her as event photographer for both the preview and the auction. She skipped school and circulated through the crowd snapping candid shots, panoramic views, close-ups, even a few pictures of the band.

Livingston arrived hours ahead of schedule and paced between the house, the band, and the auction tent.

Sally waited, anticipating the questions he knew would come as soon as prospective buyers arrived. He had to be careful—a lot of people knew of his real-estate reputation and would needle him for information. Was he interested in the property? Did he know who was? Why was it being offered at auction? A typical question, one Landon warned them about. The standard answer? The piece was being offered simply as a liquidation of assets to generate future investment income. Vague, but official sounding. The owners, who preferred to remain anonymous, didn't plan to develop the property in any way and simply decided it was a good time to convert the land to cash. Highest and best use—the real-estate mantra. Keep the buyers calm.

Once Landon advertised the auction, the serious investors were only a few mouse clicks away from knowing the owner. Click—County Tax Records. Click—Individual Holdings. Click—By Address. Click—Livingston Carr, owner of record, deeded by will and testament. Soon after the first people arrived, they converged on Livingston like refugees on a Red Cross supply truck, and he became an overall detraction. Pacing, circling, mumbling to himself. When his arms weren't flailing back and forth, shooing away the people and their questions, his fingers were snapping on one hand and flicking fingernails on the other. Landon and Sally corralled him and with Ethel's help, got him inside her house, where they'd left him with instructions not to come out under any circumstances. The arrangement suited Livingston and they had little trouble convincing him, but not before several people had noticed and formed opinions.

What Landon and Sally feared to be a negative actually became a plus. Even with the recent influx of new residents, Mason still operated under small town rules and protocol, which required those who'd witnessed Livingston's behavior to tell someone else at the first opportunity. Auction explanation provided. *Did you hear? The owner's gone bat-shit crazy. Flipped out, lost his mental faculties, gone around the bend, left the building. The family's forcing him, probably his kids. I heard they tried to have him committed. PTSD, I heard. Wasn't he a Vietnam Vet? Gulf War? Used to be a stoner, bad acid did it. He's a nut. Tragic. Didn't his daddy get smashed by that plane? Refuses to take his medication.*

Sally and Landon didn't confirm the suspicions, but they realized immediately there was no reason to deny them, either. Who would know any different? Livingston's name was on the deed, he was the only one required to sign the official paperwork to complete the sale. The agreement on splitting the money was written and signed between him, Sally, and Ethel, and the three of them signed the auction contracts with Landon reflecting how the proceeds would be divided and the final checks written. None of that was public record, none of it acted as proof. Everyone could believe what they wanted to believe, as long as they believed. No proof required.

Ethel stayed out of the speculation. It wasn't difficult, most of the crowd steered clear, even avoided eye contact with her. Sure, Brittany talked to her, and Boot Jackson said a few words, but everyone else was . . . well, afraid of her. Like Sally, she had her reputation, and she'd worked hard on it. And like Livingston, more than a few rumors existed, most of them well-earned.

Once they settled Livingston inside, Ethel moved her lawn chair to the shade of her oak tree, where she was content to sit and watch as more and more people arrived, drinking the day's first rum and coke from a large, insulated Dale Earnhardt mug, smoking her Pall Malls, and scratching the dog's ears as he lay beside her. When the band started, the dog howled and loped down the path, disappearing into the woods. Ethel refilled her drink, checked the pre-registration table to make sure all the groups on Landon's hot list had arrived, then sat back in her chair, smiling and nodding at anyone who forgot they weren't supposed to make eye contact.

An hour and a half passed. Landon and his crew herded everyone toward the trailer where Landon made a few general announcements, did a little last minute, hard-sell marketing, and answered questions before beginning the auction. A few stragglers pulled up and hurried to join the throng. Ethel strained to see the late arrivals, thought she recognized a few but decided it wasn't worth leaving the comfort of the shade tree for a closer look.

Landon rattled and rolled for almost a minute before the first bidders hand appeared in the air. Five thousand an acre. Landon asked for ten and six hands shot skyward.

Sally, who'd gone inside to check on Livingston, came out and squatted next to Ethel. "So, whatta you think?" He asked.

"Landon's done a helluva job," she told him. "With my help, of course. Just look at all these people. And got ten grand an acre already. We're shitting in high cotton, now, Salvador Hinson. You should've partnered up with me years ago."

They listened to Landon's chant. Twelve-five, then fifteen per acre. Sally laughed. "You might be right."

"Damn right, I am." The bidding slowed and Landon took advantage of the moment, did a little more puffing and the bids started climbing once again. Ethel told Sally, "Look yonder, see that big woman, the one wearing that paisley muumuu?" She pointed toward the concession tables.

"Mary? From the church?"

"I don't know her name, me and her ain't been chatty. She's the one come up with Bill Tucker that day, the one I fired off the warning shot toward."

"Yeah, I know."

"Bet if I went up and said *boo*, she'd crap her granny panties."

"Play nice, Miss Ethel. Who's that man talking to her?"

"The butterball in the Braves hat? I don't know, probably

just driving by and smelled the cakes, like one of them radar things. Huh," she said, "wonder why Landon's stopped calling bids again?"

Sally stood. "Looks like some sort of commotion off the side of the stage."

Ethel got out of her chair and squinted her brow, trying to make out what was happening. "That no count son of a bitch. I'll wring that little peckerhead's neck."

"What?" Sally asked.

"That damn James. No count hoodlum been bird-dogging my Brittany for a couple years. I knew he was trouble, ain't worth shooting. It's him in the middle of that commotion. What the hell's he doing with a shovel? Idiot. Come on."

"Wait a minute. That looks like Kat."

"Who?"

"Katherine Sardofsky. I know her. She teaches at the college. We've kinda been seeing each other. What's she doing with the kid, and who's the other guy with them? And why are they here?"

"She's been out here a couple times. Looking at some spindly flowers back on the property that Britt took pictures of."

"The Schweinitz sunflower? On *our* property? Damn it." How did he not put it together? How would he explain it to her? Would she understand? Sally started jogging toward the stage.

Ethel struggled to keep pace. "Slow down, Sally," she huffed, "I want first crack at him."

They reached the back edge of the crowd and Sally paused, waiting on Ethel before he started elbowing his way through the crowd to Landon.

When Ethel caught up, she asked, "What's the big deal about the flowers?"

"They're endangered. Kat's researching them," Sally answered over his shoulder. "If the place gets developed . . . I've gotta talk to her." He pushed closer to the front.

Ethel grabbed the back of his shirt and followed in his wake. She didn't exactly know what Sally meant by research, but she knew endangered. Endangered meant the government sticking its nose in the thick of things. It meant *60 Minutes,* undercover reporters, the local news all with cameras and microphones. Endangered meant Greenpeace and eco-terrorists and tree-huggers standing in front of bulldozers. It was un-American, them hindering decent, hard-working folks trying to make a dollar. Normally not a problem, the money machine always won out, the mountain top got blasted, the off-shore well drilled, the spotted owl had to fly to the trees in the next county, but the timing on this was wrong. They could drag things on for years, years Ethel didn't have.

Maybe it wouldn't be too bad, it was only a flower. Hell, you could dig them up and transplant, Ethel did it all the time. City folks and Yankees, they didn't know squat. College professors knew less than squat. She'd straighten them all out, even if it meant she had to shovel the stupid flowers and replant them herself. They wouldn't stand between her and payday, endangered or not.

Ethel barreled her way around Sally. A few more feet. Landon was still on the stage, standing over James, Kat, and the strange man with the pipe. Two of his auction crew positioned themselves between them and the stage as a buffer. Most of the buyers on Landon's hot list stood between Ethel and the group, trying to decipher what was taking place and what bearing it might have on the property they wanted to buy. Get past them and Ethel would have everything back on track in short order. She lowered her shoulder and made the final push.

THEY PARKED ON the side of the road, a hundred yards away from the house. Culpepper drove his van slowly past the cars but when he came to the driveway, someone wearing a golf shirt with Landon Auction and Realty embroidered on the pocket told them they couldn't park there.

"I wonder what's happening, why all the cars?" Kat asked as they started toward the house.

"I have no idea, but it's certainly an inconvenience," Culpepper answered. "Don't forget the buckets, James, all four."

James wrangled the five-gallon plastic pails from the back of the van and slid the bails over the shovel handle. "It's an auction sale," he told them.

"A what?"

"You know, an auction. Where they talk real fast. People bid and stuff. I seen a flier at Red's."

Kat stopped. "At this house? The older lady's?"

"Naw, Granny Combs ain't selling. That ornery old woman ain't leaving unless she's ten toes up. It's the land what joins hers. I had . . . uh . . . an interest in it myself, but it didn't work out."

Kat's finger flew to the tip of her nose. "Sally," she whispered.

"What? What's wrong? You look as if you've had a fright." Culpepper sucked on his unlit pipe.

"A friend of mine. He mentioned a real-estate deal he was working on, told me they were thinking of selling at auction. I had no idea . . . damn it, I can't believe he didn't tell me."

"Well, then, you'll talk to him, explain matters," Culpepper continued walking toward the crowd of people.

"What do you mean, *explain*?" She intended to talk to him, alright, but he was the one who'd do the explaining. How could he?

"Your flowers are endangered; the area will be protected."

"I don't know that. Even so, it could take months, maybe a year or more, before . . ."

"They can't sell our land, Katherine, not until I've conducted my research. I'll see to that." Culpepper increased his pace, Kat and James hustled along behind.

The plastic buckets were sliding back and forth on the shovel handle, banging James in the back. He skipped in front of Culpepper, turned and stopped. "Listen. If we ain't gonna be digging holes, I'm putting these buckets back in the van. They're aggravating me to death."

"You'll do no such thing. Now move along," Culpepper waved his pipe.

As the three of them made their way toward the auction trailer, Kat scanned the crowd but didn't see Sally. He had to be there somewhere. He didn't talk much about his work and he'd only briefly mentioned the possibility of an auction, but this must be it. Why hadn't she taken more of an interest? He was such a good listener and when they were together, well, she felt different. She *was* different. Kat could deliver a lecture so efficiently she made her last point exactly as the class time expired. With Sally, she'd ramble on and on, one topic morphing into the next, like an undergrad sorority girl at a mixer. She suddenly realized how inconsiderate she'd been, how selfish. Maybe she thought him a good listener because she never stopped babbling long enough for him to open up to her.

But he was a good listener, which meant he knew. He had to know, how could he not? Kat frowned. Sally knew what protecting the flowers meant to her.

"Hurry up, it looks as if they've begun," Culpepper snapped and broke into a clumsy jog. When they reached the stage, he started to climb up, but two of Landon's crew came over and stopped him.

"Can we help you, sir?"

"Who's in charge?"

"Rick Landon's the auctioneer. Do you have questions, maybe I can help?"

"Is that him?" Culpepper pointed toward Landon, who was asking for the next bid and made a quick glance in Culpepper's direction.

"Yes, but . . ."

"You must stop this auction," Culpepper shouted.

"Sir . . ."

"This land harbors a rare and endangered flora species. You cannot proceed with this sale."

"Ladies and gentlemen, excuse me for a minute," Landon put down the microphone and walked over to the edge of the stage in front of Culpepper. "Is there a problem, sir?"

"There certainly is. I'm Dr. Aldus Culpepper, this is Dr. Katherine Sardofsky. The Schweinitz sunflower is growing on this property and it's a protected species. You cannot continue until the matter has been addressed."

Landon's brow furrowed. "I don't know anything about that. I searched the deed, checked the zoning regs . . . didn't find a thing about any sunflowers. Now, if you don't mind . . ."

"I do mind. It is also possible that this property contains artifacts of the Waxhaw and Sugeree Indian tribes. I'm here to collect samples. If they provide evidence, this entire property will be protected under general statute seventy dash one and seventy dash two, which states the owners refrain from excavation or destruction of grounds containing Indian artifacts. I'm prepared to contact the authorities." Culpepper raised his cell phone above his head.

"Sir, I appreciate what you're saying, but I don't know a thing about Indian grounds or sunflowers or much of anything else. I do know that we're not here to excavate or destruct. All I'm trying to do is sell the dirt. You can take it up with the new owners."

"Hold on, Landon." It was the guy from the Sugeree committee. "I'd like to hear a little more of what the man has to say."

"Yeah," another bidder from the hot list, "We're not interested in buying something if the government won't let us develop. What is it you're trying to pull here?"

More shouts, more grumbling. Growing louder and more heated. Somebody called Culpepper a college nerd, somebody else called him a commie tree-hugger. He offered Neanderthal and in-bred capitalist in return. Landon paced. James dropped the buckets and leaned on the shovel, smiling. The standard jostling, bumping, and posturing increased, everyone wanting to be near the front, to be heard, to hear. It reminded Kat of the tea party rally where she'd talked with Arlen Johnson. She saw Sally coming through the crowd and braced herself.

"Kat, what are you doing here?" he asked.

"I could ask you the same thing," she replied.

"You should've told me, Kat. We've got . . . there's . . . these people . . . there's a lot of money at stake. A *lot* of money. These people, they take this kind of thing serious. They've done their own research, talked to investors, arranged financing, calculated returns. Look at them. They're pissed."

"Well I'm sorry, Sally, but I take my research serious, too. And I did say something. And I gave you the drawing. You knew I'd found the flowers, knew all about them. I thought we . . . *you* should've said something. I said plenty."

Sally waved his hand to stop her. "I know, I know. We'll talk about it later. Let me grab Landon and see if we can figure this out, come up with an option." As he turned toward the stage, a woman screamed behind them, then another.

The crowd turned in unison, then began parting. Those nearest the screams were pushing and shoving in retreat, all of them staring at the ground, some pointing, their mouths moving without sound. Ethel's dog strolled between the lines of people, carrying what appeared to be the top half of a human skull in its mouth. He walked toward Ethel and dropped the skull, where it proceeded to roll toward the stage.

When Culpepper saw the thing, he dove on it with the authority of a middle linebacker on a goal line fumble. The group from the Sugeree Nation realized what it was a little late, but then piled on top of Culpepper in force. Elbows flew, feet wailed, hair was pulled. At the bottom of the pile, Culpepper's hand locked around the upper jaw, his thumb hooked in the opening once covered by a nose. Another hand palmed the top of the skull, its thumb curled through an eye socket. Culpepper gained leverage, pulled the skull toward his chest, but the fingers on the other hand locked tight. Culpepper managed to work his way onto his knees, which gave him needed leverage. He raised the skull toward his face and bit down hard on the thumb. The thumb's owner screamed and let go. Culpepper jumped to his feet and thrust the skull above his head, shaking it for everyone to see as he hollered, his voice piercing the air in a series of high-pitched and unintelligible yelps and whoops. The dog growled, but made no attempt to retrieve its treat.

"Jesus Christ at the rodeo," Ethel swore to anyone who might be listening. "That Sunflower dog got everybody rolling around like they was dancing the flathead shuffle or something. I never seen the like."

The skull was dingy brown, nothing like the bleached Halloween variety skulls. The left half of the lower jaw was in place, even had a few teeth attached, but the right side was missing. The eye sockets were set wide and in the afternoon sunlight, had an eerie, forlorn look about them. The back of the skull was typically shaped. The front, however, flattened perfectly above the brow bones, creating what would have made an excellent bookend.

Culpepper composed himself somewhat, enough that he gripped the skull in both hands above his head. He showed it to the crowd, turning in a slow circle and shouting, "It's a Flathead, it's a Flathead," like the father of a newborn. He faced Landon. "My good man, there'll be no auction, as you can see."

"Look," Landon leaned toward Culpepper. "Let's talk this over. Ethel, can we have a little meeting in your house? In private?"

"Oh, we're gonna meet, alright," Ethel answered, "but you best remember—dance with the one what brung you. Now let's go."

"Not without us." The Sugeree group circled around Culpepper and fell in behind Ethel. Several of the other groups on Landon's hot list said *we're coming, too,* nobody wanting anyone else to get any kind of advantage.

Landon grabbed the mic. "Ladies and gentlemen, we're going to take a little break to . . . to . . . address recent . . . uh . . . developments. We'll be right back." He hopped off the stage and jogged to catch up with the group marching toward Ethel's house.

Kat bristled as Sally approached her again.

"I'm sorry, Kat. I should have realized, I should've . . . I'm sorry. Let me try to straighten this out and then we'll talk. Don't leave, okay? You're right, it's not your fault, Kat. It's all mine and I'm sorry, but I've got to take care of this right now." He stopped before going inside, took Kat's hands in his, and looked her in the eye for several seconds. "Just wait, okay?"

Kat stared back, tried to glare at him, but there was something there, something she'd not noticed before. She loved his eyes, loved the way he'd looked at her before, but now there was a child-like intensity to his gaze that almost overwhelmed her, the look of a young boy peering at a new discovery he'd just made but didn't yet understand. She started to say something more, but didn't. Her heart told her he meant what he said, that he was sorry, that he felt guilty, and in that moment, she felt her uncertainties—about Sally, about herself, about them—fall away. Still, that didn't excuse his not telling her any details about the auction.

She shrugged. "Do what you have to do, I've got to talk to Aldus," she said, then turned and walked away.

A NEW SOUND. Livingston cocked his head to one side, listening.

Once Sally and Ethel left him alone inside the house, the sounds and voices in his head calmed to a degree, but not completely. The bicycle bell still ch-chinged softly. Ed Sullivan and Barbara Walters discussed network benefit packages. John Wayne counseled The Lion on matters of the heart. "*If you've got 'em by the balls,*" Wayne mused, "*their hearts and minds will follow.*" The Lion answered, "*shucks folks, I'm speechless.*" Livingston concentrated.

He heard it again, a light rapping, but louder this time.

He stopped snapping and flicking his fingers, hoping he'd hear it again. For weeks, the cacophony inside his mind ebbed and flowed like a nascent mountain stream, bubbling and gurgling in familiar unison with his own thoughts. He came to know each distinct sound, recognized the cadence and inflections of the individual voices. They soothed him. This new sound might upset the harmony, throwing everything off key, rendering the mental score trumpeting between his ears to nothing more than nails on a blackboard. Livingston had to identify it, label it, and seat it in the proper section. Quickly.

He heard it once again, more forceful now. Three knocks in succession, a pause, then three more. Wait . . . knocks? Maybe the sound wasn't inside his brain at all. It came from . . . from . . . Livingston wasn't familiar with Ethel's house. They'd seated him at the kitchen table. Ethel'd offered him a rum and coke, which he'd refused, asking for a glass of water instead. They'd told him not to move, and he hadn't. He stood, took a few ginger steps toward the hallway, convinced now the sound was not in his mind, but came from that direction.

A wide, arched doorway divided the left side of the hallway, opening into a spacious living room. The hallway continued, acting as a foyer near the front door. Several pictures hung on the right wall, most of the same girl, but at different ages and poses. Across from the opening sat an oak, one-drawer table supporting a small lamp and a half-filled ashtray. Above the table was an arrangement of four photographs. The same flowers appeared in all four snapshots but from different angles, yellow daisies perhaps, maybe some sort of sunflowers, Livingston couldn't be sure.

Again, tapping at the door.

Livingston leaned back, checking the light switches in the kitchen. All down. He checked the switches in the hallway, which pointed down as well. Satisfied, he started toward the door, fingers snapping. He reached the halfway point and stopped, mesmerized by the photos of the flowers. He still couldn't identify them, but they seemed so . . . so . . . familiar, almost as if he'd seen them before, the actual flowers, not the photos. For some reason, they reminded him of something from his past. He studied them for a moment, but couldn't recall exactly what it might be and continued to the door.

He peered through the security peep hole, but saw nothing. He moved his head farther away, thinking it might widen the angle. It didn't. Livingston leaned closer until his nose touched the door, bringing his eye only a few inches from the small glass. When the knock repeated, it startled him and he stumbled back a few steps. How could it be? He peered again, right eye, left eye, still nothing.

"Wh-who's there?" he shouted, then quickly added, "I don't live here." The volume inside his head rose.

"Livingston?"

"No, you can't be Livingston. I'm in here. Right here." He patted himself on the chest, the stomach, his hips and thighs, before looking through the glass again. Still nothing, he saw no one.

"Livingston."

Uh-oh. Voices shouting, bell clanging, horns blaring in D minor. Fingers snapping, nails flicking, Livingston rocked back and forth, left then right, lifting each foot off the floor as he leaned. What was she doing here? How'd she find out? The flier, she *did* take the flier. But why?

"Trudy?"

"Livingston, what are you doing here? Open the door."

"I can't come out," he told her.

"Can't come out? Why not? Liv, are you okay?"

"Yes . . . I'm . . . no . . . I'm fine. They told me to stay inside."

"Who's *they*? Livingston Carr, open this door, right this minute. I mean it."

Livingston's chin sunk to his chest as he sighed and eased open the door. "Hi Trudy. How was your doctor's appointment? Did she say how soon?"

"Don't change the subject. What are you doing here?" Trudy closed the door behind her and looked around. "Who lives here?"

Livingston couldn't speak. The Lion suggested, *Unusual weather we're having, ain't it?* Livingston shook his head no, but had no other words for Trudy. What could he possibly say?

Trudy took both of his hands in hers. "You're scaring me, Liv. Now tell me what's going on."

Livingston's lower lip quivered as he drew in a breath and reminded himself of all the important factors. Trudy didn't know about the land, and now was not the time to tell her, not with the baby so close. And, she didn't know he was involved with the auction. Explaining both points would be much easier if he could first hand her the sale proceeds check. Not even that really, if he could only appease her with some explanation, anything, until after the last bid was called and the paperwork signed, he could soften the news by showing her the amount they'd soon deposit. Another deep breath. Careful . . . remember what John Wayne said—don't say too much.

"Friends of mine. Salvador Hinson, everyone calls him Sally, and Ethel Combs, she lives here. Yes, she's old, and not very nice, really, and there's nothing inappropriate, not that you'd think there was, and Sally took me to lunch, but Ethel remembered my father, so they're having an auction, and I'm here to support, that's all, friends do that sort of thing, and you're a week past due, I got too excited, the heat maybe, while you were at the doctor's, and they let me rest in here with a glass of water. Would you like one? A glass of water?"

"Liv. It's okay. So, some friends of yours are having this auction and you wanted to come. You could have told me, I don't mind. I know you feel bad about not working and about being too . . . too . . . nervous to go with me to the doctor. But you don't have to spend every minute in the house, waiting on me. And when you leave, it doesn't just have to be job hunting. A little entertainment would do you good. It's fine, really, it is."

Trudy reached for a hug. Livingston leaned down and wrapped both arms around her for a moment, then kissed the top of her head. "You're not mad?"

"Well, you could have told me, but no. Auctions are fun. Mother used to take me when I was young, every Saturday night. Peanut's Auction Barn. I loved the grab bags. That's why I stopped, I thought it was, you know, an estate auction. I didn't realize they were only selling land. I didn't even know you could sell real estate at an auction."

"I'm feeling better, now," Livingston forced a smile. What next? Should he take her outside, watch the auction? Sally and Ethel said no, stay inside. He'd be fine with Trudy. No, all those people . . . they knew, they'd found out the land belonged to him, somehow. They'd swarmed, and they'd be back. She couldn't find out, not yet. What to do? Stay inside, yes, that was best. Stay inside, change the subject. The doctor's appointment, ask her about the appointment.

20

The Future, It's Right There

Sally took in all the chaos in one long, slow stare: the knot of people in front of the auction block, the skull, Ethel, the dog. Kat. As he scanned the scene unfolding in Ethel's backyard he realized, for the first time in a long time, he had no idea what to do next. He felt himself balanced on a sharp edge. Behind him lay everything he knew and understood, the safe and predictable. Before him was, what? The waning side of middle age, the beginning of the end? Or not an ending at all, but the beginning of something . . . new? Still, if one thing ends, another begins, doesn't it? Was that why he was not more eager to close this deal? That he knew it could lead to another part of his life ending? It would make Kat happy if the deal didn't close, but what did making her happy *mean*? Sure, he enjoyed spending time with her, he cared for her, but they were from two different worlds. She had her research, her career, her youth. What could she possibly see in him? But if they somehow managed to work around this Indian thing with Culpepper and get the property sold, what would that do to Kat? Those flowers meant a lot to her, her future at the college depended on them. For Sally, the past twenty years—his whole life really—had been about making money. It was all he knew. Not really a job, not a career, it was simply what he did. And, this deal *was* a lot of money, whether he needed it or not shouldn't matter. At one time, there would've been no doubt, he'd not consider any other option. But now . . . was the money worth whatever possibility might exist with Kat? Was that really what he wanted?

It might not matter; she was plenty pissed. He should've told her, but she had to cut him some slack, he didn't understand all the rules to this relationship thing. There'd been other women, plenty, but there'd never been anything he'd call a relationship. Arrangements, maybe. Conveniences, yes. But an actual relationship? He'd never considered it before. At some point, years ago, he assumed that would be his life, and he was fine with that, even preferred it. Being unattached was easier. No one to answer to, no one to be responsible for, it made sense. Then, living that way—being single; a bachelor, his line of work, making the kind of deals he made, he learned to keep his mouth shut. He didn't mean to intentionally keep anything from her. Maybe with time to cool off, she'd come around. Probably. Maybe. He'd not find the answers to any of the questions standing in Ethel's back yard. He sighed and went inside.

"YES, I'M OKAY, now," Livingston reassured Trudy once more. "This auction . . . I'm . . . it's my . . . we should go." The subject, change the subject. "What did the doctor say?"

"Oh Liv, don't you remember? The C-section, the delivery? It's scheduled for next week But, Rachel said I've dilated a centimeter. I may not be able to wait that long, it could be tonight, maybe to-morrow. It's okay."

"Yes, yes. The delivery. But wait—we must go." Snapping, flicking. "You should lie down. We're not . . . I'm not ready. Get you off your feet, so much to do."

"It's fine, Liv. Rachel said walking helps."

"Tomorrow? Oh no, tonight? No walking. Really, sit down. I don't know how . . ."

"How what, Liv? The baby'll come when it's time. You don't have to do a thing. And if not, we'll go in next Thursday just like we planned."

"After, after . . ." The sounds and voices rising in his mind offered no calm now. He needed to think, all by himself. He took a deep breath. "After our baby comes. A father, I don't know how . . ."

"Yes you will. Now stop worrying."

Livingston heard the back door open. "We should go."

Too late. Ethel bristled in, followed by a parade of other people. Livingston put his hands over his ears, but it didn't help. Was the auction over? They'd tell Trudy. How could he . . . what would he . . . Ethel was yelling at him. He wanted to ask what all the people were doing inside, but couldn't put the words together. The voices were shouting now, drowning his thoughts. Ethel poked her finger in his chest, then she was gone and the crowd pushed past him, into the living room.

"What was she talking about?" Trudy asked. "What deal? What money?"

"The auction . . . I can't remember my father . . . too young . . . he left me . . . he left me . . ."

"Liv, calm down. Your father didn't *leave* you, he died. Now what was that old lady talking about?"

"No, no, no. He left me . . . auction . . . over a million . . . but . . . but . . . what about our child? Something to leave . . ."

"Livingston, you're not making any sense." Trudy frowned. "What are those people arguing about? I wish they'd shut up. Let's go outside where we can talk. You've got to tell me what's going on." She took his hand, but Livingston pulled away.

The voices in his head shouted, the bell blasted, someone called his name but he didn't recognize the voice. The room started a slow spin. Livingston put his hand on the wall. He tried steadying himself on the table behind him, but still the room twirled. Faster now. He heard his name again, a different voice this time.

"Liv, why are they talking about you?" Trudy asked.

His name again, a different voice still. Others joined in, the room began to shift, colors blurred. Orange, blue, violet, red, red, red, the colors bled together, pulsed and wavered. Livingston thought he smelled honeysuckles. The colors faded to gray, then white, then everything was gone.

ETHEL DIDN'T WANT all the people traipsing through her house, but what else could she do? She was *this close* to the money, a couple of bids away from having everything she wanted—her legacy, something for people to remember about her; providing for Brittany; and most of all, pissing off her ungrateful kids for all eternity. That damn Culpepper, the pompous bastard. She didn't like him the first time she met him, and now this. And the dog ... after all she'd done. Let him into her house and he picked today to come dragging that skull to her feet. He was as bad as her kids.

She led the group inside, muttering to herself. Brittany and James followed behind her, then Sally. Landon, Culpepper, and all the bidders brought up the rear. She saw Livingston and his pregnant wife. "Jesus Christ at the rodeo," she mumbled, "like I ain't got enough problems." Ethel turned to remind the group behind her not to trash her house. James bumped into her when she stopped. "You shit-fer-brains, here I am telling folks to wipe their feet and mind the furniture and you come bringing that damn shovel in the house. Were you born in a barn?" James told her no, but he kept the shovel.

Ethel confronted Livingston. "Keep your shit together, fruit loop."

"Wait ... I can't ... I don't ... what's going on, why are these people yelling at me? What did I do?"

She gave him a quick explanation, hoping it'd keep him calm, then stabbed her finger in his chest. "Don't start that looney tunes shit of yours, and we might be able to save this deal. And take your hands off your ears, you look like a fool."

Livingston lowered his hands to his side, fingers snapping softly.

Ethel tried to position herself where she could keep an eye on him, but the crowd pushed her further into the living room. As Culpepper started rambling, she caught Sally's attention and nodded her head toward Livingston, hoping Sally'd get the message.

This was her chance at one good thing in her whole entire life, and she sensed it slipping away. She was so mad she could spit.

AFTER CULPEPPER FINISHED his speech, Sally knew there'd be no auction. He'd seen less stop a land deal, plenty of times. Sometimes, deed restrictions caused a problem, but those could be settled. Throw money at it. Local governments presented a tougher case. Zoning issues, right of ways, water and sewer, those were public matters and required more finesse. Money solved those issues, too, but it involved campaign contributions, closed door donations, or secretive land swaps. Even then, things didn't always work. Election year promises, other favors owed, better offer from the competition, an official fought with his wife—anything could kill a deal. But this, this was Federal, and neither Sally nor anyone else in Mason had the money or influence to work around those boys.

He gauged the room, surveying the reactions to Culpepper's pitch. Hard to tell. Nobody appeared convinced one way or the other, but all the faces were painted with a level of doubt that said it was over. He searched for Kat, but didn't spot her anywhere. Landon started damage control.

Things didn't go well. The bidders didn't care for Culpepper's suggestion that the land couldn't be sold, not at all. One of the lesser players, someone Sally didn't know, held the high bid when Landon stopped the auction, but he wasn't saying much. The others made up for it, and they were turning on both Culpepper and Landon.

"I think you planted that skull," one of the men from Southern Exposure shouted at Culpepper. "How do we know it's from some Indian?"

Another started, "We came here for an auction. I went to the bank, got certified funds, now let's get to it. You got no proof about Indians or anything else."

Landon saw the opportunity. "Technically, Culpepper, he's right. We should go ahead, then you and whoever can work this out with the new owner."

"Now hold on. That could be my ancestor," the Sugeree representative argued. "You can't disturb Native American burial grounds, it's federal law. Culpepper's right."

"Maybe you're in on it, too, just to get that damn casino." Southern Exposure again.

"Look at the forehead," Culpepper held the skull above his head and pointed at the brow. "That's indicative of the Waxhaws and the Sugeree . . ."

"Indicative my ass . . . I'll show you indicative."

Shoving started. More yelling. Landon's shoulders slumped, his chin sunk against his chest, defeated. Culpepper looked terrified. Ethel bulled her way to the kitchen and poured another rum and coke. She came back and stood next to Landon, put her fingers in her mouth and whistled. Everyone stopped.

"We're having this damn auction sale," she told them. "Rick Landon here's got a contract saying as much. Nobody else has got a thing that's official. Now . . ."

Landon perked up.

"You ain't got a dog in this fight, Ethel," someone shouted. "What difference does it make to you?"

Landon slumped again.

"Me and Sally . . ."

Everyone in the room turned toward Sally. Muttering and mumbling followed. *Knew he was involved . . . probably scammed the crazy guy out of it for a song . . .*

"What Ethel meant to say was . . ." Sally didn't get a chance to finish.

"Don't matter," a voice from the other side of the room. "We all checked the tax records. We know Livingston Carr owns the property, not Ethel or Sally. He's the only one can say one way or the other. He's got to sign the deed. It's him."

"Yeah, it's Carr . . ."

"Where's Livingston Carr?"

"Get him in here . . ."

A loud crash sounded in the hallway. The oak table collapsed, sending cigarette butts and the contents of the drawer down in a heap around Livingston. Sally moved to help him to his feet, but stopped short. He faced a new problem, one he'd not anticipated.

JAMES COULDN'T BELIEVE it. A real live Indian skull from back in the bow and arrow days. And Culpepper was right, it did have a flat forehead, it had to be from the Waxhaws. That explained everything. They'd planted the pot on sacred Indian ground, and then did the voodoo ritual. He'd offended them, and they took his weed, simple as that. It was a sign. Brittany showing him the land, that day at the college he wanted to take a class to learn to shoot a bow and arrow, then he started reading all that stuff about the Waxhaws, taking the job with Culpepper. It was all leading up to this, it all meant something for *him*.

But what? He didn't know, but it all swirled around *him*, he was part of it. From the moment Culpepper raised the skull, the whole time in the house as he explained, while everyone argued, during it all, James could feel a tension welling in his chest, spreading over him. The power of it scared him a little. He'd been chosen for ... for ... *something*.

James turned to Brittany. "I didn't know my job would have all this excitement. You got my text, didn't you? About my new career?"

"You're digging holes, James. That's not, like, a career."

"But you said ..."

"I've got plans. That's what I'm talking about. I'm gonna be on *Survivor*, Luna Marze, remember? Use that to let people know about my photography? You never listen to me. I'm gonna be a famous one day. What are you gonna do?"

"Well ... I ... this Culpepper dude knows about Indians and stuff. I like Indians, I've been studying up on the ones he's talking about, the Waxhaws. He can teach me, I might could be one of those archeologist things. That's a plan."

"Like joining the Marines, or growing weed? Call me when it happens."

"No, listen, Brittany. This is different. I'll ..."

She spun on her heel and stomped to the kitchen, leaving James in the hallway, wanting to explain. Brittany didn't understand this *was* different, and it bothered him that she wouldn't listen. Maybe he couldn't explain it just yet, not exactly, but it sure *felt* different. It felt like the future—his future right there in front of him.

The arguing aggravated James. He wanted to say something, to speak up, tell them they couldn't go on with the auction, show Britt he was serious, but who'd listen to him? James fidgeted, shifting his weight from one foot to the other, leaning on the shovel. If they sold this land, if something happened to the burial ground, it would be just like everything else. School, the Marines, growing weed, everything. Another door closed. That couldn't happen, he had to do something to make Britt understand.

James gathered his courage. When Ethel whistled and announced the auction would continue, he stepped inside the arched doorway. Before he could say anything, the crowd turned on the crazy dude standing just behind him. James had seen him earlier and kept an eye on him once they came inside the house. The guy was definitely a six pack short of a case. Sure enough, when everybody turned toward him, the guy just fell out, right there in the hall.

The midget screamed and backed up a step or two, steadying herself against the wall, both hands on her round belly. The crazy guy tried to get up. He'd knocked over the table and was grabbing it as he rose, hoping for balance. Just as the guy made it to his knees, the drawer came out of the table and all sorts of stuff scattered on the floor, making it hard to get his footing—spools of thread, Graceland shot glass, cigarette butts, envelopes and papers, hard candy, a flashlight . . . then James saw it, just as Livingston's hand fell across the grip. Granny Ethel's pistol.

Livingston clutched, grabbing at anything to help him get upright. When he stood, he was wild-eyed, stumbling and careening against the wall, the revolver waving in his right hand. The crowd backed away.

"Livingston, it's me. Sally. Settle down, now." Sally backed past James toward the kitchen, away from the gun. James didn't move.

"He's got an itchy trigger finger," Ethel yelled. "Somebody get him."

Nobody moved. Everybody stared at Livingston, who held the pistol above his head, pointed at the ceiling. He turned left, turned right, waved the gun, flicked fingernails on his free hand.

"My father gave it to me," he whimpered.

"He's talking about the land," Ethel volunteered. "Livingston, put my damn pistol down and let's talk about this before you hurt yourself."

James took a step closer. Livingston stared at the gun in his hand, a look of surprise on his face. Ethel and Sally stared from Livingston's left hand to the right and back again. Left hand, flick . . . flick . . . flick. Right, the gun trembling. Left hand, flick . . . flick . . . flick. Right ha—snap. The bullet went through the ceiling and out the roof. Plaster fell around Livingston.

The room was silent except for the ringing in everyone's ears.

"My child. It's for my child . . ." Livingston whispered.

"Livingston, I told you to keep your shit together. Now put my gun down before you piss me off. Think about the money."

"Livingston." It was the midget, her voice low, almost a whisper. She'd been out in the hallway, but now she'd moved closer. She had both hands on her belly and was staring at it, too. She didn't look so good.

Livingston glanced at the hole in the ceiling. He didn't acknowledge Trudy. "No auction," he said and lowered the gun toward the crowd in the living room. The barrel rotated in small, random circles.

"Livingston. Oh . . ." Trudy again, her voice quivering.

Livingston looked in her direction. Liquid puddled around her feet.

"It's time, Livingston. My water broke."

Livingston's hand leveled, causing the gun to shake directly toward the crowd. The fingers on his left hand flicked faster. He mumbled something incoherent to Trudy. James felt the tension that had been steadily growing overwhelm him.

He raised the shovel by the blade end and brought the handle down across Livingston's wrist. The gun went off again.

Livingston stumbled back against the wall, Trudy never moved, fourteen cell phones dialed 9-1-1, and James fell to the floor.

"Ow, ow, ow. Damn it to hell." James rocked backwards and forwards, holding up his left ankle with both hands, a neat hole in the top of his Converse and another on the bottom, blood staining Ethel's carpet. Brittany rushed in and kneeled next to him.

"James. Are you alright? What happened? You're bleeding."

"Aw, this shit happens all the time," he told her. "It'll match my right one." James looked at her and smiled. Britt smiled back. "Heal up in no time. I don't think it'll hurt my future career none."

21

And the Sunflower Dog

A few of the bidders helped Trudy and Livingston into the living room. Trudy leaned back against the wall, Livingston sat on the edge of the chair, fidgeting. Brittany wrapped a towel around James' shoe to staunch the bleeding. Landon and most of the others filed into the backyard.

Ethel stood in the center of the room, dejected. Ceiling plaster and strands of insulation dotted the floor, dust swirled and settled on everything. Between Trudy's water and James' blood, the carpet in her hallway was ruined. The oak table, which had belonged to her grandmother, lay shattered against the wall. The house smelled of gunpowder and defeat.

A heavy sigh escaped Ethel as she walked toward the back door and the remaining bidders in her yard. As she passed James, she said, "You're paying for my new carpet," without slowing or making eye contact.

Outside, she joined the group under the oak tree and stood next to Sally.

"No, I don't see how . . . sorry folks," Landon apologized. "He's in no condition to sign the contracts, and it sounded like he's changed his mind anyway. We can't continue the auction."

Culpepper smiled. The men from the Sugeree Nation slapped him on the back and shook his hand. The other bidders grumbled and glared at Sally and Landon. What else could they do?

"If anything changes, I'll let everyone know," Landon continued. "Thanks for coming out, and I'm really sorry about all this."

The crowd began drifting away, the church group started loading food and folding tables. Culpepper, his fingers laced through the eye sockets of the skull, and the Sugeree members stood near the back of Ethel's yard, close to the path leading toward the property. Kat stood next to him, glancing toward Sally whenever she thought he might not notice. Lots of nodding and gesturing, pointing toward the trees, more smiling. Landon, Sally, and Ethel watched them without saying anything.

"Your girl looks like she's ready to tell you the what-for," Ethel nudged Sally.

"Yeah, I got some damage control to do," he replied.

"I hope she knows some tricks," Ethel gruffed, "but she sure don't look like a million-dollar piece of ass to me."

"It's not Kat's fault," Sally answered, his voice flat.

"Maybe not," Landon chimed in, "but she was the one who brought that Culpepper fellow. That dog didn't help."

"Of all things," Ethel replied, "taking in a stray done me in. Should've shot that mutt first time I saw him. At least called the pound." She gazed toward the trees for a minute and the silence settled back in around the three of them. In the confusion, she'd forgotten about the dog, and now she wondered where he'd gone.

"Well, I guess that's that. Seen a lot of things ruin an auction, but this beats all." Landon attempted a smile. "It was kinda funny the way that college fellow jumped on the skull, though, don't you think?"

"What about our advertising money?" Ethel asked him.

"Now Ethel, we all took some risk here. The advertising had to be done, that money's spent, regardless of the outcome."

"So I guess you're saying we can kiss that good-bye, too?" She shook her head.

"I did the advertising. It's been paid for already."

"Landon's right, he did his part," Sally agreed. "Hell, Ethel. You don't need the money, you were planning on buying the piece to start with, right out from under me."

"I'm an old woman on a fixed income. Besides, it's the principle. I had plans."

"Plans? At your age?"

Ethel didn't answer, didn't think Sally deserved one. *At her age.* What did he know, what did anybody know? Did they think, once a person reached a certain age, they were supposed to just give up? That wasn't in her, never had been. It would've been easy enough to quit when her husband was killed, but she hadn't. Or, when her kids drifted away, ignored her, she could have moped around, felt sorry for herself, but no. When the DMV took her license, did she stop driving? No. She did what she wanted to do, what she had to do. Planning, dreaming, was part of it, what made her get up every morning. It was the American way and she didn't intend to stop. Sure, she was doing it for Brittany, at least the money part of it. The other part? That was for her, one more thing to show the world and everyone in it that it didn't matter what came her way, she could handle it.

But mostly, it was for Jesse. They were so young when he'd died, young enough she could have remarried. Ethel'd never considered it. How could she? Every day she thought of him. Each morning, she looked at their wedding picture before she got out of bed; it was the last thing she saw before going to sleep each night. Jesse had looked handsome in his suit, and she had been proud of him. But it had been hot that day, hottest of the summer, and he had on no tie in the picture. Ethel knew it was stuffed in his left jacket pocket. *That noose makes my neck itch,* he'd complained as the photographer took picture after picture. *Besides we could've just gone to Lancaster and got hitched. instead of this stand-up funeral.* They'd been so young; their time together too short. But that day, that day was perfect. She knew Jesse'd be proud of her, too, proud of the life she'd lived, the way she lived it, and she meant to keep it that way. Ethel loved him as fiercely now as on their wedding day, and nothing would change that.

"Yeah, I got plans at my age, Salvador Hinson. And I expect, if you study on it, you might one day come to understand what I mean. I know you, your life. Floating along, making money hand over fist. What good's it done you? You got a fancy Lexus and a nice house. Hell-fire, go take a look in that shed yonder, you'll see a brand-new Cadillac. Don't mean nothing. And that house of yours? I bet it's so empty your farts echo. Them things you can't count on. Think about it."

Sally shrugged. "I didn't mean anything by it, Ethel. I'm aggravated, that's all. I didn't mean anything."

"Well, alright, but you just remember what I said." She looked at Kat, then back at Sally. "You think on it real good."

Sally nodded and turned to Landon. "So, what happens next?"

Landon grimaced. "Livingston owns the property, it's up to him. Culpepper and the Indians will have to get the government involved. If there are remains buried there, he can't do anything with it, not without their okay."

Ethel snorted. "The government thinks they're having a time dealing with those BP assholes and their oil spill down in the Gulf, wait'll they meet Livingston. He'll make a preacher cuss."

Soon, all the crowd was gone, along with Landon and his crew. Sally too. The EMTs left with Livingston, Trudy, and James. Ethel poured another rum and Coke and sat in the shade, gazing toward the trees on Livingston's property. She nursed the drink for nearly an hour, letting her mind wander. She lit a cigarette, exhaled, then put two fingers in her mouth and whistled. The dog raced from the woods and sat beside her, facing the trees.

"You know I'm pissed off at you," she told him.

The dog arched his muzzle skyward and looked backward at Ethel, his tongue drooping from the side of his mouth, his face smiling an apology. Ethel took another draw from the Pall Mall and started scratching him behind the ears. *At my age,* she told him. "I ain't dead yet."

JAMES RECOGNIZED THE EMT but didn't say anything at first.

The EMT wrapped gauze around James' foot. "You'll be fine," he said.

"Yeah, I know. Got one just like it on the other foot." James picked up his tennis shoe and inspected the sole where the bullet came through.

"Allman Brothers injury," said the EMT.

"Like the band?" James asked. "My buddy, C-note, likes them. Why do they call it that?"

"During the Vietnam War, one of the brothers, Duane I think, got a draft notice. Had his brother shoot him in the foot so he'd be 4-F. Damn hippies."

"How do you know about the war stuff? I mean the hippie part of it?" James asked.

"Hobby. Well, and it has a lot to do with my regular job. I'm a Marine recruiter, just do this part-time." The EMT sat in the chair across from James and looked him in the eye. "You look familiar. Don't I know you?"

James grinned. "Sort of. I'm James Flowers. Failed your test three times. You told me to find something else to do."

"I remember now. You found anything?"

James looked away. He wished Britt had stayed, but once his foot was bandaged and she helped him to the chair, she'd gone to check on the pregnant midget and the nut job he'd bashed with the shovel. It didn't seem worth telling the Marine dude about his job.

He shrugged, still looking in the other direction. "I'm kinda working with the college teacher, but it ain't much. Won't be enough to pay Granny for the carpet."

"It took some stones, what you did."

Why couldn't Britt have stayed to hear that?

"Whatever. The guy's a nut job," James answered.

Another EMT wheeled in a stretcher. "I don't need to go to the hospital," James said. "I didn't last time."

"Let 'em check it out, get you something for infection. But really, that was quite a reaction, from what they told me. Said you didn't flinch, didn't hesitate. You plan on sticking with this job, or . . . I mean . . . well, are you interested in taking one more shot at the ASVAB?"

"The Marine test?" Why? James wondered. This guy's as crazy as the other dude. Failing the test again sure wouldn't help things with Britt. And besides, he really did like studying about those Indians. "Naw, your test kicked my ass. I don't think that dog'll hunt. I'm thinking about being one of them archeologists, like the college teacher."

"That's a good plan, a damn good plan. You know you'll have to go to college."

"Huh. I figured I could start at the bottom, you know, like digging holes for the teacher. Work my way up from there."

"I don't think it's that kind of job. It's more a career. You'll need some education."

A career. Education. "Hmm. I might have to rethink it, me and school don't jive."

"You need discipline, structure, that's all. You could do it with some good habits. And money. College is expensive."

"That ain't happening." James hung his head. Why did everything have to be so hard? A half step forward and three back, always something standing in front of him. Maybe Britt was right. Maybe he had no future.

"You know, the Marines could provide the discipline you need, give you some focus. They'll pay for college after your first enlistment, too."

"You know well as I do, I can't pass the test. What's the point?" For the first time in a long, long time, James thought he might cry. He bit his lower lip.

"What you did today impressed me. You might be Marine material after all. Hell, going after that gun, that's the same as running toward the bullets."

"The test . . ."

"This foot heals up, you come back to see me, take it one more time. I got an idea you'll pass it this time, no problem," he winked at James. "You hearing what I'm telling you, Marine?"

James looked him in the eye. "Why? Ain't nobody ever done me any favors. And what about the Allman Brothers? Hell, I've been shot in *both* feet."

"Times have changed. Shit son, in Afghanistan, we're patching 'em up and sending 'em back after lots worse than what happened to you." He handed James a card. "You call me in a couple weeks. Need to schedule a time when I'm there. We'll take care of that test for you."

James took the card as the other EMT told him to lie on the stretcher. James looked from the card to the stretcher to the recruiter. Why this guy? All he ever wanted was a chance, and now this guy, the same one who told him to go to trade school, was holding a door open. All he had to do was walk through it. This guy didn't know him, didn't owe him a damn thing, but here it was—a chance. His chance. James wanted to hug him and he wanted to cry, but he didn't figure a Marine would do either. He sucked in his breath and looked him in the eye. "Thank you," he said.

The other EMTs hurried around him, pushing the gurney with Trudy and guiding Livingston along behind. Brittany followed them. She glanced at James, but only for a second. He stood as straight as he could, even put a little weight on his left foot. "I'll walk," he told them, loud enough for Brittany to hear.

SALLY STARED AT the framed drawing hanging on his wall, same as he'd done every night for the past two weeks. And every morning. He didn't know what else to do. Culpepper and the folks from the Indian Nation were already working with Livingston on the land deal—meeting with the zoning department, designers, developers—he was out of it, and not a dime to show for all the work. They didn't even need his opinion. And he had nothing else lined up, no possibilities, no plan. Nothing.

He'd not seen or heard from Kat since the day of the auction, either. He thought she'd have called by now, but it was beginning to sink in just how wrong he was for not telling her more about the deal earlier. If he'd've just mentioned the location to her . . . but no. It never crossed his mind that she'd found the flowers on the same property. Why would it? Still, she could've at least called by now.

For two weeks he'd been replaying it all and when Sally closed his eyes, everything about the past year scrolled through his mind again. This time, his screen stuck on a moment from several months earlier. He remembered the girl from the bank, what was her name? Lucy? Leena? No, Luna, Luna Marze. That was it. Girls like her, *girls*, didn't even see men his age, didn't see him. He wasn't there, didn't exist to them and now, right now, realizing that . . . he knew. Kat saw him, saw him for everything he was, everything he'd been, the good and the bad. And she didn't mind. Of course she hadn't called. Why should she? What he understood now, she already knew. He needed that in his life again. He needed her.

He looked at the drawing again. *Helianthus schweinitzii*. Schweinitz Sunflower. He swirled the ice around in his glass, but didn't take a drink. Instead, he put the glass back on the table and picked up his phone. He scrolled Kat's number, hesitated, then hit *call*.

Epilogue

The main entrance to The Wisacky was understated and offered no indication of how the resort came to be. No mention of voodoo rituals, weed farmers, real-estate scams, or the unemployed and delusional. Nothing about research grants, tenure, or the Interactive Life of Jesus slash Santa's Wonderland theme park. Instead, tucked several feet off the main road and ensconced in hardwoods, two columns of stacked stonework supported an archway above the drive. The center of the archway held a masonry plaque with the name etched in relief. Very little landscaping surrounded the base of the two columns. The area, protected by a small, stone border, was filled with hardy plants that produced brilliant yellow flowers in September and October. The entrance was so unobtrusive, first-time visitors often missed the turn and had to double back.

After passing beneath the entrance archway, the drive meandered through more hardwoods before dividing in two directions. A low wooden sign showed one arrow pointing right to the restaurant and casino, and one pointing left to the gardens and museum.

As far as Arlen was concerned, The Wisacky was a once-a-year restaurant, at best. Captain Steve's Fish Camp was his usual first choice, as it was this night, but Mary wanted to go to Jud's out on the boulevard.

"We went there Saturday," he whined.

"They have fried chicken livers," she countered.

"But Thursday's are all-you-can-eat salt-and-pepper catfish, and we missed last week."

"Well," she paused, "I'm changing if we're going to Captain Steve's. And it's the *Survivor* final tonight, so we gotta be home by eight."

He lumbered out of the recliner. "I'll get my jacket."

"Are you wearing that hat?" Mary asked.

"My Braves hat?"

"It's filthy and all frayed around the bill," she said.

"But it's my good-luck hat."

"Not if you wear it tonight."

He picked the NASCAR hat she had bought him a few weeks earlier instead.

When they arrived at Captain Steve's, the line snaked out the door, down the walk, and disappeared around the corner of the building. He drove slowly past and whistled through his teeth. "Some crowd."

"I'm hungry. I don't want to wait in that line."

"By the time we drive to Jud's, we'd have a table here."

"Well, pick someplace close. You know I'm hypoglycemic. If I don't eat, I get all light-headed. And it's *Survivor*, remember."

"I know, but there's nothing close."

"The Wisacky's just up the road."

"The Wisacky? It's too expensive. That's only for special occasions."

She reached across the console and patted his thigh, then winked. "You take me there and tonight might be a special occasion."

He turned the truck around.

On the way in, they passed a tall, thin man, his wife, and their young son emerging from one of the nature paths in the shadowy light of dusk. She thought she recognized them, but she couldn't be certain. The woman was a little person, she'd have remembered that. Mary started to speak, and the son—a happy-looking boy who appeared to be four or five—smiled as she did, but the man nervously looked away, as if he didn't remember her, or if he did, he didn't want to chat. Just as well, Mary thought, *Survivor* waited.

Arlen held Mary's hand as he led her up the stone steps and inside The Wisacky. The hostess seated them immediately and their waiter appeared seconds later. The meal was remarkable. Two appetizers, salads, Mary had the ribs with baked potato and a side of onion rings, he had the "Big Chief" steak, all twenty-four ounces of it. Two desserts and a bill that blew their monthly budget, but worth every penny. On the way out, she spotted an old . . . acquaintance, and wavered for a moment before deciding to make the introductions. Sure, they had a history, but that was in the past. What harm could it do now?

"Come on, I want you to meet someone. But, don't start no long conversation. *Survivor*, remember."

She called out from a few tables away, "Bless my soul, it's Salvador Hinson."

Sally nodded, then stood as the couple approached the table. "Hi Mary. It's been a while. How've you been?"

"Oh, fantastic, Sally. Just great. How about you?"

"Fine, thank you."

Mary looked at the lady seated across from Sally, then stuck out her hand. "Hey, I'm Mary, like in the Bible."

Sally forced a smile. "Mary, this is Katherine Sardofsky. Kat, Mary."

"Pleased to meet you." Mary looked at Sally. "Don't look so nervous, Sally, I won't tell her any of your secrets." She turned back to Kat. "I heard he'd been keeping company, I'm glad to finally meet you. I've known Sally for years."

"Well, Mary, to be completely truthful . . ." Sally tried to correct her.

"Oh, I almost forgot," Mary interrupted. "You heard I got married, I'm sure. This is my husband, Arlen Johnson. Say hello, Arlen."

Arlen stuck his pudgy hand toward Sally. "How you doing? Good to meet you." He looked at Kat and nodded. "It's nice seeing you again, ma'am."

Mary jerked her head toward Arlen, then Kat. "So you two have met. I didn't realize."

"Mr. Johnson—Arlen, did some work for me a while back."

"I see. Hmm." Mary looked at her watch. "Well, it was good seeing you, Sally, and nice to meet you Katherine. Come on, Arlen."

At home, Mary scooped two bowls of ice cream, brought Arlen his, and turned the TV to *Survivor*. They ate and watched in silence through most of the show. Jeff Probst tallied the final votes. *Luna needs one more vote to win,* he said.

Arlen pointed his spoon toward the screen. "I know that girl. She used to live around here."

"You knew Sally's girl, from the restaurant, too. Just how many other girls do you *know* that you've not told me about?"

"Aw, Sugar Britches, don't be that way. You're my princess, the only one for me. And besides, how is it you know that Sally feller so well? You and him have a thing I should know about?"

Mary shook her head and opened a bag of Oreos, offered one to Arlen, which he took. Jeff Probst paused for effect . . . and the winner of *Survivor Aranati—Luna Marze!* Confetti fell, the crowd cheered.

Luna Marze screamed and danced in circles for a few seconds, then dashed to the edge of the stage, where a young man in Marine dress blues waited, shoulders squared, back straight. She leaped into his arms, and the two of them twirled around and around as if nothing else in the world existed, and they twirled and twirled until the station cut to commercial.

"I THINK MARY had a thing for you. Anything you want to tell me?" Kat smiled and took another sip of her wine.

"Oh yeah, we were a thing. Hot and heavy." Sally grinned. "You know everything there is to know about me and Mary. If not for her . . ." his voice trailed. The meal was delicious but he concentrated on pushing the last bites of food around on his plate, his nerves gripped his throat too tight to get another bite down.

"If not for Mary what?"

Sally drew in a deep breath. "I just . . . well . . ." He put his fork gently on the plate. "Look," he started again, still staring at the remaining peas. "I never thought, I mean, you tell yourself things, make a decision and move on, you know, and at my age, it's just who you are and you don't think about it, but then . . ."

Kat laughed. "Sally, you sound like Livingston Carr. Say what's on your mind."

"I can't explain it, you know," he glanced up at her, then shook his head. "I'm really screwing this up, I sound stupid as a seventeen-year-old kid. I'll shut up now." He leaned back and stuck his hand in his pocket. He paused there for just a second, long enough to roll the buckeye between his finger and thumb before grabbing the ring.

"Here," he said.

She drew in a sharp breath as he put it on her finger, but the expression on her face didn't change.

"You know I'm not much of a romantic, and it's not like we're kids or anything, but we're good together. I can't give you a scientific explanation; you know what I mean," he offered.

"You're right about not being a romantic." She held up her hand and admired the ring, turned it this way and that, the light catching the facets in brilliant flashes.

"You want me to get down on one knee or something?"

"One knee? Whatever for?"

"Well, to propose, I guess."

"As in marriage, that kind of proposal? Hmm."

"You're killing me, Kat. Come on. Will you marry me?"

"One of the first things you learn as a scientist is some things science can't explain. Love, stray dogs, archaic customs for creating binding partnerships between two people," Kat smiled.

"See, that's what I love about you."

Kat dabbed at the corner of her mouth and dropped her napkin in her plate, "Let's skip dessert."

"Is that a yes?"

"Yes, Sally. It's a yes. Let's go."

The air was crisp, the first cool night of fall. It felt perfect and Kat suggested they stroll down one of the garden paths before leaving. "No need to rush," she wrapped both her arms around Sally's, "I said yes. We've got the rest of our lives." She squeezed his arm and leaned her head on his shoulder.

Sally squeezed back, then freed his arm, slipped it around her waist and hugged her close.

Before reaching the parking lot, they stopped once along the path. After making sure no one was looking, they stepped around the protective border where Sally and Kat leaned their noses into the blooming cusp of the rare sunflowers that grew on the property. The flowers smelled of earth, of the past, the fragrance reminiscent of old letters bound in an antique drawer, and yet, an aroma fecund and fertile, a hint of things yet unseen.

Author Notes and Acknowledgments

Sunflower Dog is a work of fiction. The plot, the characters, the locations, the buildings, etc. are fictional. Most of those featured in this book in no way represent any real persons, places, or things (living, dead, or undead). Some readers may recognize similarities to real people, places, or things. Those similarities are purely coincidental—and by coincidental I mean the world we experience leaves some indelible marks on us; bits and pieces of it linger in our memories and choose to resurface reshaped and reformed in any number of ways. Some of the places, however, may appear as more realistic than others. For instance, several of the highway descriptions and designations are of actual roads, a few of the restaurant names may ring vaguely true, and Mason County may remind some readers of Union County, North Carolina.

Other parts of the novel are true and bear acknowledgement. The Schweinitz Sunflower (Helianthus schweinitzii) is indeed a protected and endangered flower that grows in only a few locations of North and South Carolina (the largest concentration being in Union County, NC). The Waxhaw, or Wisacky, Native Americans were a real tribe from the Waxhaw, NC, area who were eventually absorbed by the Sugeree Tribe and then the Catawba Tribe. Early settlers in the area called the Wisacky tribe "Flatheads" due to their broad brows, which resulted from their custom of placing river rocks on the foreheads of sleeping infants to form the desired shape.

It's often said writers write in order to figure out how they think and feel about something they "see" in the world around them. If so, then the true parts are what led me to write this book. What I "see" is that the verisimilitude of (or, the realities reflected in) Southern Literature tropes—staples such as a sense of place and a strong connection to the land, familial and regional histories and how those histories inform tradition, and the concept of noblesse oblige in its heroic characters—no longer apply. These foundational ideas are disappearing at an ever-increasing rate only to be replaced by a capitalistic, voyeuristic shallowness steeped in narcissistic greed, all of which leads to an existence which lacks grace and dignity. Granted, there are many Southern "traditions" that need to disappear, but we should not throw the proverbial baby out with the bath water. The modern-day Southerner—the native, multi-generational Southerner, yes, like myself—still struggles to find balance, to find solid mooring, to know with certainty which traditions to proudly hold high and which to discard. This story, I hope, suggests the first steps in finding our answers lies in embracing Love and cultivating Laughter, laughter at ourselves and the absurdity of the world around us.

There are so many people who played a role in this project becoming a reality. First and foremost, many thanks Steve McCondichie, the entire SFK Press family, and my agent for believing in the novel and for all the help and guidance throughout the process of taking it from manuscript to press. I am indebted to Fred Leebron for his continued encouragement and support from the very earliest stages of my writing career, and through Fred, I owe much to the Queen's University MFA program and faculty, especially Elissa Schappell. Thanks to those who read early drafts of this work. Of those, special thanks to Pinckney Benedict, David Payne, Eugene "BG" Cross, Ashley Shealy, and Greta Wood for comments, suggestions, and advice along the way. Taylor and Amelia Winchester have gone far beyond the role of family support in bringing everything related to this project together, and I'm proud of them beyond words. Much gratitude to Chris Duncan for publishing early excerpts of the book in "Ray's Road Review," and to Becca Gummere and Eileen Drennen for assuring me the humor was working. The information and resources I found through the Museum of the Waxhaws, the Hilton-Pond Center for Piedmont Natural History, The Heritage Room of the Union County Library, and especially the Ethel K. Smith Library at Wingate University were invaluable.

There are two people without whose encouragement and unwavering support I would never have completed this book. They have read and re-read every single word countless times, offered critiques and suggestions, were always honest in telling me what I needed to hear instead of what I wanted to hear, and most importantly, they believed in this book at times when I doubted it. They were always there—always. Simply put, you would not be reading this were it not for Claudine Geurtin and Amee Odom. They will forever hold a place in my heart. This is a better book because of their input and I am a better writer because of their guidance. I am forever grateful, and I am endlessly humbled by their love and friendship (and their critiquing / editing skills).

Finally, I have no words to adequately express my appreciation for Terri Lilly, whose heart is so big it overwhelms me, whose fierce spirit sustains me, and whose companionship ever assures me.

About the Author

Kevin Winchester is a native of North Carolina, where he now lives, writes, and teaches. His short story, "Waiting on Something to Happen," won the 2013 Thomas Wolfe Fiction Award. His short story collection, *Everybody's Gotta Eat*, was published in 2009. Other short fiction has appeared in *Gulf Coast Literary and Arts Journal*, *Barrel House, Story South, Dead Mule School of Literature, Barren Magazine*, and the anthology *Everything But the Baby*. His creative non-fiction has appeared in the Novello Press anthology, *Making Notes: Music in the Carolinas, Tin House Literary Magazine*, and a variety of other publications. Winchester holds an MFA in Creative Writing from Queens University. He is currently the Director of the Writing Center at Wingate University, where he also teaches Creative Writing. In his life outside of writing, he is one of the contributing songwriters of and plays bass in the band Flatland Tourists, and also plays guitar in his solo project. He still has an active auctioneer's license, is a former real-estate broker, and was once a level II certified fork lift driver. His spare time is spent with his family, and he enjoys hiking, riding his Harley, and growing vegetables.

Share Your Thoughts

Want to help make *Sunflower Dog* a bestselling novel? Consider leaving an honest review of this book on Goodreads, on your personal author website or blog, and anywhere else readers go for recommendations. It's our priority at SFK Press to publish books for readers to enjoy, and our authors appreciate and value your feedback.

Our Southern Fried Guarantee

If you wouldn't enthusiastically recommend one of our books with a 4- or 5-star rating to a friend, then the next story is on us. We believe that much in the stories we're telling. Simply email us at pr@sfkmultimedia.com.

Do You Know About Our Bi-Monthly Zine?

Would you like your unpublished prose, poetry, or visual art featured in The New Southern Fugitives? A bi-monthly zine that's free to readers and subscribers and pays contributors:

$100 for essays and short stories
$50 for book reviews
$40 for flash/micro fiction
$40 for poetry
$40 for photography & visual art

Visit **NewSouthernFugitives.com/Submit** *for more information.*

Also by SFK Press

A Body's Just as Dead, Cathy Adams
Not All Migrate, Krystyna Byers
The Banshee of Machrae, Sonja Condit
Amidst This Fading Light, Rebecca Davis
American Judas, Mickey Dubrow
Swapping Purples for Yellows, Matthew Duffus
A Curious Matter of Men with Wings, F. Rutledge Hammes
The Skin Artist, George Hovis
Lying for a Living, Steve McCondichie
The Parlor Girl's Guide, Steve McCondichie
Appalachian Book of the Dead, Dale Neal
Feral, North Carolina, 1965, June Sylvester Saraceno
If Darkness Takes Us, Brenda Marie Smith
The Escape to Candyland, Yong Takahashi
Hardscrabble Road, George Weinstein
Aftermath, George Weinstein
The Five Destinies of Carlos Moreno, George Weinstein
The Caretaker, George Weinstein
Watch What You Say, George Weinstein
RIPPLES, Evan Williams

Made in the USA
Columbia, SC
18 June 2020

11419707R00190